Praise for Kay
TROPIC OF CR

"The real mystery in SF these ~~...~~ ~~...~~ Kay
Kenyon better known? She writes beautifully, her
characters are multilayered and complex, and her
extrasolar worlds are as real and nuanced as any place
you've ever visited on Earth, while at the same time
truly alien. If you missed the Kay Kenyon train when it
first left the station, fear not: *Tropic of Creation* is a
perfect place to jump aboard—for what, I promise, will
be an exciting, fascinating, mind-blowing ride."
—Robert J. Sawyer,
Nebula Award-winning author of *Calculating God*

"Kenyon draws vivid characters you care about, both
human and alien, striving on a harsh and memorable
distant world." —David Brin

DON'T MISS THESE OTHER PROVOCATIVE BOOKS
BY KAY KENYON

THE SEEDS OF TIME
"A fast-moving plot and a memorable heroine. You
couldn't ask for a better first novel." —Mike Resnick

"Kenyon has created a winning heroine, a gripping
adventure, and a setting that shows some imaginative
thinking on current theories of Earth's ecological ruin
and of time travel." —*Publishers Weekly*

LEAP POINT
"An extraordinary genre writing achievement—exciting,
involving, chilling, comic, deeply disturbing and
altogether enthralling . . . *Leap Point* should firmly
establish [Kenyon] among the very finest science fiction
writers in the nation."
—*Statesman Journal*, Salem, OR

ALSO BY KAY KENYON

THE SEEDS OF TIME
LEAP POINT
RIFT

TROPIC OF CREATION
A Bantam Spectra Book

SPECTRA and the portrayal of a boxed "s" are trademarks of
Bantam Books, a division of Random House, Inc.

ISBN 0-553-76317-2

Published simultaneously in the United States and Canada

Bantam Books are published by Bantam Books, a division of Random House, Inc. Its trademark, consisting of the words "Bantam
Books" and the portrayal of a rooster, is Registered in U.S. Patent
and Trademark Office and in other countries. Marca Registrada.
Bantam Books, 1540 Broadway, New York, New York 10036.

PRINTED IN THE UNITED STATES OF AMERICA

For Donald Maass

1

Two suns beat down on the eroded hills, cooking the air, making it hard to see the landscape except through a wavering mirage of heat. Captain Eli Dammond removed his hat, wiping the perspiration from his forehead, and peered for a moment at the sun—not the primary, but its dwarf sister: small, red, and swelling in the sky. The dwarf star was no bigger than his thumbnail at arm's length, but even so, it seemed to stoke the morning's heat to a near boil.

This far from camp the landscape lay barren and uniform—gully and dune, gully and dune—for miles. It looked like so many lands in the Congress Worlds: blasted and sere from war. But here on Null, nature alone had done the job.

At the crest of the next gully he saw Corporal Willem waving his arm.

"Captain Dammond, over here. It's here." Corporal Willem pointed into the wadi and skidded down the far side, disappearing from view.

Young Sascha Olander looked up at Captain Dammond

for permission to run ahead and see Corporal Willem's prize.

"It's no place for a youngster," Willem had groused on the hike out from camp, and he'd been right. But Eli was not about to deny the general's granddaughter her small adventure. At fourteen, she was beyond spoiling. The word had no meaning for a young woman who would have every privilege and never think twice about it.

"Go ahead, then, Sascha," he said.

He caught a glimpse of her grin before she was sprinting down the lee side of the hard-packed dune and up the next one.

Eli set out after her, his boots crunching over a litter of sticks protruding from the soil. He went heavily armed, the range gun a comfortable bulk at his hip. Though the armistice had held for over a year now, if the ahtra broke the peace, no one would be surprised. Some, like Corporal Willem, hoped for it. The corporal had a regen arm and eye and looked forward to a little payback. As bad as regen limbs looked, the eyes were the worst, swollen translucent fruits that nevertheless gathered light and saw the world as well as the original, *alpha* eyes—better, the enlisteds vowed.

Still, it was an uncharted world, and he had his people go armed.

Topping the rise, he saw the three of them waiting for him in the wadi, poking at the dusty hulk that Corporal Willem had found earlier that morning. Next to Willem stood Luce Marzano, captain of the ship and 112 crew marooned on the planet for the past three years. Like Willem, she wore the brown uniform of infantry, patched in places, and faded by now to the color of sand. Alert but relaxed, she'd had plenty of time to ferret out trouble if there was any. But she'd made her report: the locale was devoid of life, inimical or otherwise. The enlisteds called the planet Null; in three years, they'd had no occasion to change their minds.

The massive continent dominating this hemisphere was a quiet, scoured land, rumpled only by fingers of wind through sand. The most action this place would see was the dwarf star, coming round for a visit after a four-year absence, and bright enough now to cast a shadow at night.

Sascha was already climbing on the bank above the contraption, kicking sand from around its metallic sides.

"Sascha," Eli called. He waved her away from the device. The thing might be booby-trapped. But in three years, Marzano's crew had found twenty-eight similar objects—now twenty-nine—and none of them was wired to detonate.

Captain Marzano met Eli as he strode down the bank into the wadi. She cocked her head toward the machine—a craft, by all appearances, just like the others. "Looks like this one's newly minted," she said. "Hell, it's in better shape than I am."

Eli smiled at that, then fell back to neutral. Best to remember he might soon be a witness in an inquiry into her possible desertion from duty . . . But he liked Luce Marzano. She was tough and confident, and at forty-some, still handsome. And also gone missing the last two years of a war that had bled off the better part of a generation. Now, a year into the armistice, Eli's ship had found the marooned crew and the ruined ship *Fury*, presumed lost in action. Or now, it would seem, just lost.

"So they've been here recently," Eli said, walking with Marzano toward the hexadron. It was half buried, like all the others, in the soil. Maybe it was good they went armed.

"Recent enough," Marzano said. "They used this place for *something*. Training, maybe?" She squinted at the small vessel before them.

Corporal Willem wiped a small section of hull clean of dust. "Like it's right off the assembly line, sir."

When Willem said *sir,* he looked at Captain Marzano, instead of Captain Dammond, a slight that Eli ignored for now. He saved his object lessons for bigger lapses.

Marzano's crew didn't like him snooping around the crashed *Fury* looking for signs of cowardice. Hell, *he* didn't like it. But Marzano herself was pushing hardest for a thorough search, urging Eli to inspect and document every ship system, mangled or not.

There were things in her favor. Even if she could have repaired the giant fighting ship, it had no launch capacity from the ground. She had pulled off a minor miracle just negotiating an atmospheric entry and controlled crash-landing. So she wanted a clean bill of health exonerating her of sabotage, not an ambiguous report that would dog her career . . . and by God, he would give her that respect. It wasn't as though he had better things to do. Here he was, thirty-seven years old, a captain of the Sixth Transport Division—advancement prospects slim to none—with a grimy kettle of a ship and a crew that said his name like a wad of spit shot out. He wouldn't wish that fate on anyone, least of all Luce Marzano.

" 'Spose there's ahtra bodies in this one, sir?" Willem asked.

"That's what we'll find out," Eli answered.

Willem's eyes were flat. He hadn't been talking to Eli Dammond, and probably didn't like being answered by an alpha captain who wore the blue of Transport while better men wore the brown of battle.

From the exposed section of the vessel, Eli could see the ship was a miniature of an ahtran warship, at least in its shape, with six sides, sloping slightly toward the top. The craft, like the others Marzano's crew had found in the vicinity, was big enough for two ahtra, maybe three in a tight squeeze. The intriguing difference with this particular hexadron was that beneath a coating of dirt, it might be of recent origin—might even be in working order.

Since his arrival here Eli had seen several of them, and like Marzano, he took them to be landing craft. But they found no vestige of the late enemy, no electromagnetic signature as they scanned the planet. Nothing odd about finding implements of war strewn about, Eli admitted. Half of known space was littered with skeletons of metal and bone from thirty years of mayhem. Except here there was no sign of battle. Add to that, some of these craft were old—weathered, time-battered carcasses slumping to ruin. And some were newer.

It was as though ahtra had been coming here for hundreds of years. By twos and threes.

A slap of wind came out of nowhere and grazed sweat from their faces, cooling their skin just when they felt they might see flesh split open from the heat. Turning into the breeze, Eli scanned the horizon where puffs of clouds massed like suds—a rare sight, Marzano commented. She'd had crew set out basins against the possibility of rain for the last five days. But each afternoon the sun struck the clouds back with hammer strokes of 115 degree heat, and the basins lay hot and empty. The only water was beneath the ground, sucked up by the nearby stand of desiccated pillars that passed for trees: the copse the enlisteds called the Sticks. The trees hoarded the water inside, in cisterns. From these, the crew tapped and rationed out water, pure as snowmelt, hot as geysers.

Sascha was prying on the hatch door of the hexadron.

"That will do, Sascha," Eli said.

She obeyed, stepping back from the alien craft. She bumped her hat off her head, letting it hang down on her back by its straps, and allowed her black hair to escape its long braid in sweat-soaked strands. The freckles her mother so hated were popping out by the minute. *Pocks,* Cristin Olander called them, the same as the enlisteds called the ahtra.

Corporal Willem released the hatch covering. As Eli peered into the dusky interior, he thought he caught a whiff of the ahtra smell: sweet and sour, fermented. A thread of memory released sounds, like birds startled from a bush . . . deep, throaty shouts and distant screams. Even the ahtra could scream, though they showed no fear, not even with a domino gun shoved into a pocked cheek.

But it was empty.

Eli hoisted himself into the craft, sitting on the edge of the curved seat to gain headroom. The interior had a spare look, despite the characteristic ahtran patterns over every square inch of the bulkheads. A simple control panel faced him on one wall, showing quirky instrumentation with depressions where switches should be. Forty-five years of contact with the species, and Congress Worlds still had no clue why they covered their ship walls with concentric squares . . . where they came from . . . why they lived in world ships . . . how they functioned with bicameral brains . . . or how their star drive got an extra twenty percent of speed out of pulse engines.

In the end it was that twenty-percent advantage that forced CW to bend knee—in what was euphemistically called an armistice—so ahtra kept the riches of the Neymium Belt for themselves, ceding a pauper's share to CW, and the warring parties backed off, licking their wounds.

Eli's grandfather could remember the days before the Great War when, for the first time, fast ahtran ships made trade between the human worlds worthwhile, but the honeymoon was soon over.

"Captain Dammond," he heard from outside. Marzano was crouching and probing under the hexadron. "This is curious."

He joined her to look under the craft. The underside contained a plate, stuck in a half-open position, revealing a round mechanism within. Marzano reached up to pull the plate fully open, but it didn't budge.

Eli crawled under the craft, lying on his back in the dirt, staring up. Willem handed him a lamp from his kit, and Eli aimed its beam into a circular maw of metal teeth. He lay there, absorbing this view. As he reached up to touch the serrated edges, a whisper of soil tumbled into his face.

His brothers would know what this was. Hell, *he* knew what this was.

Marzano's face was in shadow as she crouched next to him. "What do you make of it?"

Getting to his feet, Eli slapped the dirt from his uniform. "Where did you say the other hexadrons were found?"

She shrugged. "They're everywhere. In the Sticks. The wadis. Buried in hillsides, embedded in the dunes."

"And you never noticed anything like that mechanism?" He gestured to the jammed, half-open plate.

"No. The others were smooth-sided. Or we assumed they were." Defensively, she offered: "We've had more pressing matters. Like surviving."

Marzano gestured Willem to take Sascha up the wadi, and the corporal left with the girl in tow. Sascha looked back to where the action was, pleading with great blue eyes for the captain to countermand the order, but he didn't.

Looking down at his feet, Eli sorted the possibilities. Two shadows, one faint, one dark, spread out from the soles of his feet, as though there were two of him standing there. He squinted up into the beady eye of the dwarf sun.

"What is it, then, Captain?" Marzano asked.

"They're not landing craft." He looked at her straight on. "They're burrowing craft."

Luce Marzano pursed her lips and frowned, as though unable to reverse her opinions on the instant. Then, with Eli, she looked down at the baked soil of the wadi with a long, appraising gaze.

2

Luce Marzano and Master Sergeant Ben Juric leaned over the screen. The soundings showed an underground tunnel with a side branch to the east. So far, readings were showing a uniformity in dimensions, fueling speculations about mining shafts, a secret arms cache, and lava tubes.

In this case, one was half the size of the other.

"A natural system of tunnels isn't proportional," Eli said.

Ben Juric looked at him, gracing him with a crumpled lip. Juric didn't talk unless he had something to say, so Eli had learned to read his face. *Tell me something I don't know,* the master sergeant managed to convey.

From outside the tent, the noise of grinding gears erupted, as the techs put the craft through its paces, digging down a yard or two; digging back up. The engineers cracked the control system easily. The controls were simple; hardest were the calibrations for depth, and the techs were closing in on that.

Techs had been swarming over the craft since the gradiometer reading had revealed the tunnels earlier that morning. The soundings crew were now some half mile up the wadi, still following the main tunnel, measuring the gravity-gradient changes that implied subsurface structures.

"Ahtran tunnels, I say," Marzano concluded. Maybe she hoped they *were.* He couldn't blame her if she was eager to fight the war she'd been denied, eager to forget the past year's truce with the enemy.

At the mention of ahtra, one side of Sergeant Juric's face hardened—the alpha side that still bore normal expression. Eli would have welcomed his assessment, but the sergeant was wary of him. There was no history between the two of them, no loyalty. Like the general's daughter and granddaughter, Juric was merely hitching a ride on this quick run down through Keller Space.

Only now the shuttle run had taken on a different complexion. They both wished he could radio for orders. Armistice or no, if you had a cache of arms down here, and God knew what ahtra surprises, you damn well got your orders from Command, especially if you're just a stinking tub of a transport with a tarnished officer in charge, occupying a post a better man would have had if most of them weren't dead or in regen baths. But radio was down, as Marzano had told them. If they hadn't discovered her Mayday beacon in orbit, they would never have found her—even though they *had* been looking for her. The satellite wasn't broadcasting—whatever electromagnetic interference disrupted the surface transmissions also extended well into the planet's exosphere—but on retrieval the ship's techs had decoded its message.

Eli caught Sergeant Juric's eye, just long enough to lock on. "We get the kinks worked on that digger, I'm sending someone down," Eli said.

Juric nodded. In the three months of their acquaintance, Eli had never seen Juric show surprise. If you were a veteran of battle, you *didn't* show surprise, not at an officer's order. If Eli had said, *Take a spoon, Sergeant, and dig your way down to that tunnel,* Juric would have nodded in just that same way.

"Let me send one of my people, Captain," Marzano said. It was her plea, maybe, for a chance to salvage something from Null. Maybe she looked at Eli and hoped to God she'd never fall so low. He didn't think she would. Patrician Luce Marzano, of good family, of the right connections, looked a little different to Command than up-through-the-ranks Eli Dammond with top scores, no connections, and a worse crime, by some lights, than desertion.

"We'll see who goes. We'll see if we *can* go." He turned to Juric. "Sergeant, keep the tech teams working here. Give them some backup for a complete scan of the tunnels. See how far they extend."

"Yes, sir. And the ship?"

Luce Marzano's ship, the *Fury,* was still out there on the flats with Eli's crew combing its systems for evidence—one way or the other. "Keep working," he told Juric, and Marzano nodded, relieved no doubt that her situation wasn't upstaged by a more interesting one. "Box up what you have and transfer it to the *Lucia.*" The *Lucia,* a sweet name for his ship of command, which was little better than a bathtub with fusion drive. And it'd be a full tub once its complement of 157 lifted off.

He heard a gentle cough outside the tent.

Juric cocked his head toward the flap. "Mrs. Olander, sir. Shall I send her in?"

"No."

Juric's face said, *Got the balls to snub the daughter of the general, do you?*

"I don't think she likes to camp," Marzano said, managing a wry smile, even as Eli ordered all her crew's damning evidence boxed and loaded up.

He hardened his heart toward Luce Marzano and strode out of the tent to deal with his civilian passenger.

"Let's walk, Mrs. Olander," he said, according her a nod, and then striking out at a brisk pace across the floor of the wadi, toward the hexadron. But it was no good acting busy—and damn it, he *was* busy. Cristin Olander attached herself to him like a burr, matching his long strides, jumping to the point:

"Captain, we don't need all this." She waved at the crews at work in the wadi. "You've done your mission, and it's got nothing to do with these . . . balls of junk. I've got business at home. We're overdue."

"Yes, ma'am, I'm well aware." *I have my duty,* he wanted to remind the daughter of the general. A duty to bring her home and also to swing into the binary system— where the *Fury* was known to have been headed when last heard from—and look for clues to the ship's fate. Now, with the leisure of the armistice, MIAs were a priority to the army—if not to this general's daughter who had the wealth to earn a doctorate in math and the leisure to present a paper at a seminar of alphas with more neurons than they knew what to do with.

"If you were *well aware,* we'd be halfway home by now." She stopped with Eli some paces from the hexadron, eyeing it with loathing.

The engineering team—Marzano's crew—were stripped down in the heat to undershirts and fatigue pants, flaunting their regen forearms, deltoids, fingers. They waved desultory salutes at Eli.

"There she is," Cristin Olander said, pointing into the distance where Sascha could be seen with her father, silhouetted against the caustic blue sky, scrounging in the dirt for specimens. "She'll be ruined by the time we get home. No matter what I do."

Eli looked at Mrs. Olander, wondering how much she could know of *ruin.*

She gave him a twisted smile, eyes making contact. "I know what you think of me, Captain. That I throw my weight around." The smile broadened at his discomfort. "You must think so. Even I do sometimes." She gazed off in the direction of her daughter and husband up on the rise. "You must wonder why I fret over Sascha—why I don't just let her muck in the dirt, let her study biology."

Eli knew that biology was no avocation for a lady. He'd learned that much cooped up with Cristin Olander on the three-month junket from Keller's star.

She continued, "It's because my general father won't permit it." She gave him another twist of her lips, a surrogate smile. "You think people like us can do what we will, but you don't know a thing."

Before she could unburden her privileged woes any further, he said, "I have the responsibility to investigate that ship, Mrs. Olander. The careers of 112 officers and enlisteds are on the line." When she had the grace to remain silent, he added, more softly, "Perhaps you could send your paper on ahead."

"With radio out?"

"We'll be outbound in a few days. Send it then?"

They held each other's gaze. Finally Cristin nodded, saying, "Fine," in a tone that made it clear it wasn't. She glanced out at the ridge. Sascha was disappearing down its far flank. "Maybe you could talk to her, Captain. She'll listen to you. She likes you."

It offered a quick exit. "If it will help." He excused himself and walked away from her, up the wadi, in the direction of the youngster who was gathering fossils and freckles, ruining her nails and her pretty alpha skin.

A shadow skittered over the plain, just missing Eli. Above, a cumulus cloud sailed in a massive, bleached globule, carrying its load of moisture far out of reach. The other side of the planet must sprout these things, Eli thought. In that great shallow ocean, animal life, marine life, might flourish. Given half a chance, Geoff Olander would be wading in that shallow sea right now, prodding at mats of algae, sampling pillows of bacteria, with something close to rapture.

Given the hand Geoff Olander was dealt on this temporary stop, the parched fossils of this hemisphere would have to do.

Eli found Geoff and his daughter in a deep, wind-scoured ravine revealing slabs of crumbling stone and, in the near distance, the hump of another hexadron, half caved-in with age. Geoff waved to Eli—a brief, cheery hello—and bent over his work once more. Sascha held a sack half her size, the satchel of their finds.

"How's pickings?" Eli asked Sascha.

"We have five bags of specimens," she said. "Great definition, full body skeletals." She rummaged in the satchel for an example.

Geoff shaded his eyes, looking up at Eli, with the same piercing blue eyes as his daughter. "Not reining us in, I hope?"

"Might be best if you stayed in camp," Eli said. "A precaution." *Against what? Against the social taboos of an overprotective mother?* But he let Geoff draw his own conclusions.

The man looked down the ravine with longing. "Best site we've found so far." He tapped at a slab of rock with his small hammer, sloughing off a crumbling layer of mud. Then he sighed and stood up. "Couldn't you give us a few hours?"

Feeling Sascha's eyes burn a hole in his back, Eli said, "As soon as you can, then."

Geoff snorted, but said civilly enough, "Caught between two Olanders, eh?"

Eli was saved from answering by Sascha sidling between them, shoving a transparent specimen bag into Eli's hand. It contained the remains of a small creature, a jumble of dust and bones. "Nice fossil," Eli said, playing the dolt, goading Sascha the way she seemed to love.

"It's not a fossil. It's a skeleton. Real bones. We found the whole skeleton together, and it looked rather like a frog, except for spinules on the back." She traced the long spinules with her index finger. "I found it, so I might get to name it. Something *olanderi*. Or, I could immortalize *you*, Captain. I could make this one something *dammondi*. If you were nice and gave us an extra day to make scientific history."

Geoff raised an eyebrow, daring Eli to deny her.

Eli found himself smiling. "I'll take your request under advisement."

"Kiss of death," Sascha declared, gently placing the bag in her satchel like a fine piece of porcelain.

"A lot of bones here, then, Mr. Olander?" Eli saw for himself that the ravine was littered with them.

"Yes, a world of them. A biologist's dream."

"Then the place had life once," Eli said, meaning the bones, but looking at the hexadron.

"Still does, somewhere, I expect. Drought's driven them off." Geoff twisted a bone fragment in his hand, a narrow span with an odd socket joint.

Eli knew it was more than an odd bone to Geoff—it was the chance to pierce a mystery or leave it forever buried. But he saw it in Geoff Olander's eyes more than in the bones.

"We'll never come back here," Geoff said softly. No challenge to Eli's authority.

"I doubt it." The planet was so far off the service routes that the *Lucia* was lucky to have found Marzano and her crew at all.

Geoff sighed at the waste. "Five, six billion years of life—and all we have is what's in those sacks. I'd almost stay behind, you know?"

Eli knew. Knew that urge to bend the rules when they needed bending.

Nearly overhead now, the yellow sun lapped up the very shadows at his feet, wrung sweat from his hairline. Down the ravine, the ancient hexadron still had a metal glint beneath the baked-on dust. He gazed at the thing, his mind looking for ways to bend the rules. . . .

Noting his gaze, Sascha asked, "What about the underground cave, Captain?" He was marshaling his arguments. *If there are ahtra down there, it will take an officer to handle the encounter; its a political matter, not a firefight . . .* but the justification could come later. *The longer you think, the worse your decision,* went the army adage.

The chance of a lifetime rang in his ears. After a beat, Eli answered, making up his mind. "I'll be going down."

"Can I come with you?"

"No place for a lady," he said, straight-faced.

She regarded him with an icy stare. "Will you bring Captain Marzano with you?"

"I expect not."

That seemed to mollify Sascha, who monitored the doling out of adventures with great acuity.

Eli picked Sascha's hat off the rock where she'd discarded it and handed it to her. "Mrs. Olander will be happier with me if you wear this. Help me win some points?"

Sascha sighed and donned the hat, a world-weary expression flitting across her face.

Geoff Olander nodded in the direction of the next wadi. "Think there's something down there, then?"

I hope so, sprang to Eli's mind. It was a Dammond brother's response. Always a nose for trouble, drawn to the action. Sometimes the action was more than they bargained for. Now three of his four brothers were dead, killed in the war—the real war, Eli's father said, not the elite officer's war, cushioned by command, out of the fray.

Once, coming back from officer candidate school, Eli and his father had duked it out over whether Eli thought he was too good for enlisted rank. Neither could remember who swung first, but they both landed some hard blows. Later, spent and gasping, they washed up together and sat down to dinner at the big family table. Nobody said a word about their bruises, swelling like bread dough.

Geoff was still waiting for his answer.

"Only one way to find out," Eli finally said.

From the distance came the grinding shudder of the hexadron, having another go at the hard pan floor of the wadi.

3

Sascha Olander and her parents had a deluxe tent, officer-quality issue straight off the newly arrived *Lucia*. Nearby, Captain Marzano's tent sagged from three years of peeling-hot sun. Geoff Olander had offered their tent to Marzano. But she had declined, as she should.

In the middle of that spacious tent, Sascha sat on a chair as her mother rewove her braid in front of the silver-edged mirror that she'd hung from the tent pole.

Sascha pursued her point, though her mother was weary of the topic: "Why do you hate him so?"

"I don't hate him." Cristin pulled the braid so tight Sascha's temples ached.

"Despise him, then."

"I neither despise nor hate him, dear. I seldom regard him at all." She secured the braid with a band, frowning at the wisps that sprang loose.

"That's so . . . dismissive," Sascha returned with some heat. "You're just like all the rest."

Her father looked up from his worktable, catching Sascha's eye, conveying his rebuke.

For his sake, Sascha toned it down a notch. "We're friends, Mother. I just want to watch him go into the mine. Or whatever it is."

"It's a military matter. You'll just be in the way." Cristin checked her own hair in the mirror, the short-cropped, stylish cut of a woman graduated from girlish braids.

Sascha needed a deep, cooling breath, but when she inhaled, all she got was a chest full of Null's hot, yeasty air.

From the shadows in back her father's voice came. "It may not hurt, Cristin. I'll go with her."

Cristin turned on her husband with ferocity. "You always give in. Each little thing just encourages her. You don't remember what it's like, the obligations she'll have. She's nearly grown, Geoff."

"Then, for God's sake, let her have a few more days of childhood."

Sascha could see the fire stoked in her mother's eyes. "You think that's going to make it easier on her? You don't *see*, do you? Already in camp she's got an *enlisted* friend . . ."

"It's only electronic chess, Mother," Sascha interrupted.

Cristin rolled on past, still locked on the enemy, her husband. ". . . with a vocabulary that could singe metal, and hair that looks like it *did*."

"Nevertheless," Geoff said, attempting a neutral end, to salvage a truce.

"That's regen hair, and Nazim's lucky she's got *any*," Sascha mumbled, invisible—and oddly beside the point—to the dueling adults.

Cristin looked at her husband a few beats. Finally, all she said was "She can't take no for an answer, God help her."

Geoff continued in the usual way, which was to give the verbal win to Cristin and then do what he chose. "This will only take an hour. Then she's yours for the day." He stood up to make his intention clear.

Mother hated to lose these contests. Suppressing the delight on her face, Sascha offered, "I'll study differentials when I get back."

Cristin waved her hand in tired dismissal.

Sascha headed for the tent door. Her father opened the flap. "Hat," he said, donning his own.

She dashed back, swiping her hat from the table. Too late, Cristin caught her gaze. "Be careful who you pick for heroes, Sascha."

"What do you care who my heroes are?" Then she regretted saying it, knowing it could refer to her preference for her father over her mother, for biology over math, and she tried so hard not to fuel that rivalry, and not to force any edicts over whether she should study a man's science or a lady's.

"I care," Cristin Olander said.

Feeling guilty now, Sascha backed away, toward the flap door. "I'll be back."

She thought she heard her mother say, barely audible, "I doubt that."

Sascha burst into the bright wall of light just outside. Her father raised his eyebrows, she raised her own, and off they set for the hexadron.

They passed the rows of tents, and the wood huts that supplemented Marzano's military-issue hutches. Salted in among the tattered quarters were Captain Dammond's crisp new igloo-style tents. These were the quarters of those soldiers with whom she'd shared three months' berth, and who therefore had had time to hate her. *Privilege,* their eyes said when they looked at her. *Money. General's whelp.* Some of the enlisteds were cleaning weapons, sitting in the last of the morning shade.

All the long way from Keller's star—Congress World Four—she got a double dose of education. The formal

one, in math and manners from her mother, who finally
had her daughter entirely under her thumb at close quarters; and the informal one, learned from the ranks of the
enlisteds, on envy and the art of despising, even over such
a small thing as the Olanders having a ship berth large
enough for ten enlisteds and taking their meals with the
officers.

Thus it was that when assigned to the *Lucia* for transport to their new post—and seeing how the soldiers sneered
at Captain Dammond behind his back, Sascha came to
take his side. Whoever the enlisteds hated was someone
very like herself.

To catch the meager shade, she and her father walked
along the edge of the Sticks, those tall spines of wood that
sprouted like quills from the land, and which inspired her
father to dub this the Gray Spiny Forest. Of the two camps
established by Captain Marzano, Sascha and her parents
were assigned to Charlie Camp, where the water require-
ments of ninety-four people engaged a harvesting operation covering two square miles of the Sticks. Baker Camp,
established far enough away to assure its own water supply, exploited the eastern stick cisterns.

What the enlisteds saw as sticks were actually plants
of great complexity, ranging from short stubs to pillars over twelve feet high. Many of them were vertically
striated with ridges, between which tracings of green
appeared to carry on the plants' photosynthesis. The
grooves were deeply folded into the wood, as though hiding from, as well as benefiting from, the sunlight. The
trees had a central shaft that at lower levels harbored
modest reserves of water, tapped from the aquifer below.
Burls of gnarled wood disturbed the symmetry of some of
the trees. A few of these were great potbellied growths of
enormous density. Beneath the gray spiny trees was no
understory at all, only the dusty millennial mats of fallen
companions.

Two suns fired the sky. Captain Marzano's people called the smaller one, the one in elliptical orbit, a red dwarf from its smoldering, reddish glow, and no amount of science could dislodge a good name once the enlisteds dubbed something. But her father liked her to call it a brown dwarf, because technically it wasn't a red dwarf, and not really a star at all, emitting its light from gravitational energy and reflected light from the primary.

Sascha spied the bright yellow cable that snaked through the Sticks between Charlie and Baker camps. With radio useless here, it was her only link to her friend, the elegant and profane Badri Nazim.

Private Nazim was Sascha's friend—despite the fact that they'd never met in the flesh and had only known each other a few days. Nazim was just five years older than Sascha, but was old enough to have a regen skull, from which sprouted bone white hair in stark contrast to her nearly black skin. Sascha enjoyed Nazim's exotic looks, worldly vocabulary, and their shared devotion to electronic chess. But she liked the vocabulary best—Nazim's arsenal of expletives and ripe expressions. When Sascha posted a chess query on the electronic bulletin board, Nazim responded within the hour. "Delighted to play chess" was how Sascha related the message to her mother. What Nazim actually said was "Chess at 21:00. Just don't mess your pastel panties if you lose."

Stepping over the cable, she and her father hurried on, sparing no time for the Gray Spiny Forest and its modest wonders. The hexadron would soon be put to its task, an event that both intrigued and worried Sascha. "What will he find underground, Father?"

"Abandoned war bunkers, I should say."

"He's going alone?"

"So he says."

"That's brave." She caught the flicker of a smile at the edge of his face. "Well, it is."

"Yes, of course. I would never detract from the man's virtues, Sascha." Earnestly said. Teasing.

She took his hand. "But I love you best."

"I'll remind you of that when I'm in my dotage, and whining for my slippers."

After a time she asked, "How will he get back up? How does it work against gravity?"

"Ahtra technology, I suppose. They've got ships forty-percent the speed of light, don't forget."

"But how will he know how to run it if we can't even understand their technology?"

Her father smiled. "It's just a digging machine, not a spaceship. The techs worked it out."

They stood at the head of the draw where, below, Dammond and Marzano chatted, accompanied by a group of officers and enlisteds. Her father held firmly to her hand, keeping her beside him.

"He won't care if we go down," she protested.

The digging machine sat in the wadi like a dark egg, tucked away by some feral, metallic beast. This did not seem like a very good idea all of a sudden, this *going down*. She stood, letting the breeze fill her blouse and wick the sweat away. A rumble caused everyone to look in the direction of several towering clouds with scoured, gray bottoms.

"Why is he going alone? Shouldn't he bring a few soldiers?"

"Well, if there's to be trouble, one soldier or three won't make much difference, I suspect."

"Then it's a very brave thing. . . ." She glanced at her father to see if he agreed, but as usual, he maintained a neutrality toward Eli Dammond, a habit of long practice, to remain aloof from military gossip.

At last Captain Dammond waved them down and Sascha, conscious of the group watching her, managed a graceful slide down the sandy hillock.

Captain Dammond wore plain fatigues, no insignia,

and his head was bare, showing a mass of sandy hair that he wore rather longer than the military style. The hair softened scoured features that made him seem uncaring or self-contained. The gray eyes, in particular, were flinty, and when angered she had seen them harden to black. But she had also seen him smile, and thought him handsome in any mood.

Looking to her father, the captain said, "Lieutenant Roche is in charge until I return." Roche, standing next to Captain Dammond, was a veteran of war, a tall, burly fellow. Captain Marzano's face was fenced in, no wisp of emotion escaping.

Her father nodded at the courtesy of the information. It was none of any Olander's business who commanded, not strictly.

But Sascha was distracted from the conversation. There was something about this hexadron she didn't like. For a machine to transport soldiers, it looked wrong. It was too small. It had no proper Congress Worlds design but that odd ahtra shape, those six sides, waiting to engulf Captain Dammond and keep him. No, this was not a good idea.

Eli was talking to her father. Then he smiled and said something to her, she hardly knew what, and he was climbing in. She wanted to cry out, put a stop to this event. What did it matter what lay below ground if they were leaving and never coming back? What harm to leave these bunkers and their war trophies behind? Even if ahtra lurked in the those tunnels, they were at peace now; no one need discover them or their purposes.

Just as they were closing the hatch, Sascha darted forward. The inside of the hexadron glowed from temporary lights the techs had rigged. She looked at Eli and said, "I've decided to name my spiny amphibian after you, Captain."

"Thank you, Sascha. That would be an honor." Looking at her closely, he finished, "See you in a little while, then."

"Yes, but . . ."

He was watching her as he always did, patiently, as though he cared about what she might have to say.

"Sascha . . ." came her father's warning voice behind her.

She swallowed, struggling with whether to speak, whether to say, *Don't go, Captain. Don't go down.* . . . But there was no reason why, no argument a soldier would listen to.

"Hurry back," she said, at last, and conjured up her best smile, though it felt hollow as a spiny tree.

4

Inside, the hexadron was spare and simple. A small control panel contained finger-sized depressions cradling touch pads for boring and hatch controls. Eli sat with his knees drawn up and his neck slightly bent, his 5′10″ frame a tight fit in the capsule. His hand rested on the panel, but it was Sascha's face he saw before him, a fleeting look of fear darting across her eyes. *Why are you doing this,* she seemed to say. *Don't do this.*

He'd seen that look before, on his mother's face, when she watched four of her five sons and her husband enter the mines day after day, year after year. Eli wondered why she always expected the worst of the mines when it was never mining that killed her boys, but only the war—the one she'd been proud to send them off to. Three came home again in body bags. And Eli, despite many battles, had never taken so much as a scratch. So despite the combat decorations, Eli lacked one badge—the indelible one—of regen.

He pressed the declivity to engage the digger. Gears churned, and the frame shuddered so hard his teeth clattered. He clenched his jaw and braced his arms on the seat. After a few seconds the drilling took on a high-pitched whine paired with relentless grinding. Rock and dirt raced through the conveyor tubes of the hexadron's hull, spewing the tailings behind as the craft sank into the ground. Soon there would be only a trembling mound of soil at the surface where the digger had been.

It took longer than Eli expected. He switched on his lamp. His hand on the small range gun at his hip was damp with perspiration as the hexadron warmed to its task. It was a descent of 120 feet. Next to him was a tank of air, in case of trouble on the way down or back up. He didn't expect trouble, but that's just when it would probably happen. His father and brothers would have been at ease in such a place, deep in the bowels of a planet; but Eli had vowed he would never be a miner, and his parents chose the only other option: they sent him for a soldier. The draft would have snared him eventually anyway, and it was an honorable calling; until Eli showed an aptitude for an officer. Then he saw his father harden toward him, as though Eli's rise in rank set his brothers lower by default. If enlisted was good enough for them, it was good enough for Eli. But now that three of them were dead, how could he ever compete with that?

His ears were plugged with noise. Rocks ground beneath his feet as the hexadron lurched downward in small, shuddering jolts.

It felt like going into combat. Times like this were what a professional soldier trained for, maybe lived for. Times when the mental world peeled away, leaving you in the center of the moment, doubts left behind along with every other piece of cognition. He thought of the many times he'd slammed a shuttle down into atmosphere, ready to debark and fight . . . the old combat high . . . distant memory now after missions of transport, supply, administration, and routine. He still had his rank, despite the carnage that was not—at least officially—his fault in that last battle. Not the last battle of the war, by any means, but *his* last battle . . .

With a final lurch, the craft stopped.

Dead quiet crept in, replacing the roar of teeth against stone. His bones rang with harmonics, skin tingling. Pings of small rocks skittered off the hull. He fingered the hatch control. A sickening delay, then the scrape of the panel. Beyond, only black—and the piquant rush of oxygenated air.

Eli powered up his lamp and crawled through. The beam flashed on walls to the side, and the floor, a short drop down from where he stood. The techs had nailed the calibration to within inches.

He stepped out, leaving the hexadron mostly buried in the wall, all but the egress side.

The beam of the lamp revealed a shelf cut into stone, stretching out beyond the cone of light, but far enough to convince him that this tunnel was a construct. Some ten feet high by eight feet wide, the place had the look and smell of decay.

Standing now in the middle of the tunnel, he listened. Profound silence surrounded him. After a time, he heard faint sounds, buried sounds: hissing of air, dripping water, creaks of sediments giving way to gravity. Once—though it was surely imaginary—a remote shout. On another level, he registered only silence. It was as though his ears carried background noise, the reverberation of things heard before, erratic snips of sound lost in the maze of the cochlea.

He set off in the direction of the most extensive tunnels as mapped by the survey team. There was no machinery, no litter of artifacts, no rails or tracks, yet the walls themselves, in their regularity, spoke of purpose and permanence. In places, water seepage traced rusty fingers from ceiling to floor.

Pulling out his comm unit, he made his call to Roche on the surface. It was no surprise to him when it went unanswered. If radio didn't work on the surface, no reason why it would come to life 120 feet below ground. But he *would* follow procedures. It would all be done according to procedure.

Turning back, he secured his tether to the hexadron with a staple. When he glanced up from that task, he noted the walls again. Something odd about them, regular but pitted, gray with what might be a pinkish cast.

The place had to be ahtran—who else could have built this? If true, it was a momentous discovery. Command would want to know about this, and soon. Because ahtra were never known to use worlds other than their great metal spheres, the world-habitats. They were creatures of their metal worlds, only fighting on planetary surfaces for the rare ground offensive against Congress World targets.

If they mined here, what did they extract? No substitute for neymium, surely, the cause of decades of war. Neymium was the door to interstellar journeys, a fuel source so compatible with the fusion drives that ships were freed from the weight of massive fuel cargoes, freed to move fast enough, far enough. When Congress Worlds discovered the Belt, however, they found their trading partners had long since staked their claim, and weren't happy to share. Congress Worlds looked at the Belt and thought of freedom, wealth, and converse among their worlds without dependence on ahtra traders. The ahtra looked at the Belt and thought, *Keep out.*

Damn likely the ahtra had a similar view of the place where he now stood.

But they were at peace, Eli reminded himself. Still, it was a fragile construct, a thing of words and promises between two alien combatants. Perhaps, to the ahtra, agreements meant nothing. Of course, having a system of tunnels on a backwater planet did not break the peace. If that was all it was. But he felt certain there was more. And if there was, he'd find it, showing Command that he could pursue the ahtra when it was right to do so. Could pursue them as far as need be.

"To hell and back," he whispered. His own voice was a startling, almost a tangible thing in this quiet world, and made him feel vulnerable for the first time.

He came to a side tunnel. A profound smell of mustiness hit his nostrils. Playing out the tether, he turned down this branch. In the beam of the lamp around him, Eli noticed that, at the base of the walls, there were long ropes of soil. Kneeling, he picked up a tubelike section, fingering its dust as it spilled through his fingers.

He came to an enlargement of the corridor. As he swung his lamp he saw that he was in a large cavern with curious walls. The closest section contained nooks perhaps three feet wide, filled with tightly rolled material. He moved forward to touch it, judging it to be cloth from the threads that dangled from frayed edges. Pulling on one roll to dislodge it, an entire section of cloth separated, releasing a thin stream of sand from the center. He took a better grip and pulled again, this time removing the entire roll, which finally dropped out of the nook onto the floor, raising a small eruption of dust. Then it was a simple matter to kick open the roll. As it unwound, the cloth split in protest. Eli stared at the contents.

Bones. Human bones. No, surely ahtra bones. It was a burial chamber. The nooks contained hundreds of bodies. Eli looked back down at the bones he'd dislodged. If ahtran, the skull should show the junction of the data tendril. As he knelt down for a closer view, a sound came to his conscious mind, a noise he'd been hearing for the last seconds that he'd thought came from his own ears. Someone was approaching, running.

He stood, dousing his light and withdrawing to the wall. He could feel a burial roll pressing against his neck.

In another moment, light burst into the cavern and two ahtra appeared. Eli had time to notice their full armament, their guns drawn, before they spied him. His own gun was pointing at them and they hesitated. One of them spoke and brought his hand up in a slicing motion. If there were only two Eli might bring them down, but his situation was ambiguous. He appeared to be grave robbing, or at least desecrating. To them he was an intruder.

Besides, it was peacetime. He wouldn't be the first to fire.

He slowly lowered his gun.

The two ahtra advanced, circling him and herding him away from the burial cloth and its contents. As he stepped backward, Eli came in view of the corridor down which he'd come. Ten or fifteen ahtra stood there, holding greenish-yellow lights, casting their gray faces in a ghoulish light.

The first ahtra—whether male or female, he couldn't tell—spoke again, in that deep register characteristic of the species, their language unintelligible. Eli held his hands up, palms out, in a gesture even the ahtra knew.

He was surprised when the blow came, the butt end of the gun crashing across his temple. He sprawled backward from the force of it, felt the breath erupt from his lungs. As he fell, his last thought was *Ought to make a hell of a scar . . .*

King's pawn four, came the opening gambit.

Badri Nazim made a conventional opening, clearing the way for her queen to swoop out on one of its killing missions.

Sascha countered with king's pawn seven and the game was under way: nineteen-year-old corporal and veteran of the Great War against fourteen-year-old heir apparent to the Olander fortune. Nazim saw their chess games as a war of the proletariat against the entrenched monarchy.

But at another level, Nazim was utterly indifferent to the politics of status. To Sascha's delight, she just wanted to beat Sascha's pants off.

On the split screen, Sascha saw both chessboard and Nazim's tent, shared with her five buddies. It was a view that might at any time include varying states of undress, blistering language, and an easy—but to Sascha's mind, highly codified—six-way banter.

Nazim was fingering her unlit cigarette, flipping it over and under the digits of her left hand. Moving another pawn, she flicked her eyes at the screen. "Heard from him yet?"

"No." It had been five hours, and they hadn't heard from Captain Dammond. "It's still early," Sascha said. Hoped.

One of the enlisteds came up behind Nazim, putting his hand on her shoulder, apparently watching the chess game. He was smoking a cigarette.

"That was smart, figuring those fuckers for digging machines," Nazim allowed.

Sascha hadn't heard Nazim say either good or bad about Captain Dammond, so the compliment warmed her.

"Yeah, probably was," Sascha responded, practicing the laconic style of Nazim's world, a world where a man could put his arm around your shoulders and it didn't mean anything. Unless it did . . . The private's index finger was moving along the inside of Nazim's collar. All of which Nazim ignored, but easy, smiling a little. It was wonderful to be so easy around men. Noncommittal, friendly, but holding your own. Sascha committed the style of it to memory, but feared it wouldn't do in any social situation she could imagine. In her world, one must always have something to *say*. Preferably witty, or at least intelligent. Or knowingly gossipy. One didn't sit mute while a man stuck his finger under your collar.

Nazim moved her queen's pawn to a vulnerable d-4

position, which forced Sascha to decide between taking a pawn or continuing her attack on Nazim's rook.

"Well, son of a bitch," Sascha said, admiring the move. Nazim often thumbed her nose at chess theory; her approach could be summed up as *whatever works*.

Sascha made her decision—she took the pawn—so she could concentrate on the other half of the screen where the maneuvers were even more interesting.

From a cot in the back came the comment, "Marzano's all the captain we need," making it clear where the loyalties lay.

Nazim held her expression and her companion smirked. The game went on: chess, and finger in collar.

Sascha wouldn't win an argument in this venue, didn't want it to come between her and Nazim. Especially not tonight, when she'd hoped the captain would have been back, reporting on a moldering cache of weapons, long forgotten by the ahtra . . . or with a bloody but superficial wound, having taken on a bunker of thirty aliens.

Tonight she didn't want to hear the barracks' side of things, the stories of the alpha captain, the coward captain. She'd no heart to hear him vilified, his wrong background, attending the wrong schools—his hasty field promotions in the wake of the fifty million dead. She'd heard it all before—and deflected it all with cool disdain. She knew jealousy when she saw it. Eli Dammond was a self-made man whose humble background might never earn him a colonel's bars, but who loved the infantry, the command of troops. It was said that, given a new company, he knew every enlisted's name within a week and where they hailed from. With his prodigious memory, he could recite the RSC, Revised Starship Code, from front to back. Thus even the story of the *Recompense* made not the slightest wobble in her conviction that he was unjustly despised.

Nor would she hear of it tonight, of all nights.

Nazim was looking at her with a raised eyebrow, no more than a white scar arching over her eye. Sascha's mind had been wandering. How had Nazim threatened both the pawn and rook in one move?

"One of 'em's dog meat, Olander." Nazim could smell blood, and Sascha sat forward, concentrating.

As Sascha sorted through her moves, Nazim casually reached up and tugged on her companion's shirt, bringing him down to her level, kissing him full on the mouth. To Sascha's astonishment, when she released him, she exhaled a plume of cigarette smoke in a long, sinuous spurt. Sascha tried not to stare, but her concentration was blown.

It was purely the most elegant and sensual thing that Sascha had ever seen, both for its outrageousness and its casual execution. Already, as though it hadn't even mattered, the enlisted with the lit cigarette was moving away, talking with someone else. Unconscious of, or taking for granted, Nazim's playful and artistic act.

Sascha was deeply envious. It was an odd feeling, having consistently been the object of jealousy, to so desperately want a thing someone else had. She wasn't even sure what it was that Nazim had, that she wanted. Maybe it was a particular grace, in a woman whom Sascha's mother would judge to have none at all. Or perhaps it had to do with freedom, with ways of being a woman that had never occurred to her, or with being superbly suited to the place you chose. Again, the word came to mind: *grace*.

"Your move, Olander," Nazim said.

Sascha was three pieces down, but she hardly cared. "I am outmatched," she murmured, and Nazim smiled, taking the compliment as her due.

5

Deep in the flow of data, Maret Din Kharon became aware of a disturbance. Something was pushing on her body. This would be highly discourteous in the public data lobe where she had gated in. Reluctantly she disengaged from her devotions.

Vod Ceb Rilvinn stood at her side, nudging her shoulder. His gritty digger clothes were noted with sidelong glances by those nearby.

"Maret-as, attend me!" he said, careful not to touch her again.

"I am here, Vod-as." In truth, she was struggling to return. She released the data plug, and curled the tendril to her neck. "What is it?"

"Nefer Ton Enkar. She calls for you, but you haven't heard a thing; you've been wasting yourself with kin wagers." His expression conveyed what he thought of her devotions.

Maret's skin prickled at the mention of Nefer. "She calls me? When?"

"Now! For the past span and more." His agitation drove him to his feet again, tugging at her.

If Nefer was calling her so urgently that even the diggers knew, then she was very late. More debits against her. Nefer would rejoice.

Vod hurried her along with a discreet touch at her left elbow, urging her past others who found this little side way conducive to their data needs. No one would interrupt here—unless it was Nefer Most Prime herself.

Vod fumbled at the portal to the nearest travel chute, opening it wide for her. He had paled in his emotional distress, causing his markings to recede. Vod was ever too emotional, but his concern was sweet.

"Vod-as, why hurry me to my detractor?"

"So she won't debit you beyond recovery."

"I am ever in her debt."

"She'll ruin you," he growled. His eyes held hers in a gaze that would be rude had they not been friends so long.

"Nefer needs me." She was Nefer's Chief Data Illuminator. It was not a trivial position.

"Then don't keep her waiting." He slammed the hatch behind her.

"Nefer Ton Enkar," she vocalized, and the sled shot away, an approved transit from Nefer herself, no doubt, and a luxury of mixed benefit that Maret had come to associate with excruciating audiences with her static mistress.

Eli fought his way back to consciousness. Through blurry vision he saw a small room without ornament or furniture other than the pallet on which he lay. But it was less a room than a smoothly carved space, walls meeting ceiling in an uninterrupted line. He was bound firmly, lying on his side.

An ahtra knelt before him. He or she wore loose

long pants and a cropped shirt, cut from a richly patterned material in brown and red. From his one previous encounter with ahtra civilians, he recognized the typical garment pattern of squares within squares. Males and females dressed alike, he knew, but by the drape of the shirt he guessed this individual was a female. The face, hands, and forearms were covered with the faint circular markings for which humans gave ahtra the sobriquet *pocks*. This individual bore a large oval pattern precisely between the eyes.

Eli spoke. "I am Captain Eli Dammond, of Congress World Sixth Transport Division. I meant no harm, coming here." If they hadn't heard the war was over, he hoped they'd take the news well.

The ahtra gave no indication of having understood him. Eli noted the thick data tendril that curled from the left side of the back of the bald skull. It was folded tightly against the head, reaching almost to the neck.

The ahtra leaned in closely, staring at him, eyes profoundly dark blue, the whites no more than a halo around the extended iris. A nictitating membrane closed up from below as it blinked. Its graceful lips parted to reveal small white teeth and an expression that might have been a begrudging smile or a heartfelt sneer.

They left him alone then, tightly bound, ignoring his calls of protest. When they finally came for him and summoned him to his feet, it was a relief to move.

They led him out of the cell, and down a brightly lit corridor with a ceiling just a little too low to look proper. He was taller than his guards, a full head taller, but it wasn't a great advantage when they were armed and he wasn't. Passages diverged frequently from the corridor they followed, revealing a bewildering array of tunnels and stairwells. All were covered in a slightly irregular, rubbery-looking material. He took pains to remember this route, trying to maintain his orientation to his entry point.

Though he'd been stunned or drugged, he thought he had been conveyed some distance from the burial chamber on a mechanized transport.

Bad luck that they'd come upon him in the burial chamber—but his reception might bode worse than offended sensibilities. He had discovered an extensive underground warren; this labyrinth was no longer an ahtran secret. Unless they killed him . . .

His escort brought him to a room where a patterned carpet covered half the floor.

Two ahtra faced him, one seated on the carpet, the other on the bare floor. One of them—from the discernible oval in the center of her forehead—might be the one who had inspected him earlier. The other individual was seated off to the side, wearing more simple attire, yet patterned. This aide—if that was the designation—spoke:

"I have your speech, and will signify for Nefer Ton Enkar, who requires your attention."

The accent was an excellent approximation of Standard. "I understand," Eli said. Perfume saturated the air, bringing a slight nausea upon him. Or perhaps it was this close view of the hairless, bronze-skinned creatures, aliens he *had* seen before, had seen close up . . . and under worse circumstances.

The one called Nefer spoke, articulating the guttural ahtran speech.

The interpreter said, "My mistress wishes to know how you came to the burial place."

He decided on the short answer. "In the digging machine, which we found on the surface. We meant no harm."

"How many came with you?"

"Just myself."

The interpreter spoke now to Nefer, and they conferred for some time, with Nefer keeping her gaze on the carpet. Complex symbols nested in squares within squares, like a mandala in reds, black, and gray.

The interpreter translated. "Why did you venture to disturb our departed kin? Do your people not tend to show honor to the dead?"

"It was an error of ignorance. I couldn't guess it was a burial site. My people don't bury our dead this way."

"You would not be aware of human catacombs?" the interpreter asked without reference to Nefer.

Old Earth had societies where catacombs were used. It astonished him that the ahtra knew this. "Yes," he said, "but it is a very ancient custom, no longer much known. I apologize for the offense."

The blink came from the bottom up. "Perhaps you were careless?"

He ignored the rebuke. He had no wish to convey undue deference. "Please translate my apology for your mistress."

As far as he could tell, his interpreter did so. Hearing this, Nefer raised her hands slightly in a gesture he took for acceptance, but which might also have been a shrug of indifference. Nefer looked at Eli for the first time. He thought he had seen more sympathetic eyes on drill sergeants. But ahtran eyes were very large—larger than a horse's. It was disconcerting, and perhaps accounted for their look of a raptor. Seeing the two ahtra together, he noticed that this Nefer looked different than the interpreter, with less prominent markings.

The interpreter spoke again. "My mistress would know your rank and mission among us and how many are with you . . . above."

He told the truth, since it wasn't clear to him if more or fewer troops would be to his advantage. He explained the situation of the marooned group, and that he had intended to leave the surface within a week, having stayed long enough to collect evidence in regard to the absence from duty of Luce Marzano and her crew. The discovery of the working hexadron and the tunnels, however, prompted an investigation, armistice or no.

There was a long silence as both ahtra stared at the floor. Finally, Nefer asked, through the aide, "What armament have you brought with you?"

"We have little. We are a transport ship. No threat to you."

When the aide translated this, he noted that the lead ahtra's data tendril jerked, almost like a startle reflex. The interpreter looked up at him. The dark eyes fixed him in a disconcerting, long gaze. When the gaze was withdrawn, it was like a sentence being passed. The room grew stifling—overwarm and more perfumed.

"Release my bonds, as a courtesy," he said. "You have my word I intend no violence."

Nefer granted permission and the aide came over to unfasten the ties. The aide's facial patterns were mirror images on each side, with the largest ovals resting on the cheekbones.

"What is your name?" he asked.

The ahtra's head turned to the side, avoiding his eyes while working the ties. The light caught the skin tracings in high definition for a moment, showing gradations of bronze coloring, deepening to brown. "I am Maret," the aide answered very low.

Eli rubbed at his wrists and arms while the aide moved back into place. Before questions could resume, he said, "My superiors will want to know the purpose of your presence here. How shall I answer them?"

Nefer took a long time to answer.

Maret translated. "We occupy this world as is our right. Below."

They sat for some time, waiting for Nefer to continue.

When she did not, Eli ventured, "You abide by the treaty terms?" Not that he would believe their answer.

"It happens we have always been here. It is not forbidden by treaty."

"I am free to go?" The silence greeting this was rather longer than he would have liked. "It would be against the treaty for you to keep me here."

"Yes. This presents a difficulty."

He filled the silence by saying, "Perhaps I can help you with your difficulty."

Nefer turned to the interpreter and spoke softly for a time. Then she rose and moved past him, toward the entrance. She spoke something directly to him for the first time. The words were like rocks ground together. She left the room, ushering in four other ahtra, who remained standing by the door.

Maret looked at the floor as she translated, "My mistress says she is very sorry."

The heat in the room was mounting. "I hope she has no reason to be sorry for what she can still avoid doing." The gaps in their conversation were swollen silences, with a presence of their own. He waited.

Finally Maret looked at him. "You cannot leave now."

"Then when?"

"As you measure it, you would say . . . a few weeks. I am very sorry."

"My people will grow alarmed at such a delay. It will attract military attention." He thought that might not be true. They could leave without him, assuming he had suffocated in the capsule or in the tunnels.

"Yes, regrettably."

"What is the difficulty? Your position, if you hoped it to remain secret, is likely to be exposed, even if you never release me. There's no point in keeping me here, and much reason to permit my return."

After a slow blink, she said: "I very deeply regret to bear the news to you that your people will all die. I am very sorry. There is nothing we can do."

He stared at her.

Her dark eyes were calm as she said, "No one will survive—above. I am sorry."

He fought back his alarm. "If you attack, Congress Worlds will find you and destroy you. These tunnels can't protect you." That was no bluff. They would come, for the general's daughter and granddaughter—eventually.

"We will not attack. It will not be our doing. You have no armament . . . to speak of. You will tend to be overwhelmed."

"Let me go back, then, to warn them." She was standing up to go. He also rose, aware of the guards shifting behind him. "No matter who attacks my people, you will be blamed. The armistice is fragile. Maret, do you want war?"

"No."

"Then help us. Let me warn them."

"This would not be possible."

Her passivity was maddening. He found himself stepping toward her, gripping her by the forearm. "By God, it *is* possible!" As he held her arm, she visibly paled.

The guards grabbed him from behind, and he allowed them to restrain him for the moment.

Maret's eyes took on a glaze as she stood taller and brushed at the place where he had grabbed her. "They are as dead already," she said placidly.

He surged forward, despite the restraints. Strong hands locked him in place. Maret hastily backed away from him, retreating toward the door. He cried out after her: "No, this will not happen!"

She paused in the doorway, saying, "No one can hear you." Then the door closed behind her with sucking noise.

* * *

A thin stream of dirt cascaded onto Vod's head from the bare rock overhead. He looked up into the blackness where foam girders held the lid of the tunnel in place. So far from the comforting walls of DownWorld, the smell of dirt and the sight of oozing water claimed his senses. He was uneasy, though he'd spent his whole life working amid the dirt and the wet.

The tunnels here were *wrong,* no matter what the Prime Engineer said.

They had eighteen increments of rest before work resumed. Around him, his fellow workers slumped against the walls, fatigued, plugged in. Crouching among the shavings of the tunnel, he sank his tendril into the temporary gates strung along the work shaft.

His backmind swelled with data.

Nefer Ton Enkar commandeered a forward position for her latest data. It hove into view, bragging of completion rates, hexals of ways dug, rebored, renewed, and inspected. She bragged of safety records, projected outputs, maintenance cycles, and increments of cost. He bypassed this propaganda with irritation, barely suppressing a pallor of disgust. Nefer and her numbers. Slime data.

His backmind quickly scanned the data streams. News strands were full of the human among them. Wagers clogged the fields: the human would stay, for how long; he would leave, by when. Nefer would kill him, the choice of execution style. Some wagered that there were more humans, their true numbers, what they would do. Some bet on war.

Vod noted with chagrin that Maret was assigned as the human's custodian. A flurry of exploratory wagers flickered into view. She would fail, by when. She would lose favor, she would fail in training, she would achieve ronid, she would not. So this was the path, Vod thought, by which Nefer would ruin Maret. He forced himself to attend to the wager streams. There appeared a shocking wager on which past kin the human had defiled in the reliquary. Many calls for censure greeted this wager; it was withdrawn. Then a flood of sentimental remembrances, wagers in honor of past kin, a show of devotion, many half-hearted and skimpy, an emotional crest in the data flow soon subsumed by the general flood of speculation on the human captain and the baleful events that his arrival must portend. Events that fluxors saw as *interesting* and statics as *ominous*.

All in all, it was an uproar. A fine distraction that he would not put it past Nefer to have orchestrated. Diggers were dying in the relentless boring through DownWorld. *But now we have a human among us to breed new fortunes in the wager fields.* Well, Maret was less and less the fluxor to lead them from their misery. Maret tended strongly to study, and though scholarship was all very well, scholars were not leaders.

Nefer herself groomed Maret for scholarship, funded her. So Maret studied. Already she knew more than most of her teachers. She knew mathematics, history, her kin to the twelfth net, and even spoke the human standard language. It would be so like Nefer to use Maret's strengths against her.

In the tendency of dwellers to be either fluxor or static, Maret was, Vod believed, more central on the scale than most. Though a fluxor, she tended more toward tradition and caution than most fluxors—more than himself, certainly—and therefore had appeal as a leader who could command the respect of statics. Vod had alienated most dwellers at one time or another. But it was his birth stamp, his pattern. Dwellers do not change their markings, the saying went.

As his tendril disengaged from the gate, he noticed Irran sitting next to him along the tunnel wall. Her scent stirred him. But already the diggers were moving back to work, and he abandoned the idea of finding a side lobe with her. Irran was always one to rush the season.

Along with Harn and Wecar, he traipsed back toward their stations in the borer.

Wecar spoke. "The human," she began. "Maret-as will show you the human before we see him." She was curious to see this fabled creature.

Vod hurried to answer before the machine drowned out all talk. "We'll see what Nefer decrees. Maret has no say in this."

"They say he is pale as a mushroom," Wecar said.

"And bad smelling," Harn added.

"Nefer Ton Enkar will kill him," Wecar said. She climbed onto the borer, into the driver's well.

Before Wecar could close herself in, Harn threw back: "Nefer won't *kill* him, she *sent* for him. Otherwise, how could he be here?"

There was no good answer for this question. But if Nefer had sent for him, Vod mused, why? *We are done with war.* They had fought the humans to their knees. Hemms, who even Nefer must attend, bragged that the humans had sued for peace. And ahtra granted it, even though it would have been only justice to kill them all.

As Wecar slammed the driver's well door, Vod and Harn took their places in the cab. The cutterhead growled to life, biting into stone.

Vod's tendril no more than touched the data plug when he knew something was wrong. The pressures had mounted to limits of tolerance, ground shifts signaled from all sides. He beat the warning system by a breath, shouting over the voice path, "Out, out! Get out!" He heard the driver's cab door open, heard bells clanging. Through the cab window he saw the First Engineer racing away to safety, a sure sign from a cowardly static that a ground shift was under way. Vod found himself outside the borer amid pandemonium. The Second Engineer tried to urge Wecar to return to the driver's well to back the machine out, but she refused. Now Vod was in a crowd of workers shoving to get out of the tunnel even as the ground creaked around them. Sand cascaded from overhead. Rocks spit onto their helmets.

Vod stooped beside Wecar, her helmet dented by a great stone. As he dragged her forward, a roar sped toward them from the habitat of death itself. Billowing dust overtook them, followed by a deluge of rock and soil. It caught Vod's feet, pitching him headlong, then carried him forward in a monstrous wave of dirt. It struck the breath from his chest and locked his arms in place, ripping Wecar from his grasp.

Soil drilled up his nose, and he knew the terror of suffocation . . . but then a draft of cool air touched his head and his face. He snatched a breath. The dirt fell over him again. He was pinned in the slide like a boulder. He felt someone—Wecar he hoped—squeeze his ankle, once, twice. He lay rigid in the weight of the spill, wiggling his head a little to form a hole by his nose. Then he heard voices and someone was freeing the dirt around his head, then his shoulders. As strong hands gripped under his armpits and pulled him free, he saw Wecar's hand protruding from the snub end of the slide.

"Wecar," he gasped, looking into the faces of his fellow diggers. "Find Wecar."

They left him propped up against the wall and returned to the fray. Moments later a rumble heralded a further slump of debris. He scrambled back to the massive incursion of soil, digging with bare hands alongside his co-workers.

Much later, when all hope was spent, he staggered out of the fresh dig, past the terrible faces of kin assembling down-tunnel, carrying the rugs of those they feared dead.

But it was Wecar's hand reaching from the soil that long remained in his mind.

6

During the night the rains came. At first, lying on her cot and awakened by the noise of droplets on the tent, Sascha thought that someone was showering the tent with pebbles. She lay listening to the staccato beat, her body tingling, as though registering the taps herself. In the dark, her body was vast, her mind a gentle curl in the midst of a hot, dark realm.

A puff of wind punched at the tent, carrying the smell of mud and rain. She looked over to her parents' cots. "Father?" she whispered.

"I hear it." His voice was barely audible.

"Rain," she said. After a pause: "They said it never rained."

"They were wrong."

The mirror on the center tent pole shone with a blue iridescence, reflecting Cristin's nearby computer screen, still active, running her mother's equations. Sascha thought she might sleep, lulled by the soothing white noise of rain. She remembered a line from an old poem: "For rain, it hath a friendly sound/ To one who's six feet underground." She wondered if Captain Dammond could hear the rain. She wondered about him constantly, one moment hoping he was alive, and then—considering his entombment—hoping he had died swiftly.

Sleep was impossible. She sat up, hearing voices outside.

Her mother's drowsy voice: "Go back to sleep, Sascha."

But Sascha found her boots and went to the tent flap. Peering out, she saw a sheet of rain lit by the nearest camp light. "It's raining, Mother," she said.

"Yes. And now we shall have mud as well as heat."

More voices. The camp was waking up, though morning was nowhere in sight. A few people stood in the aisles between the tents and let the rainfall wash them. Sascha put out her arm, feeling the rain like small stabbing needles. Her body shivered in the cool lashing. She had seen many rains, but this one was so different. Perhaps she reacted to the crew of the *Fury*—without rain these three years—gathering outside, seeing it with the eyes of wonder.

By dawn, it was a revitalized camp. Everyone remarked on the rain, enjoying the clean, cooler air. Soldiers wiped down items that had been left out and were now spattered with mud. Remnants of clouds scudded overhead, receding as the sun took over, boosted by its dwarf twin.

She wandered through camp, jumping the queue at the mess tent, and grabbing a piece of bread. Munching on it, she sloshed through puddles, already disappearing into the sand.

Captain Marzano and Lieutenant Roche were standing in the clearing at the center of camp. Marzano's brown uniform and Roche's blue—Infantry and Transport, respectively. As Marzano and Roche conferred, Sascha wished she could eavesdrop as they discussed the subject on every-one's mind.

Captain Dammond had been gone two days. The first few hours were the worst, with everyone waiting for his return or expecting—though no one spoke it—an attack if ahtra were below. From snippets of conversation, Sascha knew what the enlisteds were thinking; that Dammond got caught in a rocky grave trying to play hero. They had never thought ahtra hid below; everyone knew that pocks lived in hexadrons. If the ahtra came to this world, as it seemed they had, perhaps they, too, tried to investigate the tunnels, and failed—as Dammond had.

Now Lieutenant Roche's Transport crew were ea-ger to leave. They'd finished combing the wreck of the *Fury*. The evidence—neither condemning nor exonerating Marzano—was boxed up and loaded on the *Lucia*. But they waited, giving Dammond the benefit of the doubt.

Shamelessly, Cristin added her voice to the arguments, urging a return to what she called civilization. Sascha saw clearly what civilization would mean for her; a life like her mother's, talking and steering conversations, attending to people and their endless social stirrings. Sascha might have an avocation, a ladylike pursuit such as math or physics, but she would not go mucking about in the wilderness, not once grown. So Sascha stayed just one step this side of womanhood. But she felt—with a numb certainty—that once she wore the dresses of the general's granddaughter, everything would betray her at once. Her bosom would show itself beneath the thin silks, her first blood would come. And it would all be over.

She made her way among the uniforms, the soldiers winding their way to breakfast, eyes averted, except those regen eyes that seemed to focus in all directions at once. She had seen a soldier in a regen bath once, floating like a sea plant, a small nub appearing at each of the three severed limbs. The limbs would grow perfectly, except for color, which rumor had it could be done better and wasn't, by design. The enlisteds liked their fleshy medals of valor.

A sheen of iridescence caught the sun, a long ribbon of pink and lavender at the bottom of the ditch. This trickle was all that remained of the small torrent that swept through last night: a mere line of moisture, bubbling before sinking into the dirt. Sascha walked closer, kneeling next to the rivulet. Instead of bubbles, the froth was composed of a myriad of tiny insects, their backs draped in the diaphanous shawls of their wings. She had to lean very close to see them.

From behind her came a voice. "Mind they don't bite your pretty nose."

She looked up to see Sergeant Ben Juric. With the sun behind him, his face was backlit, and she couldn't tell by his expression how much sarcasm he intended. "They must like the water," she said, pointing at the insects. "Or what's left of it."

"They do. Crawled right out of it."

Sascha looked more closely. She'd assumed they'd flown and alighted there. But even as she watched, the gnats crawled from the mud, wings slicked back and rapidly drying in the sun. She squinted up at the sergeant. "Most people wouldn't notice something like that."

"I pay attention."

This was the longest conversation she'd had with the sergeant in their three months of shipboard acquaintance.

Emboldened, she asked: "You think he's coming back?" No preamble needed for the question on everyone's mind. If he answered yes, he'd be on the captain's side; if he answered no, then not. People showed their hearts by what they hoped for and what they thought they'd get. Like the disappointment her mother saw every time she looked at her daughter.

The question got him moving. He strode past her, his left side to her, the side they said was all new growth.

"No," she heard him say, low and certain.

Sascha stood up, unwilling to leave it. "It was a brave thing, to hunt them out down there." When Juric didn't stop, she added, "All by himself."

Juric paused then, turning to fix her with one cooked eye. "Don't confuse brave with stupid."

She tramped up to him, the words cascading out. "What have you got against him, all of you?"

Juric probed at his teeth with his tongue. "Well, let's see. How about your alpha captain taking an old man's job in Transport? How about your captain skating through twelve years of war and never taking a wound? Skin as smooth as a baby's bottom."

"Those aren't fair reasons to hate a man." She had an urge to shake some sense into him as he stood there with his ugly grin.

"Every soldier knows *fair* when he sees it, princess."

She advanced a step. "Don't . . . ever . . . call me that."

His grin broadened, and he gave a mock salute, leaving her fuming in the heat.

Later that morning she and Nazim hooked up for chess. Nazim looked to be alone in her crew tent; no subtext to their chess game today, then. Sascha was mildly disappointed, but thought she might therefore have a better chance to win, undistracted.

"Hey, Olander," Nazim said, advancing a pawn onscreen. Her unlit cigarette rested behind one ear like an extra weapon. Sascha knew that Nazim had given up smoking. Keeping the cigarette at hand was sheer bravado.

"Nazim, you ugly bastard," Sascha threw back, enlisted-style.

"I feel real lucky today, Olander. Gonna beat your alpha ass," Nazim said cheerily,

"Bull*shit*," Sascha said.

But perhaps Nazim's white hair might be proof of luck. Then again, getting half her skull blown off might be proof of *bad* luck.

7

Maret hurried down the PrimeWay, fury in her chest and a fine mask of calm over her features. She spoke to those she should, according respect, but moved on as quickly as propriety allowed.

Data stewards beckoned to her from posts along the way, promising strands into the flow. When they saw her, they offered tidbits of archival data on the human species, along with wagers on the human's fate. Failing to close a deal, they tailored wagers for her kin nets, issues that her kin had once followed and would wager on now if they lived. Most times she would have placed a wager or two, remembering her kin as though they still strove in fluxor affairs and surrounded her with close relation.

Pausing, she purchased a few remembrances of those lost in the tunnel cave-in, and then resumed her course to the galleries of Nefer Ton Enkar. It was well that Nefer had locked her out of access to a chute this time. If Maret had arrived in Nefer's presence earlier, she would have disgraced herself with a display of emotion. She wasn't sure which emotion would have exposed itself: anger at being denied access to Tirinn Vir Horat, her Data Guide, or fear that Nefer had at last turned on her as Vod always predicted she would.

Nefer was her benefactor. Nefer opened the gates of opportunity for Maret, lavishing resources on her, enabling her to perform prodigious devotions, and sweeping aside every obstacle to study, paying for almost unbridled access to the data flow. Sometimes Maret thought that Nefer had some feeling for her.

She believed this less and less these days.

The PrimeWay was fragrant today. Lorel blossomed from cultivated patches on the walls, beckoning with a new odor, tailored to the coming season. Maret stopped to pluck some, taking sustenance for the interview with Nefer Most Prime—ever an exhausting prospect.

A steward nearby whispered to her, "It's been many spans since I had a wager of you, Maret-as."

She turned to face him, her reverie impinged. "Tomorrow, Bir-as, tomorrow." She hurried on, shunting to backmind the obligation to Bir and also backminding how much she could afford to wager. Sometimes backmind was more cautious than prime mind; but in matters of wealth, this was proper.

Striving to maintain her color, Maret hurried on. All along the way, dwellers watched her for a sign of whether the human among them was a portent of disaster. All humans carried the scent of carnage and war. For Maret, their odor carried a further strand of revulsion. . . .

She was in training for ronid. She was the last of her bloodline; if she died in war the thread of her lineage would dissolve, except in the deep wells of data where nothing was lost.

Nefer looked at her with a friendly expression, taking up a tiny wand of snuff and inhaling.

"How fares the grave-defiler?" Nefer asked, as Maret seated herself on the adjoining rug.

A small plate of food lay between them. Maret ate a morsel for sociability, answering, "He hides his distress poorly."

"Yes. I have been most concerned for him. But he is now calm."

"Drugs?"

Nefer raised her hand, confirming it was so and of no importance.

If the human was drugged, Maret doubted she could win his confidence as she was expected to. "He may resent the drugs."

"He was raving."

"What did he say?"

"He voiced your name."

"Why was I not called?"

A pause before Nefer answered. "You were determined to see Tirinn Vir Horat. We tried to reach you." Nefer adjusted her position, seated cross-legged in front of Maret. "Hemms Extreme Prime must wonder if you neglect your duty."

"But mistress, the human has reason to be in distress. I cannot much help him and I have many other obligations—such as ronid."

"I cannot say how you will perform your duty." She looked at Maret, still friendly. "Can I?"

Maret was shamed by the rebuke. "No, mistress. I will attend him." She leaned forward to refill the snuff wand. "The flow swells with agitation over this event," Maret went on. "The human camps will perish. Who among the human worlds will believe we did not kill them?"

Nefer answered, "Who will know they died? The first ship was lost for three years. Now another ship will have disappeared. Who will care now that never cared before?"

"Yes. But the human claims they will know."

"He would."

"Yes. But if he is right?"

Nefer sat very still, her color holding. "When was a fluxor admitted to high counsels?"

"Forgive, mistress." Maret stared at Nefer's rug, woven with her ancestral designs.

"There is much to forgive lately, Maret-as. One tends toward exasperation. But if you share in the regrettable agitation of your inferiors, I will assure you that we are ready to fight if the humans attack. Did you think me defenseless?"

"No, certainly not." Maret looked steadfastly at the floor. "But . . ." Though the silence was a great weight, Maret pushed through it. "Why bother with this single human?"

Nefer waited a long time to answer. "Though we are not afraid to fight, it may be well to avoid an unnecessary conflict. This may require us to have a survivor. One who can vouch for us. To say what killed them."

Maret looked up at her, barely containing her surprise. "Why would he do us this favor?"

"It will not be a favor. It will be the truth." Nefer held Maret's gaze as she added: "And though he will hate us, he will come to admire you."

Maret concealed her disgust at the notion of the human forming any fond opinion of her. She would much rather have his hostility.

Within Nefer's placid face, her eyes were unrelenting. Nailing home her point, she added, "This is the Extreme Prime's hope, and mine."

And so, Maret thought with a sinking heart, it was a command.

"One thing in addition," Nefer said, taking another small line of snuff. "The matter of ronid."

Maret held very still.

"Such a distraction from your work." Nefer wiped a

remnant of snuff from her upper lip. "It is very disagreeable, is it not, to place oneself in needless danger? One must admire those who attempt ronid. A deeply proper occupation, certainly. But I have withdrawn all resources supporting your further training with Tirinn Vir Horat." She pushed the plate of cella forward, encouraging Maret to partake. "One might leave such things to fluxors of— lower capacity. Might one not?"

At this statement, Maret felt her skin cool in anger. Nefer herself could never summon the courage to enter a freshly dug tunnel, much less attempt ronid.

Nefer watched Maret with a close gaze. "You do look well when you are distressed, Maret-as. A static pallor, might one say? You should have been born a static. It would make my job so much easier." In the heavy silence that followed, she murmured, "Your genome is to study, Maret-as, as mine is to lead."

Then, liking to finish with such a fine homily, she signaled the interview at an end.

He dreamed he was a young boy, walking through a puzzle.

It was a maze in a field, like the one he had once gone to with his father. The farmer had trodden down the cornstalks, creating paths that twisted in endless serpentine patterns. Looking up at the corn around him, Eli found himself in caverns of gold. A matching maze of blue above was the sky. By the time he looked ahead again, his father was gone, and he ran to catch up. But at the turn there were two directions to choose from, each one long and stalky and yellow. He called out, but the only answer was the scrape of husks in the wind. He ran on, taking all right turns, thinking to himself, *First I'll try right, then left . . .* but there was no logic to the corn maze, and his father was gone, though from time to time he thought he saw, through the sea of husks, a flicker of the man he sought. He pursued that flicker; it was all he had. When at last he saw a figure at the end of a row, and approached, it proved to be a creature with bronze skin, and the marks of a leopard. . . .

"Captain Eli Dammond." The voice was low and cooing. "Eli Dammond, you will please make an effort to wake up."

It was the voice of dry corn husks.

Again his name was spoken. This time by a goblin. He blinked as the room came into focus.

"If you wake up, I will remove your restraints."

He thought of plunging back into the maze; it was preferable to where he feared he really was. But he opened his eyes. He was in a small round room devoid of furnishings except for the pallet beneath him. The ahtran at his side was the one with matching oval pocks on each high cheek.

"You are thirsty. Drink this." The goblin had pulled him up into a sitting position. It put a tube in his mouth that delivered water. The goblin had a burnished brown skin with silver rings etched just below the surface, the size of a baby's fist, a chicken's egg . . . but his vision blurred. Events of the last few hours came back to him in nauseous snatches. They had drugged him—whether before or after the beating, he wasn't sure.

"You are awake now."

"Drugged, damn you."

"So you will be calm."

So he would be helpless.

"My troops . . ."

"No, Eli Dammond." Her voice sounded like a deep purr. "We will not speak of them."

He rose up, braced by one hand, and tried to get his feet under him, but the room morphed into odd shapes, dizzying him. Rage swelled in his chest. "Back . . . let me back . . ."

"You called for me. But I will leave if you tend toward this subject."

He reached for her arm and managed to latch on to it, yanking her close. The goblin's eyes were sapphire blue. Within the orbs, a lighter iris was set, and within that an inner ring. Worlds within worlds. Bonds within bonds.

He hauled her closer, pushing the words into her face: "My troops, my camp."

"If you return you will die."

"Don't care . . ." he said, still gripping the slim wrist.

"My mistress does not permit you to die."

"Then she is . . . my enemy." They all—all were his enemy. He had fought his guards, and blows came. Then drugs. They were cowards to subdue him so. He tried to tighten his hold on her wrist, but the power in her hands was extraordinary.

She pried his fingers easily off her wrist. "Quiet yourself."

"Kill me. Then I'll be quiet." His voice sounded like an ahtran growl. He sipped at the water from the tube. The room began to settle into a consistent shape.

Maret settled in front of him. "Now I will tell you how things are disposed to be for you." Her voice was low and eerily calm. It stoked his fury, but he banked that for later. "You have shown unseemly agitation to your guards. Such outbursts shall not be tolerated."

"They needed correction," he mumbled. They had taken him into some awful communal bathroom where he was urged to void his bladder. Somewhere in that trip he had come to blows with his guards.

She looked at him with a long, slow blink. "You came among us as a criminal, insulting our dead. Leaving aside that graceless act, you came armed into the heart of

DownWorld. We did not look for you or ask for you. Your ships above are unwelcome, and incline toward deep offense. Yet we do not retaliate. Odds are, no one of you will survive above, but that is not of our doing. We know you are a soldier and your disgrace will be to live. Do not lecture me on human psychology. But what you want is not noticed among us. Nefer Ton Enkar wishes for you to remain safe and for me to see to your comfort. Her reasons will not be questioned. If you are violent, as is your birth stamp, you will be subdued. I do not wish to remove your last realm of freedom, your mind. Do not bring this upon yourself. Do not presume to have information of me. You will have information as may be permitted by the graciousness of Nefer Most Prime. Among the ahtra information is not free. I am very deeply sorry for the coming deaths of your command. But we have no responsibility for them, neither causing them nor shirking our responsibility to intervene. Be obedient, Eli Dammond. I am very deeply sorry to tell you of your harsh circumstances. Accept what you can and resolve to be calm."

"Go to hell." He closed his eyes to shut her up.

But she wouldn't let him be. "That would be a human insult, Eli Dammond, not an ahtran one. You must study your enemy to know a proper insult."

Eli thought her neck fragile enough to know a good insult. But he bided his time.

She continued, "It is a very human mistake to measure all things against yourselves. Your culture is young, and you tend to immature error. Thus you will not have a perspective to understand the ahtra. You believe, for example, that Hemms Extreme Prime is female, inferring female leadership from my position and my mistress'. Do not assume a gender bias in our culture because one exists in your own. Gender is irrelevant among us. Of much greater import is the tendency toward fluxor or static. You may take some liberties with a fluxor, Eli Dammond, but when in the presence of a static, you will do well to conform. That was a static guard who gave you the disfiguring bruise, you apprehend."

He opened his eyes to look at this creature. "And what is your tendency, Maret? Toward beating your prisoners, or not?"

"That would be an offensive question."

An ahtran insult. Good. He closed his eyes again as a wave of nausea overtook him.

The creature Maret remained silent then, watching him as he fell back into a stupor.

The usual pictures played out on the back of his eyelids. The bridge of the *Recompense*. Screens on every side, each one filled with fire, fire from the *Fidelity*, from the *Raptor*. Radio channels clogged with shouts, some incoherent, some all too clear. He thought he heard the ship hull scream, metal torqued beyond endurance.

The *Recompense* shuddered under a hit, lights failed, came back, failed again. In strobelike frames, Eli saw the bridge crew in random moments of chaos—Lieutenant Nule's face was bleached, his eyes always on Eli, waiting for orders.

All the while the bridge filled with noise like the world cracking open, releasing monsters, bellowing.

8

The forest was changing. The enlisteds said so. Sascha had seen the grass sprouting in camp like a patchy beard. But she wanted to see the forest.

Sascha waited for one of the torrential rain squalls that lashed the camp and made a dash past the desultory guards on the perimeter.

Though both camps were officially on alert, few believed in the possibility of ahtran attack. Captain Dammond was missing from mischance, not malice. Meanwhile the enlisteds awaited the decision to leave. Soldiers stood around in tight knots, resigned to more waiting. Oddly, the ones that had been waiting three years seemed more patient than the ones that just got here. But for everyone, life was suspended until they dug the captain out or gave him up.

The digging reports were ominous. Field bots morphed into diggers had initially gouged out a crater some twenty feet wide and six deep, but the walls slumped in during the first rain, creating more of a mud wallow than an excavation. From gradiometer imaging they knew the hexadron was buried deep. If Captain Dammond was alive, he'd be in the tunnel below, perhaps unable to activate the hexadron for the return trip. The plan, which every hour looked more desperate, was for the two bots to drill their way down and morph into a machine capable of repairs to the hexadron.

Sascha ran in the opposite direction from the digging operation, toward the Gray Spiny Forest, rumored to be outgrowing its name. After four days of pacing the compound, ducking her mother, pestering her father at his desk, and—in her mind—clawing out that muddy in-filled shaft with her own fingers, she needed a cheering sight.

Smells of wet soil and mud surrounded her. In the distance thunder ground out a swallowed roar, but the lightning was missing. Something was always missing. This world was bound up in secrets, like the hexadron to nowhere, like the fate of Captain Dammond, like the precursors of all those bones in the valley where she'd found her amphib.

Her father tolerated her nickname, amphib. By the dentition and morphology, many of the specimens they'd collected resembled amphibians. Now that Null revealed its water, the classification began to fit.

She was in the spiny forest, standing in an eddy of light. The squall had passed, leaving her feet sunk halfway in mud, her shirt adhering like a droopy skin. A patina of pale green shone from the stick trees. It was an intermittently green world, where one slant of light brewed a verdant palette to the forest, another a gray-brown. On the nearest tree she noted that the inner grooves of nascent green now bulged as though swollen with water—ballooning over the ridges of the bark grooves, and grown lighter in color with the expansion. Sascha took out her knife and sample bag, cutting into the curdle of green, the first blush of an unguessed-at spring. From the tops of a few stick trees a green growing tip protruded from the sheath of gray bark.

Fingers of morning sunlight released fog from the forest

floor like smoke from a banked fire. She took off her hat
and stood in place, steaming like the forest itself. Around
her, in a bubble of life, small flying things, barely distin-
guishable from pollen, swooped in unison. She thought of
the captain in his own bubble of life, that metal container.
She had known it would kill him. She might have told him,
but instead gave him that false, cheery good-bye. . . .

Sascha hurried on, trying to leave these thoughts behind. Striding through the ravine, deepening here in this
wood, she made her way toward the cleft where she and
her father had collected skeletals.

When she got to the ravine she found a swift stream,
partially obscuring her boneyard. Rivulets cascaded down
the flanks of the hills, carrying water opaque with silt. In
the growing heat of the day, the water tempted her to leave
her clothes in a pile and wade in, letting the waters renew
her as they had the Sticks. She closed her eyes, letting the
sun warm her eyelids. Through the slit of her eyes, she saw
prisms, ripples of color chasing over the landscape like a
slick of oil set alight.

A disk of color blossomed up on the ridgeline. She
opened her eyes to stare.

A great yellow-green cloud undulated there, not fifty
feet away. It flashed pink, then yellow-green, then pink
again. In the midst was a dark center, and from it came a
soprano wailing. Sascha stood up, shading her eyes from
the sun which just now rose over the ridge, backlighting
the miasma—and clearly silhouetting a human shape in the
middle. She thought the screaming sounded like her mother.

Sascha scrambled up the muddy hill, slipping on the
glasslike clay. Closer now, Sascha could see that it *was* her
mother—surrounded by flying insects with colorful wings,
butterflies perhaps, with downward beating wings flashing green, and upward, pink. They covered Cristin with
bright fur and surrounded her as she ran along the ridge,
screaming. She was careening away from Sascha. Then,

reversing in panic, she began running toward her. Her mother flapped her hands around her face, fending off the flying swarm. Sascha plunged straight into the cloud of insects. There in the blind buzz of wings, she reached out to her mother. Slapping hands pummeled Sascha before her mother registered the sight of her daughter.

As Cristin shouted, a butterfly flew into her mouth as into a red cave. She spat it out again, coughing, as around them fluttered the green, and then pink papery wings. Finally Sascha pulled on her mother's arms until they both fell to their hands and knees. Cristin buried her face in the mud while Sascha swept the winged cloud from her mother's hair. She noted that the slower she moved, the less they flocked, until, abandoning her swipes, she wrapped her arms around her mother's trembling back and found a pocket of insect-free air to breathe in the crevasse between their bodies.

What frightened her more than the swarm was her mother, lying huddled in the mud, shaking. Sascha whispered in her ear: "I'm sorry, I'm sorry. . . ." She would never hear the end of this.

After a time she felt a firm hand on her shoulder. It was her father. The swarm had disappeared. She looked up into his face, mouth set, eyes hard. Mother sat up, catching her breath, and began pulling wings, legs, antennae from her person.

Cristin looked up at her husband, then at Sascha. "Hat," she said to her daughter and rose to her feet with calm dignity, as though she were not covered with mud and bug juice.

Sascha's father pulled her to her feet. It was then she saw the soldier with him, rifle drawn, facing outward, scanning down both sides of the ridge. She'd never thought her father one to bring a gun where soap and water would do.

His rigid arm fixed Sascha in place. "Stay right here," he said, moving then to his wife's side, saying something to her in a whisper. Beneath the layer of filth, Cristin's face flashed alarm. A noise from the other side of the ridge grabbed Sascha's attention. Two more soldiers, fully armed, climbed up onto the ridge from below.

Cristin latched on to Sascha and urged her along the ridgeline, with soldiers leading and at the rear, watching everything.

"What's happened?" she asked her mother in a low voice.

Cristin's face was streaked with mud, sweat, and butter-fly pulp. A pink wing with a lacy pattern was pasted onto her cheek like a tattoo. She spat to one side, an action that Sascha had never seen from her mother, much less in public. Evidently the prospect of swallowing bug juice overcame her scruples.

"Something bit one of the men. It must have been venomous," her mother said.

"Is he all right?"

"No. He's dead." Cristin brushed bug litter from Sascha's face and braid, but Sascha broke away to walk next to her father.

When she started to apologize, he stopped her. "Sascha, you'll stay out of the forest now," he said softly.

"Yes, sir." His gentle tone drove home his edict more than any lecture.

All the way back to camp Sascha checked the backs of her hands, finding scratches that might or might not be bites, and listening to her body for evidence of venom.

9

Hoisted on the shoulders of dwellers, sixteen rugs wound their way to the reliquary. Vod knew the procession was under way and he wanted badly to be there, but only kin were excused from the digs to bury the dead. The digging must go on. Unless, as now, he was favored with one of the Paramount Borer's regrettable lapses of efficiency.

The borer was broken. By the look on the Second Engineer's face, the delay would cost several spans of digging time. The old static looked directly into his face, as though it were Vod's fault the day's lineal output was ruined. Coworkers gathered around, staring balefully at the great borer with its mangled blade. A broken machine was ever a reminder that DownWorld could strangle as well as nurture. From the diggers' expressions, Vod thought he could tell which of them had wagered on the output numbers, and which were losers.

With the impassive skin of a true static, the engineer kept her color, but gazed long at the borer as though searching for a sign—perhaps a miraculous recovery from its broken condition. Engineers were a superstitious lot, putting great store in the timing and type of breakdowns, reading them against historical maintenance trends, discerning patterns. But to Vod, the meaning of breakdowns like this one was clear enough: dig too fast and the rock will kill you.

As static maintenance workers swarmed over the borer, Vod slipped away from his work unit, aware that he must hurry before the borer growled back to life.

The contusions on his body from the slide were nearly healed after the ministrations of the physiopath, but one knee protested his hurried pace. Limping, he hurried past fluxors digging side tunnels. They hailed him as he passed, and he acknowledged them, knowing each by name and many up to the third kin net.

Vod slipped into a downway. A temporary stairset, it was a raw, crumbling place, without a growth of hab and supported by foam beams. He blinked so frequently from the suspended dust that his sight seemed to be a succession of pictures rather than a seamless reality. But this was error. The Data Guides said that all life was a process. It was error, they said, to believe in separate things and particles. All matter and all events were interrelated, all ways interrelated, as the realm of the submolecular was said to demonstrate. No one thing is fundamental; all is relational.

But he was no scholar. He had dug since he was a child. The HumanWar required that everyone work, and many fluxors chose the patriotic way of digging and physical work. He had not got far with philosophy. Only as far as politics.

He passed portals leading to the multilayered digs, where fluxors carved new ways forward. A major portal led onto the extension of the PrimeWay, the major undertaking of every digger's life in the constant migration through DownWorld to replenish their dwelling. The rolled dead were left behind in successive reliquaries, where now Wecar was borne on the shoulders of her kin.

Vod continued into the DeepReaches. Where a minor way dead-headed in an unfinished lobe, he came upon many rug looms, once lovingly stored, now forgotten. Threading his way among them he came to the hidden portal—also long forgotten.

Here was the entrance to his wondrous find, a secret he had not disclosed even to his nearest friends. The statics would certainly come and tidy up this place, if they knew of it. It was ancient and unmaintained, dangerously unmonitored: a relic of the past. For this reason, Vod loved it. Here was a separate and ancient chute, the original digger chute that carried workers to and from the new region six thousand cycles ago, to dig the new ways that would become Ankhorat.

He sidled through the portal and crawled a short distance to the cab, waiting where he had left it, its door filling the portal. He entered the cab in utter darkness. The lights didn't work, but he knew from explorations that it contained thirty-six seats, the hard foam deeply carved with messages from the past—fluxor names, all the workers who created Ankhorat with their hands and lives. He stabbed his fingers into the overhead console, connecting to the simple on switch, and felt the cab lurch forward, carrying him along the deep, forgotten path.

In this very chute his ancient kin had traversed the fresh regions to renew DownWorld. The chute brought them to a forward position where they set to digging a new PrimeWay, boring back to meet the digging from the other side. Once the two sides broke through to each other, the chute fell into obscurity. But Vod knew the ways; had made it his life study. A scholar of digging; that perhaps described him best.

He hurtled along in blackness, under everything, steeped for this brief ride in timelessness, surrounded by the hum of the cab's ancient motor. His fingers traced the etchings in the seat beneath him. Under his fingers he felt the grooves that marked where a digger had carved a name. For a moment he thought he felt the name Wecar . . . Wecar, now as dead as the ancient digger who had once sat here.

Arriving at the end of the line, he scrambled out into another forgotten lobe in the DeepReaches. There, an oversized way housed a region of industrial noise. The ominous sound of water vats sloshed nearby amid the rumble of power generators and supplemental food refineries. He noted that a team of statics labored on an exposed flank of the hab, reconstructing networks embedded behind the sheath. They eyed him, a fluxor out of place. He hurried through this tunnel of noise.

In three spiral turns of an upway he came to a subminor way and saw the tail end of the reliquary procession. In this region were simple kin dens, the ancestral apartments of humble fluxors. More accomplished fluxors lived Over-Prime, where their sensibilities would not be offended by the sight of rolled rugs. Vod fell in behind the line of mourners, their shadows hunching against the walls, thrown in relief by pockets of phosphorescent cella.

Proximity to apartments required strict inwardness. He neither looked to the side, nor, in foremind, noticed much outside his immediate purpose. Through the portals he saw that dwellers slept and studied and played with progeny and sat their rugs, but he registered little of all that. Walking next to a fellow digger, the fellow nodded at him, but kept the silence of the walk. He noted some static maintenance workers had joined the procession in a show of support.

And then, at the next curve of the way, stood Maret Din Kharon. She fell in beside him.

"Here are rugs we will never see again," he muttered by way of greeting. "All for the whim of Nefer."

"We renew our home, Vod-as. I have two sadnesses for the deaths, but sometimes there will be a lapse in safety."

He spoke close to her ear. "Her *whim*, those tunnels."

"We must renew our world," she whispered.

The vision of Wecar's hand protruding from the slide prompted his bitter reply: "You sound like a static." At the rebuke, Maret fell silent. "If you will speak like a static, best you don't come to lay the rugs down."

Maret dropped back, and Vod stopped with her for a moment.

"Best you don't come farther, Maret-as, if you still keep your color." *While those with murdered kin pale with grief.* He thought it, but kept it to himself.

She nodded gravely, standing calm as stone while the procession retreated into the depths.

The sixteen rugs were borne along, tightly rolled, pattern facing inward. The footfalls of the mourners were the only sounds, as dwellers stopped their errands to let the procession pass by. With every step, Vod dug a deeper groove in his heart, hating Nefer Ton Enkar.

When at last they lay the rugs in their resting slots, several fluxors looked to him, as though he must be censored for what he failed to do. For failing to win Maret to their cause. His connection with Maret was the one strand of digger hope, the only access to power.

Other diggers said their devotions, mumbling of vone and UpWorld. These were simple dwellers, fluxor and static alike, who clung to their myths. Above, the sunlit world delivered to the dead their rewards, as the vone decreed. Many of the kin gathered at this reliquary were the sort who thronged to the PrimeWay dramas, never tiring of the stories, and worse, sometimes *believing* them. It was maddening how otherwise rational ahtra minds could hold at once a scientific understanding of the vone, and at the same time imbue them with mystical properties. When pressed, a dweller given to devotional tendencies would say it gave the vone honor. *Superstition, more like.* Vod set little store by such notions. This life was all they had.

All the more reason to make it count.

"My mistress wishes for you to walk with me, Eli Dammond."

Eli had risen when Maret entered his cell. The effect of the drugs had passed, leaving him steady on his feet and clearheaded at last. The only lingering discomfort was his stomach cramping from a diet of fleshy mushroomlike segments. He was beginning to recognize which kinds made him most nauseous, and left them untouched.

She had said *a walk.* So far he had only walked from his holding cell to the communal bathrooms, and once to Nefer's interview room. And he remembered every inch of those paths.

"As you wish," he said. He could pretend at conformity, and gladly, if she would show him more of the layout of his prison.

"Your demeanor is agreeable, Eli Dammond. Much improved."

"I do better when not poisoned by your drugs."

"Yes, certainly."

He was getting used to her placidity, though it galled. She spoke of the attack on his crew and passengers as though it were a terrible inconvenience. Worse, she spoke of it as being imminent, and then claimed the right to remain uninvolved. She claimed it would not be ahtra who attacked—who then? And why were the ahtra helpless to prevent it? Perhaps it was some natural disaster they spoke of—but if so, why did they probe for how much *armament* the camp possessed? Under threat of drugs, she expected him to remain calm, as though a display of emotion was more notable than a pending breach of the armistice.

He had asked her, earlier: *"Who is your enemy? Who threatens the surface of this world?"*

"We have no enemy except yourselves, Eli Dammond."

"But we are at peace . . ."

"Enemies may be at peace."

He was coming to know this individual named Maret: arrogant and dismissive of him, yet seemingly pleased when he let himself be guided or instructed by her. She was a *fluxor,* she said . . . perhaps some system of psychological grouping—though the skin markings of fluxors were considerably more pronounced than those of the ones who Maret referred to as *statics.*

"My mistress wishes you to have some understanding of us," Maret said, "so that you may come to learn that we mean you no harm, despite your unfortunate circumstances among us."

Again, the insistence on ahtra innocence. It rang hollow, as did the implication of some unnamed threat. But he only nodded at her to continue.

"Therefore, we will walk today along the ways. While we do so, you will remember that my people may be surprised or alarmed to see you, though all have heard of your presence here. Therefore, you will remain strictly courteous. For example, you will not move from my side, nor make sudden movements that may appear threatening. Humans are prone to violence in social situations, a tendency that is alarming to the dwellers."

"I would not wish to alarm such peaceable people."

She took time for one of her slow blinks. "You may give me your word that you will be apt to observe these rules."

"Of course."

He followed her to the door, which she appeared to unlock with a flick of her skull tendril against a pad in the door frame.

He followed her into the corridor that she referred to as a *way*. This way, like others he had seen, was about five feet wide and eight high, with the ceiling forming a curved arch. The wall surfaces appeared similar to those in his cell, where the irregularity looked like a knobby gelatin substance that gave slightly to pressure of a finger, soon resuming shape.

At intervals along the way, screens arose from the walls on fleshy nubs, displaying ahtran language texts and figures. Individuals stood to view the screens, some with their data tendrils inserted into cables. Without fail, his presence caused every other activity to stop while ahtra stared at him, data tendrils popping out of their holds—the equivalent, perhaps, of jaw-dropping. Maret had said the ahtra had been here a very long time, an intelligence that confounded human assumptions that the ahtra lived exclusively on world ships.

He concentrated on the system of corridors, noting side passages teeming with shadowy ahtra—*dwellers,* as she called them. Several times he'd seen work crews massed around a rupture in the wall, using tools on what might be a deeper mechanical system. In addition to the side passageways, stairways led to what were likely other levels. Somewhere, relatively close by, was the personal transit chute leading to the point he had entered this place. And by which he would escape.

They passed a section of wall where a mass of pale blue mushrooms sprouted. Ahtra freely plucked at them as they passed, eating them as they walked. His stomach spasmed, remembering those blue morsels.

Maret noted his gaze. "In places, the hab is host to these fruiting bodies. Behind the hab, their mycelia form a network in the deep soil. We produce most food chemically, but this would be our traditional food, which is now a—parasite—you would say, on the hab. A beneficial one."

"The hab is alive?"

"Yes, certainly. The hab is a . . . symbiont, you would say. Ahtra and hab have lived in relation for a million cycles. Ours is a built environment. But of the living UpWorld, the hab is a sole and precious remnant."

"Alive . . ." Eli scanned the spongy corridor walls with new interest.

"What else? But do not be alarmed, it is . . . domesticated."

"It's an animal?"

"That would be your word. To us, it is the hab, of ancient lineage. Cycles past remembering, these were fierce burrowing creatures. We shared our dens with them, and trained them to protect us. They burst from our holes to devour our enemies, and it tended to provide safety for us. Our wastes supplied a source of food for the habsen."

Eli looked around him with new sight. "But now the hab . . ." He struggled to find the words that would express how a creature could turn inside out, if that was what it was.

"Is inverted, yes." She smiled. "As I said, cycles past remembering."

"How old *are* the ahtra, Maret?"

"You cannot imagine. Since ancient days the hab has depended on us, as we on it. But it is not everlasting, so we move forward, through DownWorld, in renewal. Where it has died, we leave."

"We always thought that you lived in world ships. . . ."

"Some of us tend to do so. But the—world ships— would provide a subsurface dwelling of a sort you apprehend."

Ignorant. We have been ignorant of our enemy. And the ahtra preferred it that way to judge by this hidden place.

She led him to the right as the corridor split into a Y before them. The tunnel now grew more crowded with both heavily marked and lightly marked ahtra. He impressed the route into his memory, alert for any clue to the way he had traversed from the transit chute to his cell. Though he'd been drugged and beaten at the time, by God, he would remember.

With a turn of the corridor, the way became yet more noisy, and before long they came upon an arch that opened onto a stunning sight. Beneath a massive, arched ceiling lay a tunnel wide enough to contain the *Lucia.*

The ceiling rose some fifty feet over their heads and extended in a straight line as far in each direction as Eli could see. Hundreds of ahtra gathered here, some standing in knots around the ubiquitous—but, here, larger—screens which shifted with displays of ahtran symbols. Many dwellers seemed riveted by what they watched. In pockets along the corridor some ahtra sat like proprietors next to their screens, sharing wall space with what Eli took to be vendors of various sorts. In the center of the way moved a swarm of pedestrians, most talking and gesturing in a hubbub of interaction.

"This is the PrimeWay," Maret explained. "My mistress wishes you to know us, as much as you are capable. The PrimeWay is the heart of us." She touched his elbow, guiding him forward.

He controlled the urge to yank away. He would *conform,* as she put it. For now.

They moved into the throng of ahtra. He could see over them, from the vantage point of his height, down the cavernous tunnel, across the smooth skulls of thousands of individuals. As they proceeded, a path opened up for them. Dwellers brushed up against others standing next to the screens, who in turn swung around to stare at the human among them. From all directions, large dark eyes turned to watch him.

For the first time Eli believed in Maret's claim of the antiquity of this subterranean world. Here was the scale that suggested an extensive population, here was the cacophony of their voices, the interlocking lives, cohering in groups, clusters, eddies; here was the variety, density, and disorder of a long-dwelled-in city. He wondered what else this *DownWorld* had of vaulted spaces, tributaries of *ways,* and caverns of unknown purpose. All in all it was a staggering discovery.

And since they had taken such pains to hide, Eli had little hope they would allow him to leave. In that case his display here on the PrimeWay must have some purpose other than what Maret had claimed.

They walked down the *way.* Eli tried to guess what ahtra roles and occupations he was looking at. By dress, some looked less prosperous than others, but none were shabbily clad. There was no evidence of military presence—no combat uniforms nor visible weapons. He saw that among the ahtra, there were large and small individuals, portly and thin. Some with many oval markings on face, neck, and bare arms, some with fewer. Markings ranged in shading from bright silver to light gray.

"What does Nefer wish me to see?"

Maret answered in her well-modulated manner. "To see that we live as you do, proceeding with our lives, a peaceful community."

With a few notable lapses . . . Ignoring the public relations, he asked, "Who is Nefer among you?"

"My mistress is Most Prime, and orders all affairs of our dwelling. She also orders my life according to her design, as she does yours."

"Who is above Nefer?"

"That is Hemms Pre Illtek. You will not have reason to know him."

Someone in the crowd plucked at his sleeve. The individual was staring at him most pointedly, but Eli and Maret kept moving. Apparently not all ahtra disdained to touch him.

"What are the screens showing?" he asked his guide.

Maret stopped in front of one, where the screen filled with ahtra runes, displayed in concentric squares.

"Different things," she replied. "This one displays wagers."

A dweller who sat next to this screen sprang forward and began trying to engage Maret in a conversation. She answered him, in her speech. By the screen, several ahtra had inserted their head tendrils into jacks in the wall.

"Wagers? Gambling, you mean?"

"You might say so. We love to guess how things will occur. We win and lose." She smiled for the first time, a strange sight. "This one is about you, Eli Dammond. You are of high interest here, being new. As you stay longer among us, interest in you will wane."

The individual who had touched Eli a moment before was back again. Seeing this, Maret turned from the screen and hurried Eli away. However, the individual refused to be left behind, keeping pace with Eli and Maret. When the ahtra moved, the cloth of the dweller's white robe took on sheens of red or green, distinctively different from the subdued fabric worn by everyone else Eli had so far seen.

"Ignore her," Maret said, quickening her pace. "This is only a gomin."

But the gomin pursued them, finally moving to bar their path. She spoke to Eli, looking up at him eagerly, and then to Maret, as though she might translate. She didn't.

As a small crowd of ahtra gathered to watch this fracas, the gomin made a distinctive gesture with the palms of her hands, a gesture directed at Eli, and which was followed by a stir among the gathered ahtra—a reaction that Eli sensed was an angry one.

"Do not look at her," Maret said, now pulling on Eli's elbow, and attempting to navigate around the gomin.

But she was blocking his path. Eli looked down at her.

The crowd of ahtra grew loud, with some shouting at the gomin, and others at Eli. Feeling something push him in the back, he pivoted in that direction. His quick movement took those nearest him by surprise, causing them to swerve back from him. Conscious that every movement had meaning, Eli tried to adopt a calm exterior, keeping his face expressionless, looking at no one.

Meanwhile Maret was trying to push past the gomin once again, and succeeded in putting her off balance. For a moment the gomin jostled against Eli, gripping him firmly by the upper arm. Then other ahtra were pulling the gomin away, which she did not resist, but began repeating something, chantlike, which was soon subsumed by the answered chant of the crowd.

Maret was fairly hauling Eli down the way, herding him toward the side of the PrimeWay to an opening where a side corridor led away from the tumult. Keeping her fingers on his elbow, Maret steered him down a narrow way, and then into an even narrower set of stairs, where they climbed to the next level. She paused at the top of the stairs, then chose her direction and silently herded him along the corridor.

"We will go back to your cell, Eli Dammond," she said, her skin having taken on a slightly pale cast.

She was taking him on an alternative route, unwittingly giving him a further view of the labyrinth. They passed open doorways. Within, groups of ahtra mingled, sometimes sitting on rugs or engaged in various activities. Once, he saw what he thought might be a loom. Then they were descending a stairwell. After the vast cavern they had come from, the smaller ways and especially the stairwells seemed cramped and overwarm. The ceiling here barely cleared the top of his head.

She steered him by the arm, muttering, "You did not honor your promise."

"What happened down there?"

She stopped suddenly. They were very close together, forcing him to look into the dark shafts of her eyes. This close she did not look humanlike—not anything like. "Your *promise*," she said, "to remain calm, to be courteous."

"What is the courteous response to a mob?"

Resuming her pace, she turned them into a corridor he recognized. They were approaching his cell.

After a moment, she said, "It was your scent." After a beat, she added, still hurrying him along: "You are different from us. But it is your human way, so you cannot be at fault."

"What is the human way?"

"To be ready for sex at all times."

She noted his surprise. "Your scent conveys a sexual meaning. Though it is alien to us, some perceive it strongly. Such as the gomin. This one was attracted to you. Then you looked directly at the gomin—as I instructed you not to— and she became agitated, which those around her found worthy of censure. And the happenings tended to disorder."

He recognized the vicinity of his cell. He knew the place, the corridor, the environs. It was as though his very body remembered every turn, every advance, every retracing of steps. And more, he thought he knew where the access to the transit chute lay . . .

With Maret standing by the doorway, he walked into his prison. After gazing at him for a few moments she said, "Gomin are unnatural. They can participate in sex at any time, like humans. My people observe a time with sex and a time without. When the red season comes, we hunger for each other; otherwise not. Your human ways are peculiar to us. Nevertheless, since your scent upsets the dwellers, I will see that your needs are met. Do you require a sexual partner to be at ease?"

He looked down at her, diminutive as she was. Powerful as she was. "Leave me alone, Maret. That would make me at ease." He didn't plan to stay long enough to upset the dwellers.

She paused, blinking slowly, the lid arising from the bottom, and barely reaching the zenith before retracting. It was, Eli concluded, a kind of sigh of confusion or exasperation.

"We do not understand each other very well, Eli Dammond."

"You can say that again," he muttered.

She looked as though she might literally repeat her statement. Then, with the utmost dignity, she turned to the door, summoning it open. And then closed again. He stared at the door, acutely aware of the acrid odor of his own sweat.

10

Sascha had been lying on her cot in a state of sensory deprivation, eyes closed, with the relentless rain masking all sound. She tried to sleep to escape her dark thoughts.

They had abandoned the search for Captain Dammond yesterday. The hole the bots dug was now full of water, seven feet deep. Lieutenant Roche pronounced the captain dead. How convenient for them, Sascha thought, that Captain Dammond should obligingly die just when they could no longer make headway against the pit of mud. She raged and argued, but her parents were the only ones she dared speak to, and they were tired of the subject. Sleep was the only answer, but she had slept enough to last weeks. Now all that was left was a state of semiconsciousness, alternating with her mother's structured lesson plans. The high points of the day were trips to the mess tent, accompanied by her parents. Watchful. Afraid.

In two days of unremitting rain three soldiers had died. The venom of Null's creatures was swift. Paralysis came within seconds, then death. The men died by suffocation, when their diaphragms froze up—a bad way to die, the enlisteds said. You couldn't *will* your chest to rise and let in air, not if your automatic nervous system was disconnected.

Cristin and Sascha felt no ill effects from their encounter with the butterflies—or what Sascha's father had agreed could be *called* butterflies until the insects could be examined. It wasn't the butterflies that killed the men, it was small semiaquatic creatures about as long as a hand, not including the tail. The enlisteds called them lizards, but what they really were could not be determined from the body of the only one in their possession—a blackened corpse, the target of four laser guns at once.

Through the drumbeat of rain, Sascha thought she heard a counterpoint. Voices shouting. In another moment, she was sitting up, swinging her feet off the cot.

"Easy does it," her mother said, turning slowly from her work at the computer. She raised her hand, palm out, to stop Sascha from moving.

Geoff Olander walked to the tent flap, peering out into the encampment. "Someone's coming. It'll be Baker Camp coming in." Baker Camp would be consolidating with their camp in readiness to move out. To debark the planet. "I'll just check to see," he said. Cristin looked at him with that *be careful* look she used so liberally.

Sascha bolted across the tent to his side. "Father, please. Let me come with you." If Baker Camp was on its way in, Badri Nazim would be with them. She swung around to face her mother, plead with her. "The only ones that died were right next to the stream." They called the ditch running through camp a stream, for it was now a permanent watercourse.

Geoff shook his head. "Stay with your mother." He was weary of her entreaties, or perhaps of Cristin's counter-entreaties.

Sascha locked eyes with her mother. "You can't protect me forever. You can't protect me from my own *life*."

Geoff looked at his wife for a long moment, challenging her to respond. Cristin took it as another of her husband's small betrayals. "Go, then." At Geoff's hesitation, she waved at them resignedly. "Go."

They plunged out of the tent without further argument. Sascha's clothes were instantly drenched in the pelting rain. Through the cascade of water, Sascha could barely see the tents sharing a row with their own. With the rain leaching the color from the world, the camp and the hills beyond had gone gray and white. Beyond the camp perimeter Sascha watched great banks of fog rolling through, masking the low, jagged hills. She knew those hills were changing. In moments of abating rain Sascha had seen a green fur lying over the toothed ridges. It was grass sprouting.

The camp had awakened one morning to find the mossy fuzz everywhere, sprung up from the ground where rhizomous roots had lain dormant. Grass was a remarkable plant, her father had said—a strange comment, for Sascha had thought grass the simplest of growing things, the least worthy of consideration. But grass, her father said, had the odd characteristic of arising from underground structures without any growing tip protruding. Upon this quality depended all the grazing animals of all worlds, which otherwise might chew their local grass crop out of existence. And upon the grazers depended many a human settlement. So grass made human life possible, in a sense.

Well, if so, Null was indeed coming to life. And this miracle was occurring just as they were leaving. Just as they were abandoning Eli Dammond. When he came back—and Sascha was sure that he would come back—he would find the land changed. Perhaps he would hardly recognize it for the hot, scoured place it had been when he left. The only proof he would have that he was even on the right planet would be the sodden remains of their camp.

This lonely vision filled her with more dismay than the thought of his death.

A large crowd of enlisteds had gathered at the perimeter to see what the commotion was. It wasn't, as Sascha's father expected, the contingent of sixty-three soldiers coming in from Baker Camp. It was a military detail leaving. The corporal next to her murmured, "They're going to bring in the *Lucia*. 'Bout time."

A unit of twelve soldiers was forming up under Lieutenant Roche's direction. They learned the mission would be led by Captain Luce Marzano, tasked with hiking the six miles to the transport ship and flying it back. Marzano would be landing on the wide field to the south of Charlie Camp, but she'd have to wait for a break in the weather to maneuver down and avoid the ridge. There had been talk about evacuating on foot, but the ground was soggy and turning to marsh, the presumed niche of the poisonous lizards. Though some argued deploying on foot was safer than risking the *Lucia* on a tight landing, Lieutenant Roche made his decision. He had civilians to think about: *the general's granddaughter,* for God's sake.

Despite the eagerness to be rid of the place, the enlisteds were in a better mood, now that Marzano was going after the *Lucia*. With a little luck, they could lift off by the end of the day.

"Shoulda taken a dog with her," the corporal next to her muttered.

Sascha saw that Captain Marzano was indeed leaving on her own, without the escort of a bot. The versatile machines were about the size of a dog, and dubbed accordingly by the enlisteds. Apparently Charlie Camp's two bots would be reserved for defense of the camp.

She sidled her way closer to Lieutenant Roche and his officers, hoping to overhear any scrap of news that might relate to Captain Dammond or the dig, but in the downpour, the officers' voices melted. She could see their faces well enough, though. Roche looked sour, as though command didn't suit him, not after losing five enlisteds. The expression on Luce Marzano's face, however, couldn't be mistaken for anything but glee. Today she had a small command and a chance to pull off a difficult mission, and no question of her fleeing army justice in the *Lucia,* for where in the eight worlds could she go?

As Marzano's unit moved past the camp perimeter, the gathering broke up, except those that watched the line wend off, skirting the edge of the Gray Spiny Forest. Sascha and her father were among those who watched.

"I'm sorry, Sascha," her father said.

She knew what about. Marzano's mission was Dammond's sentence of death or exile. Sascha tried to believe that Congress Worlds would send a ship out for him: a mop-up mission for the mop-up mission. But word had it, no one would ever be coming back here. Not for one man. A man who was probably dead.

All at once, Sascha found herself resting her head against her father's chest, warm tears springing out to join the cold rain on her face. His arm cinched her close. She had no right to cry for Eli Dammond. She was only a girl who could barely presume to call the captain her friend.

Someone had come up next to them, saying: "Mr. Olander, got something for you."

Sascha disengaged from her father's arms, embarrassed to see Sergeant Ben Juric regarding them with a critical stare. She hated to be seen crying, by him of all people, a man so tough he'd been known to saw a soldier's blasted leg off with a pocketknife.

"What've you got, Sergeant?"

"You'll have to tell *me.*" Juric twisted his chin to the left, indicating where they should go.

They followed Juric through camp, avoiding the deeper puddles whose depths were suspect. As they walked, Juric said, "Couple of my men been hunting." He offered nothing more, but led them to a tent deep in the lower enlisteds' section of camp.

As they entered the tent, two soldiers looked up from a game of cards on the bunk. One of them glanced to the middle of the tent where, on the floor, a covered washpan lay. A thick pane of clear plaz lay over the top. Juric waited by the tent flap as Sascha and her father stepped forward. Within the pan a small lizardlike creature skittered from one side of the pan to the other.

Geoff looked sharply up at Juric.

The sergeant shrugged. "You wanted to see a live one."

Sascha noted its triangular, flattened head and four short legs and tail. The only remarkable feature was its smooth skin, gleaming silver, banded by black lateral stripes. Then it revealed its other remarkable feature: a jaw full of tiny, stiletto-sharp teeth.

The pan clattered gently as the creature began dashing around the perimeter of its cage.

"This what killed those men?" Geoff Olander asked.

The enlisted sitting nearest them said, "Yeah, and now we gonna kill *it*." He flipped down a card on the mattress, with a flourish that roundly displayed his regen hand, pale as a fish belly.

"No," Geoff said. "*I'll* kill it."

The one with the regen hand frowned at this appropriation of what he clearly considered his property.

"Dissection," her father said.

Sascha ventured, "Looks like a salamander." The smooth, moist skin would allow water evaporation, and the slits on the head might even be gills, such as some salamanders kept into adulthood.

Geoff Olander pursed his lips, nodding to Juric. "Perhaps your men would bring this over to the med tent, where I'll be able to borrow some instruments."

Meanwhile Sascha hunched over the pan to peer at the

creature, which froze in the shadow she cast over its cage. In the next moment it had gathered its hind legs under it and leapt straight up, tipping the lid to one side and catapulting itself into the air. Startled, Sascha fell onto her back as the tent erupted into action, the two enlisteds scrambling for weapons and Sascha's father lurching toward her, arms outstretched in warning. She swiveled her head to locate the lizard. She saw it poised by one of the soldier's feet. Unaware, the enlisted turned from side to side, pointing his gun at everything that moved. Then, just as she said, "By your feet," the creature bounded into the air again, landing in the middle of Sascha's lap.

She froze.

Her father was shouting for the men not to fire as the two soldiers pointed their guns at Sascha's solar plexus.

She stared at the creature. The world collapsed swiftly into the present moment: hot tent, silver lizard, golden eyes, pressure on her pelvis from its feet. The animal looked like a porcelain statue except for the eyes, which seemed to return her gaze in friendly fashion. Then it sprang.

Sascha was knocked flat by an arm. When she scrambled up again she saw the lizard impaled on the tent floor with a knife through its midsection. Orange-red blood began pooling under it.

As her father pulled her away from the creature, she saw it was still convulsing on the knife that Sergeant Juric was methodically twisting back and forth in the creature's gut. At last Juric stood and, bracing the toe of his boot against the creature's body, pulled his knife out.

Sascha felt a shudder pass through her, the tremor she couldn't allow herself a moment before.

One of the soldiers swore. "God*damn*." Then he laughed. "It's a leapin' lizard. A goddamn leapin' lizard."

"Shut up," his friend said, holstering his gun and wiping the sweat from his upper lip.

Juric cleaned his knife on a cast-off sock.

"Thank you, Sergeant," her father said softly.

Juric nodded. Then he turned on his men. "You *alphs*." They bristled. No enlisted wanted that name, especially these two who sported their regens with pride. "Helpless without your guns, aren't you? Ever kill anything with your bare hands?" He smiled, a terrible half grin that seemed to carve a painful course into the working side of his face.

Sascha's father had regained his composure. "Perhaps you men would get that specimen back in the pan?" They jumped to the task, using a rag to lift the creature by the tail.

As they handed Geoff the pan, he said, "We won't talk about this. We don't want to upset anyone over what might have happened here, do we?"

The two men nodded. They had no more wish to face Lieutenant Roche than Sascha wished to face her mother.

"Well, then," her father finished. He clamped a hand on Sascha's shoulder and gently steered her toward the tent opening.

As Juric held the tent flap for them he said to Sascha, "You've got steady nerves, Ms. Olander. Put my *alphs*, here, to shame."

Despite the glowers from the two enlisteds, Sascha let herself smile at Juric. "Thanks, Sergeant."

He didn't smile back, but she had no wish to see *that* particular expression again.

Word came that evening from Baker Camp. They weren't coming. It was the first time since they landed on Null that Sascha saw her father worried. Her mother always worried, and therefore was no barometer of events. But now Geoff Olander's eyes took on a watchful, edgy cast that signaled he was paying attention to something beyond biology.

It was 2 A.M., but every light in camp was on. They didn't

think that Marzano would attempt a night landing, but the rains had stopped—and if she made a run for it, they wanted the lights to mark the spot. Of course, no one knew for certain that Marzano was in fact sitting secure in the *Lucia,* much less pondering how she might exploit a break in the monsoons to do a night run. Everyone acted as though she was, but no one knew. Not now that they'd heard from Baker Camp.

Sascha was sitting on her bunk trying for the sixth or seventh time to get through to Nazim. Perhaps her friend was asleep. Her connection to Baker Camp faded and surged, promising a bad transmission even if she did get through, but Sascha continued to try.

In the other corner of the tent her mother, who, like Sascha, had abandoned sleep, was busy inputting at her screen, revising her paper endlessly, as though the act of editing imposed much-needed order on the world. Geoff was sitting with the officers in Lieutenant Roche's tent. It made Sascha proud to think that they considered her father an important resource in their current problems. His dissection proved that the venomed creatures were more like amphibians than reptiles, and that the poison was delivered by spray, not fangs. It meant that you didn't want to get even close to the amphibs, much less have one eyeballing you as it sat in your lap.

"Nazim," she repeated again. "Nazim, wake up, you lazy rotten enlisted." Outside, the breeze rippled the tent walls. After all the rat-a-tat-tatting of the rains, the wind possessed an extraordinarily calm sound, rather like the breathing of a somnolent world, asleep after a purging rage. Sascha sat cross-legged, balancing her screen on her knees, poking the reconnect button at regular intervals.

When an answer came, Sascha was so surprised she almost dropped the slate. Cristin turned around from her screen.

"Hey, Olander," Nazim said. Her image on-screen was slightly twisted on the diagonal.

"So," Sascha began, "you patches afraid of a little hike in the woods?"

"Shit, no." Nazim's usual devilish grin was twisted to the side. "We'll meet you halfway, Olander. By the bridge."

It was such a relief to hear Nazim's confident tone, Sascha almost wept. It would all be all right. These seasoned troops weren't going to panic over a little trouble.

Still . . . "What bridge?"

Nazim hunched something closer around her shoulders. It looked like a blanket, but the screen was seeded with holes, and aslant. "Our camp dog is out there building us a nice bridge. We didn't like the narrow one."

"Bridge over what?" Sascha asked.

"Bridge over the black river."

Sascha and her mother traded glances at this obscure remark. Nazim closed her eyes for a moment as though she would fall asleep in the middle of their conversation.

"Did I wake you?"

"Yeah. But I was having bad dreams."

"What happened?" After a pause to let Nazim answer, Sascha prompted, "We heard you lost six. That's ugly."

"Yeah, we lost Olivetti and Ganz to the lizards. If you stay away from the banyans, they don't come at you as much, but sometimes they hit you from ground nests." Sascha didn't know what banyans were, but she didn't interrupt. "By the time we got a few hundred yards in, we couldn't see shit, it was so dark in the canopy and the everfucking rain. Couldn't march in a straight line, with the roots getting in our way." She seemed to be talking to herself, not explaining anything, just replaying her memory. "So we went around them and ended up switchbacking all over the pocking jungle. That's when we found the river." She stopped to take a swig of something from a cup.

"What river?"

Nazim said fiercely, "The goddamned black river, that's what." Her fervor caught Sascha by surprise. "You guys didn't know about the black river, did you? You said, come on down, come in to Charlie, so we took the straightest path we could, and yes, there's a pocking river in the middle of the Sticks! "That's where we lost the others." Her expression was impossible to read on the slant. "Don't go wading in shallow rivers, Olander." The connection went out.

Sascha's mother came over and sat beside her daughter on the cot. In another moment Nazim was back again, continuing, ". . . went after him, to help. Then he starts floundering, too, and we see what's got hold of him, maybe same thing that got Fortney. It's a big bastard, 'bout as big as you, Olander. It's got very large front pincers in front, on a flat body. It had eyes on the top of its back, and a tail with a stinger like a lance. We zapped it the best we could, but our guys went down into the black river. They went down, Olander!" Her voice cracked, or the connection was garbling her. "And they never came back up. So we got the dog to work on the bridge, and it did a narrow one. Perez volunteered to go over, and he was fine, got over just fine, and then we lined up, and when Barent went over, there was a thrashing below the bridge, and he just toppled in. After that, we retreated. We left the dog to do a wider bridge, but we weren't going to wait. Perez, on the other side of the river, he was supposed to go on, to try to get to Charlie Camp. We finally made it back, sort of. . . . And you guys, you never saw Perez, did you?" When Sascha didn't answer, Nazim spat out, "*Did you?*"

"No," Sascha whispered. Then louder, "No, Nazim, we haven't yet."

"Yet?" Her tone was menacing. "You *expect* to see him come waltzing in?"

Sascha felt her mother's arm around her shoulders. It was the kind of comfort that Sascha wanted to give Nazim, but all she could say was "I'm sorry, Nazim."

Her friend shrugged beneath the blanket that she kept snug around her. In a more even voice she said, "I'm not going back there."

"We're bringing the *Lucia* into Charlie Camp," Sascha told her. "We're going to get out of here."

"Have a nice trip," came the bitter reply.

"We will. As soon as you get here."

"We figure to go around the Sticks tomorrow. The long way around," Nazim said.

"See you tomorrow, then."

"On a nice day it would take an hour, hour and a half."

"Maybe it'll be nice tomorrow." Even to Sascha it sounded lame.

Nazim stared. "I think we're about done with *nice*." Then she reached toward the keyboard, and the disconnect button. "Don't go walking in the woods, Olander," she said, and the screen went blank.

11

Eli wiped a gob of paste from his sleeve. Somewhere in the tour of the PrimeWay, he had picked up a sticky wad of something. It stuck to his fingers for a moment, and he threw it to the floor, where it joined the unfamiliar litter of his prison cell.

He went to the cell door and listened, trying to discern the rhythms of the place, and when the corridors might be less used. He knew the route to the transit chute. But avoiding meeting a dweller would be difficult, given that he couldn't predict ahtra periods of rest or low activity. They didn't sleep at regular intervals, it was known. But when they did, it was a profound and unmovable sleep. It was little enough information to have at his disposal. Ahtra hid themselves and what they were. At the same time, ahtra undertook to study human ways. Maret's familiarity with his culture might easily come from the radio communications of Congress Worlds, over hundreds, even thousands of years. But ahtra, to their great advantage, did not leak information, by radio or otherwise.

Just now there were voices outside, and shuffling feet in the corridor. He waited.

His thoughts went to the encampment on the surface. Sometimes he thought that by sheer concentration he could see what was happening there. Sometimes he envisioned a blasted place, an enemy attack, everyone dead. Other times, a tidy departure. They had waited, then left, thinking him dead. Or they were breaking camp at this very moment, preparing to leave. He pressed his ear against the door, straining to hear.

He thought of the moments where everything hangs in the balance. Pivotal moments carried in the stream of ordinary events. Like fragments of space rock, they shot past you—or through you—out of nowhere. Sometimes you didn't realize their importance until you found blood later. Other times you knew them with dead certainty, right away. That day on the *Recompense,* the event came upon him like that. Even at that moment, he knew it would make him or ruin him.

The screens were registering nothing. The bridge was cool, but the electronics, as always, cast a miserly heat, enough to release a gummy, chemical odor. Colonel Suzan Tenering had just left the bridge, passing the helm to Eli, and the crew relaxed a notch. Someone made small talk in low tones. It was the calm, ordered atmosphere of combat readiness with an underlying anxiety, each crew member knowing they could join the fifty million dead today, depending.

Then it appeared on-screen, no more than a speck, but the techs had its signature, some jumping to conclusions, whispering the word that galvanized the bridge: *world ship.* Colonel Tenering was in the elevator, three decks down, heading lower. Then her voice burst into his ears, over the headset, while the bridge crew scrambled, hailing, analyzing. Eli conveyed the gist of it to Tenering, now riding back up to her command, but too late to be at the center of events as was Eli Dammond, first officer of the *Recompense*. Lieutenant Nule stared at Eli, awaiting the order to launch missiles, looking like a man set on fire. Everyone else stared at the screen, just trying to figure out what they were looking at, the view no human had laid eyes on before, more than a fleeting glimpse at vast distances. "Captain?" Lieutenant Nule said. Tenering's voice hammered for assessment. Lieutenant Nule asked again for orders. The crew turned to Eli, all frantic. He spoke. His words left an imprint in his body, a fleshy callous.

"Hold fire, Lieutenant . . ." he said.

At that moment Colonel Tenering burst onto the flight deck, even as the event came hurtling through, taking with it chunks of what had been, until then, Eli Dammond's life. . . .

Sweat dripping down his sides, Eli got up from his crouch near the door and paced his cell, walking nine steps in one direction, nine in the other, and back again. Sometime in that hour of pacing he thought he saw a movement. The gob of paste that he had thrown down was inching along the floor. Amoebalike, it scrunched itself up and extended its forward portion, drawing up the back.

Eli sat down and watched it. It was heading for the wall, where it stopped, wriggling in place, then disappeared inside. The wall closed up behind it, leaving a small bruise-mark.

He sat for a very long while, watching the bruise lighten. Then it began to swell. He watched with amazement as a white bubble half his size ballooned from the wall. From within the sack, a voice came, barely in hearing range. "Move closer."

Eli probed the bubble with his finger, slipping it inside to no ill effect.

"Inside, inside, can't you?" came the voice.

The bubble elongated, almost beckoning. With nothing to lose, Eli moved toward the wall, entering the bubble.

He found himself sitting in a small gallery, knee to knee with an ahtra in what must be a virtual environment, utterly flawless in its detail. The individual wore odd, patternless clothes that, in the folds, flashed iridescent green. It was, he suspected, the gomin that he had encountered in the PrimeWay.

"I can't stay long. I hope you don't mind," the gomin said. "Would the words tend wrong? I've been studying." The gomin spoke softly, the deep voice almost a purr. "Yours is Congress Worlds Standard, would that be wrong? I hope I haven't been backminding all this span without success. I've worked hard to get here, Eli Dammond. Don't waste my time. There isn't much of it."

"I can understand you."

The gomin's data tendril jerked in surprise at the sound of Eli's voice. "This meeting verges on improper ways. Decide now if you will risk any consequences."

Any meeting his jailers would find improper, Eli was most eager for. "I accept."

The gomin relaxed her position. "You are conducive to our converse, then?"

"Yes."

"That is very commodious of you. You give me two happinesses." The gomin relaxed even further, slouching and drawing one knee up to support a languid arm. "Eli Dammond, do not tend to believe what Maret Din Kharon says about me. She inclines to be conventional. I will tell you about me. I am susceptible to censure for being like you." She looked about her, her eyelids closing up for a moment. Opening her eyes again, she said, "We do not have much time. I have tried to find a way that would not offend."

"Speak, then, if we don't have much time."

"Thank you, I take that for permission." The robes

rustled, flashing colors in response to movement. "You are predisposed to be the enemy, Eli Dammond. But gomin like me have an—interest—in human ways. Because we tend like you in that we have no seasons. I would know some matters about you. How alike do we tend to be, how do you function without chaos, and is it a perfect life? You can't answer all at once," she said. "Start somewhere, please."

Now, this might be exploited. Maret had said that information was not free among her people. So then, if the gomin wanted information, the gomin would pay.

"Let's start with what *I* wish to know. Then I'll tell you what *you* wish to know."

"That would not be fair. I risk that you, as the enemy, will be unlikely to honor your side of it. Please realize I would not speak so bluntly if our limited time together did not preclude courtesies."

"Then we'll alternate, answer for answer."

The gomin sat up, more attentive now. "Answer for answer. That would be fair. I begin."

"You have already had one question. I answered that I am willing to converse with you."

"Ask, then. But do not ask me about escaping. I tend to be a gomin, but I am no traitor."

Jumping to the heart of it, Eli asked, "What is happening to my people on the surface?"

"That would depend on the . . . vone."

"What are the vone?"

"They are . . . as they are." The gomin fidgeted with her robes. "Objects of devotion, you might say."

"Myth or reality, then?"

"Oh, both, certainly. It is a continuum, you perceive."

Eli waited. "But what *are* the vone?"

"I answered."

"Poorly."

"The vone," the gomin continued, "are understood as

death and life, with the power over us all. They might be, in your view, our gods. Above, they may accept or reject us. Soon Maret Din Kharon will ascend to meet them."

"Maret is going to the surface?"

"That is another question, Eli Dammond."

Eli resolved to frame his questions more carefully. "Your turn."

The gomin blinked again, this time keeping her eyes closed longer, as though listening to something. When she opened her eyes, she said, "Perhaps there will be no point to all this. When you leave, all will be disposed as it was. Knowing of human things, might I not be more miserable than ever before?"

"Is that your question?"

"No. Thank you for that allowance, Eli Dammond. I see you do not take advantage of me. My question: How free are you humans among yourselves with matters of close sexual contact, and knowing who is conducive to receptivity and when? Would it be wonderful? Would it be—this is your word—*paradise?*"

Eli plunged ahead: "We can ask if the other person is interested." He thought of Luce Marzano, and how he would have pursued her but could not, under the circumstances. "Sometimes we don't take any action, because the other person is clearly not available, such as being someone else's partner, or being under your power or command."

"That would be complicated."

"Sometimes."

The gomin said softly, "You didn't answer about paradise."

Paradise is the place you used to have, that you can't return to. But he answered, "No, it's not paradise. But maybe it's good enough."

The gomin blinked, long and slow.

Eli took his turn. "What does Nefer want from me?"

"One can't know the Most Prime's mind, certainly."

"Guess," Eli insisted.

"Nefer might want to punish you." She plucked at her robes.

"That's not much of an answer."

"Neither was yours," the gomin countered. "But perhaps she seeks a way to use you to gather power. It happens she is an important static, but thwarted. Hemms is only four years her senior, so Hemms Pre Illtek will live long, forever shading Nefer Ton Enkar in his leadership."

The gomin posed her question: "Again about paradise, do your rules surrounding close sexual contact suggest that you are constantly unfulfilled and therefore not deeply happy?"

Eli answered: "Our ways are all we know. But I'm glad we aren't—censored—as you are. For some of my people, sexual rules can be troubling. But we are freer than you. As for paradise, that changes with circumstance. For me paradise is rejoining my command. Do you see?"

The gomin hesitated. "Would that be your next question?"

"No." Eli asked: "Tell me what it means to be static or fluxor, and why you set such store by it."

"I think you may have asked two questions, Eli Dammond."

He shrugged.

The gomin drew up her knees and folded her arms around them, as though lost in thought. "Static and fluxor. That is the slant of our lives. You see it all around you. By chance, I am a fluxor, for instance.

"Things are not separate and—fundamental—you perceive. They are in relation to each other, so we are taught. In relation to other fluxors, and certainly, statics, I am an extreme. I tend toward unusual interests. Curiosity—your word? This may entail risk and higher emotion. Sometimes one tends to bend the traditions. Statics will find this offensive. But I do not despise statics, though they may despise gomin. Statics are our leaders of late—for the last thousand cycles. They are prone to administration of affairs. One would find weariness in such things. And of course, statics are not conducive to sexual converse, so one is grateful to be a fluxor."

"It is confusing, these roles of static and fluxor," Eli said.

"These are the ways we know," the gomin said. "But now it is my turn . . ." Suddenly she closed her eyes. When she opened them, she looked alarmed.

The bubble evaporated, and Eli was aware once more of his cell. In the next moment, the door opened, and a guard entered, bringing food.

It was the chance Eli had been waiting for: a single guard, the door left ajar.

Maret's face hovered in front of him. Someone had sawed off the back of his head. Her face came closer to him. "I have sent for a physiopath, Eli Dammond."

They had bound him, arms and feet, where he lay on the mat in his cell. As his sight cleared, so did his memory.

"They said you fought harder than they thought a human would tend to do. Therefore they had to beat you harder. I am very deeply sorry, Eli Dammond."

He turned his face to the rubbery wall, hating the sight of her.

His escape lasted as far as the third side corridor, where he walked among the dwellers, remaining calm, acting like he had business elsewhere. As he did. They tolerated this, it seemed. But at the next turn, the guards were waiting.

He had time to think that their markings were very pale, and thus they would be statics, who would be harsher with him. Then he took out the nearest ahtra, turning to the next.

They did not understand street fighting, which gave

him a considerable advantage for the first fifteen seconds. Then, once he was down, they set on him, beating him exclusively on the right side of his body.

Maret explained this was their tradition, not to hit on the left side, near the side of the head where the data tendril was seated. She seemed proud of the fact that the guards showed such restraint.

"Nobody ever taught you folks how to fight," Eli muttered.

Maret was very quiet then. "You break the rules when you fight," she said almost inaudibly.

So I've been told.

12

Maret sped through the chute, stretched out in the flattened car, making herself a fleshy bullet. The privacy of
the chutes was worth paying for today. Although it was
her right to purchase a Data Guide's services, Nefer's ire
called for discretion.

Nefer had always paid, and now Maret saw the folly of
handouts. By her patronage Nefer controlled Maret. Cutting off funds for training purposes, she forced Maret to
access the few credits her first kin net had reserved for her.

Maret tried to remember how it was that she had become so dependent on Nefer. The Most Prime Nefer had
sought her out when Maret was still a child. According to
Nefer, Maret's gene scans showed a promising scholar,
and Nefer had need of a scholar-servant, finding meaning
in the richness of the Well. Maret dispatched her role as
Data Illuminator with scrupulous confidentiality—unlike
the powerful Data Guides whose discretion Nefer did not
trust. In her more cynical frame of mind, Maret thought
it served Nefer's interests to use her as an intermediary.
For those tracing data draws could not tell whether Maret

accessed information for her own scholarly pursuits—
which were many—or for Nefer's secretive administrative
and political needs.

Leaving the chute, Maret lost no time crossing Prime-
Way. At this extreme end, a small crowd had gathered at
the Meridian, watching as the sun line elongated increment by increment along the wall, informing the hab,
from the remote ocular UpWorld, of the approach of the
season. More than a tradition, light relayed from above
was the hab's last link to sidereal time, a link that must
never be broken.

As she hurried across PrimeWay, the sun line seemed to
point at her, saying, *Hurry, hurry. . .*

Arriving at last at Tirinn Vir Horat's imposing lobe,
Maret found the forward gallery teeming with workers.
Some were plugged into trunks clustered like cilia over the
data pedestals. They moved about with the distracted look
of those fully engaged, researching issues in backmind
while developing heuristics and pattern searches in foremind. Tirinn's Paramount Locator noted her standing there
and motioned for her to enter. Nemon Es Marn accorded
her his personal attention, graciously choosing to ignore
whether Nefer paid or did not. He conducted her into a
narrow way just outside the busy lobe, where they passed
other dwellers seated on a bench along the wall, who looked
up resentfully as she passed by the queue.

In front of Tirinn's chamber, Nemon gestured forward
a Second Data Custodian. She carried a tray bearing a
small tube of water and a plate of lorel. For courtesy,
Maret took a sip of water. Nemon and the custodian then
retreated, leaving her to summon calm. She never knew
what she would find in the chamber before her. Since it
was a data stage, it could be anything.

Once it had been the surface of a traveling hexadron.
They had conducted their lessons hurtling through space,
with radiation setting off quick fires in their eyes. Other

unsettling exercises placed her UpWorld, with sky and things that swelled out of the ground. DownWorld was a place of routine and safety, but UpWorld was a realm of chaotic and shifting perils. Tirinn's job was to accustom one to such an experience. For those like Maret, ascending for the first time, it was a daunting task. She had studied UpWorld. But she had not felt it.

She opened the portal and entered Tirinn's stage. He was surrounded by noisy free water. From this inauspicious locale, Maret gathered it would be a bad session.

As she looked more closely, she saw that her teacher was seated in front of a waterfall, on a shelf of rock. Maret gathered her resolve and approached him. At the foot of the falls, a WaterWay disgorged its contents while canyon walls rose up on both sides, laden with disorganized plant growths. Here were bottomless skies, and many kinds of fecund life, some mobile, some fixed, some edible, many poisonous, some lower on the food chain. Some higher. She *knew* these things, didn't she?

"Shall we stand and gawk, or shall we begin?" Tirinn Vir Horat asked, his grating voice carrying despite the roar of the falls.

Maret picked her way through the plants crowding the edge of the WaterWay, her feet wallowing in soupy gravel. The smells of the place disoriented her. *What does a vone smell like?* all candidates wished to know. Like a meal of sweet lorel and like offal, myth said.

As she seated herself on the rock, a disconcerting mist of water sent chills through her scalp.

Tirinn shifted his perch, creating a rock indentation that allowed him to sit more comfortably. He left her sitting on the flat rock. His loose-fitting caftan was soaking wet, clinging to his body, revealing rolls of fat at his waist. He turned, searching her face. "Ah. So you have questions, do you?"

She found herself blurting: "Will you send me forward?"

He spit to the side. The gob fizzed as the mist fell on it. "Impudent. Ask me something else."

"Will Nefer prevent me from going Up?" It was discourteous to imply that Nefer might subvert Tirinn's decision. But statics were always trying to manipulate ronid decisions, to support their wagering for personal vendetta, or to indulge personal genetic preferences.

He looked up to the vivid blue sky, as though in exasperation. "You think I'd admit to corruption?"

"Will she find some other way to ruin me?"

"She may try. Is it worth the risk, is that your question? If you don't know the answer to that, why are you wasting my time? This is the busy season for me. Did you see the line out there?" He waved at the portal, now a large flower with progeny flowers sprouting by the moment from its edges. "A few of those candidates are very promising. I've put my hopes on several of them. I can't waste time with slackers."

"I'm not slacking. I'm paying for the training myself."

"Yes, paying. And the price hurts, does it? Maret-as, are you blind as the hab? The risks are commensurate with the payoff."

Anger crawled up from her belly. She was paying dearly, and getting little. Was it cowardly to fear Nefer Ton Enkar and the ruin she could bring?

Ponderously, he rose to his feet, facing the WaterWay a few moments. Then he carefully removed his caftan and jumped in, naked.

It was a shocking thing, to see someone jumping into a flow of water without any warning.

She couldn't see him for a moment. Then he reappeared in the writhing pool where the falls met the WaterWay. "Ho!" he cried. "Here is what I see! You are Maret-as. Your siblings are Nirid, Rumir, Hoz, Diret, and Garl. Your prime is Ellod, your second prime is Talik of high repute. Your second kin net from Birim, Ellod's sibling,

are Berd, Rullat, Fon, and Falaam, as well as Rez's progeny, Lassem and Zir; finally, Rumir's progeny, Ninim. All
names of distinction. And that is only the beginning."

He floated on his back, squinting into the bright ceiling
of sky. He spoke softly, but she could hear him whisper in
her ear. "Deeper than Talik, the flow speaks of your kin
and your lineage. They stand, Maret-as, foot upon shoulder, each net supported by the one beneath in cycles past
knowing."

She saw a vision in her mind of prime supported by
prime supported by prime, each standing on the shoulders
of the one beneath. Between her feet she saw Ellod's dear
face looking up at her. Ellod stood on Talik's shoulders,
Talik's features grown darker in the data well. Talik stood
upon her prime's shoulders, a fluxor of surpassing beauty,
whose name Maret knew, as she knew them all to the
twelfth net. The pillar of kin threaded deeper, past the
twentieth, fiftieth net. Maret's sight was so keen, she could
discern their expressions, their patience, and their faith.
Some had been standing for one thousand cycles, and some
for five thousand. She saw their faces. Some looked outward into the well, still called by the flow of the world,
still remembered in the wager fields, if only in batches. A
few craned their necks to look straight up from their posi-
tions in the ladder, gazing past feet and shoulders, looking
Maret in the eyes, holding her gaze with a binding force.

Tirinn called out: "Ho!" The WaterWay now ran backward, up the falls. "Here swim your bold descendants, or
they would be swimming if there were any. In some ways I
hold out more hope for them than you. And some of them
are excellent swimmers. They don't sit whimpering on the
sidelines, afraid to get wet!"

She thought she could see gleams of arms, flanks—
future kin, born of her imagination. . . .

After a time, Tirinn climbed out of the WaterWay,
grunting with the effort of hauling his bulk up onto the

rock. She thought he could just as well jump up to his seat as make such a production of it, but Tirinn did as he wished. A great fluffy towel was around his shoulders, and he began to vigorously dry off, wiggling his rolls of fat with the towel and buffing his skin to a bronze sheen. As he dressed, he said, "So what was your question again?"

Maret bowed her head. "There is no question, Tirinn-as."

He took his seat again. "Sure? We've got plenty of time." He smiled out at the WaterWay—now flowing in the right direction.

"I'm sure."

He shrugged, a movement she had seen Eli Dammond use. For a moment she had wondered what he knew of the human. No doubt, with Eli's escape attempt, Tirinn would think she had failed at that commission as well.

The Data Guide's voice was relaxed and self-satisfied. "Now that we've had our little chat, let's train."

He smiled with great kindness. "Swim," he said.

She rose and removed her clothes.

"By the way," came his voice, very low. "You aren't the only swimmer today. Some will tend to be hungry."

Holding on to her color, she hesitated only for a moment before diving in.

13

The Third Engineer looked up at Vod dubiously. Vod stood on the lip of the Paramount Borer during one of its brief down increments.

"Please, Third Engineer. This will be quick."

She was one of the older statics, and had always seemed friendly enough. He thought he could count on her discretion. "Only an increment." Vod ducked inside, leaving the door open. Soon he heard her lumber in behind him.

The cab brightened as they entered, its data displays bristling with light.

"What is it, Vod-as?" She glanced out the door to see if Second Engineer was watching. Apparently satisfied that he wasn't, she turned a pointed gaze at Vod.

Now that he had her attention, Vod felt a pang of impropriety at what he was about to do. It wasn't his place. Nor was it Wecar's *place,* that narrow slot that now held her bones. Vod plunged on. "It's the latest digs."

He inserted his forefinger into the display nub on the control panel where his configuration was primed up. Onto the heads-up display came a flood of lines, a schematic of tunneling, with colors showing projected build-out of current patterns.

The engineer's data tendril jerked in surprise as she looked at the display. "What are you doing, working this data?"

"I'm showing you the digs."

"Yes, certainly, but this isn't your job, Skilled Digger."

"Just look, will you?" Vod turned to point at the display, but the engineer went on, disregarding the data. "This is engineer's work. You're way out of category, here, Vod-as. Diggers don't model tunnels." Statics had a tiresome weakness for truisms.

"I didn't model them. I just plugged into what *engineers* had already done." If she would just put one of her minds to this, they could be done and out of here before anyone saw a high engineer and a low digger consorting.

"Why would you need to look at the modeling? You're a digger. A worthy job, Vod-as, or don't you think so anymore?"

"By the deep dark well, Jindaal-as, will you just *look*?"

A splotch of discoloration appeared on the engineer's cheeks. "Since when did you think stepping out of category was a fine way to spend downtime?"

Releasing an explosive breath, Vod grabbed Jindaal's wrist and fairly dragged her out of the borer and down the freshly dug tunnel.

The anterior feeding flaps of the hab were grazing through the loose spoil of clay, sand, and gravel, as though this tunnel were the same as any other.

"Vod Ceb Rilvinn, what in DownWorld has come over you?"

Thus far the engineer allowed him to propel her into the tunnel, but Vod knew he was on shifting ground. He tried to placate her with formality. "Third Engineer, it is vitally important that I show you something for the safety of our dig and our lives." He had hoped she'd come to her own conclusion about that, but he'd be lucky just to keep her attention.

In the sudden gloom of the deep tunnel Jindaal snapped her headlamp on, as he did. "This better be worth—"

"Your valuable time. Yes. It will be." The old static wasted twice this much time wagering on the job, but Vod knew to defer. "We'll walk the latest dig, Third Engineer. Then you'll see."

He had her gently by the elbow, walking her as quickly as they could manage in the semidark, so that she could imprint the digs. All dwellers kept a map in backmind of everywhere they had ever traversed. In a few increments Jindaal would have the lay of the digs without resorting to an engineer's display called up by a *digger*. So he took her on through the tunnel, and into a downway, back through another tunnel and into an upway.

Trickles of free water slithered down the open walls of the digs, a sight both he and the Third Engineer were hardened to. Still, they averted their headlamps from the rivulets. As they walked the deserted tunnels, Vod fancied he heard a deep thudding now and again. It was an odd sound, not like the creak of the foam girders or the echoes from active digging elsewhere DownWorld. But soil and rock shifted, he knew; the deep world was not a silent place.

When they'd stepped through the entire path, Vod turned to her. "So do you see?"

The engineer stared at him.

He added, "They're too close. The entire new portion of the network is unstable."

In the gloom he searched her face for response. Beyond the safety issue lay the more interesting question. Why would the engineers allow faulty pockets of tunnels? But when he looked into Third Engineer's static face, he found only cool contempt.

"Perhaps, Vod-as, you need to rest. The shock of the recent slump . . ."

"Slump? It was a collapse!"

"But these tunnels are holding."

"You can see for yourself it won't last." But he was in no wise certain what the engineer could see.

"Fluxor hysteria," came the dismaying answer.

"I'm not hysterical!"

"Keep your color, Vod-as. I only meant that you tend to overreact."

To his chagrin, he felt his skin pale. This was worse and worse. "Jindaal, this whole section may collapse. Do you want that responsibility?"

"That's an engineer's judgment."

"Yes! That's exactly what I'm asking for. An engineer's judgment."

This seemed to mollify her for a moment, but then she said, "I'd be asked how I came to my opinion. It would look very bad for you if I told about digger meddling."

"Then lie."

"You're asking me to lie?"

"Vone take me! You're twisting everything."

At that moment a grinding creak issued from all around them. A bone-weary pluck on the sinews of the deep. Third Engineer looked up at the ceiling. Her face had turned the color of the hab in off-season. A sheen of sweat coated her face. She began backing up, heading toward the lighted digs.

He'd lost her interest. She was now interested in getting as far away as possible. Though her fears only supported his position.

"Don't worry," he muttered. "It won't fall down until it's full of diggers." But already she was scurrying away. Statics ever coveted their personal safety.

In high frustration, Vod kicked the tunnel wall with all his strength.

It held, for now.

*   *   *

Nefer sat before Eli on a richly patterned rug. He remembered her distinctive markings, especially the double oval between her wide-set eyes. This was the first time he'd been with Nefer alone, without Maret to translate.

"You would be well, Captain Eli Dammond," she said in Standard, with a guttural accent so heavy that Eli leaned forward to hear her. Nefer drew back.

He knew ahtra reacted to human scent, but for this meeting, at least, they'd allowed him to clean himself thoroughly with a cleansing clay and a vacuum hose. His clothes, temporarily taken from him, were returned stiff and clean.

"I am alive," he responded. He adjusted his position, favoring the side of his body not swollen with bruises.

"Alive—yes. That shall be agreeable to me."

"I do strive to be agreeable."

"I would not have said so, Eli Dammond. You are regrettably unruly for one who has been offered my protection."

"It is a gilded cage, Nefer-as."

She blinked. "One has difficulty understanding you. Your language has a—proclivity to error."

In other words, she was still learning. In the pause that followed her statement, he asked, "Are our two peoples at war?" If they were, it would explain why she didn't worry about provoking Congress Worlds in her actions against his mission.

"Would your ships coming here show such a tendency?" she countered.

"No, as I've said already. The first ship suffered equipment failure. My ship was to rescue them."

"One hopes not to give offense by saying one doubts. Failure of equipment in the FarReaches is a most seriously regrettable safety lapse. Perhaps humans tend not to be adequately prepared for venturing into FarReaches?"

"In the recent war, the FarReaches held some surprises for ahtra as well."

"One remembers." She licked her teeth. He noticed her tongue seemed to have a nap. "But the HumanWar is concluded. Now we are conducive to more delightful topics."

She helped herself to a morsel of food on a plate in front of her. The food looked like fragments of fungus. After chewing slowly for a moment, Nefer pointed to the plate in a graceless gesture for him to help himself. There were no noxious varieties displayed, but he declined.

"Eli Dammond, we will speak of things Above. Shall that become agreeable?"

"Yes." She had his full attention now, and she seemed more keenly focused on him as well.

"One will try to explain as much as your flawed language may tolerate. Please forgive any unintended error. The risk may be that you become outward with your feelings. One wishes you to have the understanding that if you make a threatening gesture toward one's person, you will immediately receive injuries that shall be regrettably difficult to remedy."

"I will remain calm." He sat very still, to show how calm he was.

"Yes," Nefer continued. "As one has already said, your ship and its contents are dead."

She was new to the language. But he wondered if her choice of words was deliberate.

She reached for a short, narrow stick resting on a plate at her side and inhaled from it a powder. Sniffing noisily, she continued, "Do you know what tradition is?"

"Yes, it's a long-standing way of doing things."

"Even among humans, I would guess, some things seem like they shall be longtime-standing ways."

"Like protecting those under one's command."

"Yes, very like that," she said with some satisfaction.

"In the case of ahtra, we do not venture UpWorld except under traditional—happenstances."

"But you sometimes travel in ships at your whim."

"Ships." She blinked. "Yes, you call them ships. But that, Eli Dammond, would not be UpWorld. That would be away from the world. You discern the difference?"

"When do you venture UpWorld?"

Ignoring this, Nefer continued, "Given that we shall not pass UpWorld except for our traditional ways, we cannot remove the bodies for burial. Generally, there will not tend to be bodies in any case, you apprehend." She paused, pointing at the plate of fungus.

He controlled his response with difficulty. "It is deeply offensive to offer food when discussing news of disaster."

"One forgets courtesies. Your language drifts so easily toward error, does it not?" She watched him with great intensity. Her large eyes seemed to gather up all the light of the room. At last she continued, "One does not rejoice in the misfortunes of others . . . but one might wager on them."

She watched him as he shifted his position, stretching out a leg that had begun to throb with his cross-legged posture.

She went on: "Thus we wager on happenstances, such as when and in what manner all of your people died. Of course, winning or losing still proves nothing. It would be a tradition."

Fire flicked across his skin, and in his gut. "Understood. We have traditions like that. Such as taking revenge against betrayal. It proves nothing, but it's satisfying."

"Certainly," Nefer replied. "We do the same. We have much in common, I think."

He held her gaze. "If it's war you want, there are easier ways to get it."

"One does not look for war. You will tell your betters

that to pass UpWorld is our high tradition. You would not be permitted to return in this season."

"Even if it might lead to reprisals?"

"The stakes are thrillingly high, you apprehend."

"You risk calamity, and blame it on tradition. Unless your command of my language lends to error." He let her digest this insult, then slipped in the question: "What do the vone have to do with the alleged deaths of my people?"

She paused. "You are accustomed to speak of the vone?"

He did want to guard the source of that intelligence, so he merely shrugged.

"Maret makes very free," Nefer observed with a feral smile.

"Do the vone attack my encampments, then?"

"Perhaps. You must pray they do not."

"What are the vone?"

She took a morsel of food, chewing slowly. Then she answered: "Beasts. Horrors of the sunlit world. Some of your people killed themselves rather than face them. One could understand the tendency."

"Others of my people would hunt the vone, if they are beasts."

"Yes, certainly, they would be disposed to try."

"If you faced a vone, Nefer-as, how would you prevail?"

She had a startle reflex, the smallest twitch of her tendril. "One does not."

"Prevail?"

"Face the vone," she said, very low.

"If you did, would you fight or retreat?"

A long silence. Then: "Neither one or the other."

"Perhaps my people will react similarly, doing neither one nor the other."

"The odds are against this."

It was not lost on him that she used, at last, the present

tense. *The odds are against this.* "Even so. Traditionally, we do not give up."

"Then they suffered longer than they might have."

"Yes, perhaps. But I would wager they are not all dead."

She blinked. "Do you offer a wager?"

In the next instant, he responded, "Yes."

"But one discerns you have nothing to wager."

"There's always something to be gained and lost."

"Yes." She took another piece of fungus. "Describe your wager."

"Someone survives, UpWorld. Some of my people. If I'm wrong, I'll give you what you want from me that is in my power to give."

"That would be?"

"You tell *me*."

Her lips slid away from her teeth a fraction. "Perhaps one could think of something. . . ."

"But if I win, you will give me what I want that is in your power to give."

"One has interest in this wager, since everyone is dead, and therefore one risks nothing. . . . Understanding that one would not break traditions."

"And understanding that one will not use traditions to cheat on the wager, or to influence the outcome."

She regarded him.

"Take it or leave it."

"An apt expression." She stared at her plate of fungus for a long time. Then she looked up at him, her eyes wide with pleasure. "One takes it." She made some movement that called the guards. When they came to escort him, she said: "That would be your expression, 'to take it'?"

"No," he answered. "We say 'done.' "

"Done, then."

"I hope you'll abide fairly by the wager," he said. Though he had no such hopes, he also had little to lose.

She smiled, showing small white teeth. "Eli Dammond,

it has been long and long since I have received such delightful insults. One is apt to enjoy conversation with you again. Would that be conducive?"

"I'm at your disposal," he said with mock courtesy.

"An interesting phrase," he heard her murmur as he was led away.

14

Sascha awoke to glorious sunshine. Peeking out of the tent, she beheld a steaming world.

Split rays of low morning sun streamed through the Gray Spiny Forest, some one hundred feet away. The forest was no longer gray or spiny, its pillars growing a foot a day. The growing tips bore upward the green vines and mosses that were hitching a ride to the best light.

The *monsoons*, the enlisteds called this deluge of rain. Without more detailed study, the term might suit, her father said. Half a world away, winds crossing the great ocean were heated ever warmer by the approach of the red sun. Bearing higher moisture content than in the dry season, the moist winds rushed in to fill the void left by rising hot air over the land. And so once in four years it rained. And rained.

Her mother stirred, one eye always on Sascha—even, it seemed, when Cristin Olander was asleep. "Don't go outside, now."

"No, Mother." She stood in the tent flap opening, the boundary line.

Her father was melded into his cot, not budging after an all-night session with the commander and his lieutenants.

Already at least ninety degrees, the air sucked up moisture from the forest, the camp's drainage ditch, the tents, and the enlisteds who, soaking wet, were just returning from sentry duty. Behind wisps of dissipating fog, the sky flickered neon blue. On such a day, Sascha could almost forget the unsettling conversation with Badri Nazim, the fate of Eli Dammond. Except it was the second day of clear skies, and still no sign of the *Lucia*. Nor of Baker Camp.

Outside, one of the off-duty sentries walked by, nodding at her.

"Quiet watch?" Sascha asked.

As he passed her he said, "Gets louder every night." He was a corporal, with black skin splashed here and there with the mottled regen that proclaimed his battle history.

She thought of all the young men and women whose lives were interrupted for a time—or permanently—by the Great War. By the time of the armistice, two generations of young lives were winnowed down to a surviving few, all patchwork bodies, with what some said were patchwork hearts to match.

Then she heard the sound. It was a human wail. In the distance, from across camp, came a long scream. And it didn't stop, but grew louder, more insistent. Her father, who'd slept in his clothes and boots, charged past her, commanding her to remain, while her mother sat on the side of her cot, shoulders slumping, as though she would not be surprised by any bad news the screams might herald.

The terrible howls were now punctuated by some dozen gunshots. Sascha peeked out the tent flap. Soldiers dashed to their squads under the shouted orders of their officers.

Sergeant Ben Juric was standing in the aisle between the tents just in front of her. He was facing away from her, away from the source of screams, watching the forest. He held a Dominator Gun, called a domino, loosely in his left hand while running enlisteds parted around him like a river around a boulder.

Sporadically, the screaming pummeled them from across camp. Finally, when her mother could stand it no more, she stalked to the tent opening and ducked outside, threatening Sascha with disinheritance if she followed. But after a long interval of quiet, Sascha judged the crisis over and, emerging from the tent, hurried in the direction of the crowd of soldiers. The ditch running through camp had been covered in a dozen places by sheets of metal matrix, forming bridges. But in their hurry, some of the enlisteds now hopped over the open ditch, defying the water to produce monsters such as those, rumor had it, that lived in the new rivers of the forest. Sascha used a bridge, determined not to get busted for a minor infraction of rules.

As she wound into the crowd, she heard soldiers swearing, using combinations of profanity she had never heard before, not even from Nazim. Just in front of her, an infantry private was talking to his buddies, filling in what he knew for the benefit of the newcomers.

". . . four to a tent," he was saying. "One moment these guys are sleeping, then those things are inside and grabbing hold. Nobody calls out, nobody wakes up. When we killed them, they just dropped off our guys, all full of blood, too full and happy to care if they got blown to kingdom come." To a question, he answered, "Dead? Yeah, they're dead. Twenty of our guys never gonna wake up."

Turning, he saw her standing behind. He grinned at her, wild-eyed. "You wanna see?" He made as though he would hoist her up to have a look.

A commotion off to their left made him pause a moment. Then he turned back to her. "Did I say twenty? Oh man, *should* have been twenty! But it was only nineteen, 'cause one patch, see, he just sleeps through the whole thing. No little bloodsuckers on him, but when he wakes up he finds his three tent-mates are white as your behind." She wished he would stop, wished he wasn't looking at her with that flat, eager stare. He chewed on his upper lip for a moment before continuing. "Now, Farley, here—he's the screamer—he must wonder how nineteen good buddies can die in such peace and sweet quiet. He must wonder how we all can be lying asleep and dreaming of goin' home, and wake up hoping for bacon and eggs, all the while monsters been sucking the life out of guys like they was nothin' but a milkshake."

He grinned at her as she backed away from him. "Makes you wonder, don't it?" he repeated.

She broke eye contact, sidling away from him. He was crazy. It couldn't be true that nineteen enlisteds had died last night. Nineteen lives gone, gone as *food,* he had said. It was worse than murder, worse than war. . . .

Flanking the largest knot of the crowd, she finally worked her way forward to see medics tending to the bodies. They hoisted a woman onto a canvas stretcher, her face as pale as her blond hair. No wounds or blood, but as Sascha surveyed the area near the tent, she saw a gout of blood lying under a small animal body. Her father was bent over this carcass.

Sascha could only stare at the very large pool of blood, the casual food of the rodents, or whatever these creatures were. About the size of a rat, the creature was smooth-skinned and bore splotches of dark color, rather like CW camouflage fatigues. From its snout protruded four saber teeth, two pointing up, two pointing down, that could well be the device that had locked on to the soldiers, perhaps delivering a quick poison before feasting at leisure. Long hind legs with muscular hip joints suggested the creature jumped onto its prey. It was plump, but growing less so the longer it bled onto the ground.

Her father approached her, putting his arm around her

shoulders. In the milling crowd of soldiers they formed a pocket of stillness. After a moment she asked, "Father . . . why didn't anybody know?"

"They never called out. No one heard a thing. The animals gnawed through the tent walls, probably driven by scent. When they got in they must have paralyzed the occupants all at once."

"Did they suffer?"

Geoff Olander started to say something, seemed to think better of it, and gazed over her head at the Gray Spiny Forest. At last he looked at her and said, "Sascha. You should realize what we face. You're almost grown now." He looked at her with dismay, as though he wished she were not almost grown, that he didn't have to speak to her as an adult. She thought again how her body was betraying her, to cause her father such a bitter moment.

"The *Lucia* isn't coming in."

"But Captain Marzano . . ."

He shook his head. "She didn't make it to the ship. If she had, she'd have been here by now." His voice was gentle, his eyes more so as he said, "I'm afraid for this camp, Sascha. It pains me to tell you . . . the danger is very serious." He glanced toward the tents. "No need to upset your mother about this."

"What will we do, then?" He always had an answer for a question like that.

But this time he only said, "I want you to be watchful, Sascha, and to stay close by. Promise me you won't take chances. This isn't a game anymore. You see?" His eyes searched hers as though plumbing her thoughts, as though he was afraid she *did* see.

"Yes . . . I promise."

He gazed into the distance, in the direction of the *Lucia*.

A shuffling noise interrupted them, and they turned to see an enlisted, helped along by two others.

"The survivor," her father said under his breath.

The man walked in a kind of slow motion, his eyes serene with tranks. On spying Sascha, he stopped abruptly. "Kids?" he muttered to one of the medics. "We got kids?" He started to smile, then broke into a ruined laugh, saying, "Oh, no, Christ almighty, whose idea *was* this?" He looked directly into Sascha's eyes as the others tried pulling him away. "Whose fucking idea was this worthless bloody mess?" As they hauled him past Lieutenant Roche, he shouted, practically in his face, "This your big stupid idea, you raging asshole? *Was* it?" Roche looked as though he was ashamed of himself, as though it had been all a terrible blunder on his part. He winced as the soldier started wailing, "Oh, no, no . . ."

"Get him out of here," Roche told the medics. "And shut him the hell up." Roche turned, resuming his talk with Lieutenant Anning, the bot specialist. Anning was halfway through morphing one of their two bots into a squat machine on rollers. The verbal codes sounded like a language where she knew only every other word. The bot housing shifted in a liquid-looking wave, a mutable housing for the platforms of nano beneath. Flat black, the machine looked like the finest metal matrix, silky in texture, catching a shimmer now and then as the plates exposed the working nano beneath.

Roche caught Geoff Olander's eye. Sascha should not be so close to the military-grade nano.

As her father escorted her back to the tent, Sascha could hear a fizzing in the distance, as the bots got to work, defoliating an area just outside the west camp perimeter, improving the landing site.

She said good-bye to her father outside the tent. Together, they watched Sergeant Ben Juric leaving with the remaining bot, heading into the forest on the east side of camp.

Under his breath, her father said, "Damn him."

"He can't kill the whole forest," Sascha said.

Geoff Olander snorted. "He can try."

"He's trying to protect us, though."

He sighed. "We're getting out of here, Sascha. Do we have to leave a wasteland behind us?" He smiled, shaking his head. "Never mind. Go keep your mother company. Lace up the tent flap behind you."

Cristin delivered no lecture, no cross looks. They waited together throughout the morning as the tent approached broiling temperatures. Each lay on her cot, drinking sparingly from their now-rationed water. Catching rainwater was inefficient, but no one wanted to venture close enough to tap the trees. As Sascha lay there, she listened for any hails from the camp that might signify that Nazim and Baker Camp had made it in. *On a nice day it would take an hour and a half. . . .*

Gradually, as the sweltering day wore on, they each came to understand that they would be spending another night on Null.

Late in the afternoon, the rains began again, keeping up a steady barrage into the evening.

When the sounds of muffled explosions came from the forest, Sascha heard her mother at the tent flap asking the guards what it was. "The bots . . ." she heard. And then: ". . . pushing back the edge of the Sticks." They always called it the Sticks. No matter what it was becoming, they stuck to the version they liked better. Sascha slept fitfully, now and then aware of forest-muffled detonations amidst the rain, and the sickly odors of chemicals burning.

15

Through a haze of nausea, Eli noted that the communal elimination chamber was blessedly empty. Having accompanied him this far, Maret withdrew with the guards to the far side, facing away. She had learned his fastidiousness, though she thought it strange.

Here the hab was swollen in places, creating thick vertical cords that plunged into the pits below the toilets, feeding on wastes, no doubt.

He cleaned up with the air brush and then managed the walk back, with Maret speaking in low, guttural whispers to the guard, her expression betraying flickers of what he took for anger.

When he was settled back in his cell, she gave him a sack of water. He sipped through the straw, his eyes closed.

"You are sick," she began. "I am very deeply sorry. The food makes you sick."

Sick. No, that wasn't it. He was dying. He hoped.

When he had made his decision, he thought it might be born of lack of sleep and despair. But when he woke, he hadn't changed his mind. It was the last thing he had to gamble: his life. He reasoned that if the ahtra wanted him alive, he might have a bargaining chip. The fact that he expected to die, and did not any longer greatly care, gave him power for the first time since he entered the hexadron and burrowed down.

Fingering the mushrooms in his pocket, he assured himself that his wafers were still there. These were the common blue fungi that made him violently ill and that he'd been conserving.

Maret was talking again, in her low, calm voice. "I wish to take charge of your feeding from now on. I was not summoned when you first became sick. Now I tend not to trust what is happening."

"Join the crowd."

Her smile showed her pleasure at knowing the idiom. An ahtra smile was not a response to humor, Eli had learned, but a sign of enjoyment.

Then she became serious again. "Among my people," she said, "we say we have two sadnesses, held in the two chambers of the mind. I have both sadnesses now."

He sat staring at her, his arms resting on his bent knees. "Why? Why be sorry?"

"Because I tend to believe you are being poisoned, regrettably, and against all orders for your safety. I have called for a chemipractor."

"Don't bother, Maret." He put his hand in his pocket and took out a few of the mushrooms. "I'm leaving."

Maret's large eyes fixed on the blue fragments in his hands.

He took one and placed it in his mouth, chewing slowly, letting the oily and bitter liquid drip down his throat.

"I will take these from you, Eli Dammond."

"I'll get more. They grow everywhere." They had to take him along the corridor to the communal toilets. They seemed oblivious to the concept of individual latrines.

He popped another fungus in his mouth. His mouth flooded with saliva. Swallowing, he gagged, but kept them down.

"Do not do this," Maret ordered.

"Like I said, I'm leaving."

"You do not wish to live?"

"No."

"Ahtra do not kill themselves," she said, pedantically.

"Humans do," he said, eating another.

Suddenly, she thrust out her hand, leaning forward and touching his wrist. "Why?"

He shrugged. "To express outrage. To die without doing further harm to my people."

"You do not harm your people."

"It's a human concept. Guilt by inaction." She must be certain of his resolve. She must understand it.

"Nefer forbids this act," Maret said in growing agitation.

He snorted in a half laugh. "To hell with Nefer."

Maret's hand dropped into her lap. She remained silent. Then she spoke very low: "What do you want that will make you stop this?"

He reached for the water tube, and sipped, trying to keep the poison down.

"What will be persuasive?" she pressed on.

A wave of nausea left him sagging limply against the spongy wall. He whispered, "You're going Up to the surface."

She leaned closer to hear him. "How do you know this?"

"Word gets around. When you do—go Up—I want you to help my people, my camp. Whatever it takes, I want you to promise to help them. Whoever's left."

She remained still as stone. In turn, he remained locked in place, ready to make a meal of the buttons, or cast them down.

The room grew cooler, along with his thoughts. He had a new peace, now that he could finally act. "I don't accept that they are all dead. I don't accept it." He chewed another mushroom.

As he did so, she whispered, "They may yet live."

He had forced her to say it. But still—it was all the hope he had.

She went on, "But they are like babies set into a raging river. Without great courage—of the sort they cannot have—they will tend to die swiftly. But in truth, we cannot know."

"Why? Why will they die? They're seasoned troops."

"Because they are not accustomed to UpWorld. It will have terrors, for which they are unprepared without guides to teach them. We undergo deep training, encountering our weaknesses many times. Then, UpWorld, we are prepared."

"Maybe surface worlds have more terrors for you than for us."

"Perhaps. But we are hardened against mercy that might make us soft."

He looked at the mushrooms in his hand. They had tiny spots on the outer edges. Toward the center, they deepened in color. The detail of each cap impressed on his sight with preternatural vividness. The caps rested in his hand amid the lines of his palm as though in some meaningful alignment to his life. "Well?" he asked. "Will you help them? When you go Up?"

Her voice was a shadow. "Yes."

He closed his eyes. Now that he had extracted her promise, he wondered if it was enough. If he had sold his death too cheaply.

"Eli," Maret said from what seemed very far away.

He rested his head against the wall. His body was loose, floating, but his mind was firmly anchored in each passing moment.

"May I have the food?" Maret asked.

Eli slowly raised his arm, allowing a spattering of mushrooms to pass from his hand to hers. He gazed at her with a detached interest, noting the patterns on her smooth skull as she bent over the mushrooms.

"What can I do for your comfort, Eli?"

He could barely hear his own voice. "Get rid of the smell." The perfumes in the room added to his nausea.

Maret went to the data plug by the door, then returned to sit cross-legged in front of him once more. The air freshened. He breathed it in like nourishment.

Maret spoke very softly. "I never knew—an individual—to kill themselves for the sake of another."

He cocked his head. "Isn't that what war is?"

"Yes. But this was different." The tone of her voice was hushed, as though she knew how sensitive his hearing was at this moment just after death had passed him by.

"One learns very much from you, Eli."

She was using just his given name for the first time. It sounded strange, a little unnerving. He squinted at the glowing walls. "The lights are very bright."

Rising, she went to the data plug again, and the lights dimmed, releasing the needles that had been plunging into his temples.

They sat in the dim quiet for a while. The chemipractor came and Maret dismissed him at Eli's insistence.

In the semidark, Maret's voice came to him. "I once had those I would have died for."

He sipped from his straw. The water ran down his throat as though for the first time, tracing a cold path.

"Before the HumanWar," she added.

"Millions dead . . ." Eli said, half to himself.

"Among us, there were fewer dead," she said. "But we are smaller in number than you. Vastly fewer. And so each death was a blow."

"Even the fifty million dead," Eli mused, "each one had a mother who grieved, a father who grieved."

"We do not use those terms. They are very strange to us."

"Mother and father. Everyone has a mother and father. . . ." He felt that he was speaking in parables. His mind took him to absolutes and obvious places. He was peaceful, a little crazy.

"We do not. We have only all our kin. And for myself, I have not even that."

Looking at her face he noticed that the markings exposed on her face and hands were darker—considerably darker—than before. She had been more accented for days now, he realized.

"Where are your kin, Maret?"

"Dead. In the Human War. The war took all but me. All my first net and second. Now that I am alone, I often think I would have gone in place of any one of them. Sometimes to be the sole survivor is a terrible thing." She said this last looking at him instead of the mushrooms in her hand. "That is why I must be permitted ronid . . . to continue my bloodlines. And why I must not fail in my duty to Nefer, who might ruin all. Regrettably, she might influence the Data Guides who decide who will go Up."

"Why do you go Up, Maret?"

Her voice was now only a whisper. "UpWorld . . . is the place of the bloodlines, Eli."

"But sex is very free down here, you have said."

She looked toward the door as though confirming that they were still in complete privacy. "It is not a polite conversation, to speak of UpWorld." She glanced at him and he held her gaze until she continued. "DownWorld we bear only sterile issue. To be truly fertile, we must go Up. Humans do not express distinctions between sex-for-pleasure and sex-for-progeny. But for us, there is sex, and there is ronid."

"Why are you only fertile UpWorld?" When she kept her eyes pointedly down, gazing at the floor, he remarked,

"It must be a dangerous place to have babies, your Up-World."

Her data tendril twitched in apparent surprise. "Of course. How else?"

She urged more water on him, and he drank, though his stomach warned against it.

"And you, Eli?" Maret continued. "What of your kin? Lost in the war also?"

Lost—always easier to say than *dead*. "You know the concepts of sister and brother?"

"Yes, we have those concepts."

"I have—I *had* four brothers. Two died in the same battle. Then later, Quinn was killed. It's eight years ago now. . . . But we don't forget."

"No. One does not." She helped him to raise the water tube to his lips. "You should drink more."

He acquiesced. The sack was empty. Maret replaced it with another.

"Nefer wishes to avoid war," she said. "My mistress is a cruel individual, but she is not wrong about all things. She hopes that you will help to avoid war by speaking for us and explaining that we did not kill your people."

"If it's true, then I'll tell them. But what I say won't carry much weight."

"They will not listen to a ship's captain?"

"Among your people, you have those of high and low degree, yes?" When she nodded, he went on, "I'm of low degree." At her look of surprise, he said, "Don't place your hopes on me, Maret. I'm one in disgrace. Like a gomin, you might say."

"Your people are very strange. To despise such a one as you."

"They have good reason."

"If war comes, neither your sorrow or mine will much matter," she said, so quietly it was almost inaudible.

"It will matter. Even then. Because we remember." It

was bizarre to think he had just used the term *we* to describe himself and an ahtra. But he let it stand.

The dim light of the room shimmered in Maret's eyes.

Maret kept vigil as Eli fell into an exhausted sleep. He dreamed of open skies and lying with a woman, while the sun warmed their bodies toward conception, and monsters roamed nearby, snapping branches under ponderous feet.

16

They may yet live. Eli paced in his cell, nine steps in one direction, nine back, thinking of how his crew might defeat the UpWorld threat—which was, Nefer said, *perhaps* the vone, the monster gods of the ahtra. Maret had said the survivors would be those without mercy. If so, they would be the hardened veterans: Luce Marzano . . . Sergeant Juric . . . and a few of the enlisteds with the mercy soaked out of them in regen baths. And he knew who would be the first to die: his civilian passengers. Young Sascha . . .

A movement at the far wall. A bubble swelled, beckoning Eli. The gomin was back.

The gomin was seated on a rug and gestured Eli to sit opposite her. "Eli Dammond, you have been ill. No longer, I hope?"

Eli shrugged. "The food. I've been better."

"Yes. You—languish—would that be the word?"

"Close enough."

The gomin spoke very softly. "I have so regrettably failed you."

"How?"

"It would be like paradise, you said. To return to the place that you have lost, to be among your people. Even if you die of it, it tends to be a worthwhile gamble. For paradise."

"Yes."

"Eli Dammond, I have not behaved with all courtesy toward you, for which please forgive."

"I've taken no offense."

The gomin waved her arms, agitated. "No, I have failed in courtesy. I was inclined to learn of your sexual ways, and your path of happiness. I am disposed to many weaknesses, curiosity for one." She closed her eyes, listening. When she opened them, she began speaking very rapidly. "The task was to tell you to leave us. But I have delayed. Now you have very little time."

"Leave?" The gomin had his full attention now.

"Please forgive my many errors."

"Tell me, then." He reached out to urge the gomin to speak, but his hands pressed through the image.

"There would be danger. If one is caught, one suffers."

Eli thought she spoke of herself as well as him.

The gomin continued, "Now remember, everything. Do not ask me questions that one will tend to fail, and that will waste time."

"Quickly, then!"

"At the next meal your door will not be barred. Proceed—you would say, left—down the way. As the season is near, some guards waver in their attention. There will occur a distraction for the guard near your door. You will proceed to the nearest downway, taking it to the next way. One will leave a robe for you, where possible. Watch for it. Proceed right again to the fourth downway. . . ." The gomin continued in this manner, reciting right, left, downway, several times.

Eli concentrated. There were four rights, after the first

left. There were five ways to traverse. Only once was the
next downway not the first one. This was on the second
level, where he was to take the fourth downway. He
would forget nothing; it was etched like acid on stone.

"You're telling me to go down. What about up?"

"No, down, down! Then you will come to the old
downway. There, one has been told, the hab is dead, very
dangerous. Proceed as far as you can down. There is a
probability someone will be there to guide you farther.
You will go to an ancient way, beyond memory. From
there, you may go up." She looked at him, blinking. "It
being dangerous, you would still engage the risks?"

"Yes. But in case I fail, I want a way to speak to my
people. Just once. By radio."

"No, no," the gomin said, fluttering her hands. "We do
not speak with those Above."

"You don't. But maybe I can?"

"No, the Well does not permit such. No radio."

"What Well?"

"Our great Well, our . . . ancestral data cistern. One
has the wrong words. But all our memory loops around
the world in a great field. It forbids radio waves, while giving camouflage. It holds all knowledge and memory and
all our kin nets. If you would speak to your people, you
must ascend to the OverWoods."

"What place is that?"

"It is where the vone dream, such dreams that we have
fallen from, but struggle to know imperfectly, in intervals."

"Myth or fact, gomin?"

"It is said that myth tends toward a condensed truth.
Among us, everything is an approximation of truth. How
can one know absolutely with so much uncertainty?" She
closed her eyes, then stood up abruptly. "Eli Dammond, I
am glad I learned that your sexual ways are not paradise,

nor are they chaos. Life is imperfect, in all realms, one is tending to believe. Even so, one hopes you find your paradise."

"And you yours, my friend."

"Lastly, no matter what the happenstances, do not trust Nefer Ton Enkar."

"I wouldn't trust her as far as I could throw her."

The gomin fluttered her hands. "Such a statement strays to delicious discourtesy." She smiled broadly. "I will miss our talks, Eli Dammond."

The bubble evaporated.

Far below PrimeWay, in a deep UnderPrime lobe, Vod stood facing Harn, his arm trembling with the desire to strike his coworker. They had exchanged words lacking in all courtesy, a breach of form that might well erupt into something worse. Just down the way, he could hear the clatter of the maintenance crew, intent on the DownWorld delivery systems behind an exposed flap of hab. The whole vicinity was darkened as the hab dealt with the intrusion.

Harn's cousin Belah accompanied him. She gestured at them, urging them to retire around the curve of the way, out of sight of the statics. It was conducive to fluxor pride to keep disputes from the notice of statics who would be eager to feed the information into the common flow.

Affecting nonchalance, Vod sat on the rusted arm of an antiquated soil crusher. "Leave it be, Harn-as. I don't answer for Maret." He would have *liked* to answer for Maret, if she would ever listen to him, but events had veered too far in one direction now.

"Maybe not," Harn allowed. "But then, where's all the gip we contributed when we *thought* you answered for her?"

Vod had long been accumulating contributions against

the day Maret would lead them. Until now, diggers had given freely. "Your funds are safe," he answered. "Do you want yours back?"

"Maybe I do. And what about everybody else that thought they wagered on Maret?" A crop of cella growing nearby lit Harn's face with a ripple of light. Vod tried to calm himself. The threads of the mycelium linked Down-World in a net of nourishment, like dweller kinship itself. There was no call for argument, especially among diggers.

He spoke reasonably. "It was never a wager. It was an investment."

"A bad one, if she's going Up."

"She'll be back." He said it automatically.

Belah exchanged glances with him. They were both against Maret, Vod saw.

"She won't be caring about diggers in any case, not like you led us to believe. Some think you strayed a hexal or two from the truth, Vod-as."

Vod jumped off the crusher. A strand of anger coiled in his stomach.

"Not your fault. You were out of the flow on this one."

Fairly said, and meant to mollify, but Vod rode a crest of emotion. He fought for his color, but it drained like free water into dirt spoils.

Then Harn added, "Your humble Maret serves Nefer. And now she serves the human."

As Vod opened his mouth to protest, Harn added: "Maybe serves him more ways than one."

Vod struck. It was a strong blow connecting to the dark side of the digger's head, avoiding the tendril. And Harn went down. After a moment he struggled to rise, then lay flat again.

Vod pulled in warm gulps of air, feeling queasy. He had never struck anyone before, much less a fellow digger.

Belah hurried to Harn's side. For a moment, Vod felt a strong attraction to her, despite the circumstances. Was she responding to him? The atmosphere was gravid with tension and pleasure.

Vod was backing up, both relieved and disappointed to see that Harn had begun to regain his senses.

Belah looked up at him, her eyes mocking his lapse of control.

"So, Vod-as," she said, her voice seductive and ironic, "the Season begins at last."

Around them, the hab glistened with humidity. A trickle of water edged down Vod's hand where he leaned against the wall. He wiped his hand on his clothes, stammering his apologies to Harn, but all the while looking at Belah, and her tacit offer of sex-for-pleasure. Then he turned and fled.

17

Sascha lay on her cot, pretending to sleep. Every light in camp was on, though it was the middle of the night. Her parents sat on folding chairs, each armed. She knew her mother had never shot a pistol such as now lay across her lap. She gripped it as though she might just as easily beat to death as shoot anything that came through the tent flap.

Through the drone of her parents' whispered voices, Sascha could hear occasional gunfire at the perimeter. The enlisteds shot at anything that moved. Sometimes a staccato burst would shred the rain-filled night; at other times, a short volley of shots. Each time, Sascha hoped for one more fallen enemy—though the enemy, of course, was without end.

In the morning, Charlie Company was leaving on foot, hiking the six miles to the *Lucia*. They had given up on Baker Camp. They'd leave Badri Nazim behind, alive or dead. Sascha turned over so many times on her cot that the blanket was wrapped around her like a cocoon.

She felt the cot sag on one side. Her father put a hand on her shoulder.

"Can't sleep?" he asked. His eyes were sunken into dark cavities. Behind him, Cristin watched the tent flap, sitting tall, perfect posture even in the cheap folding chair.

"Nazim," Sascha said. "She's still out there."

Geoff looked at the tent wall, in the direction of the sporadic gunfire. "Nazim survived the Great War, remember."

Sascha thought of Nazim's hair, altered forever, but still growing. "I don't give up on her."

Rain pelted the tent, filling in the spaces when conversation faltered.

Nearby, a shot fired. Cristin rose from her chair, then sat again when quiet returned.

Sascha noticed that her father was holding something in his lap. He placed it next to her pillow. "This is something I had made for you," he said.

"Why don't you just give her the pistol?" Cristin mumbled, her back to them, still keeping watch.

Geoff's mouth flattened, ignoring her. "You've never fired a gun, Sascha. But you've used a flashlight." He patted the cylinder lying between them. "This is a modified light spectrum lamp. The techs put it together for me."

Sascha pushed herself up on one elbow to look closer at the thing. It was dull gray, with the look of nano-housing. A bulb on the front protruded from a neck, a design that would allow light to flood in all directions.

"When we set out in a few hours, I want you to carry this. You can put your arms through the straps so that it rides on your chest." He handed it to her.

"But it won't be dark when we leave," she said, fingering the lamp. She sat up, facing her father. She was dressed, as they all were, to move out in a moment's notice. Cristin had insisted she sleep with her boots on. They were army-issue, lug-soled web boots. They weren't officer-caliber such as her father and mother now wore in anticipation of their march, but basic enlisted boots, the smallest in camp. Sascha felt proud to wear a private's boots, like Nazim's—Infantry, not Transport boots, she noted. Infantry always got the best boots.

"But it *is* dark," Geoff said. "The clouds and rain make it darker than when we arrived, darker than the dry season."

He turned the lamp on. The tent burst into light, probing all niches, creating a great shadow of her mother against the tent flap. He showed her the switch, and she turned the light off.

"The fauna don't like bright light. I think they're adapted to a wet season existence, going dormant in the dry season." He was speaking in a low, middle-of-the-night voice, calming and matter-of-fact. It almost seemed like a normal time, except for the gunfire.

"The enlisteds found the animals don't like bright light, especially directly in the eyes—but what we've got here may even be better." He tapped on the lamp housing. "This light matches the spectrum of light from the primary sun. I'm thinking that the wet season happens in several years' long cycles, tied to the approach of the dwarf star. So we skewed the spectrum away from the dwarf toward the primary sun's wavelengths, to give the locals a nice headache."

Put them off their feed, came to Sascha's mind, and she wished it hadn't.

In the pause, Cristin's sigh was unmistakable. Under her breath she said: "Good Lord, a *flashlight.*"

"Why don't we try that for the camp's lights, then?" Sascha wanted to know.

"There isn't time to reengineer things now. But it's why we've kept the lights on every night."

Cristin twisted around in her chair to look at them. "Geoffrey, just give her the gun. She's old enough to shoot a gun."

Geoff swallowed, but shook his head. "We're starting to shoot *each other* with the damn things. We're not going to win with force." He held his wife's gaze.

"I'm glad we didn't take that tack with the ahtra," she said, staring back.

"These creatures aren't the enemy, Cristin. They're animals, exploiting their food resources. If we think in those terms, then—"

Cristin interrupted. "The food resources are *us,* have you noticed? We don't need to study them when killing will do." She looked at her daughter, and doubtless saw for the thousandth time that Sascha would follow her father, always her father. Cristin turned back to watch the door.

Her father patted her arm and returned to his vigil by Cristin's side, their voices again mixing with the rain patter. Finally Sascha fell asleep, clutching the lamp.

She dreamed of the two suns, the red one in an elliptical orbit around the other. She watched from her balcony as the dwarf sun grew larger, bringing summer, and heat, and chaos. Below her, in the city, people frantically danced and made love. A few hailed her, calling her to do the same before it was too late. She retreated from the balcony and their voices. . . .

A hand was on her elbow, pulling her. She woke in an instant. A soldier was standing in the tent door, wind and rain beating in around him. Her father was urging her to her feet. "Hurry" was all he said.

With Cristin, they rushed from the tent into the night. Gunfire spattered around them, along with the *thunk, thunk* sound of the dominos.

"Roche's tent," her father said, grasping her by the upper arm.

They ran toward the center of camp. Amid shouts and gunfire, soldiers dashed to their posts.

For an instant Sascha saw a shape. Three feet high,

much larger than anything they'd seen before, with an odd, strutting motion. It disappeared between the tents. Shouts came from the perimeter, along with the zinging noise of the bots as they hurled hot plasma. The smell of cooked flesh drifted among the tent corridors, mixing with the smells of mud—a thick paste that sucked at their feet as they ran.

In the next tent aisle, Sascha saw more of the creatures, running in a pack, jabbering what sounded like words as they ran. *Real words.* Narrow heads bobbed up and down, heading away down the aisle, babbling in a high-pitched litany: *Fire! Here! Run!* A domino clattered only twenty feet away and a soldier screamed, dreadfully cut off. Cristin had latched on to Sascha's other arm, her eyes wild.

Sprinting toward the command tent, the three of them joined Lieutenant Roche and Sergeant Juric, who were crouching on one side of it. Sascha's knees sank deep into the mud as her father shielded her against the tent with his body.

"Wait here," Roche barked at her father, as though they would even venture into the melee.

Ben Juric's face fell into sudden blackness as a near section of camp lights failed. "Split us up, Lieutenant. Last chance, I'm thinking."

"No. We'll pull back to a smaller perimeter."

"No perimeters! Christ almighty. Give me five men and I'll get through, with or without a bot."

"I said, no one leaves."

Juric spit to one side. "Don't get it, do you? We're a restaurant, sitting here. Those stalkers are *attracted* to us all together. Send us out in units of five or six." A wave of gunfire came nearer. "Last chance," he snarled. "Or you think you're still fighting the"—here he swiveled and sent a volley of shots down the aisle to fell a creature running full speed toward them—"goddamned battle of Mi Pann?"

Cristin was holding Sascha's arm in a tight grip, her other hand pointing her pistol out toward the rain and the night.

The tent collapsed. Behind it were two upright creatures with gray beaks and long legs, covered with fur that now glistened in the streaming wet. In the next instant they ducked forward, heads bobbing down, legs flinging up to tear at the group. Roche was caught in the throat. Cristin was pulling Sascha down, but not to safety, only down because she was shot, the side of her head erupting in fragments, and Sascha stumbled backward, losing her mother's grip. In shock, Sascha stared at her mother. Then Geoff was running forward to where Cristin lay, just as a creature turned toward him and brought its long leg up in the air and then down, slashing, letting loose a spray of blood. Sascha heard herself screaming, standing in the rain, screaming.

A bot was jostling beside her. A sharp twang next to her ear, and when she looked again, the attackers were dead, their flesh smoking and sizzling in the rain. Beside them, three human bodies, Roche and . . .

Juric yanked her to her feet and began loping across the compound, but she ripped her arm from him. "My father!" she cried.

"Too late," he growled. He dragged her along as she fought him, digging in her toes.

"Medic," she said, "medic . . ."

"No medic for them, gal. They're gone. Now you save yourself." He hauled her to a barricade, where twenty soldiers had piled planks and equipment.

"We have to go back!" Sascha cried. "My grandfather will say you have to go back. . . ."

Juric pushed her onto the ground and crouched next to her, his face a couple of inches from hers. His regen eye looked like the dominant of the two, the tough member of the pair that could look at anything. "Don't be bringing up the big general, gal. Nobody cares about generals right now. Lie down flat and shut up."

Lieutenant Anning was in charge, trying to organize a defense, but everyone was shouting at once. The lights were all gone except for one spotlight that loyally held on. The stalkers and soldiers mingled in battle all around, with Anning shouting to hold fire, and no one listening, only firing in long, pointless bursts. Shaking, Sascha heard herself moan, "Medic, we need a medic. . . ."

"Fucking hell," someone in the bunker cried out. "What in the hell?" The enlisted, a female private, crouched below the barricade, saying, "I saw him. Perez! Don't shoot, I saw him!"

"Perez is dead," somebody muttered.

"No, I saw him." She licked her lips, eyes darting to the others. "But," her voice cracked, "but not exactly . . ."

A burly corporal with his regen paw clutching his rifle said, "Not exactly what, private?"

She opened her mouth to answer, then closed it again.

Perez was a name Sascha knew. Perez was the enlisted stuck on the other side of Nazim's black river, back when her life still held together in all its parts instead of, as now, scattered and bleeding in pieces.

"Perez is as dead as asshole Roche," somebody else said. "Asshole waited until we were surrounded, then he wants to take a stand."

"Jesus," somebody was muttering. "They talk, the things *talk*."

"Sergeant," a private said, eyes glazed, "how can they talk?"

Ignoring him, Sergeant Juric was arguing with Lieutenant Anning.

"Put 'em on automatic," Juric was saying.

"We lose their versatility. No."

They were talking about the bots. Both were in the bunker. One was clinging to the top of the barricade, aiming needles of fire into the rain.

"What happens if you go down, Anning? Nobody else's got the bot commands. On automatic, they can still fight after those birds pick you apart."

"We'll lose fifty percent of the capability," Anning said. "I'm saying no, Sergeant."

Then Juric's pistol was against Anning's forehead. "Yeah, and I'm saying yes. Do it."

Anning's eyes were blank as he sized Juric up. "You're finished, Sergeant. I'll run you out of the corp."

"So demote me. Now switch the dogs over."

A twitch took over Anning's face. "You patches are my witnesses," he snorted. "You remember this." He turned, calling the bots to his side, alarming, silver-black beetles. Sascha was eye to eye with them, wondering if they would kill her if she moved. Their bodies had morphed into walking guns. The footpads of the nearest one looked strangely amphibian. Its splayed toes left star-shaped prints in the mud.

Sascha heard Juric cock his gun, saying, "Make any mistakes, I'll kill you good."

From her viewpoint on the ground, Sascha watched as Anning coded the bots, one at a time, reciting the string of commands that identified his authority to program them, and releasing them from their previous orders, placing them on general battle and defense for whatever unit of soldiers they could find. From now on, the bots used their own AI judgment.

The sergeant took Sascha by the upper arm and pulled her to her feet. Now, in a lull in the fighting, the soldiers sharing the barricade watched him with both hope and terror.

Juric nodded at them. "We split up now. Leave here in

four groups. Buddy up as you want. Whoever gets through, wait one day on board. Then get the hell out of here, and never look back."

The soldiers looked from Sergeant Juric to Lieutenant Anning and back again.

"Ignore that order," Anning said. "We're staying."

Sascha hoped they would stay. They couldn't just leave her parents in the mud, but she knew Sergeant Juric cared nothing for that. He had her arm in an iron grip.

He turned to the enlisteds. "If you stay here, guess who's coming for dinner?"

One of the men nodded. "I'm in with you, Sergeant." Others muttered their agreement.

Still aiming the gun at Anning, Juric growled at the unit, "You assholes need a fancy invitation? Move."

In another moment everyone was running pell-mell out into the murky dawn, and Sascha was running with them, remembering at the last moment to turn on the lamp, where it hung on her chest like a flame.

18

Maret stood before the Extreme Prime's galleries, waiting
for her interview. She hoped to find Hemms Pre Illtek in
a conducive mood, but in Red Season he was often snap-
pish. Her own mood was restive. *Up, up,* her thoughts
tended. She was ready to go, her body primed, responding
to the hab's nectar. But she was still *down* as others ascended.

Hemms, a friend to her dear prime, Ellod, was disposed in her favor. With Nefer growing colder toward her,
she had need of a powerful supporter. Hemms was likely
to approve her traditional choice to bear progeny, though
it meant jeopardizing her studies. *Her studies.* She thought
of Eli with confusion and shame. She had studied humans,
she now realized, only to hate them more fully. . . .

In her hand she carried a scroll on which Nefer had
painted data coordinates. This was an official commu-
niqué from Nefer Most Prime to Hemms Extreme Prime,
and Maret was to deliver it personally. She was to make
sure that Hemms, often absentminded, attended to the
scroll, though Nefer had told her nothing of the subject

matter. Perhaps, if Hemms needed data interpretation, Maret might offer some small service to him. It was regrettable to admit, but without Nefer to administrate, he would have made a less than satisfactory leader, despite his splendid genotype.

When the attendant led her inside, she found Hemms seated on his carpet, where skilled weavers had traced his rich ancestral line. The huge carpet placed him at a considerable remove from her. He was alone, Maret noted with relief. Sometimes interviews did not go well if attendants were there to whisper in his ear.

"Maret-as," he said. Then, without preamble: "Recite."

She began the chant, still holding Nefer's scroll, still standing, not even being asked to sit.

After reciting to the sixth net, Maret paused, hoping to be given permission to execute her mission. She had recited his lineage for him before. It was almost a tradition between them, and seemed to give Hemms great pleasure.

Hemms' eyes, half-lidded with relaxation, snapped open.

She plowed on, to the seventh net, a level of recitation that only his close attendants were expected to perform. But the seventh net was very long, and her time slipped away.

At last she finished. Surely he would not require her to go further.

He did not. "You misspoke the seventh," he said, allowing some irritation to show. He picked at a piece of lint on his pant leg.

Maret cast into backmind to see what had gone amiss. With chagrin, she realized her mistake. "Forgive my inexcusable and shameful error, Extreme Prime."

He waved a hand, saying peevishly, "You should study more, Maret-as. Nefer gives you leave to study, does she not?" Without waiting for an answer, he said, "It is a very

great privilege to study, but one's dwellers are immersed in wagers and entertainments, a shameful waste of resources."
He glanced up at her.

"Yes, shameful indeed."

"Many cannot even recite to the sixth, and if they can"—here he glanced at her again—"they make errors, and tend toward self-satisfaction."

"Yes, Hemms-as, this is a sad thing, when it occurs."

"When it occurs!" His voice rose beyond all propriety. "You think it would be seldom?"

"No, one does not disagree. . . ."

"Disagree." He nodded to himself as though confirming an ugly opinion. "What right have you to disagree with your high prime? Have you such a right? Have you?"

Maret was so surprised by this attack that she hesitated to answer. By then it was too late.

He rose to his feet. "You are not as pious as one thought, Maret-as, may your prime, Ellod, forgive you. Your kin nets are very faint in the flow. Who carries your kin names forward? Are all your kin as lax as you?"

"My kin, Prime of my life, are all . . ."

"Yes, your kin! This neglect becomes very deeply regrettable."

The room pumped out odorants to cover his agitation. It was shocking for Hemms Extreme Prime to display such temper. She feared he might be ill.

"You waste your days, Maret-as. You prepare for ronid. Let others undertake such things! One is in entire agreement with Nefer Ton Enkar on this matter. Furthermore, you embarrass us by fraternizing with the Human, who is our hostage."

She jerked her head up in surprise.

"Did you think one took no notice of such things?" He paced around her, and she dared not follow him with her eyes. He circled her, muttering, *"Lost, lost."*

Maret's distress now was beyond containing. Was she fraternizing? How had her conduct fallen so far from his pleasure?

But he had veered back to the topic of study. "A very sad thing it is to see you waste your heritage, Maret-as. Study, that's the thing!"

Maret stared fixedly at the eighteenth concentric circle in Hemms' ancestral rug. She dared not answer.

"Well?" He glared at her. Then, pausing at a wall sconce, he indulged in a wand of snuff.

"I have failed to please you. Please forgive this inadequate person." She would have studied all her life and been content. But study would have to wait.

Calmer now, Hemms settled himself on the rug once more. "One doubts, Maret-as," he said sadly. "One doubts those around one." He looked over her head, toward the door. "Everywhere, there are dwellers who oppose me, against all tradition. You knew?"

"No," she said in alarm. "Oppose you?"

"Oppose, we say! Who plot for their Extreme Prime's ruin, who loose their rogue strands of lies into the data flow, who forget our lineage, who bring barbarians into the heart of DownWorld, who falter in their seventh kin net recitation, who fail in their studies!" The hab pumped and pumped, but his distress came to her nostrils like a burning wick of flesh. She heard herself indicted in his list. Maret, the most loyal of his subjects.

Then his shoulders slumped, and his voice was so soft, she barely heard him say, "Well, give us the scroll. Or must one beg leave to read one's missives?" His skin had waxed pale, smudging the aristocratic lines that had bred true for a thousand cycles.

She approached his rug and handed it to him, leaning over it as far as she could without stepping on the sacred threads. The scroll fluttered as she placed it in Hemms' palm. He murmured: "Our dwellers neglect their devotions. Scandalous. So many lost in the Human War, and so few remembered in the flow. We had thought that you, Maret-as, would never stumble in devotion. One can never predict the outcome of genetic gifts. We are very sad." As he unrolled the scroll, a data plug descended from the ceiling, and his tendril snapped into it.

Scanning the coordinates, Hemms shunted the results onto a wall screen.

To Maret's consternation, the screen showed Eli Dammond entering a reliquary. He shone a light about him, disturbing the peace of the rugs. She watched in horror as he pulled a rug from its rest, laying open the contents, bending down to inspect the sacred bones. . . . It would have been far better not to have provoked Hemms Extreme Prime with a remembrance of that unfortunate happening, but now Maret learned that Hemms was more than provoked.

He sprang to his feet, barking, "Shame! Shame!"

His reaction so startled her that she froze, unable to speak or defend herself.

The door flew open as attendants flooded inside. They stood, wondering at the high tension in the room, while Hemms sputtered, "This! This!" He pointed at the terrified Maret. "This *fluxor* defies us! This *fluxor* caters to a barbarian who desecrates our dead!" He stalked close to her, bending low to look into her eyes as she crouched at his feet. "You knew?"

"Yes, Extreme Prime . . ." And she had thought *he* knew. Could it be that Hemms was so out of the flow?

". . . knew," he was saying, "and walked publicly with the—the . . ." His lips quivered as he fought for an epitaph.

The human, Maret filled in for him. *The human. How easily Nefer has arranged my ruin.*

Nefer had kept Hemms ignorant of the desecration. All this time, it wasn't Hemms who required her to attend on the human. It was only Nefer.

"My mistress commanded me to attend the human. Please forgive—"

"You dare to blame your benefactor, Nefer Most Prime? Shame, Maret-as, shame! Nefer has told me you are *not* obedient." He turned to his astonished attendants. "Not obedient! Our dwellers are not obedient! Our kingdom sickens before our eyes." His face collapsed into open, displayed grief. "One had thought Maret-as the best of you, though she is only a fluxor. But if Maret is the best, then one is lost, lost . . ."

As the attendants led her away, she heard Hemms ranting after her, "Your bloodlines are shamed! Your descendants do not exist!"

The words struck her like blows. The attendants let loose of her, not wanting to touch one so cursed.

19

Just as Eli turned into the first downway, he looked behind, back the way he'd come, seeing a soldier standing with the gomin, talking. He knew it was the gomin by the sheen of her clothes, and by the fact that she was naked from the waist up, by which he understood that she was distracting the guard by offering sex. He slipped into the stairwell.

His muscles were tense enough to lift a piano. Six steps down he spied a lump of cloth that, once shook out, became a cape and cowl. He rammed his fists into the sleeves, noticing the powerful smells of the fabric, to mask his humanness. He took the stairs two at a time; then, hearing voices above him, he ducked into a narrow lobe and turned aside to hide his face.

The voices faded down the steps.

In the stairwell, he repeated the gomin's instructions: *left at the downway, right at the way, right at the downway, right at the way, and two rights again on downways and ways . . .*

But despite the specificity of the directions, he was in

trouble. He had not thought to ask her how to tell the difference between a downway and an upway. Each stairwell, Maret had said, was used in only one direction. And
downways might lead to different levels than stairwells
designated as upways. Furthermore, each time he turned
into a stairwell and rushed down, he knew that he might
meet an ahtra coming *up,* and so betray himself, cape
or no.

Right, then right, then left, but right into the downway . . .

All his life he had remembered things in excruciating
detail. Dates, numbers, useless facts, names, faces, songs,
and things said and done, and things not done, the lost
moments when things could have been set to rights. It
stood him well in academics, vaulting him to the top of his
classes. While his fellow students sweated over the minutiae, Eli read it once and had it. Some felt he was getting
something for nothing, that he had an unfair advantage,
despite his protestations that being able to forget things
was a great gift.

Now left . . . As he turned down, he saw someone coming up, and he stepped quickly back and walked to the
next stairwell with as much dignity as he could muster. He
didn't think the ahtra had had time to notice his misstep.
He hurried on, sweating copiously under the cape, his
thoughts turning on how, by going down, he would eventually go up—and whether the gomin was part of some
plot by Nefer to use his escape to finally kill him, despite
the puzzling desire of someone here that he be kept alive.

The tunnels and ways were strangely dim, a change
from the bright ambient light usually emitted by the hab.
Perhaps the gomin had arranged this as well, or whoever
assigned the gomin her mission to *tell him to leave*—and
he thought he knew who that might be. In any case the
dim lighting worked in his favor, as he passed two ahtra in
a way, deeply involved in conversation, intent on each

other. They paid him no notice. He began to hope that he might succeed, might find the *ancient way*, and the one who would *guide him farther*. It could only be Maret. He looked for her, hoping that by some stroke of fortune he had stumbled on the *right way*.

But now, after five or ten minutes he was hopelessly lost. He had come to the end of the gomin's lefts and rights. He faced down an endless, dim way with many stairs. And it looked exactly the same as the one he had just come from, and the one before that. *Maret,* he thought, *where are you?*

Voices, again.

He ducked into a stairwell. Someone paused to look at him from the way. Was he descending an upway? He casually continued down the narrow stairs, which quickly swallowed him from the view of whoever had stopped in the corridor. He listened for the sound of their steps in pursuit, but all was silent. He plunged down, sweat streaming, throat parched.

Down, down. The stairway was the longest continuous stairway he had seen. The gomin had said nothing about such a downway, but he descended, passing great shelves of fungus, similar to those he'd seen in other stairways and ways of the place. The smell of the fungus pressed in on him. The stairwell was so narrow, the very walls seemed to sag toward him, but he went on. He must.

At the bottom, he found himself at a dead end. Here was a vast, hexagonal room, full of cubby holes. Many of them were occupied. Ahtra lay very still in the slots, perhaps a hundred or more . . . but not rolled up in rugs—just lying very still. *Asleep,* he thought. *They sleep communally.* He slowly backed up, then heard a noise behind him. He pivoted around.

It was Maret. Her markings paled, and she steadied herself against the door for a moment. "Eli, quickly," she whispered, and he hurried to her side. They turned out of the chamber and she led the way, dashing up the stairs. "The guards are everywhere, searching for you—if they find you it will not be well."

They crossed the first way and wound into the next stairwell.

"Maret," he said, between gasps of breath, "the gomin said to go *down*."

She took him by the elbow and hauled him forward. Though a full head shorter and slim, she had surprising strength in her hands. "No, Eli," she said. "We go up." For a moment they paused as she faced off with him, blue eyes to gray. "Back to your den."

His limbs hardened, locking him in place on the stairs. He looked back down the way he had come.

"You are hopelessly lost, Eli. What made you believe you would ascend against all tradition?" In her deeply patterned skin, her eyes and mouth were merely two more disfiguring ovals in a pockmarked face. "It was a gamble," he said, voice flat. *Friend*. How could he have thought an ahtra would be his ally?

Her nostrils flared in an ahtran sneer. "A poor one." Then she turned and walked up, leaving him to follow or not.

He stood his ground, contemplating his chances. Then, from below, voices. A group of ahtra approached on the stairs, stopping to stare when they saw Eli, his cowl thrown back. With rigid calm, he turned and walked up the stairs, joining Maret at the top where she waited for him. As they walked down the way, several guards trailed them, uncertain, because of Maret's presence, whether to approach or not. But it was over.

Returning to his cell, he found a visitor waiting. Nefer. Behind her, workers had pulled back a flap of the hab where the gomin's virtual bubble had emerged. Pinkish blood pearled up on the severed edges.

Nefer looked from Eli to Maret and back to Eli again.

"One has been uneasy about your disappearance, Eli Dammond," she said in Standard.

Eli gazed back at the creature, wondering if it was true that ahtran skulls were delicate, and how many he could damage before he sustained injuries that would be regrettably difficult to remedy.

Then he heard Maret say, "We have been walking together on the way. As my mistress commanded."

Something flickered across Nefer's face. As the pause among them lengthened, an attendant offered Nefer a dusting of snuff on an ivory stick, which she inhaled, murmuring, "One is reassured by such obedience, when it occurs." She gestured at the workers. "This den would be infected by a worm, one discerns. One regrets any impertinence by the *unnatural*. One deals with the gomin as she deserves."

She moved to the door, then turned at the threshold. "Given that you had a private walk where few saw you, Maret-as, one surmises you would have missed the Extreme Prime's news strand."

Maret looked at Nefer, her eyelids fully retracted.

Everyone in the small den watched the two of them, even the workers who turned for a moment from their repairs on the wall.

"One surmises that the Extreme Prime disapproves of your frequent walks with our hostage enemy. One must admire his judgment. Therefore you are required to correct your behavior, Maret-as. You will return to your studies, and one will monitor your expenditures carefully. It is your happenstance that ronid is beyond you now." Her lips parted in a fragment of a smile. "Perhaps next season?"

She left, chatting with her attendants.

*   *   *

Vod bent down for a closer view of the artifact. It was a mask from an ancient play. It crumbled to dust in his hands as his headlamp shone on it. Here, where the hab was blackened and petrified, was a way that no ahtran had seen for a million cycles.

Tirinn Vir Horat had told him where the place lay buried, far under all. The Ancient Way, Tirinn called it, before Ankhorat. Even before Longorr habitat, before data stages and the Great Well. Before dwellers cared to build world ships and roam the galaxy. Before they cared to build warships to confront the humans. In ancient times, DownWorld was enough, buried deep and safe, beyond any predation. Vod had thought that his secret digger chute was old and forgotten, but this place was far deeper than the chute, accessed by an almost endless downway in such disrepair that he thought it might cave in on him just from his footfalls.

He let the mask, now all threads and dust, fall to the floor, as ruined as his attempt to eject Eli Dammond from DownWorld. Tirinn had said Eli would be in a certain way confluent to a certain downway, but he had not been. Nor was he in the next downway, or the next. Then the flow announced that Eli was escaped, and almost as fast, that he was captured again. Then Vod had plunged downward, following Tirinn's directions, though now it had no greater purpose.

What Tirinn's greater purpose was, Vod didn't know. He had been summoned to the old guide's presence, high AbovePrime. Surveying Vod's grimy workman's garb, Tirinn growled, "Ask no questions. You can't afford me." Then he gave him explicit instructions, which Vod memorized into backmind. One of the instructions was "Keep your tendril flat," by which Vod knew the information he now possessed was dangerous, completely outside the flow.

No old mountain of flesh was going to order Vod

around, high fluxor or not. But Tirinn's interest was the same as Vod's: get rid of the human. So he agreed to the plot, making a mess of everything.

The human was still among them, pale and ruinous. And Maret's reputation unraveled—though Hemms' condemnation of her might actually give her a boost among fluxors. Hemms cared nothing for diggers' lives. And while the Extreme Prime recited his kin nets, better dwellers were buried alive in rubble . . .

Vod returned to the AncientWay the next day, wandering with dark thoughts, shining his lamp, thinking of his kin who'd once added their numbers to the thronging PrimeWay, thinking of other cycles when fluxors had ruled, when safety and long lineage were due both static and fluxor.

It was on his third foray into the subworld that Vod first heard the noises. It began as pinging in his ears, produced, he thought, by his own head, the depths to which he was unaccustomed—for he was a half hexal under Ankhorat. But he walked forward, pausing at upways and downways to listen.

He stood at the foot of an upway where once fluxors had passed UpWorld for ronid, in the days when all ascents went on foot instead of by conveyance. Here, the noises had more variety: thuds and pings and buzzing, dripping down from high overhead, as though drawn by gravity. For an instant he thought he might be hearing UpWorld itself, the ghastly sunny realm that he would never see. A superstitious dweller might think it was the sound of departed kin, denied their rugs, still roaming there. A superstitious dweller might listen for whispers telling him how he might save Maret, or save his people from a digger's death, buried in slumps of stone, forgotten by mad Hemms, driven by the clear-eyed Nefer.

Vod listened harder. And then he was ascending.

The stairset turned and turned in relentless coils. As his

footfalls echoed, he almost felt himself accompanied by terrified fluxors who chose to ascend, who proved their worthiness. He followed the helix upward.

He passed an agricultural lobe, long abandoned. Here lorel still bore its fruit in patches, the latest generation of the unbroken line from earliest times. It was as close to immortality as Vod could imagine, these fruiting bodies sprouting from the vast plait of mycelium crisscrossing DownWorld. He broke off a tidbit to chew, replenishing his energy, and continued his climb. Coming upon way stations where the ancient fluxors had adjusted to depth changes, he rested there, too. Then he went on, climbing, his legs aching, then numbing.

At the top he faced a wall of dirt. And began to dig, feeling the vibrations from up ahead.

In a sudden fall of soil, he poked through a hole to the other side. A cool draft of air hit his face. There, before him he glimpsed the source of the noise. It was a foundry, a great cavern, crowded with workers. They were no dwellers he knew. But he knew what they built.

Voices mixed with the pounding noises of metal and machine. He was high in the wall of a great cavern where no hab lived. It was a gallery defined by stone. Within this nest, many hexadrons took shape. Warships. Massive ships, larger than any he had ever heard of. Down a cavernous tunnel to one side the ships massed in a long line to the limit of sight.

Backmind told him what lay above this foundry realm. It was the latest fluxor dig. There lay the hurried and pointless shafts that Nefer required, the long digs that never seemed in relation to Ankhorat. Instantly he knew why Nefer wanted those shafts, and why they needn't be executed with care. They would provide egress for the ships. Nefer was orchestrating a massive collapse of the fragile, riddled soil. Freed of their nest, the beasts would fly.

Nearby, a fluxor turned to stare at Vod. It was a face he

remembered, kin from a world hexadron, kin he hadn't seen since she'd come home for ronid last season. Then he saw that she wasn't looking at him, but gazing at the vast, high ceiling, as though dreaming of the moment when the warships would ascend.

He backed up into his hand-carved tunnel, but as he jerked back, his headlamp toppled away, clattering down into the great cavern. Vod quickly packed the short tunnel full again.

Plunged into darkness, he sat stunned. The scale of the thing . . . Yet how methodically and neatly it had all been carried out. To build such a place, such ships—it had to be *years* in the undertaking. And all beneath the very noses of those Nefer had duped. All on the backs of those digger lives lost in the *disposable* tunnels.

The great, hulking ships . . . the globes of war. It would all begin again. The great slaughter would engulf them all once more. She had never accepted the armistice. *Hemms' armistice.* Likely she had never accepted Hemms, either. All these spans he'd thought that digger's lives meant nothing to Nefer, but his eyes had been plugged with soil.

Ahtran lives meant nothing to her. Now, like Wecar, they would all be buried before their time.

He began the descent of the long, long stairset, staggering at times in the absolute dark, the only light a flame in his two minds, burning away the last hiding places of Nefer Ton Enkar.

20

Eli sat on a shaved-off pinnacle jutting a thousand feet or more into the air above a green, foaming jungle. At night he dreamed of tossing and turning, rolling close to the edge. They fed him now and again. Guards climbed from below, bearing food trays. Puffing and sweating, they deposited the tray on the plateau, then secured their repelling gear and returned to the base of the pinnacle.

He would watch their feat, trying to discern the telltale shimmer of a virtual environment. But it was a perfect rendition, aside from the one-handed climbing. He wasn't sure why they had chosen a jungle setting for him, but they had designed it beautifully, from what he could tell at this height.

Hours passed, and perhaps days—if days existed anymore. Sometimes Maret climbed up, staying just below sight on the cliff-side. "Eli," her deep voice would float to him. He had sworn at her and heaped some highly creative curses on her relatives. But she'd never been other than his jailer, though he sought information from her, then hope, then connection. The familiar behavior of the kidnapped.

It rankled him, despite the multitude of his more serious problems.

"I am very deeply sorry, Eli," she said mournfully.

He would be happy to never hear that expression again.

The sky darkened into night as the red sun followed the yellow one to the horizon. They couldn't know what pleasure it brought him to see sky and day and night again, even in simulations.

"Eli," Maret said in the dark. She lurked just out of view, as though in response to his anger. Or perhaps she couldn't penetrate as far as the guards. "We are in a club, Eli." She had taken to the phrase "welcome to the club," when he'd responded to her statement that she'd lost everything.

Reproachfully, she said, "If you would have told me about the worm, I could have saved you from error. The gomin is not clever, and has only made things worse."

"She was teaching me things."

"Do not believe what she says."

"She said the same thing about you. What is Nefer going to do to her?"

"Oh, she has already done it. She has cast her from the flow. Disallowed her access to the Well."

"Is that a harsh sentence?"

"Oh, certainly. One is cut off from our ancestral converse."

"I regret that she suffers for my sake."

"Do not worry about such a one. I wonder more who sent the gomin."

"I thought it was you."

Maret sighed, a mannerism she copied from Eli. "How could you think I would so turn from my duty?"

He watched the stars overhead, imagining new constellations. "Friendship. Sentimentality. Rebellion. Any number of stupid impulses."

After a beat: "We are very different, Eli."

"Are we? How do you feel about your Nefer, now that you know she used you?"

"One is hers to use."

"Like hell. You're in Shit Creek Club, Maret, and you can thank your Nefer. She had us parading around together, ruining your chances for UpWorld. Is that about it?"

Maret's voice was very soft. "Yes, that is true. I have lost all affection for Nefer Ton Enkar."

"Really?"

"Irony," Maret said in a forlorn voice. "I have been thinking of why Nefer has ruined me. Now I tend to conclude that she perceives me as a threat to Hemms. That she always saw me as a threat, and hoped to keep me safely in scholarship, and barred from the glory of ronid. She is regrettably foolish. All I ever hoped for was study, not revolution."

"I suspect she hates you for her own reasons, not for Hemms' sake."

A virtual shooting star scudded across the sky.

Her voice was soft. "I hated you once, Eli. I have reveled in your suffering. You suffered so outwardly, so vigorously. Through you, I grieved all my lost kin, in ways that I could not in all propriety do myself."

He turned away from her voice, but she went on.

"Now, however, I cannot blame you for what my own fluxor kind have done. Nefer says the HumanWar was brought on by fluxors, because we wanted outwardness and trade with humans. We had never, in all our history, met another sentient race. Fluxors lobbied for trade while statics were reluctant. So all this began with fluxor error. Compounding the error, I have been in your company improperly. If I had observed proper ways I would have descendants. And you would not be in such danger."

"I was always in danger, Maret."

"But worse now, Eli, because I have shown you our

world. Nefer will never release you, given what you know of us. She will not allow you to use your knowledge against us. She has used me to ruin you."

He heard her shift position on the lip of stone where she crouched. Her voice came nearer to him. "My foolishness is beyond repairing. But Eli, there is one thing I can give you. Such a small thing . . ." She paused. "Nefer will come to you, one believes. When she does, she will command the Well to be disagreeable."

So, he thought, *now comes the part I expected all along.*

"She will search for things to distress you. But my mistress does not know human ways and may be inclined to error. If she guesses correctly, do not respond. She will wish for you to respond."

"What does she want from me, Maret?"

"Nothing, anymore. Now she will . . . toy with you. She is pursuing an instinct. It is Red Season, Eli. Sex is very free among us now."

"You've lost me." At her momentary hesitation, he rephrased, "I don't understand."

"Idiom," she said absently. Then, "Statics—Nefer is a static—have only a vestigial interest in sex. They sometimes . . . require high stimulation to feel conducive."

"She wants to have sex with me?" He would have much preferred more garden-variety torture.

"No, certainly not. Not *with* you. *Because* of you. It is hard to explain." After a moment she continued. "Fear is a stimulation of long-standing tradition. She will want you to fear."

In the long silence that followed, Eli squinted up at the star patterns, seeing one or two click into place. He realized he'd already been used. If Nefer wanted fear, he'd given her plenty in their last interview. It was why she described the deaths UpWorld. That he had unknowingly given Nefer pleasure was a worm in his gut.

"Eli," she said, "I have two sadnesses over you. Please forgive my many errors."

"I don't blame you, Maret. I chose to come here. It was my job."

"It shames me that you forgive my debts so easily."

Lying on his back watching the sky, Eli thought about debts and what it took to forgive. And whether some things were beyond forgiving. *If you forgave, would you betray those who suffered, who were dead, and therefore unable to forgive? What did the dead want of us, or we of them?*

"No," Eli said. "That wasn't it. . . ."

"What?"

"It wasn't my job. To come here."

"You are a soldier."

"I was, once. It was what I wanted to be. An officer of Congress Worlds. None of my family ever graduated from an upper form school. To four generations, we worked the asteroids and took enlistment in the army. But I wanted something more."

"You are a captain of ships, Eli. That is a high office."

"No, not of the ships I have now. Luce Marzano, she is—or was—an officer of the army. She had a real command."

"Luce Marzano," Maret said. "The captain of the first ship . . ."

"They hated me for holding myself superior to her. I hated it myself."

"It was your job."

"Yeah. Like your job was to parade me around. Sometimes the job is a nasty one." He knew then that he would tell her everything. He didn't want to be stuck with her admiration. It was starting to fester.

A pause while he gathered his thoughts. They were close to hand, as always. "Suzan Tenering was old army," he began. "You would have liked her. Big on tradition. By the book."

"By the book . . . she followed the rules," Maret said.

"Yes, the rules. There are the rules written down, and the ones in the margins."

"Sometimes the rules in the margins are the most important ones," Maret said wistfully.

"We were patrolling in a squadron. I was assigned to Tenering's flagship, the *Recompense*. Oddly, the *Recompense* was the only ship that survived. It took a hit on the external solar array, and one of the cargo bays took a bad crease. It looked like a bad parking job, nothing worse. . . ."

"Is the rule you must die when others do?"

She startled him, jumping to the heart of it so fast. But he said, "Only if you're in charge."

"This is called 'the captain going down with the ship,' is that the phrase?"

"No. Yes. Hell, if I knew the rules maybe I wouldn't be here now. Don't ask me what the rules are. But I'll tell you what happened."

He told her the best he could remember it, which was perfectly. The expressions on the bridge crew's faces; who said what; what happened and in what order. At the hearing it took a long time for him to tell the story, and the panel of officers stopped taking notes after a while and stared at him as though they would rather have a shorter version, not one embellished by Captain Eli Dammond with good reason to concoct a version to save his neck. In the end they dropped formal charges. He had fought bravely in the boarding party, so it was hard to charge cowardice and make it stick. They left it that he'd discharged his duty; badly perhaps, but not dishonorably, or not the sort of dishonor they could openly punish. Sometimes dishonor is in the margins.

There were on their way to a CW world, a way station, not a battle zone, but they were combat-ready and searching, as always, for ahtran warships. If they caught them at first blip, they had a chance to fry them. The balance of power was Congress World numbers against ahtran speed. CW could stand to lose the ships it did, at the rate of thirteen to one, the infamous Baker's Dozen rule. By that day the tally was eighteen to one, so they were overdue for a hit. Soon after that day they sued for peace. It was war by the numbers, and the numbers had been against them for a long time.

So when the blip came that day on the *Recompense*, they'd been more than ready for engagement. But in the next instant, word came it wasn't an ahtran warship, it was something else. An asteroid, but under propulsion . . . And then Lieutenant Onaka said it was a world ship, the construct seen only a few times before, the habitat of the ahtra, presumed to be carrying its cities, its culture. Its noncombatants. Always, the world ships fled at ahtran speed.

But not this one. Techs said it might be crippled. Later Eli would understand how much more deadly that made it.

With Colonel Tenering off the bridge, Eli had said, "Hold fire, Lieutenant," speaking to Lieutenant Nule, who would have shot first and thought later. But Eli ran the numbers. At the dimensions of these world ships, they'd be housing two hundred thousand individuals, Intelligence estimated. And such world ships had never fired on CW ships . . .

That was the progression of his thoughts, in the space of a second.

"Captain?" Lieutenant Nule's eyes were wild. He looked to the door through which Colonel Tenering, just five minutes before, had walked off the bridge. "Captain?"

Slightly forward of the convoy, the *Raptor*'s captain was on comm, standing by to engage. Tenering, on her way, was barking over the headset, "What's happening? Report!"

And then the *Raptor* disintegrated in pulsing blooms of incandescent color, and in a sickening one-two punch, the *Fidelity*. In a heartbeat, Eli gave the order to fire.

Colonel Tenering came bursting onto the deck shouting, *"Fire, fire!"* The gunners hit it with everything on board. One nuclear-class pellet struck home, and another. The screen glowed with the conflagrations of the sister ships, pretty squares of fire, casting an orange glow on the faces of the crew on the *Recompense* bridge.

The transport ship *Hera* was calling for evacuation, the vessel now commanded by a pale eighteen-year-old ensign, the last one left on the bridge. On another channel, they were hailed by the world ship. As Tenering continued firing, Eli heard the ahtran screams. The translator barked in his ears, "One agrees to withdraw, agrees to withdraw. . . ."

Tenering, desperate to salvage the battle and her career, gave no quarter. She wanted the world ship, its submission, and its treasure of enemy intelligence. She ordered a boarding party, and sent Eli commanding it. Once admitted by the crippled world ship, Eli's detail found a nightmare world of labyrinthine corridors filled with the dead and dying enemy, some of whom fought the intrusion with suicidal forays. Spiraling out of control, the mission took losses, then fell back, fighting hard, with CW troops wild, firing on the ahtra regardless of threat. Eli ordered restraint, and his men responded by turning off the comm units in their radiation suits, all the while firing, firing. The corridors echoed with bass ahtran screams. . . .

A few survived that boarding party. But only Eli Dammond survived it without wounds.

Then, having used the time to regain flight capability, and after the CW shuttle was clear, the world ship fled.

The battle toll was: the *Raptor*, all hands lost, 146; the *Fidelity*, all hands lost, 117; the transport ship *Hera*, damaged collaterally by a slug of molten drive-matter from the

Raptor, 68 lost; the *Recompense* boarding party, 31 lost. In total, 422 soldiers died, including the ones that never made it out of the regen baths. And though no one was reprimanded at the hearing, the very mention of the *Recompense* came to stand for disaster, and in the army way of things, Suzan Tenering's career was effectively over. At fifty-eight, she took an early retirement. Eli was thirty-three.

When he finished his story, he sat staring out over the jungle canopy seeing, as though with Olympian sight, the struggles of humans far below.

Maret was silent for so long he thought she might have left. But at last he heard: "It was mercy. . . ."

"Mercy?"

"Yes," Maret whispered. "Mercy that you held off to fire. They despise you because of that."

"Cowardice, some called it." After all these years he still couldn't say which one it was. He had never thought himself a coward in battle. But it was courage of another sort to make a hard decision, a decision that will damn you one way or the other.

"Eli," she said in a small, low voice, "it was that world ship where I lost them. All my kin."

By the love of God. He closed his eyes. But he wasn't surprised. The battle returned and returned, like a phantom ache in a severed limb. Eventually he found some words. "I'm sorry, Maret. With two sadnesses."

Silence then. What was there to say, that would not give the nightmare more power?

After a long while he heard her climbing down the cliff face, her slippers shuffling against the rock sides.

"About Nefer," he said softly, "thank you for warning me."

In a husky whisper she said, "Do not think much of it," mangling the idiom.

*   *   *

Through the night, Eli had been hearing noises in the jungle below: human cries, and the roar of beasts.

When it was light enough in the virtual dawn, he could see figures far below, appearing now and then in the clearings. They were so small, he couldn't see whether the ahtra had somehow divined what individuals in his command looked like. They all wore army brown, so Nefer's minions didn't pick up on that detail.

The details they did best had to do with killing. The denizens of the forest pursued their prey with fan, beak, and claw: alien predators of horrible aspect. The figures in brown died and died.

He heard Nefer's voice behind him. "You wanted to join your people, Eli Dammond. One is so limited in how one can help. Forgive one's halting attempts to be useful."

Turning, he gave her a thin smile, mimicking ahtran placidity. "Quite all right. One is able to participate. It is very satisfying." He managed to watch impassively as a pack of tree climbers converged on a soldier who had unwisely taken refuge in the dead-end upper branches.

Beyond the cruelty of the game she played with him, there was more to Nefer, he knew. He intended for her to have no satisfaction of him, but he worried what else she meant to have. Her assigning Maret to him was a ruse, nor did she ever plan for Eli to speak in their favor. She seemed indifferent to the threat of war. In fact, he feared she sought it.

Nefer settled herself cross-legged. A rug materialized under her. "One should punish you for the matter of the gomin," she purred. "But one relents. One grows . . . fond? Is that the word? Fond of you."

The beasts roared as they ate. "Regrettably, one can't return the sentiment."

"Of course. The matter of your failed command. You will tend to blame me."

"As to that, it appears the soldiers of my command still live." He gestured to the jungle below. "Does all this commotion mean I've won our wager?"

"Your wager was that they would survive. They are not, as you observe."

"Some of them are dying. But it's a big forest down there, and I had a lot of soldiers."

"One hundred fifty-seven, so you affirmed."

"Is that what I said? That was on just one ship," he lied. "I had two ships. Forgive any inaccuracy. I had a head wound at the time."

"No matter. The more of them, the worse it will be. The monsters will abandon pursuit of more cunning prey and exploit the ready meat. Your people will tend to herd together, as humans do. So regrettable. One understands your distress."

"And I yours."

A slow blink. "One does not feel distress."

He seated himself in front of her. "Among my people, when one has served—an organization—for a long time and is not advanced, there is cause for distress."

Her markings, unusually pronounced today, lost some of their edge.

"For instance, it's distressing if one is overshadowed by a more gifted person, causing one's own talents to be eclipsed." He shrugged. "I understand that Hemms is young and in fine health. Although one would not begrudge good fortune in others."

A cry erupted from the base of the cliff. A long, slow, painful-sounding death. Nefer sat very still before finally taking a dab of snuff. Then, speaking in a pinched voice, she said, "Is one disposed to slow deaths, or quick—to allow satisfying participation?"

"Slow is more realistic. More like war, which I am well used to."

She murmured, "One had thought you had more . . . compassion . . . is this the word?"

"A liability for an officer. My job is to lead soldiers to their deaths."

"One wonders if one has mistaken you, Eli Dammond. One is ignorant of human ways. You must teach me." She rose in a languid movement.

"Before you leave, Nefer-as, there remains the question of our wager."

"The outcome of the wager is awaiting happenstances."

"But you hold to the wager?"

"Certainly."

He meant to pin her down, slippery as she was. Maret had shown him the ahtra data screens and the wagers registered there. So, by God, he would have his wager public.

"If you hold to our wager," he said, "I would register the wager in the flow. Otherwise, one fears you will only honor it if you win, and not if you lose."

"Such rudeness is surprising in an individual so beholden to one."

He shrugged. "It is a human way, to be suspicious of treachery."

The rug she'd been sitting on broke up into spots of color and evaporated. "It does no harm to register our wager in the flow. It shall be a token of one's fondness for you."

Another cry erupted from the bottom of the cliff. "You see?" he said, turning to watch the slaughter. "A few are still left."

"It is a construct, you perceive."

"A convincing one. My compliments to your techs."

That night, the cries went away.

21

They lay in the high grass, hugging the ground. Upwind, a herd of rippers was dozing in the sun, some standing on one leg, beaks turned into furry torsos. Every now and then, one of the birds muttered a croaking word or two, like *fire, sweet cheesus, behind joo*.

"Fucking chickens don't even have feathers," Private Brad Limon muttered. Known as Lemon for his personality, he was skinny as a bird himself, with nervous eyes that seemed to dart independently of each other. Juric and the others ignored him, too parched to talk. Besides Lemon and Sergeant Juric, there were privates, Leo "Chi Chi" Vecchi, Bill Tafoya, and big "Pig" Platis.

Sascha lay on her back, filling her eyes with light, as though her brain needed drying out.

Of course they don't have feathers. "What are the chances that feathers would evolve twice in the galaxy?" she whispered. "Think about feathers, how improbable they are."

The bot was humming next to her. They hoped it wouldn't attack the herd, betraying their position. For now, the bot seemed to be on siesta. But a bot on automatic was a dicey proposition, relying on AI judgment, the last resort of battle. Sascha knew that the bot couldn't save them. She expected to die, and the thought kept her from despair.

Lemon spared her a quick glance, taking in her posture of openness, when everyone else was belly-down in the dirt. "I joined the army never to have to learn shit like that."

"Shut up, Lemon," Juric whispered, "or you'll get a close-up lesson on chickens."

Sascha watched the grass sway in the hot breeze. Each stalk was jointed, like what her nanny used to call horsetails. Interspersed were wildflowers with blooms remarkably like an insect. The petals were like wings, stamens like antennae . . . all to trick an insect to attempt copulation with the flower while fertilizing the plant with pollen-laden feet. In her mind, she held a conversation with her father. The jointed plants were arthrophytes. The flowers were mimicking. It was important to remember everything so it could all be written up and not lost. That way, it would all be for something. She reached up and snapped off a flower, tucking the specimen into her pocket.

Somehow, they had survived their first night out of camp. Three groups had fled the bunker. That might be all that was left. Two groups each had a bot, and the race was on for the lander. Juric let her keep her lamp on, though the men argued for the cover of darkness. When morning found them all still alive, the lamp idea got more respect. Now its bulbous eye was pointing at the two suns, recharging.

They'd seen dead lizards everywhere. The patches wouldn't call them amphibs, and Sascha knew better than to correct them. The men stepped on them, grinding them under lug heels, grinning like maniacs. They pranced for one another's benefit, who could stomp more lizards. It surprised her, how silly grown men with stubble beards could be. But their smiles were as thin as bubbles. Underneath was something more like panic.

Somebody wondered out loud what killed the lizards. But Sascha knew. Life killed them. They emerged from the lakes and streams famished, feeding their short lives with vast supplies of bloody fuel until, breeding accomplished, nature abandoned them. Just in time to avoid the emergence of the rippers. Blood was the best fuel for a short life-cycle. She'd said as much to the men. But some of them seemed to feel that by understanding the creatures, she was siding with them. The way they looked at her, it was clear they had no love of their baby-sitting job. She heard them mutter that they should leave her behind. But she wasn't slowing them down.

The mud was slowing them down. They sank in most places past their boots. And it was time-consuming to search for the best fording points of the numerous rivulets and streams. So far, they'd managed not to wade.

"Fucking Christ," Private Tafoya whispered.

Sascha scrambled up to look in the direction he was staring. Every ripper head had emerged from its dozing position, and was stretched high, eyes alert. Guns snapped into position.

But in another instant the rippers bounded off in the direction of the Gray Spiny Forest, with a speed that soon took them from sight. Whatever prey they'd sighted, Sascha felt sorry for it.

"Let's go," Juric growled. They set out over somewhat firmer ground, hunched down, though the grass was six feet tall. Using its own judgment, the plate-shaped bot morphed into a hammer shape, making a shurring sound as its matrix sides brushed against the grass. Sascha hoped it would survive them and carry her report to her grandfather.

"Remember this," she'd whispered to the bot late last night. "My mother died by the fire of our own guns during the attack, and my father died when he ran to protect her from the rippers." Those were the facts. She reported them as though they pertained to someone she barely knew. "Captain Marzano lead out a detail a week ago and was never seen again. Baker Camp fought honorably in the Gray Spiny Forest. And Badri Nazim was very brave," she added, because she was sure it was true. "When the camp was attacked, we separated to make for the ship in bands, to throw the animals off our scent. Captain Dammond took it on himself to investigate the ahtran craft that dig down below. He gave his life to be sure it was no ahtran outpost. Grandpa, he inspired everyone with his sacrifice. Make sure everyone knows."

They heard a rustling noise inside a fallen log. For a moment they glimpsed the first few inches of an insect with many legs. Now the enlisteds took to arguing about how long the thing really was. Judging by what she'd seen, Sascha guessed a good five feet. Insects with tracheae could be large here, her father had theorized, because of elevated oxygen on Null, which would work well for insects that absorbed oxygen through the skin with a few tubes to distribute it to the rest of the body.

Sascha walked with her lamp on. She liked walking better than hiding. While walking there were things to observe, catalogue, sample, and investigate. There was putting one foot in front of the other—no mean feat in some of the mud wallows—and she concentrated on these things rather than the unthinkable night before last. It hovered around her, saying, *Remember, remember*. But first there was walking and cataloguing. Later, remembering.

They came to a river. It flowed slowly and broadly through the valley. Though in the molten sunlight, they could see to the bottom, they stood well back from it. The bot wandered off, reconnoitering, its movements traced by the parting grasses.

"Tell it to stick around," Vecchi suggested to Juric.

Juric looked at him like he'd just suggested a swim. "It doesn't take orders anymore. But that's OK, Chi Chi, 'cause it's got more smarts than your whole family put together. I'd rather have that dog than you. So never mind about the dog." He licked his lips and grinned at the private until Vecchi broke eye contact.

Hurt, Vecchi walked off to stand near Pig, who was watching the river with disgust, carrying the heavy domino like a baton. Baker Camp's reports on the dark rivers of the Sticks had raced through Charlie Camp faster than radio. The enlisteds weren't used to enemies in the water and didn't like the prospect of it.

The grass behind them rustled. They heard the whine of the bot's firing, followed by an eruption of bird screeching. The grass thrashed. Backs to the water, the men started firing in the direction of the commotion. The first ripper sped out of the melee and was caught in midair by lobs from the domino. Then they were everywhere, beaks with eyes on both sides, swiveling heads looking for, then locking on targets.

Sascha was forced into the water by the retreating men who now ignored the river's dangers for the immediate attack on three sides. She was hit in the face with someone's blood, then knocked to her knees by Juric, by accident or design. Under the gunfire and shouts of the men, Sascha heard distorted croaks of, "run," "bot," "cheesus." As she struggled to rise, she turned. Behind her, two yards away, a pair of long pincers emerged from the glittering water. She glimpsed a flat-bodied creature as big as a dog, with eyes on its back. Grabbing her lamp to aim its beam, she shone it in the creature's face. It backed off in slow motion and pincers snicked shut on the arm of someone nearby. It was Tafoya, floating facedown. Sascha stood up and chased the creature with her lamp as it backed into the deeper water. It released Tafoya and disappeared beneath the surface.

When she turned around again, the rippers had disappeared. Many of them lay in the grass, slaughtered by bot and human fire, their long legs twitching. While Pig pulled Tafoya from the river, Juric and Vecchi scrambled to a small rise to see if more remained. Sascha fled the water and joined them.

Across the shallow, grass-filled valley, the rippers loped in tight formation, their heads appearing in unison above the grasses on every stride. In close pursuit, a taller creature ran, matching long strides with rippers. Muscular and upright, the creature's lower body was obscured in the grass, but they saw a very long, jointed arm reach forward and haul down the hindmost ripper.

"What the hell was that?" Vecchi said.

The bot trundled up the hillock, deploying a pole from its center. Aiming the periscope, it followed the retreating animals with what seemed its own brand of amazement.

"The top of the food chain, maybe," Juric said softly.

"Lucky for us," Vecchi said.

"You feel lucky, Chi Chi," Juric said, "you check out that river, find us a place to cross."

"Maybe I don't feel so lucky after all."

They watched as the creatures disappeared over a rise in the distance. Then Juric led them back down to the river. "Who's hurt?" he growled, as though anybody being hurt would be held against them.

Pig nodded down at Tafoya's body, mangled by a ripping claw down his centerline.

"Blood attracts the eurypterids," Sascha said.

Juric smiled down at her, using what the men called the "sunny side" of his face—the side that could still move. "Don't show off, girl; just tell what you saw."

"It was a water scorpion, or looked like one. Pincers, stinging tail."

Pig said, "It don't like her flashlight."

Juric glanced at the lamp hooked on her chest strap, still shining.

Late that night, when she crawled a distance away to pee, she snapped the lamp off to gain some privacy. Finished relieving herself, she was about to return when she saw a movement in the grass. By the light of brown dwarf, she saw something that so startled her she had to stare to be sure she hadn't imagined it.

It was an ahtra. She knew it must be—she'd seen pictures. . . . One pocked hand had parted the grass to stare at her in turn. In the darkness, the face was obscured by shadows, but the major features—the large eyes and oval markings—were unmistakable. The ahtra and human stared at each other in what might have been stupefaction. Both remained perfectly still. Then, after what seemed a very long while, the grass fell back into place, and the ahtra was gone.

Sascha hurried back to tell Sergeant Juric, but instead she came face-to-face with Vecchi. She could see his thin face in the dwarf light, bleached of life. A knife blade flashed. Her finger flew to the on switch, and she shone the light in his face.

"That don't cut it with me," he said, "but I'll be taking that flashlight, girl." He lunged. Then he was sprawling on the ground.

Juric hauled him by the collar into camp and kicked him to his hands and knees. At the commotion, Pig and Lemon drew their weapons, swiveling, looking for targets.

Juric stared at his three remaining men, shaking his head. "If any of you had the brains of a gum ball, we might make it out of here alive. Since you don't, I'm about ready to give up on you. We don't need stupidity. Next stupid thing I see, that man's staying behind. He's on his own."

"She shouldn't have the lamp, she doesn't fight," Vecchi muttered.

"Doesn't fight." Juric nodded. "You noticed that this fourteen-year-old girl doesn't fight. You're a scholar, Chi Chi." He walked over to Sascha, who stood on the fringe of the group, and clamped on to her shoulder. "This here, if you didn't get a chance for formal introductions, is Miss Sascha Olander, granddaughter of Gordon T. Ridenour, General of the CW Army, with enough stripes as makes no difference to any of you patches. Take a good look." He thrust her in front of him, paw still on her shoulder. "Now, your job, if you didn't figure it out yet, is to get this young lady back to Granddad. 'Cause if you don't, if any of us makes it home and she doesn't, Gramps is going to give you a lifetime cruise on a mining asteroid, if he doesn't put a fragmenting cluster up your ass first." He gave each of them in turn a deadpan stare. "Anybody confused about the assignment?"

In the ensuing silence, Juric said, "Anybody like to guess who keeps the lamp?"

Pig ventured, "The girl?"

Juric looked at him with half a grin. "That's right. You pay attention, Pig. You and me gonna fly that ship home, the only bastards smart enough to get out alive."

As the camp settled down, Sascha lay clutching her lamp to her chest, keeping her own counsel. But she whispered to the bot, "Captain Dammond was right. There *are* ahtra here."

She had no idea if the bot heard anything she said, but it went through a series of clicks like it did when morphing, or perhaps thinking hard.

22

So many carriers ascended at once, it set the hab vibrating. One did not begrudge others' good fortune . . . *one did not* . . . but one could wish the hab to devour her ere this moment had ever come. Of course, she had no right to expect ronid as her due; it was not a foregone conclusion. Thus by Hemms' decree, she had been left behind. She looked at her forearm, her hand . . . and her color held. It was always good practice to maintain camouflage.

Other sorrows beckoned: Eli's fate—and Vod's. Vod who had tried for her sake to aid Eli's escape and who now ran from Nefer's wrath. In his final gift, Vod had transferred his funds to her, a notable sum for a digger. She would expend a goodly sum now on Eli Dammond, lately her arch enemy.

She doubly bribed the guards. First, to allow her access to Eli's cell, and second, to keep their tendrils flat about it. They gave her forty-nine increments, little enough for her handsome payment.

And then she was in, facing Eli, where he stood on the high pinnacle. He looked thinner. But Nefer had allowed him to shave and clean himself, so he did not look as repulsively hairy as he had. Maret had grown used to Eli's physical form, at first so bizarre. His pale, undifferentiated skin, the disconcerting patch of hair on the top of his skull. His eyes, though small, were attractively dark—deep gray in tone—and expressive, easy to read with a little practice. To one used to reading nuances, humans were . . . an open book. How could he know such a thing could kill him?

"I thought you weren't coming back," he said.

"This is the last time I will be able to come here, Eli."

He nodded, accepting. "Try to help the gomin," he said. "I don't want that on my conscience."

"Do not worry about such a one." At his dark look she said, "That one tends to make difficulties for loyal gomin. The flow carries many tides of censure. You must forget the gomin, and worry more about yourself. Do not fight the guards, for one thing, Eli. You incur a reputation for discourteousness."

"There've been worse things said about me."

She looked to the side as a shuddering noise shook the ground. "Eli, they are leaving."

"Who?"

"The chosen. That is the sound you hear, of the carriers ascending. For ronid." It had been many cycles since an Extreme Prime had overturned a Data Guide's decision. Rumor had it Tirinn was furious.

"She really screwed you over, didn't she?"

"Sex and making mistakes?" she asked, puzzling with the phrase *screwed over*. "Sit down, Eli; one gets a crick in the neck always looking up at you."

As he did so, he reached out to brush her sleeve with his hand. "You're really here."

"Yes." She traced her hand on the sandy ground. Up-World was a world of soil and untidiness. She knew that what she felt on this data stage was a once-removed sensation, much as the dark waters she swam in on Tirinn's orders were not truly wet like the dreadful wet of UpWorld. She mustered her next words with difficulty. "I have studied that humans have tears when they are distressed."

"Yes. Or when profoundly happy."

"I thought it was only for sad."

"Humans are complicated."

She nodded slowly. "We do not cry."

"Maybe that's why you're so crazy."

She glanced up sharply, to see him smiling. "A joke?"

"Yes."

He pressed his own hand over hers, as it lightly rested on her knee.

She looked at their two hands, one cupped over the other. His light skin looked fragile against her own, bred for the season. "When my people are sad, Eli, or in other high emotion, our markings fade. UpWorld, this reduces our camouflage. So we learn not to have emotion."

"Like you're not having now?"

"Yes, like that." She smiled, proud that they could speak in this mode of irony so favored by humans. She would have liked to continue thus, but in second mind she would rather be done with what came next.

The roar of an animal in the forest below showed that Nefer had not yet given up on coaxing responses from Eli.

He looked to the edge of his plateau. "Why does she think I fear the jungle?"

He was hopeless. No matter how she tried to help him, he would be a babe in the river. "UpWorld is a forest."

He frowned. "It's a desert."

"No longer, Eli. Now the wet season has come and with it, the tendency toward growing things."

"If so, it happened fast."

"The season is short." *And my time.* She gently pulled

her hand away. "Eli, you have tended to believe that Up-World is the realm of mating, yes?"

"So you've told me."

"You will have many errors in your understanding. Now I will tell you the way of it. Our practice is that we ascend, and though many die, those who live create descendants. The vone decide who is fit to mate. We must not fear them, lest we tend to smell like their prey. If we fear them, they do not recognize us as their own."

"Their own?"

"They are like us. And unlike."

"Monsters, Nefer said."

Tradition imposed its frown and she lowered her voice. "But we mate with them. If we survive."

Now it was his turn to blink.

In profound embarrassment, she shivered, fixing her gaze on the ground.

At last Eli broke the quiet, asking, "What are the vone, Maret?"

"They are ourselves."

He was gazing at her, waiting. She plunged on.

"Our physical forms Up and Down are vastly different, but each is suited to its place," she said.

She would need to start from the beginning. This she did, telling him the story; not the story as told in enactments in the PrimeWay—those dramas of myth and ritual and poetic indirection—but the plain story, as it was recorded in the Well. "Long ago," she said, "we were like them, cycles past remembering. We lived as they did, and our society—for it *was* a society, however primitive—was unified. Then it happened that some of us hid in holes in the ground to escape the ravages of Red Season when all manner of creatures walk abroad. But there were bonds of kinship across the two enclaves, and as more chose the underground way we yet longed to be one cohesive group.

These bonds—social and cultural, you perceive—have always been strong among us. And it is our unique custom to honor such ties, as you have noticed, Eli."

"I've noticed." His tone conveyed that she had committed an understatement.

He had become very attentive. Perhaps he strained to follow her. Perhaps he could not see past the simplicity of his own people's sex-for-progeny. But now that she had begun her story, she would finish it. "Thus began the tendency to seek out each other, to breed between our two enclaves . . . even so far as to discourage intra-enclave breeding. Finally it became a taboo. During Red Season, we sought out members of the other—clan, you might say. And they sought *us*.

"Over fathomless cycles, we dug deeper. And Down-World, we changed, we ceased to sleep through dry season. We left behind true dormancy. We built our dwelling here below, we domesticated the hab—a precious reminder of the primeval, natural world. But all this time, we never lost the thread of cultural practice—to return to our first community."

His forehead furrowed in thought. "You said that sex is very free among you DownWorld. How is it a taboo?"

"Over time the taboo waned, then disappeared. But we found—as did the vone—that our offspring from such matings were infertile. I have told you we are few in number; we lacked genetic diversity. So we continued to go Up. And though statics were not disposed to venture into the sunlit realm, their fluxor cousins were. Even fluxor males, because vone need us for their fertility as well, and in the long view—and we have always tended to the long view—the vone must be viable."

"But you never used your technology to overcome the problem of DownWorld sterility?"

She suppressed her exasperation. "Eli, we never *wished* to overcome it. It is . . ."

"Cultural," he finished for her, with the hint of smile. Then he went on: "Such unions between ahtra and vone, produce . . . ahtra?"

"That depends. Most female fluxors have several issue. Some could be vone. One would hope not."

"But separate morphology. No hybrids?" Eli was thinking, as was his habit, in terms of his familiar biology. She feared her time would slip away in a morass of questions.

But she answered: "No, no mixing, no hybridization."

His eyebrow raised, his human way of showing doubt.

"We are more complex than you, Eli. We have, for example, mechanisms that prevent mixing. And, above all, we have the vone—masters of creation. If you experienced a vone, you would know they create forms. . . ." And he *would* experience a vone, soon, she thought.

But she went on: "UpWorld, if a vone bears an ahtra, the progeny dies quickly, due to the harshness of the place."

"And if an ahtra bears a vone?"

She kept her eyes carefully down, "We kill the issue, if vone. We would tend to have no choice."

"No disrespect intended, Maret. But all this is complicated."

"Inefficient, you are thinking?"

He nodded.

"Eli, you are in error to think nature is efficient. Nature is traditional, building on past biology, however imperfectly. The thread of evolution is unbroken, and today we are modifications of what we were. Your people, Eli, are built in a similar manner. On the old."

Eli was quiet for a long while. Then he said in a low voice, "The result is harsh, Maret."

"Nature is harsh. Sex and death are kin, so it seems to us. We do not flee from either. As a result, we are a strong, long-lived race."

Her feet throbbed with the grinding of the carriers as

they drilled their way to the surface. She had only a few increments left.

"We are one people," she said. "Your lexicon has a word you may know: *dimorphs*. That would tend to describe us and the vone." She paused. "I feared to meet with them. And I longed to."

Her time was at an end. She saw the guards hovering, but she spat out a warning for them to back off. To her relief, they relented, for now. She turned back to Eli, trying to finish in a hurry. "It is said, 'The vone keep our dead.' Children believe the dead walk UpWorld. But the truth of it is the vone mimic our kin to inspire terror—those they devour, they mimic. So, Eli, when you go Up . . ." She saw his expression, and it was easy to read. "When you go Up, you must not hesitate to kill the vone if you are so unfortunate as to encounter them. No matter what you see, have no mercy on them. And have no mercy on the dead, either."

She saw his eyes narrow with intense concentration. With hope.

"Maret," he said, "will Nefer release me?"

"Yes, if you force her to relent." She saw his emotions painted so clearly. There was no going back now. "Eli, I have a selfish hope that you will not go Up. But your wish is to die like a soldier, yes?" She didn't need to wait for an answer. "So, then. I will give you a 'fighting chance,' as you say. It would be traditional, to have a fighting chance."

"Have I won my wager with Nefer? Is that why you say I'm going Up?"

"No. It would be unlikely for you to win that wager. But I know another way. You understand, a 'desperate gamble'? That is what this is."

He took her hand, gripping it. "Tell me." It was a stronger grip than she had thought him capable of. Still, it was a hand that she or a vone could easily break. He was not bred for war.

She told him then, what he must do to ascend. Soon she would have the satisfaction of watching Nefer lose face and lose her prisoner. When Eli worked this scheme upon the Most Prime, Maret planned to be in the front row.

If their ruse proved successful, he would go UpWorld. There he would become that good soldier he wished to be. Therefore—though it gave her two sadnesses—it must be a good thing to release him from DownWorld, where he had no rug to hold his bones, or kin to wrap him.

23

Vod was seen and not seen. He appeared for an instant at the head of an upway; he was glimpsed jumping into a chute; he was seen OverPrime and, at the same moment, UnderPrime. Wagers began on where he would be seen again, and when. Sightings of Vod were sworn by fluxors and statics alike. He appeared in an enactment; dwellers who watched the drama thought he was an actor. Later the actors said it was all improvisation with Vod the Digger, who walked onstage and said: *The world has changed. How shall we be?*

It was a question Vod had no complete answers for. But when Maret joined him, together they would forge a change. Her brains, his fervor. The rumors in the flow gave him hope. Dwellers thought they saw him everywhere, but it was their own hopes they saw. They yearned for change, he thought, or had he become mad as Hemms?

At the head of the ancient upway, Vod dug a short tunnel through to Ankhorat, and, at the last, pierced the hab carefully to minimize bleeding. Peering out, he heard the pulsings of the recyclers and the throb of the generators.

Down the way, shadows of maintenance workers—statics who would betray him in an instant—flickered against the hab. Arching snakes of hosing loomed large, as the workers labored beneath the exposed flap. He sprinted to the nearest nub and plugged in, there leaving a data trail for Maret, code terms for where she might find him.

Slipping back into the upway, he tended the hab, knitting the flesh into place, leaving only the smallest evidence of bruising. Though by tradition maintenance work was a static function, Vod was not unfamiliar with upkeep of the hab. As a digger, he was accustomed to repairing the sheath, where its growing tip extruded into raw digs.

He scurried down the stairs, disturbed at having to descend an upway. But here, with most stairs collapsed and choked with soil and stone, custom must give way to necessity, and, liking the sound of it, he filed the notion away in backmind.

Once back in the ancient PrimeWay, Vod shone the light of his stolen headlamp on his water-collection tubes, still producing enough water for his hydration needs; as for food, the lorel proliferated here, where the hab placed no limits on its fruitings. The role of revolutionary went better on a full stomach, he had to admit.

The ways echoed with his footsteps, recalling the tread of so many who had gone before. The sheer darkness of the place coaxed images from shadows, to one unaccustomed to the dark. But when he brought his light to bear on the presumed spot, he found only the hab, creased and rigid, or a gaping portal to up- and downways, inhabited only by memories. Vod was not one to believe in the vitality of the dead. Here and now was life enough.

A thud of something behind him. He stopped, swinging his head around to shine the lamp. Nothing.

Rocks fell here, he realized. He'd seen how things slumped. Gravity would claim everything in the end. But, to his surprise, he heard himself say, "Who are you?"

Asking that question seemed to give life to the way. He imagined many voices answering. *I am Mirah. I am Vell. I am Unso. Gor. Atter. Doln . . .* Pushing the fancy aside, he listened again. Shapes bulked up out of the blackness, ink against jet.

"Who?" he asked again.

Then, "I am Tirinn," came a voice.

"If you are Tirinn, why are you following me?"

"I'm not *following* you, you young clod. I've been trying to *find* you."

A dark shadow moved into the middle of the way, a shape large enough to be Tirinn. Then he caught the Data Guide's bulk in the beam of his light.

"Turn your headlamp to the side, you're giving me a headache."

Vod complied, watching as Tirinn trudged over to an old crusher machine abandoned by the wall.

The Data Guide deposited himself on the seat. "Made quite a stew of things, haven't you?" Tirinn shook his head wearily, wiping at his forehead with the edge of his caftan. "And I still have to walk *up* all those stairs," he said ruefully.

"What are you—"

"Oh, keep quiet! I didn't come here to waste my time. Fact is, I don't know why I am here. Maybe I owe you a little help. I don't want to die with more debts than I already have."

In the murky corridor, Vod could only see one side of Tirinn's face, and that, dimly. He looked very old and sagging downward, like the AncientWay itself.

"First off," Tirinn said, "stop leaving your artless clues for Maret. She's gone. And you're giving your position away, though you're bound to be caught anyway. Beg Nefer's pardon, do it publicly, maybe she'll get a few hexals out of displaying generosity toward you."

"Maret's gone?"

"Of course she's gone! If you spent some of your ample free time collecting information instead of making trouble, you'd know what every other dweller's known for the past span. Gone, yes. I sent her Up."

"Up?" Vod was so stunned, he repeated, "Up?"

"Yes, yes, Up." Tirinn said acidly. He braced his hands on his knees and looked about himself. "This place is a mess. No wonder we built a new one."

Vod felt a surge of outrage. "This is the old dwelling!"

"Outrage, my Skilled Digger, is ill-suited to the young. Wait until you've got a few cycles on you, then you can be outraged. You'll be more convincing when you've seen as much villainy as I have." He turned to look directly at Vod for the first time. "Now, attend. I haven't got much time. I sent her Up. You understand it was my choice? Hemms has the mind of a plucked mushroom. He'd forgotten the rules. That's one thing you know well by my age. I get to choose, and I don't care if Hemms chokes on his twelfth net." He glared at Vod. "Thought he could overrule a Data Guide."

"But she'll die," Vod said, the full implication of Tirinn's words finally registering.

"My, my," Tirinn said wearily. "UpWorld: sunshine, muck, and vones. I've heard it all before, believe me. All you need to know is that when Maret gets back she'll need a few friends, and from all the fuss you've been making, I take it you're one of them. I won't be around to help her. When she gets back and bears her progeny, you help her. I have high hopes for her issue. Her genes are of the first order."

"But why did you send her? She might be hurt!"

"For her *descendants,* you dumb clod! We can't have her descendants without ronid, now can we? She's the one I've been combing the genotype for all these cycles." His chest rose and deflated in a long, weary gust. "When I saw her life unfolding in scholarship, I realized she'd never make a good leader. Too brainy. Too conflicted. But her children . . . Now, there's a wager worth making, or I've just thrown my life away."

He noted Vod's surprise and waved an impatient hand. "Don't tell me you haven't heard *that* data strand, either? And I thought I was the center of attention for once! I should be hurt." He scratched at his belly in an idle fashion, as though tired of the news already. "Nefer got herself into an unseemly display of irritation over my pulling rank on the Maret issue, and arranged to send me Up, though I'm clearly not in shape to go. She got one of her more malleable Data Guides to approve me. Needless to say, I won't be coming back."

Vod stared at the blackened hab, hardly registering Tirinn's plight. "You're giving up on her. She could have been great. A great leader."

Tirinn snorted. "Let's leave the genetics to me, shall we?"

"Now *you* attend, Tirinn-as." Vod stood and looked down on the Data Guide. He was done with giving this old fool a respectful hearing. "We can't wait for Maret's progeny."

"Waiting is an undervalued quality, I assure you."

"Listen," Vod said, strictly controlling his pallor. "We're building war machines. Right above your overstuffed head." Vod pointed at the ceiling, where far above, the war foundry begat its progeny. "We can't wait. We'll be at war before Maret leaves the birthing dens . . . *if* she comes back," he added, wishing it were not such bad form to punch a Data Guide.

"We're not at war," Tirinn grumbled, eyeing Vod narrowly.

"No, not yet." Then Vod gave him the news that was both terrible and opportune. But it wasn't until Tirinn had climbed the thousand stairs that he believed.

They sat together then, at the top landing. Tirinn was quiet for a very long time.

"It's time for us to be rid of Nefer," Vod said quietly.

They stared at the walls of the stairset: crumbling, and seeping water.

"Yes," Tirinn rumbled. But still he sat, gazing at nothing.

"We'll use the foundry to drive a wedge between Nefer and Hemms. My wager is that Hemms knows nothing of this." When Tirinn didn't answer, Vod went on: "But we'll move carefully, so as not to force Nefer's hand. The question is, how close is she to blowing the tunnels?"

"It's why Nefer hates Maret," Tirinn said, his voice flat but still powerful.

"Beg pardon?"

"Hates her like she hates a water bath." Tirinn chuckled. "It was never just a matter of power with Nefer, you perceive. It's one of ideology. Isolation, that's what she wants. A traditional ahtran way of life, uninfected by human contact. We've met another sentient life-form. And some of us wish we hadn't."

"Statics," Vod supplied.

"Not all statics. By the deep dark Well, don't turn this into *them* and *us*. It's a continuum, my boy." He turned and looked at him as though just remembering him. "You're an extreme fluxor. Not everyone is an extreme. Don't make the mistake of measuring all dwellers by your own index." He sighed. "That's the last free advice I intend to give you." He rose, heavily. "Let us descend."

"So why *does* Nefer hate Maret?"

"Vone take me for a dunce," Tirinn muttered. He shook his head and began lumbering down the stairs. "Because, besides her most excellent genes, Maret has dangerous fluxor outwardness. Maret would be one to turn the Neymium Belt situation into a trading opportunity, not a battle. She might want to *mix* with humans."

"Mate with?" Vod felt his tendril jerk at the awful notion.

"Don't be a clod. Of course not. We have to draw the line somewhere." His voice was laced with heavy irony. "I for one would draw it right there."

They fell silent as they descended, with Tirinn puffing even more heavily than he had on the way up. Vod thought the old fluxor might die just from the exertion of the stairs and the shock of what he had seen. It would have been an altogether better death than the one Tirinn was likely to get.

24

Five ahtran guards herded Eli along. They told him that the short wands they carried would fell him in an instant if he ran; he didn't doubt their prods could do the job. Many dwellers followed in their wake, eager to see the spectacle, their voices trailing in a throbbing bass rumble.

The guard to his left was the one who spoke the best Standard. From him Eli learned that he had won his wager with Nefer Ton Enkar. The first fluxors had returned from ronid, giving reports that at least some humans still survived. The guard couldn't say how many of his crew or passengers yet lived, but the news gripped Eli fiercely. He thought of his best soldiers, and of Sascha and Geoff and Luce Marzano. He couldn't let himself believe it was any of these, but the hope broke through anyway.

Now the flow was bursting with demands to see him paid off in full view, in the PrimeWay. The rabble—the diggers—were especially keen on such rituals, the guard said, and in a show of indulgence, Nefer Ton Enkar had agreed to the event. Her popularity soared. Upon losing a wager, one does not begrudge the winner, he added piously.

This ahtra had good reason to learn a bit of his prisoner's language. For tidbits of information, Eli had agreed to behave in certain ways that the guard wagered upon. Especially on what days Eli would become outward and fight his guards. The guard on his left had earned a tidy sum off of Eli, and was disposed to offer bits of information in payment.

From side ways dwellers poured forth, falling in behind what had become a jammed procession. Eli looked straight ahead of him, conscious of the train of ahtra behind him. It all fed into his plan. The bigger the crowd, the more his gambit might thrive. Much like entering armed combat, his muscles surged with adrenaline.

Nefer would be waiting for him, and that would be a battle in its own right.

Coming into the expansive PrimeWay, Eli took a powerful breath of the cooler air, finding relief in the vast arched ceiling after the confinement of the smaller ways. He looked for Maret as he and his escort pressed through the throng, but all he saw were strangers, and the occasional gomin in the typical white flowing dress. Over the heads of the thousands of ahtra crowded into the way, he glimpsed a great canopy—the stage that was his destination.

As the guards pushed him forward, Eli saw one ahtra he recognized. Not Maret, but the gomin of his virtual conversations. She looked very pale, and she turned away from Eli, but he managed to swerve closer. The guards grabbed him firmly, but Eli made eye contact with her. "Translate for me," he said, "and I will repay you."

The guards pushed him onward, and the gomin fell into step. "I am only a gomin—now less than all others."

Eli jammed to a stop. "What is your name?"

The guards indulged him for a moment as she stammered, "I am a gomin."

"Everyone has a name."

She looked him full in the face then. "Zehops Cer Aton."

"Well, then, Zehops-as, speak for me today." He twisted his head to see if she followed, but now, pushed firmly onward by his escort, only the stage filled his view. He climbed the ladder as he was bid to do, finding himself on a platform some fifteen feet above the ground. Maret had once told him that this was a favorite stage for the ahtran dramas that flourished alongside the virtual entertainments of the flow. Below him, a vast crowd filled the PrimeWay. Above the throng, a breeze greeted him, bringing the sweet and sour odor of his enemies to his nostrils.

And Nefer stood waiting there. Whatever she herself smelled, she took snuff to remedy it; one of her attendants offered a wand to her.

Her great blue eyes raked over him, then she turned to the PrimeWay. She spoke, and a hush descended. Whatever the content of her speech, it was short, and then greeted with a roaring so deep it seemed to issue from the cavern itself.

Nefer turned to him. Her entourage turned with her, as though they were her chorus in a play. She said, in Standard, "State what is your very reasonable demand, Eli Dammond, upon the winning of this minor wager." As he was about to speak, she added, "Always remembering that one has said one would not break traditions."

"Nefer-as," he said, avoiding her eyes, and looking steadfastly out to find Zehops in the crowd, "I would have my translator speak for me."

"I would be your translator. There is no other, you perceive."

"There is Zehops Cer Aton."

At the sound of this name, those foremost in the crowd

stirred, passing the news backward, and Eli heard the whispers of "*Zehops Cer Aton, Zehops Cer Aton . . .*"

Nefer's attendants engaged her in heated discussion, perhaps of protocols, but before Nefer could respond, Zehops was climbing the ladder, her robes flashing their subtle aurora. Guards surged after her, but Nefer waved them back.

As Zehops came to stand next to Eli, a murmur swelled up to the stage from the crowd below. Zehops looked small and terrified.

Declining to take notice of the gomin, Nefer said, her voice amplified: "One is ready to hear your request, Eli Dammond."

He filled his lungs and said to the crowd: "Leniency." And Zehops turned to the masses and uttered an ahtran word that Eli could only hope matched the nuance of the word he had chosen.

Nefer spoke to the crowd. Beside him, Zehops murmured her translation: "There tend to be many who would say I have been lenient with you, Eli Dammond."

He answered Nefer, looking at the rapt faces tilted up at the stage. "Not for myself. For Zehops Cer Aton." Zehops turned to stare at Eli. "Tell them," he urged.

Her translation caused a stir.

All down the PrimeWay screens showed Eli and Nefer and Zehops standing there, and from all down the corridor, Eli heard his own voice echo back to him, along with a crescendo of murmurs from the gathered throng. A shuffling ensued, and after a moment it became clear that gomin were pressing forward, threading their way through the crowd to the foot of the stage. Though it seemed to stir anger in some ahtra, others stepped aside and allowed their more colorful neighbors to come forward.

Beside him, Zehops was trembling. "They may think my translation tends away from the truth," she said to him.

In what he hoped was a confirming gesture, Eli placed his hand on the gomin's shoulder. "Leniency," he repeated.

Zehops translated.

The cavern of the PrimeWay surged again with bass voices. Amidst this clamor Eli saw some dwellers dressed in the garb of diggers push forward to join the gomin. Several hundred dwellers stood there, the grime of digging in sharp contrast to the shimmers of the gomin robes beside them.

And then Nefer was speaking. Her voice carried along the PrimeWay, and next to Eli, Zehops whispered her rendition. The speech was laced with references to loyalty and subversion and tradition. But amidst her calm words, Nefer could not help but note the rapt faces of the gomin and the diggers at the foot of the stage, looking up at Zehops and Eli. Perhaps it was this that persuaded her to grant the request, for she ended by saying that Zehops Cer Aton would have her access to the flow reinstated, provided that all her data strands were public, and several other limitations that made no sense to Eli.

When Nefer was finished speaking, Eli turned to Zehops. "Is it lenient, what Nefer is allowing?"

Zehops looked at him for a long moment. "There is a probability one can find a path of happiness after all, I come to believe."

"Is that a yes?"

"It tends to be a yes."

Eli nodded, then spoke to the crowd. "That is fair payment for my win. I thank Nefer Ton Enkar."

As Nefer turned to go, the crowd seemed fixed on Eli. He had stepped toward the edge of the stage. They knew, with their sense of spectacle, that more was to come.

"Nefer-as," he said. "There's one more thing." He searched for Maret, hoping that he would get it right.

Nefer stopped along with her entourage. Slowly, she turned to face him, her eyes as wary as Eli had ever seen them. She looked at him as though he had a weapon. And he did.

"I demand to return home," he said.

When Zehops translated, the throng erupted, their rumblings and shouts echoing along the PrimeWay and looping back from speakers. The gomin in front of the stage were louder than anyone.

"You have accepted payment for the wager!" Nefer boomed out. "Too late to ask for what must regrettably be denied—due to tradition."

In turn, Eli shouted over the tumult of the crowd. "But tradition holds that those whose names live in the flow are still with you, are remembered, are dwellers forever. I am present in the flow. From the moment I came among you, my name was a subject of wager and discourse." Over the surging voices of the crowd, Eli called out, "I claim my right to ascend."

"A human cannot undergo ronid!" Nefer responded.

Beside him, Zehops trembled and grew ashen with the stress of translation.

Eli steadied her with a grip on her elbow. Then he proclaimed, "Let the vone decide who may and may not, as they do with all who ascend."

At that, pandemonium overtook the crowd. Below Eli's feet, a wave of dwellers surged against the stage, their shouts deafening.

Next to him, Zehops shouted something, a brief salvo. And then the gomin below took it up as a chant.

At Eli's questioning look, Zehops explained, "For Eli's kin. For Eli's kin."

Then, to his surprise, this chant proliferated up and down the PrimeWay.

Nefer held out her arms. "A Data Guide has not approved him! He has had no training. It is not in accord with tradition!"

After several minutes of continuing pandemonium, Eli

noted a commotion at the foot of the stage ladder. Then an ahtra of exceptional bulk could be seen lumbering up onto the stage. His appearance caused a hush to fall over the throng. To his side, Eli heard something very like a growl from Nefer.

The new figure spoke to the crowd in a soft voice. He appeared almost weary in his demeanor, but the crowd hung on every word.

Zehops translated. "Thus says Tirinn Vir Horat: As for training, Nefer Ton Enkar has kept this human on a data stage as his prison, and tested him most thoroughly." Then the rotund ahtra turned to Nefer and spread his arms in a simple gesture that seemed to convey self-evident truth.

Zehops translated. "I say he ascends."

At this statement, the clamor in the PrimeWay made further talk futile, and Eli judged that the crowd was overwhelmingly persuaded in his favor—for as long as crowd emotions might last.

In the uproar, Nefer approached Eli, leaving her escort on the other side of the stage. As she drew closer, her stare caused Zehops to hastily retreat.

Nefer stopped just far enough away that she needn't raise her chin to look Eli in the face. Her eyes took him in with a frozen calm. "Go, then, Eli Dammond. One withdraws protection of you." A small white smile appeared and fled. "And may the monsters of the upper realm delight in you."

Eli returned her gaze, gray eyes against blue. "They can't be worse than the monster of DownWorld," he said. "But I thank you for your hospitality, Nefer Ton Enkar."

25

Sascha grabbed on to a thick root and hauled herself up the steep slope after Private "Lemon" Limon, who kicked in footholds on the way to the ridge. Behind her, Private "Pig" Platis shuffled and grunted in the effort of his climb. The lamp, hanging now on her back to keep it from banging against the hillside, sprayed its light across the valley. Perhaps, somewhere below, Badri Nazim could see this beacon—or Captain Dammond, if he had returned from the lair of the ahtra.

She'd told Sergeant Juric about her ahtra sighting. By his face she couldn't tell if he believed her or not.

Nodding at her chest, all he said was "Did your lamp scare off that pock?"

He squinted at her as she answered, "I don't know."

It had been Juric's idea to climb to the ridge above the deadly streams of the valley. After hearing Sascha's tale of the water scorpion, the unit decided that no way would they wade that river.

"Chopper at three o'clock," Lemon announced from above her.

Sascha looked up to see the small rodent flying over-head. Its tail ended in an umbrella of bristles and matted hair that carried it on the thermals. Sighting a prey, it col-lapsed its tail and dove upon its meal. The bot aimed a segmented arm at the creature, but withheld fire. Only in marauding groups were the drifting creatures much of a threat. This one was alone, its prodigious front teeth sparkling in the sun.

Sascha told the bot, "Remember this: Rodentia, small parasailing creatures that may swarm for cooperative hunt-ing when the prey is large." She thought she could hear the bot recording, the brief whispering vibration deep un-der its metal skin. Her catalogue had dozens of entries by now.

"Shut up," Lemon hissed at her.

She had come to like the bot, with its doglike loyalty, its mute acceptance of the task at hand, its shiny black body that took on gleams of blue and teal green in certain lights. It was always slightly warm, like a living thing, and adapted with enviable swiftness. For the climb it had sprouted seg-mented appendages, three to a side, gripping the vine ropes with agility.

She defied Lemon, whispering, "Each ecological niche is filled. The rippers don't come up where they'd need forearms for climbing. Their predatory role is filled by the rodentia. Prey include the rock crabs, if they can catch them before they roll up into their pleated casings. The rock crabs fling off their armor to catch flying insects, trig-gered by shadows passing over their shells, if not actual landings." The reassuring vibration was the bot's only comment on her analysis.

At last they reached the narrow ridge at the summit. Juric clambered up beside her, and several minutes behind, Pig came lumbering up.

From their vantage point they commanded a pan-oramic view. Across the valley the transformed Gray Spiny

Forest looked impenetrable, a wall of sage green. Streams webbed the valley floor, eventually meandering into the forest. To north and south, the narrow basin stretched into the distance, hazy with evaporation and transpiration. Six miles to the south, Sascha knew, the *Lucia* waited for them, the focal point of all their striving.

"Head out," Juric said, hoisting his L-31 over his shoulder and nodding in the direction of the *Lucia,* a jagged course along the ridge that would take them down as often as up, clinging to the highest point of land available to them.

Pig, still winded, was slow to rise. "Wait up," he mumbled. No one paid him any attention. Juric had made it clear: whoever keeps up is with the group, whoever falls behind is on his own.

The rodentia were back, this time a cluster of them, twisting their bodies to change the angle of their sails, coming in on a brisk thermal. The bot emitted a series of clicks, and everyone hit the ground at once to stay out of its line of fire. It spattered the air with efficient stitches, bringing down a bevy of the creatures faster than Pig could have aimed the domino. The remnant scattered on the updrafts or dropped down on their own wounded.

Continuing along the ridgeline, the group followed what seemed like a flowered road. The thread of the path was studded with flesh-colored, radial flowers. They spread out in a straight line like landing lights on an airstrip. When Vecchi kicked at one, his boot bounced off the tough petals.

"Looks like somebody planted these," Pig said. "All regular and everything."

"Yeah," Vecchi said, "them flying rats just love purty things. Like your hairy ass, Pig."

Sascha told the bot, "Flowers on the ridgeline in a row,

sprouting from continuous rhizomes. Just like the grass and vines, it all goes back to root stock in the dry season. A rhizomous world."

Vecchi, just behind her, muttered, "Who you think's gonna give a shit about flowers and flying rats? Your daddy's not around anymore to go nuts over plants."

Sascha didn't miss a step. Without turning around she said, "No one in the history of the galaxy has ever been to this ridge. My father will want a complete report."

"Dead as that flying rat back there is what he is," Vecchi persisted.

Sascha slowed her pace, feeling her face as hot as cooked tomatoes. After a moment she was standing still in the middle of the path, and everyone else had stopped, too, watching her. She looked at Private Vecchi, seeing his hatchet-face, his smirk, his flat black eyes.

"Never mind him," Pig said, his face bright pink and sprouting a hairy growth of beard. "He's got no daddy. Never had one. That's how come he's so mean."

Struggling to keep her composure, Sascha said to the bot, "Remember this: The ridge flowers store water in their petals, prolonging their growing season beyond what might be a drastically short wet season." The bot thrummed next to her as Sascha resumed her walk, and the men followed suit.

"Crazy rich girl," Lemon said. "Them rich types are all crazy."

"Quiet," Juric growled from on point.

As though in defiance of his order, a volley of shots came from the valley, the crack and sizzle of fire from the other bot. Proof positive that someone yet lived. But once all were dead, Sascha wondered, would the bots keep fighting? In their complex AI minds, was there an imperative to win when the cause had been lost? Or would they, like her, have the grace to stop caring?

Forced to temporarily descend, they picked their way down a precipitous drop in the trail, then back onto the connecting ridge, where the path grew marginally wider. In the north, drumrolls of thunder announced the approaching battle-gray clouds. Then, in a wall of wind, the temperature dropped by fifteen degrees. The bot stopped, making morphing noises, the ones that sounded like the screams of mice. Everyone stopped to watch.

"Sprouting rain gear?" Lemon offered.

In organized sequence the machine elongated and retracted appendages, reformulating them until it became something resembling a tall box on legs. Then it turned around, facing in the direction from which they'd come. Sergeant Juric turned to gaze down the trail toward the ridgeline of the previous hill. Down the bot's centerline a crack appeared, and close underneath it, a ridge, with nubs that began growing into nozzles, then barrels.

The men drew their weapons, but they still didn't know why, except that the bot sensed something.

Continuing its morphing, the bot extruded military business equipment from every side, and began walking back the way they'd just come.

They watched it go. Pig was fingering the domino with repetitive movements. Vecchi and Lemon crouched and aimed down path, while Sascha moved forward to stand next to Juric, who could be counted on, more than any of the others, not to shoot her by accident.

As they waited, Juric turned his head from side to side in that way he had of scanning things with his regen eye, which, they said, was equipped with infrared.

They lost sight of the bot in a twist of the path.

A tick caused Lemon's left eyebrow to quiver. "What's up there?" he croaked.

No one answered. The sky was swept clear of rodentia,

as the air took on a soaked green glow. The quiet was almost suffocating.

In a high, thin voice Pig said to nobody in particular, "Tell her I did good, if anything happens. Tell my mom I did good, I didn't go coward."

Vecchi cracked a sickly grin. "Ain't been proved yet, Pig."

Juric nodded at Pig. "I'll tell her." He started forward, passing them each in turn, heading down the path the bot had taken. "I don't plan to die, unlike you patches."

Lemon squeaked, "Hey, Sarge, where you going?"

Juric turned around wearily. "The fewer of us in one place the better, like I told you a hundred times, Lemon." Eyeing the group with pity he said, "You're safer without me." Behind the words Sascha heard, "And I'm safer without *you*." From down the trail came his dark mutter, "I'd give my good eye never to hear somebody call me *sarge* again."

Fat drops of rain splatted at their feet, but no one moved. There was nowhere to go but forward or backward, and the men seemed paralyzed by the choice. Rolling thunder came close upon cracks of lightning. Pig wiped the rain from his face in a dainty movement while shouldering the domino in business mode.

Then, from down trail, came zings of bot fire, joined a second later by pops from a rifle. In the next instant Vecchi was dashing toward the sound of battle, heedless of the narrow path, charging with gun blasting already. Pig and Lemon hunkered down, legs dangling over the steep side of the ridge, trying in vain to dig in. Their guns pointed down trail, waiting for the charge of God only knew what. Meanwhile, Sascha stood in the rain in the middle of the path.

She felt a tickle in her feet. Lightning tension was gathered in the ground, causing a low twanging sound. Aware that she was the tallest thing on the ridge, Sascha crouched down, feeling her whole body quiver in resonance with the electrical charge building up. When it finally discharged, it threw her up in the air. She seemed to be flying for a long while. Perhaps this was how death felt, she had time to think, like being picked up off the world.

The impact of the fall stunned her, forcing breath from her lungs. She was wedged into a crack in the hillside, unable to move. A relentless rain battered her face as she lay staring into the towering galleons of clouds. Her hearing was gone. She closed her eyes to be sure. After a few minutes she heard muffled screams and shouts. She managed, by a powerful twist, to dislodge her lower right leg, but she could get no leverage on the muddy hillside.

Squinting, she watched the ridge for one of the men, listening for voices. Thunder beat the sky in wave after wave of abuse. She most desperately wanted to see Pig and Juric and even Vecchi once more.

Then she heard the sound of someone moving down the hillside. Someone had seen her. It would be Juric who would come. Juric, who wanted to look her granddad in the face and say, "We brought her back, sir."

With a lurch of her heart, she saw a creature scaling down the vine-massed valley wall. Within moments it disappeared from view behind a hillock. But she could hear its steady progress toward her. She hoped she was wrong about what she saw.

In her terror, she began to sing. The song came from nursery times. Her voice sounded like the noises bottles make when you blow across their tops.

"Hush little baby, don't say a word, Papa's gonna buy you a mockingbird. . . ."

The creature's face and then torso loomed over her. A humming noise seemed to be coming from it.

"If that mockingbird don't sing, Papa's gonna buy you . . ."

She looked up at the monster, holding on to her song: *". . . a diamond ring."*

Its large face was a pronounced triangle with eyes as big as a baby's fists. When it stood up on hugely muscular hind legs it looked to be seven or eight feet tall. From its narrow torso sprouted two arms jointed in two places, ending in very long hands with impressive claws. As it paused, regarding her, she saw that the broad forehead bore a crenelated ridge. Great jaws were just visible under its triangular faceplate. From the muscular throat came a deep humming sound.

She heard herself sing: *"If that diamond ring is brass . . ."*

The crenelated brow ridge undulated slightly as though sensing her more fully. Sascha noticed it was studded with small holes.

"Papa's gonna buy you a looking glass."

The creature's face began to twist. The broad end of the triangular surface curled back to form a rounded cranium, while on one side a knob of flesh emerged, sculpting into something very like a human ear. The entire face was changing, but Sascha could only stare at that ear as it flowered into a delicate shell, flushed with a rosy pink color. The flesh tone spread outward in a wave. . . .

Sascha thought if she just concentrated on the ear she would be all right. She knew better than to look full in the eyes of the visage forming before her.

"If that looking glass gets broke, Papa's gonna buy you a billy goat. . . ."

But she must look.

A human face bulged, fully formed, from the creature's head, as though trying to crawl out of the monster's body.

Her voice collapsed into a whisper. *"If that billy goat don't pull, Papa's gonna buy you a cart and bull. . . ."*

She knew that face. It was Lieutenant Anning. He looked very angry. Then surprised.

Her tattered voice persisted. *"If that cart and bull turn over, Papa's gonna buy you a . . . dog named Rover. . . ."*

It bent very close to her as she sang.

"If that dog named Rover don't bark . . . Papa's gonna buy you . . ." It was very important to keep singing. She whispered, *". . . a horse and cart."*

The creature's face was two feet from her own. Lieutenant Anning growled out, "Horz an cart."

26

The grinding action of the carrier stopped, but Maret's heart beat so hard in her ears she didn't realize it. Lioth Vir Homan turned to her in the murk of the capsule, her face dark but her voice easy to read. "We are Up."

They must act quickly, before the arrival of predators, attuned to the sound of a carrier. Maret reached for the door release.

Lioth stopped her hand. "I do not know you," Lioth said in the formal cadence.

She'd almost forgotten the ceremony. There would be no mutual aid, no acts of mercy between them. Tradition held that UpWorld would cull those ill-suited for breeding. So the oath was sworn, that they were strangers to each other.

Maret responded, "And I do not know you, Lioth Vir Homan." She punched the release and the door flew open.

A soup of odors flowed over her as she bolted outside, arming the mav, the traditional ronid weapon. Behind her, Lioth sprang out, her feet hitting the ground with a splat of mud. Droplets of water hit Maret's ankles, running in repulsive warm trickles into her boots. The heat squeezed her with a suffocating embrace.

They were on a plain of stalky plants that jutted from the ground. Leaves in the shape of swords fanned out, pointing skyward. Between clusters of the sword plants, festoons of moss formed bridges, obscuring sight. Maret pivoted, scanning for predators. In the distance, jagged peaks formed a long ridge.

Lioth looked at her, her eyes wide in a face rapidly loosing camouflage. Then, looking past Maret as though she were no more than a shrub, Lioth chose her direction and bolted off, quickly putting distance between them.

Two suns shone over the world, one large, one small. Near the mountains, clouds towered, emitting pulses of light. Maret smelled ozone, humus, plants, and her own fear. As she'd been taught, she used that fear to fuel her purpose. She ran, choosing a different direction than Lioth, crashing through the moss walls, feeling their feathery scrape on her face. After a few moments, she crouched near a clump of sword plants, listening for pursuit. UpWorld rippled with noise: wind, rustling leaves, chittering. The sounds painted a jumbled picture.

She raced for the crest of a hill, then used the vantage point to scan the larger terrain. In the distance lay a gallery of trees. Such an OverWoods would harbor many vone, but at the same time, in the close growths of stalk and vine lurked a concentration of predators. But this was no time for timidity.

Running toward the OverWoods, she noticed how the moss shot out filaments to connect one bush with another. The plant created a net to more easily catch the fertilizing pollen. Maret darted from bush to bush thinking that her goal was the same.

The sky spoke in a deep-throated growl. No one who

had studied thunder could imagine that sound. It beggared her imagination. The stacked clouds, though still distant, made the sky look immensely tall. Such distance, such height, such . . .

She had stopped, gazing at the sky, but she mustn't. Maret set her legs to running again. And then, amid the sun, and the thunder, and the hard plain beneath her feet, a surge of joy overtook her. It powered her legs and primed her senses.

I am Up World. By my kin, by my bloodlines, I am here.

An hour later she was more circumspect. She'd drawn the interest of a *frajet*, a low-slung amphibian capable of disabling her with a poison-delivering tongue as long as she was tall. Though she sliced off that tongue with her mav, it was a warning to keep her camouflage intact. Humans had an expression: *Looks can kill.* To an ahtra, this had special meaning. Calming herself, her skin mottled up nicely again.

By Ellod, she thought, *I will prevail. By my departed prime, I will come to the shade of the trees, swim the dark rivers, meet ronid with all courage.*

A glint caught her eyes, a bounce of light off metal. Curiosity pulled her toward the glare. As she approached, she saw the human ships. One, as Eli had described, crashed and ruined; nearby the . . . *Lucia.* In a bizarre custom, humans named their ships, sometimes after people or human qualities. It was like humans to bring poetry to war, confusing the two.

The *Lucia* was squat and fat, surrounded by the blackened scars of the craft's descent. Maret stood for a moment, staring up at the massive and clumsy structure. She found herself thinking she would see Eli Dammond come around from the other side of the ship. He would walk up the ramp to the craft. In her imagination, he took a last look at his prison world. Then he looked at her, waiting for her to say that some yet lived.

She backed away. The ship rested in its grass nest, deserted, quiet.

Then she turned and ran on, watching as the storm clouds masked the suns, turning the valley gray and cool.

Screams drifted in from the distance. Ahtran screams. She tried to outflank the noise, but was drawn to it. Coming closer, she parted the moss to spy into a clearing. It was Lioth, writhing on the ground. She was beset by habsen, burrowing predators, distant kin of the hab itself. Erupting from the grass, one had got hold of her leg. As Lioth thrashed, Maret's fingers shook on the mav she held. Blood gushed from Lioth's leg. The habsen was still half in the ground, but its grip was sure. Another burrower tossed its head up from underground, turned toward the action. Slowly, Maret let the curtain of moss fall.

Lioth Vir Homan, I do not know you.

She ran on. The clouds flowed toward her with relentless roaring, masking the howl in her throat, a moan of terror.

Maret, came her unsettling thought, *I do not know you.*

27

Nefer Ton Enkar remained on the stage, watching. Eli could feel her drilling gaze as he hurried through the crowd. With the PrimeWay in an uproar, and the crowd surging around him, it was hard to say just what the mood of the ahtra was at the moment. Some reached out to touch his arms, the cloth of his sleeve, others jostled against him rudely. Zehops was left behind, and he was in the custody of the rotund ahtra who had joined him on the stage. This individual cut a swath through the crowd, muttering and warning off the rabble with ham-fisted waves of his arms.

"Where are we going?" Eli managed to shout at the guard who had some Standard.

"Following Tirinn Vir Horat," came the unhelpful answer.

"But where?"

The one called Tirinn turned and glared, saying in Standard, "Less talking, more hurrying, you progeny of hopeless stock!"

They quickened their step, with Tirinn sweating and

puffing ahead of them, until they came to a stairwell where they hurried up a flight of stairs, leaving the crowd, if not its rumblings, behind.

"Hurry!" Tirinn growled at them, looking over his shoulder as he lumbered down the way. "If you were paying for my time, you'd pick up your feet." He pressed on, growling, "Clods and stumblers . . ."

At an imposing portal the guards remained behind, and Tirinn swept into a gallery crowded with workers. Thick platforms jutted from the floor like growths, their top surfaces deeply pitted with depressions. Trunks of the hab trailed from the ceiling in fleshy pulls into which some of the ahtra were connected by their tendrils, hands free to work at the platforms. Ignoring the clamor his appearance created, Tirinn waved them off and led Eli down a narrow corridor and into a den.

Throwing open storage chests, he began pulling out items, and throwing them into a sack. "There are some things she can't have," he mumbled, rummaging in bins. "She'll give this stage to another guide faster than the hab can digest dirt, you may be sure. But she can't have everything." He pivoted slowly, staring at Eli. "And I suppose you can't pay for my time, can you? Don't own anything, don't know anything. You *would* be me my last client; there's a flourish to my life pattern!"

An attendant appeared at the door. Tirinn thrust the sack into his hands, saying something in ahtran, and fairly pushed the acolyte out of the room. In due course another attendant appeared at the door. Tirinn spoke in low tones, handing him the sack. "My Prime Locator," Tirinn explained when the individual left. "He's good, is Nemon Es Marn, but he'll never make it to Data Guide. Here's why: He knows too much. Head stuffed with facts, backmind brimming with information. But the secret of the prosperous guide is context, attend me. Context. Generalizations. Think of it. Without generalizations we wouldn't know anything. Anyone can do specificity! Plug in, get specific! Then what do you know?" Tirinn glared at Eli, daring him to say that something might be known.

Tirinn deposited his bulk wearily on a wide bench. "Oh, sit *down*," Tirinn snapped. "I'm not going to give myself a neck ache on your behalf." His gesture made it clear Eli was to sit on the floor.

"If we're in a hurry, Tirinn-as, why don't you get to the point?" Eli managed to fit in.

"Why don't I get to the point?" He sighed with a huge gust of breath. "Eli Dammond, if you had any idea of the point we're about to get to, I don't think you'd be in a hurry." His eyes narrowed. "And I set the pace, attend me. A little courtesy is in order for the free information I am about to impart. Not to mention the sizable draw-down I did a few spans ago to learn your cliché-ridden language."

He wiped his hands on his caftan. "It galls me, it really does, to give information away. Can't understand that, can you? In your world, information is the only thing that's free. You let your people starve, but they can be informed! Well, you'll learn. Eventually you'll be exactly where we are. That's the only consolation of the old among the young. Knowing that eventually, despite all the posturing and nonsense, they'll all end up exactly like you."

The den darkened. "I'll miss watching you blunder into the future," Tirinn said. Around them, the air sparkled as the den became a virtual environment.

The floor dropped away. They were suspended in a cavernous cylinder, with viney growths and ferns clinging to the walls. A warm tickle of air pushed up from below.

"Hold on," Tirinn shouted—but there was nothing to hold on to—as they began a rapid but controlled descent.

Eli's stomach clenched at the sudden fall. As they dropped down the tube, the vines lost their leaves, becoming skeletal roots clinging to glistening wet rock.

"Everyone has their own picture of the Well. This is

mine. No pretty, awe-inspiring metaphors. Just deep. No one knows how deep."

The notion came to Eli that every time he thought he was going up, something conspired to take him down. He had wrestled Nefer for his freedom, and now he would go Up. But first, apparently, Down.

Glowing rock walls emitted just enough light to show myriad fault lines webbing the stone.

Tirinn waved his arms. "It's all here. All the records, all the generations. Everything we know now and everything we used to know. In the Well. The names of our kin, and all their cares and wagers are here."

Their descent halted in front of a lateral shaft. They entered it, seeing scenes of ahtran life: dwellers moving about their lives. Maret appeared before them, her face lost in a rapt smile, her data tendril plugged into the flow.

"Studying, of course," Tirinn said. "Even as a youngster, always studying. She was a rule-breaker, too, and I had great hopes for her. You have to know when to break the rules. That's the sign of a leader, savior and tyrant alike."

In the central shaft once more, they were dropping again, gaining speed.

"You're getting quite a ride for free, Eli Dammond. I hope you appreciate it!"

"I'd like it better if I knew why."

"Why? Why?" They stopped suddenly with a resounding bounce. Now Tirinn was on a swing, and he kicked his legs out to get a movement going, then clutched on to the rope of Eli's swing. "Because you're going UpWorld, you hopeless dolt! And you'd better know why." He pulled Eli so close to his face that Eli could see the faintest circles within the circles of his eyes. "Context, context." He pushed Eli away, in a wild arc. "So try to pay attention."

And they dropped again.

"In my little conceit here, the deeper you go, the older

the data. In reality, it's nothing like that. When we say the Well is deep, it's an expression. But its true, if you know what I mean. Most dwellers never come here. But for you, the trip's important. So you can quickly grasp what every ahtra knows from a life of contact with the Well. Think we're deep now?"

They sped downward faster than Eli could keep his eyes focused on the walls. Beside him, Tirinn's robe billowed in the rush of air, his giant sleeves fluttering up against his face like beating wings.

Swirling around them, scenes emerged. Of ahtra going about the business of DownWorld, living in close dens, tending the hab, digging new habitat, studying, birthing, dying, rolling the dead in their rugs . . .

They fell and fell. The air turned suddenly cooler. "So much for verisimilitude," Tirinn said. "But the heat gets tedious."

"Where are we going, Tirinn-as?"

"A hundred thousand cycles and more!" came the reply. "To the beginning of your time."

"Of my time?"

"Human time." They sped downward.

"We are old, Eli Dammond, the ahtra are unimaginably old. We have been sentient for billions of years. Can you conceive of a four-billion-year history of a civilization?"

They had stopped. With a visceral shock, Eli saw himself surrounded by deep outer space. The stars were flecks of light, massing here and there, separated by dark, yawning gulfs.

"No," Eli said, responding to Tirinn. "Nothing lasts a billion years. No living culture."

He could barely see Tirinn on his swing, so faint was the light. "Ah. No living culture, you say. Perhaps ours no longer lives. We are a conservative culture. By strict observance of the traditions, we ensured that things would not change. We have not changed. We have been dormant, you might say, to outside forces. It's the static side of us. Perhaps it's why we've lasted as long as we have."

A chunk of rock careened by.

"That rock, Eli Dammond, is heading for Earth."

"The final solution? A catastrophic end?" Eli suspected, for an instant, some kind of betrayal. Why should Tirinn want him to have information? To control him? To gloat in his suffering, as Nefer did?

He couldn't see the Data Guide, but he could hear him. "No doomsday, no indeed. You amuse me, Eli Dammond. We should have had more time together. Maret liked you, and she has relatively good taste. I must say I enjoyed your trouncing of Nefer on the public stage. We could use a little shake-up like that now and then!"

He became quiet for moment.

"That's what fluxor rule was going to bring. A little shake-up. Now, I'm afraid, Nefer has arranged a tedious prolongation of static rule. Fluxors cause trouble. But trouble is the price you pay for change. For the statics, it's too high a price. Usually, I agree with them, fluxor though I am. They're suited to rule: organization, keeping the forms and formalities, that sort of thing.

"Three billion years ago, in a time forgotten everywhere but here, the fluxors had one of their short, several-thousand-year reigns. They made a mess of things, and eventually they were kicked out and sent back to the mines, so to speak. But they did one interesting thing."

Another hunk of rock, irregular, pitted, sped by so close Eli ducked.

"Don't worry. The rocks are small. About two yards wide is ideal, for proper radiation shielding."

"Ideal for what?"

"It's my story," Tirinn said peevishly. After a few moments he continued: "You humans are hampered by a blinding predisposition to faith. You have faith in life, for instance. That all you have to do is throw some amino acids into water, keep it nice and warm, and presto—you have life, eventually. Pardon me, but that's hab shit. The laws of nature, my friend, are not conniving to produce intelligent life. Far from it. Life is immensely improbable. If it weren't, we ahtra would believe in the Divine Being you humans are so enamored of. Life, arising more than once, would look less like an accident and more like a god's grand purpose. But let's leave philosophy aside."

"Please, Tirinn-as, your point."

Tirinn said darkly, "I *am* getting to the point." He drew a deep breath. "After thousands of years of space travel, we suspected life hadn't arisen elsewhere. So we made sure it did. Duck."

Another rock flew by, close enough, it seemed, to give Eli a permanent new part in his hair.

"With those," Tirinn said. "Those rocks contained the microbial seeds of life. Dormant in deep space, sent to Earth and many other candidate worlds. Buried in those rocks were bacterial chemotrophs, built to thrive in your rather tumultuous early history. But genetic information was curled up in the proteins. We needed to get a direct hit on your planet, entering at the right angle of trajectory to avoid overheating. We planned to, of course, but the distances were large, and yours wasn't the only world we pinned our hopes on. Apparently, on Earth, it took."

Tirinn watched him closely.

"You want proof? I'll tell you your proof. Our DNA. It's the same, chemically the same. To you humans, that was certain proof of God. Everywhere, the DNA is the same. Like a grand plan. Sorry to disappoint. We seeded the galaxy. I can't tell you how dumbfounded we'd be to discover similar DNA in another galaxy. Might make believers of us. But for now, if you want a Divine Parent, I'm afraid it's us." He smiled a self-deprecating smile. "Sorry."

The stars winked out, plunging them into darkness.

"Hab shit," Tirinn spat. "We just ran out of time, Eli Dammond."

They were in the well again, ascending.

"That's one thing we never learned to do well: swear. I think there are things we can learn from each other. I made *hab shit* up. Not entirely satisfying, but it's a start." They were rising fast, past the fractured light of the well.

"Why should I believe all this?" Eli asked. "And why should you care if I do?"

Tirinn sighed. "You're a practical sort, aren't you? As a military man, maybe you'll be more interested in this: War is coming. I was going to tell Maret, or her progeny, and now it's too late."

"I know," Eli said.

Tirinn was slumped against the ropes of his swing. "Clods and dolts," he muttered. "You don't know a thing. You don't know, for example, that during our fine little armistice Nefer has been building a new armada. A rather larger one than you can imagine."

Eli felt like he was still falling into the Well. Nefer did indeed want more than he could have known . . . Tirinn's words had pulled away the floor, and his thoughts cascaded and fell away. "The armistice . . ."

"Not worth the paper it's written on." They were in Tirinn's gallery again. "Despite Nefer's high hopes to beat Congress Worlds to submission, neither of our races can survive more war." When Eli remained silent, Tirinn continued: "Make peace with Nefer, Eli. Convince your people.

"We're kin. That's the thing everyone has forgotten. No one remembers what the fluxors did so long ago. If it hadn't been for the meddling of an old fool like me with too much time on his hands, I wouldn't have discovered it, either. Maybe that ancestral relation won't matter. It never stopped humans from killing each other.

"On the ahtra side of things, I thought I had time . . .

time to broker a transition to fluxor rule, to make things work with our human competitors. Outwardness is what we need, a more open mind, as you put it, for things non-ahtran, for interchange, for peace. Now, unfortunately, you may have to deal with Nefer Ton Enkar. I don't think she likes competition. Sue for peace, Eli. You won't have much choice."

Guards appeared at the door.

"Now you have your wish, at last, Eli Dammond, to go UpWorld." Tirinn rose slowly to his feet, grunting with the effort. "Sorry to say, I'll be coming with you."

Vod's instinct was to run. There was no real refuge, but he ran into the dimness of the AncientWay, fleeing the sounds of heavy, thudding feet.

Nefer Ton Enkar's troops had burst into the Ancient-Way just a few increments ago. Vod could hear them in the distance, shouting orders. He paused at a portal into Prime-Way, listening. He heard many soldiers running, arms clanking against metal belts, and, far down the way, their lamplight bouncing off the great ceiling. He darted across the PrimeWay, ascending the crumbling stairs as noise-lessly as he could. Before they caught him he must reach a data plug in the hab, and tell what he knew. Before Nefer silenced him. To tell of the foundry would force her hand; if Hemms was not conducive, she would step in as war guide, Extreme Prime, and launch her ships. But, in second mind, if he did not expose her, it would happen anyway.

Matters tended from dire to doom: the foundry . . . his lamp, with his personal code on it, tumbling into the cavern . . . Maret gone for ronid . . . Tirinn, a possible ally, sent up to die . . .

Behind him, the thud of falling debris. Extinguishing his lamp, Vod flattened himself along the wall. He heard someone running toward him in the dark. Sprinting to the first downway, Vod raced in the dark along the minor way, then into another downway.

Panting hard, he found himself in PrimeWay again. He bolted into it, running with a soft and furious lope. He wouldn't go quietly, they'd have to . . .

He stopped short in his tracks. Nefer's army stood blocking his passage. They crowded from one side of the PrimeWay to the other. As his eyes took them all in, he saw they were a miserable army. In soiled work clothes, armed with shovels, picks, hab prods.

No soldiers. These were diggers. Harn stood in front.

"We figured the numbers were against you, down here." Harn tilted his head back at the diggers massed behind him. "Guess we'll even things up."

Vod's heart surged. He saw them all, his fellow diggers, dwellers he'd worked side by side with all his life. Ooan, Hute, Ulton, Belah . . .

But he shook his head. "Nefer's guards are heavily armed. We can't stand against them."

Harn snorted. "We'll show them what digger tools can do."

Vod nodded at Ooan, Belah. They grinned back, ready for a fight. They were pale with the dare of it.

But Vod shook his head again. "We're not ready for them. Not like this."

Harn challenged him. "Still waiting for Maret to get on the path?"

Vod swallowed. "We'll see about Maret. But with or without her, we can't fight guns with shovels." It gave him a stab of pride that they *would have*. "We'll find guns, then we'll fight. But now, everyone back up. Quickly, before you're noticed missing. Our interval will come." He saw Harn's disappointment as a few diggers started to move back through the portals.

Shouts came from behind them on the PrimeWay. "Hurry," Vod urged.

Harn relented, herding the workers into the upway. Their digger tools clanked against each other, surely drawing attention from their pursuers. At the next way, Vod separated the group, sending them along routes in five different directions up to Ankhorat. Harn and Vod took two steps at a time, running until breath gave out.

"I know an old digger chute we can try . . ." Vod said between gasps.

Harn blinked. "Nefer's got that chute watched . . . her troops are everywhere."

All his secret places uncovered . . . Vod felt the Most Prime's net cinching around him. They climbed on, finally breaking out of the AncientWay, where they left a gaping hole in the hab. They dashed into the DeepReaches.

Vod and Harn crept among the industrial engines of the area, hiding when soldiers passed, wending their way to safe dens among the fluxors. They stopped at a portal along a way. Vod chose a direction and Harn followed, though he complained, "This is a bad section; it's gomin land."

"What choice?"

Harn grimaced. "Unnaturals."

"What's natural about rebellion? We've become unnatural."

Harn was stubborn. "Not me."

"Go, then, Harn-as. Go back to work, you're not in trouble." Vod looked at his coworker. "If something happens to me, just be sure to look under the new digs."

"Under?"

"Just remember. Look under the new digs. Nefer has a surprise there." Then Vod darted off.

Soon he was in the galleries of the gomin. There was no kin feeling between diggers and gomin, and Vod was acutely aware of their eyes following him as he wound through their local ways.

Before long he was aware that a number of gomin were

following him. No doubt they didn't trust him, anymore than he trusted them. At the next turning of the way a knot of gomin were formed up in front of him.

"A digger in gomin sector?" the one in front said to him.

Vod faced off with her. "As you see." He hoped not to have to fight them.

She held a garment in her hand. "You will become a gomin, then."

"I am a digger," he answered, offended.

The gomin smiled. "Yes, yes, you would be a digger. And it would get you killed."

She handed him a shimmering robe. "I am Zehops," the gomin said.

28

In the dark, knee to knee, Eli sat facing Tirinn in the cramped capsule. The roar of the grinders made speech impossible, even if there had been anything left to say. Through his boots, Eli felt the quaking of the deck beneath his feet, the vibration of the thrusters, as they bored their way upward. He *thought* it was upward. He willed it upward. Now, after everything he'd endured, the worst thought was that they were actually going down, in some final payback from Nefer.

Outside the metal walls the world howled. The screams of metal against rock, thrusters against gravity, ahtra against human. In the cacophony, ghouls and demons growled at his passage. Once in hell, one was not supposed to return. He shook the fancy. There would be monsters enough Up-World, so he'd been told—though when he'd left, nothing lived except for the people of his command. . . .

However many that might be, he meant to find them. Then he'd see about larger things like war and peace—and Tirinn's story of an ancestry so dim as might not register on the machines of war. . . .

War, the voices howled outside the capsule. For all that Tirinn thought him a peacemaker, Eli wasn't ready for peace just yet. The hatchway would open on a battlefield. He put on his fighting face. *Let's have at it, then. . . .* He'd checked his old gun, returned to him. Even Tirinn had a weapon that he held daintily, like something foul.

The shuddering stopped. Quiet filled the hexadron.

"The hatch . . ." Tirinn grumbled.

Eli turned toward the hatchway mechanism. Tirinn's hand on his arm stopped him. "As soon as we get out," Tirinn said, "start moving away from the carrier. The noise attracts undesirables."

He cranked the lever, pushing open the hatch and letting in a deluge of sunshine. It hit him like a physical blow. Wafting in with the light, a miasma of botanical smells. Up. He was Up. The hexadron was poking out of a steep hillside, forcing Eli to jump, landing hard. His feet sank into sucking mud.

He looked around him, at a world of muted green. Jagged hills surrounded him, draped with grasses thrusting up through a web of vines. Sunshine turned leaves silvery, created prisms of colors on the water-soaked world. The sky stacked over him in bright infinity.

The thought came to him that, by sheer misfortune, they'd sent him to a place far from the desolate, dry valley of his camp. Maret had said that he would find forest. But this . . .

Behind him, Tirinn grunted. The old ahtra was standing in the hatchway opening, shielding his eyes. Then, with surprising agility, he clambered out of the capsule, and half ran, half fell down the hillside, dropping his weapon. He lumbered back for it, then stood pointing it at Eli.

Eli made a brushing motion with his hand. "Aim it somewhere else."

"Right," Tirinn said, moving the gun to the side. "And let's *get* somewhere else. Rather soon."

They set out down the narrow declivity as fast as Tirinn could manage. A backdrop of insect noises pressed in on them as Tirinn began talking, puffing with the effort of the hike. "I don't have much time to help you. The first thing you need is a different smell. No offense, but you smell like a promising dinner. We'll find you some food. Seed polyps, if yellow and not wrinkled; those are best. Eat as many as you can find. Should be compatible with human chemistry, from what little research I had time to do. But, with or without food, attend me, you get to that ship. Don't stop for anything."

Overhead, occasional vines draped between short, massive tree trunks, forming a tattered ceiling.

"These trees weren't here when I left."

"They aren't trees," Tirinn huffed beside him. "They're shoots arising in a circle, so they look continuous. Don't get near them. Animals den inside them, usually with progeny, which makes them a little edgy."

They emerged from the ravine, confronting a stunning sight. Before them, a long valley stretched, bordered by eroded mountains on the right, and a forest on the left, with a network of rivers spanning the distance between the two. Tirinn sank to his knees, hanging his head, as though he might pass out.

Eli scanned the valley. It was eerily familiar. It might have been the site of Charlie Camp. Except it could not be, with jungle, and rivers . . .

Towering thunderheads glided overhead, pressing shadows into the valley. He couldn't see anything else moving below. No monsters. No humans . . .

Tirinn was muttering. "So high . . . who would have thought it was all so high?"

Eli knelt down beside him. "Tirinn-as?"

The old ahtra looked at him with eyes gone wide, lower lids fluttering as though unable to complete a blink. "The sky . . ." At Eli's questioning look, Tirinn said, "It's awful." He slumped into a seated position, shaking his head.

Eli pivoted, as down the ravine behind them a pack of small animals came running. As they came closer, Eli saw that they ran on two legs, with arms ending in long claws. He sprayed them with a pulse of fire, dispersing them if not doing much damage.

Tirinn fingered the short gun in his lap. "I'm not much of a fighter, I'm afraid."

He had traveled from a black and white, subdued world, to a stunning realm of excess: an excess of color, of jungle growths, of smells and sounds. The world was full of dizzying complexity. Amid the fecundity, he searched for signs of his people: gear, footprints . . . bodies.

He thought this might be the valley he'd left. He could convince himself he'd seen these hills when they'd been naked of grass and vines. In the distance, a rampart of green marked the foreword edge of a forest that might be the Sticks, in a new season. He noted that the flora were mostly grasses, vines, and ground-hugging plants that he could imagine sprouting in days, not weeks. It was harder to imagine animals emerging—and from where?

Like Tirinn, he carried a food pouch swelling with polyps and seeds. Tirinn staggered on, methodically collecting, and urging the sour yellow puff balls on Eli, insisting he chew and swallow. Though Tirinn had surprising stamina, he was unobservant and careless, not pausing in his foraging even when the orange-throats sprang up from the river.

The small creatures emerged from the water, three of them, pausing and swaying, neck sacks pulsing with orange light. Insects swarmed around the light, to be lapped up by a flick of a foot-long tongue. Eli retreated from the stream, pulling Tirinn backward, as several more of the

creatures strutted out of the water to eye—and tongue—
them.

"Poison," Tirinn said offhandedly, as he bent to har-
vest a puff ball. "In their tongues." He thrust the food into
his pouch, spilling some as Eli pulled him away from the
swaying creatures. He heard them plop back into the water, then turned to face Tirinn. He would not last long
without Eli.

As though acknowledging that, Tirinn sat heavily in
the mud. His face was pale with exertion and stress, but
his voice was oddly flat. Looking into the distance, he
mumbled, "No training. Trained so many, but never myself. That's the thing." He pointed upward. "It never ends,
does it? Things fly apart, nothing holds it all together, how
could it?" He began muttering in ahtran.

Eli knelt beside him. "Tirinn-as . . . I have to go on."

Tirinn waved a tired hand at him. "Go. The ship. Find
it and leave. Take this." He thrust his pouch of food
toward Eli.

"You keep it, Tirinn-as."

The Data Guide's former self flashed for a moment.
"Don't be a clod. This is for you; I can't eat that fod-
der. You eat it. You still smell like a snack for vone."

Eli shook his head. "Get back to the carrier, Tirinn-as.
Go back down. Confound Nefer. Survive."

Tirinn put his hands on his knees and stared up at the
sky, where boiling clouds rapidly closed ranks, dimming
the landscape. "Yes, yes, I'll do that," the old fluxor said,
though his great body looked like it was thoroughly ce-
mented in place. "Now go." Tirinn looked at Eli as he
crouched there, hesitating. "What are you waiting for, a
ceremony? There isn't one."

Eli wanted to say, *Don't pin your hopes on me. They
won't want to hear your news, Tirinn-as. No one will
want such kin as ahtra. No one will thank you. No one
will thank me.*

"Well?" Tirinn demanded.

Eli stood up. "How will I know a vone when I see one?"

Tirinn sighed. "You'll know. When you do see one, kill it. Even if it looks—familiar."

"Familiar?"

"Yes, yes, they eat what they kill. Then they play with forms, with physiognomy. To confuse and frighten. It's a world of disguise and camouflage, disguise and camouflage for which you are particularly ill-suited. But don't worry, the biological information deteriorates quickly after ingestion. The vone don't keep the dead more than a few hours. Don't hesitate to kill them." He shooed Eli away with both hands. "Go, go . . ."

Closing his eyes, Tirinn blew out breath from his massive chest. "I'm not afraid. Once you've made up your mind to die, there's no survival value to fear." He waved absently at the gun at his side. "Take the mav."

Eli crouched down, retrieving the ahtran weapon. As he did so, Tirinn's eyes opened for a moment. "There's something I have to say."

Eli waited.

Tirinn blinked, as though struggling to remember something. Then he whispered, "I do not know you, Eli Dammond."

The first drops of rain fell like icy pellets. Eli turned and left Tirinn, shouldering the ahtran weapon, carrying his own before him.

He found the camp at last. A heavy rain lashed down, obscuring but not hiding the awful scene. Charlie Camp lay abandoned, a scene of death.

He walked among the tents and the bones of his soldiers, jumbled near-skeletons, picked at by carnivores and scavengers. He found an ID clip here and there, recalling a face for the name, a shred of history. . . .

Holding a fistful of clips, Maret's words came to him, from that first awful meeting: *They are dead . . . very deeply sorry . . . all dead . . .*

There were other skeletons as well, of the animals that overran the camp. With so many carcasses, it showed that his people had sustained an organized defense long enough to do great damage, but not enough. He saw many long-legged, upright skeletons, birdlike; and other bones, lying in puzzling heaps.

Because their wounds had vanished with their flesh, it wasn't clear exactly how his soldiers had died.

But it was clear how Cristin Olander had died. Her skull bore a bullet hole. A gold locket around her neck and the remains of civilian clothes were all the ID Eli needed. He pulled the locket free. Next to her, another civilian, Geoff Olander . . . so keen to stay, once, now here for the duration. What had been their last moments? Had she taken her own life, or been in the line of defensive fire? He looked for a younger body, dreading to find it, forcing himself to watch for short arm or leg bones, about Sascha's size. . . .

He found Lieutenant Roche's ID . . . Lieutenant Anning's. But not Luce Marzano's, not Sergeant Juric's. No sign of Sascha. He half expected to find his own ID clip. *Captain Eli Dammond, Sixth Division Transport . . .* His place had been here, among these bones. His burrowed prison seemed long ago, like a dream, a partial death, an interim hell. And now on to the real thing . . .

There were no ahtran bodies. He examined each intact skull for the telltale ridge of the data tendril. No ahtran bodies. That was good. He didn't want to find that Maret had lied. But it somehow would have been easier to have a target for the emotions coiling in his gut: a betraying enemy, a conscious evil. But if the wilderness of the planet had killed them—like an avalanche, a forest fire—it was no proper enemy, and it was immune to justice.

He found the command tent, where he searched for and retrieved the electronic log and a reader. Then, shouldering the weapons he'd chosen for their condition and portability, he left the camp quickly, toting a pack of essentials light enough not to slow him down as he searched for survivors.

He knew there were survivors; the ahtra had said so. And one other clue gave him hope: the bots. There were no bots in camp, live or demobilized. It was the one weapon he'd omitted in the inventory he gave to Nefer.

They raised the odds. Considerably.

29

It had been raining so long, it was not possible to become any wetter than she was. Sascha had a ferocious headache from her fall, and her stomach ached like someone was pulling on her intestines. She lapped at the milk that gathered in the grooves as she clung to the great shoulder of the beast.

She dozed again, dreaming.

"Get off that thing," her mother instructed her. "What if your grandfather sees you? Tell it to put some clothes on."

Her father was walking at her side, and raised an eyebrow at Sascha, as she clung to the Singer. "Don't worry," he said. "We still have three more verses."

"What happens when the horse and cart fall down, Papa?" She had never called her father papa, *so she knew she was dreaming.*

"Let's not borrow tomorrow's trouble," he said, winking at her.

The beast was singing: "Papa's going to buy you a looking glass. . . ."

Sascha looked into the glass embedded in the back of the beast's head. She saw herself, her hair cut short and slicked back like her mother wore her own for special occasions. Her cheekbones stood out, and her lips glowed red. She noticed that her dress was cut low enough to show the swell of her breasts. "This is a stupid-looking dress, Papa. I can't even run away in it, when we get to the end of the song."

"I know." His voice sounded rained-out. "It can't be helped."

"If that looking glass gets broke . . ." the beast quavered, and the glass in its skull shattered and broke her image into a thousand fragments, some of which showed a fourteen-year-old girl with a bloody forehead.

"Papa's going to buy you a billy goat. . . ."

The billy goat turned into a cart and bull—one form becoming another—and then into a dog named Rover.

The dog was loping joyfully, nose to the ground. But when it raised its muzzle to bark, nothing came out. Dogs weren't supposed to be complicated, to have trouble barking. Why would her father give her such a dog?

"It can't be helped," he whispered to her.

When she looked in his eyes, she knew that he was in another world, that they must say good-bye. She wouldn't even be here if it weren't for the beast carrying her, protecting her with its magic.

He shook his head. "Stay until the end, Sascha," he said.

"I'll try."

The beast sang the next verse. Its great strides

began to leave her father behind. Sascha turned,
twisting her body to see him.

"You'll still be the sweetest little baby in
town. . . ."

Her father raised a hand in farewell.
Sascha wept, the source of all the rain.

She was accustomed by now to the bouncing up and down, the loping gate. She rode on a crossbar, straddling it as she would a horse. Her nostrils were full of a sharp, musky scent. Maybe it came from the milk. She had been sucking and a warm trickle rolled down her throat.

She spat it out. In a moment of lucidity, she saw the huge triangular face of the creature she thought of as the Singer. It carried her in one long arm. The arm seemed to be broken, for it extended backward in an impossible way. One of her legs was bent against the Singer's back.

Her parents were dead. She saw them die. Her mother died first, blood streaming from the back of her head. Then her father fell as the ripper jumped at him. He had run to Cristin, though Sascha could see the ripper coming. He'd run to Cristin, to help her, his face contorted in pain, more pain than he showed when the ripper killed him.

Sascha was sobbing hard now, leaning against the Singer. They were gone, both at once. The Singer might grow agitated by her noise and kill her, but it couldn't be helped. Her cries stabbed into her head like ice picks.

The Singer had stopped moving. Sascha felt herself lowered to the ground, gently placed in a hole of warm mud. Perhaps her crying hurt the Singer's ears. Or perhaps now it had leisure to eat her.

The beast crouched, dipping long hands into a rushing stream. It's haunches were massive, three times a human's girth. Compared to the lower limbs, the torso was narrow, with a thick neck supporting the great skull. A pronounced jaw sported a carnivore's teeth. The rest of its face was a triangular plate, large at the forehead, and narrow in the place where a nose should have been . . . and thin at the outer edges, so the plate could fold back and mold into a shape like Lieutenant Anning's face. If she could trust what she'd seen.

It brought water up to its mouth in the cup of its hand. Sascha began sidling away, slowly.

Then a clawed hand locked on to her ankle. It gripped her, while it calmly drank with its other hand. Sascha stared at the arm. Who would have thought the arm of the Singer could bend in that way? The arms were exceptionally long, and had an extra joint, making for a limb in three segments, not including the long hands. After drinking its fill, the Singer brought her a drink of water in the cup of its hand.

She slurped from its hand, and then again, when it brought more. As it turned back to the stream, it let go of her ankle, then turned to stare at her, as though daring her to move. Sascha remained still.

A movement—behind the Singer, in the reeds near the stream. It was a bot. She flattened herself on the ground, as Juric and the others had always done, expecting a volley of fire from the bot.

The Singer saw the bot, too. It rose to its full height— Sascha guessed it to be over seven feet tall—and turned its head back and forth, its notched top ridge fluttering slightly. From the reeds came a low whirring, the noise Sascha thought of as the bot's thinking mode.

With an absent gesture, the Singer plucked Sascha from the ground and ensconced her in its left arm, so that she was straddling its mid-arm. It strode out, ignoring the bot. As they passed by the stand of reeds, Sascha could see the bot huddled there, pivoting to watch them go by.

"Follow me," Sascha called back to the bot.

"Volo mee," the Singer repeated.

Sascha wondered if she was delirious. Her head and

body ached, and she was sleeping much of the time. She could have sworn that milk came from the Singer's arm before, but now, as her head rested against the muscular shoulder, it was only a tough, wrinkled hide. Gray skin with black whorls, oddly like ahtran pockmarks. No rosy pink . . . no perfect, fragile human ears . . .

Up ahead, she saw that the Singer was making for the Gray Spiny Forest.

"Father . . ." She mouthed the word. "Father . . ." She didn't want the Singer to repeat it. It was her word. It meant love. And gone.

30

She had known it would come to this. Tirinn had told her, had drilled her over and over. *Swim, Maret, swim.*

She stood before a broad, slow-moving mass of water. Its surface sparkled where the sun hit it, from great shafts of sunlight leaking through gashes in the clouds. Beyond the WaterWay in the distance was the OverWoods. She had seen no vone since ascending, and felt that those dark reaches would be her place of consummation. But the WaterWay barred her path.

Her main problem now was exhaustion. Other candidates had entered dormancy before ronid, emerging with fresh power. But Maret had not rested during all the time Eli Dammond had been in her charge, when her duties to him, to Nefer, to her kin nets, and to training had pressed every increment into service. When, suddenly, she was free to ascend, she was at her lowest ebb of strength.

The WaterWay flowed before her, bearing life in its depths. Maret could see lights under the surface, as the photophoric creatures swam in their water world. When she entered their domain, she would be *fair game*, as Eli called it. As with so many human expressions, she wanted to ask, when is a game not fair? Was Lioth fair game for the burrowers? Tradition said yes, but it was damp comfort, then and now.

But she would use her wits not to *become* fair game. That was tradition, also. Maret stripped off her tunic and pants, and the unaccustomed heavy boots. Now, between thunderstorms, the day burned bright, an ally to her plan. She began slathering herself with mud from the bank so that she would smell like soil instead of flesh. Turning slowly, she spread her arms to the suns, hardening the layer to a crusty pelt. As the mud dried, it tickled her skin, like small fingers tracing over her body. Gazing at the OverWoods, she hungered for its deeper pleasures.

She used her belt to cinch up her clothes, boots, and mav, strapping them on her back, with the tie biting against her ribs. Then she strode forward, entering the WaterWay without preamble, up to her shins, her waist, launching herself into the water's cold clasp, parting the glittering surface.

The WaterWay was flowing faster than she had judged. Her purposeful arm-strokes took her downstream, not across. But she swam on, drifting sideways, losing her mud disguise by the moment. Caught in this wet snare, she fought panic . . . the darkness, the helplessness as she swallowed water, learning the awful gap between virtual and real moving water.

The current carried her, ignoring her fatigued thrashings. The shore was still impossibly far, and death by drowning, the worst death, loomed in her foremind. Struggling across the current, she replayed in backmind an image of power: her chain of kin, strong females holding on to the feet of beloved daughters as they stood on muscular shoulders stretching upward into the immediate mystery of life yet to come. Someday she would hold up her own daughter on her shoulders. It was worth swimming for. She strove mightily toward the farther bank.

Then she was kneeling in the shallows of the other side of the WaterWay. Next to her, emerging from the water, a great, serrated claw. Two eyes bulged from a long body. It lunged just as Maret scrambled backward, slipping on the mud bank. A shadow fell across her as something stood nearby. A long, muscular arm grasped the water creature by the mandibles and hauled it into the air. Then she heard the loud cracking of the body shell.

Maret staggered to her feet, pulling herself from the mud, fleeing the WaterWay. Her spent legs collapsed under her. She was on her knees, at the feet of a giant vone.

It had broken the water scorpion in half and was sucking out its soft tissue. Then it lowered its arms, dropping its meal and staring at Maret, in what seemed frank surprise. Maret looked up at the great haunches, and the long, segmented arms, ending in translucent claws.

It looked at her with her own eyes, bright blue with concentric circles of iris. She was shivering uncontrollably. The river, the scorpion, the exhaustion. Fear raced over her skin. *No. Not like this. I was ready, I wasn't afraid.* But her skin betrayed her, turning as pale as the palm of the vone's hand.

It cocked its head to one side, eyeing her keenly. Then its features began to flow. Bulging here, receding there, collapsing into an ahtra face and skull, the visage of its last meal. A terrible sight, that dweller's last moment. For an instant it looked like *her.*

The vone swept down its arm, a great claw gleaming. It missed her. But, no, it would kill her with an upward stroke.

Then a hole appeared in the creature's forehead. It froze in place.

The crack of gunfire. She turned around.

Standing on the riverbank behind her was Firan Hil Assi.

"Move!" Firan snarled. Maret staggered away from the vone, as the great creature fell to its knees, as though dazed. But it was dead. It crouched in the mud of the bank, sitting upright on broad thighs. Dead.

She knew this Firan Hil Assi—but not well—as a Subordinate Data Trader in the PrimeWay. He had been UpWorld many times, she knew. He was scanning the vicinity, clasping his mav to his chest, ready to fire again.

"Firan-as," Maret said as she hurriedly dressed.

The dweller turned to her.

"It was a vone . . ." Maret whispered, half-stupid with shock.

"Next time, welcome it."

"Firan Hil Assi . . ." She looked into his face. "You . . . helped me. . . ." Against all tradition, he *knew* her Up-World.

"Get up, Maret-as, put your minds together." He didn't look at her, but kept a watch on each shrub and hill.

She fastened on her boots, keeping her mav in the crook of her arm. He had saved her life. "Firan-as," she began, wanting to ask, Why have you broken your oath?

He interrupted, "I've ascended five seasons, Maret Din Kharon." He took time for a slow blink. "I've had a little help, too."

She looked at him, stunned. UpWorld, dwellers *did* help each other. If so, it was a hidden tradition, a closely held secret of ronid.

Before she could respond, he was moving again,

hurrying off. He glanced back at her, calling out an admonition: "Run, Maret, run."

She looked over at the vone, kneeling in the mud. The face had only imperfectly recovered its former shape, leaving it a disconcerting mixture of the familiar and the strange.

Then Maret ran.

31

It was very dark in the nest, but growing lighter. Through the canopy of vines overhead, Sascha noticed shards of sky. She lay very still, not wanting to attract the attention of Watchful Singer just now.

She had been among the Singers for a day or two, emerging from her stupor only intermittently. At first she thought she was in a huge hollow tree. But now, awake and more clearheaded, Sascha took closer note of her surroundings. In the gathering light, she could see that it wasn't a single tree but rather a circular stockade of woody canes, buttressed by several pillars: the reborn sticks of the Gray Spiny Forest. Two gaps in the fortress formed what Sascha thought of as the front and back doors. Over all were twining vines, sprouting many broad leaves and lobes of fruit.

Each adult Singer staked out a circular nest on the perimeter. The one she called Triplet Singer commanded a position nearest to the nest Sascha shared with Watchful Singer. Triplet Singer had three young ones that ran wild in the nest, chasing one another and screeching. Triplet hummed constantly, louder than any of them. Brat Singer, half the size of Watchful and Triplet, harried the three younger ones, keeping them at bay. In addition to these six, Sascha thought that a very large Singer had been in the center of the nest, but had left at first light.

Watchful Singer could sense Sascha's return to consciousness. She—Sascha thought that the milk demonstrated her gender—licked at the wound in Sascha's forehead. Watchful allowed the triplets, but not Brat, to approach Sascha. Her high-pitched hums got Brat's attention, freezing the adolescent cub in mid-mischief.

Triplet began to thrash, throwing bits of sticks and leaves around her. Sascha thought the Singer was ailing.

The beasts did not talk. That had been hallucination. But they sang melodies of a sort, humming. The range of their humming sounds scaled from bass rumblings to soprano warbling. Watchful had a favorite tune, complex but recognizable by now, one that had been threading in and out of Sascha's delirium.

At last Sascha opened her eyes and looked up at Watchful, squinting at the beast, through the slicing pain in her head. Along Watchful's left haunch a mighty scar gouged out a valley all the way to her foot, and left her with a limp. No less impressive for that, Watchful was a terrible beast, capable of killing her with a swipe of her hand. Yet the creature gave her milk and protection, and to Sascha's relief, had not resumed her terrible facial contortions.

While Watchful hovered, the triplets climbed over Sascha's legs, tugging at her clothes and wrinkling their high foreheads. The thought occurred that Watchful Singer had taken her to the nest to give the youngsters hunting practice. The babies were the size of small dogs, perhaps a foot high, with teeth and claws that would have put a hyena to shame. One of them nipped at her pants legs. Reflexively, she jerked away, and the cub pounced on her shin. Crippled or not, Watchful didn't hesitate. With a powerful swing of her arm, Watchful swiped the legs out from under the cub, sending it toppling. The youngster ran back to Triplet, who was still producing a caterwauling that drowned out the noises of the woods.

Sascha saw a huge insect perched on the top of the stockade, amid the green, growing tips of the sticks. Black with many appendages, it moved with a familiar slow-motion deliberation.

It was the bot. Beneath Triplet's screams, she could hear the bot morphing, pointing a tube at the retreating cub.

"Don't kill the little ones," Sascha told it. "The Singer is protecting me. You'll make things worse." The bot was still taking aim. It wouldn't obey her, she didn't know the command language it responded to. But the bots could learn, were programmed to learn, and since it was directed to protect humans, it might not need a fourteen-year-old's suggestions on how to do it.

Keeping one eye on the metal creature, Watchful offered her shoulder to Sascha, where milk trickled amid the grooves of her skin. With a high-pitched whine, the bot pointed its warning finger at Watchful. It hesitated when Sascha lapped at Watchful's milk. It was her only source of nourishment, and she was thirsty. Then, exhausted, she lay back down, resting her hand on her lamp, still strapped to her chest, proof of her previous life.

When Sascha woke again the day was bright, even in the canopied nest.

A shaft of sunshine struck a pile of bones lying near her. Opening her eyes fully, Sascha saw a very small human skull. She stared, trying to process this sight, doubting her senses. Much of the flesh was gone from the small body, but on the back of the skull the remains of a tendril lay withered. Three feet above her, the bot was clinging to the stockade, regarding the body with interest. It slowly climbed down into the nest and approached the bones, examining them with an extruded prod.

Out of nowhere, Watchful erupted. She came charging, sending Sascha into a tight curl of protection. The Singer's hums soared ever higher, and finally out of hearing range. When the screaming stopped Sascha opened her eyes, seeing Watchful bending over the bot, and the bot bristling, nozzles pointed at the beast. The soft ridge on Watchful's head fluttered, perhaps trying in vain to smell the bot.

The Singer won the face-off. The bot reversed, sliding away from the bones and back to its perch on the tree wall.

With the crisis passed, Sascha considered what to do with the body. It stank.

She began plucking the large, round leaves from the vines around her. When she had an armful, she carefully laid them out in an overlapping pattern to form a small blanket. Then she lifted the bones and placed them in the center. Watchful hummed her anger.

"I can't sleep next to bones," Sascha told her. Then, thinking better of it, she sang the phrase to Watchful, keeping the tones low and soothing. She covered the bones with more leaves, then folded it together, tying it with a fragment of vine. She offered the package to Watchful, who rippled her forehead furiously, but remained immobile.

"I'm going to bury this," Sascha sang. As she stood up, dizziness overtook her for a moment, and she leaned on Watchful's thigh. The nest looked skewed and blurry. It had a ragtag population, some large, some small, some mechanical, some flesh. There were humans and ahtra . . . it was a mix of life, all confused in one place.

When her vision cleared, she made her way along the inside perimeter of the den, looking for a suitable gap in the braided tree-wall. When she found one, she tucked the package inside. As she crouched there, she could see through the maze of trunks into the surrounding woods. The Gray Spiny Forest had become a vast and shadowy swamp, replete with streams, hanging moss, and giant stands of circular growths, looking like massive stubby trees. *Banyans,* came to mind. Nazim's Banyans. She peered into the altered world, watching for Nazim, or any human soldier, trying not to conjure up the cruel hope of the sight of her father.

Giant eyes regarded her from the other side.

In her surprise, she fell backward, landing on her rump, and jarring her head with horrible effect.

It was a Singer. Bigger than Watchful. It had pressed its face close to the tree mass, rumbling deep in its throat, making an ugly sound, unlike any sound Watchful had made so far. Sascha stepped away from the hole, but when she passed another gap in the wall, the great eyes were there, waiting for her. The big Singer's forehead ridge curled dramatically. Its eyes watched her with a decided unfriendliness. She plucked a leaf from the vines and stuffed it into the keyhole, as she thought of it. A needle-claw pierced the leaf, and pulled it through the hole to the other side. She had a bad feeling about this Singer, with its unsettling interest in her. She named it Demon Singer.

Sascha's stomach clenched in taut pangs. She had to relieve herself, but was not about to put on a show for the spying beast. For privacy she found a thick section of the tree wall, squatting to relieve her bladder, which eased but didn't erase the ache in her belly.

Nearby, the bot had found a gap in the tree, and was intent on looking through it. From the other side, she heard Demon Singer mimicking the bot's tiny screams, unfazed by the array of weapons pointing at it. Then the lethal extrusions retracted. The bot was uncertain about Demon—about all the Singers. Its confusion prompted mouselike screams.

The nest had grown quiet. She turned. The Singers had all gathered around Triplet. As Sascha crept in among them, she saw Triplet lying on her side, humming sweetly. Between her legs lay a birth mass, which she was licking clean.

One swift lick revealed a disturbing feature of the new cub. If it were not impossible, Sascha would have said that amid the glistening birth sack lay a wriggling infant—with a data tendril.

32

Pinned down by gunfire, Eli lay flat in a shallow trench. It was the sound of an L-31. The shooter had the advantage of having seen Eli, but Eli had not yet seen his assailant. He had called out several times, but it had no effect.

After a quarter of an hour, Eli became convinced it was just one person. He or she was ensconced on a promontory forming a tower at the end of a long saddle jutting from the hills. It formed an excellent vantage point, commanding the entire section of the valley. The way to it held no cover except for a small hill a hundred yards to his left. He sprang up, firing toward the hilltop as he ran, sprinting through an obstacle course of braided ground.

He skidded over the top of the ridge, dropping into a small gully. It was occupied.

A soldier dressed in rags of infantry brown lay flat against the gentle rise, pointing a gun at the high nest where the shooter had dug in. Eli flung himself down beside the soldier out of the hail of fire.

"Sir," the enlisted said, managing a salute from a prone position.

She had short, colorless hair, sprouting from a skull composed of a puzzle of pieces like tectonic plates. The rest of her skin was mahogany brown.

"Slime alpha can't shoot worth shit," she growled.

A few feet away a bot occupied the top of the hill, swiveling a sensor in the direction of the ridge. It was the best sight Eli had seen in weeks.

"Corporal, are you coded for AI?"

"No, sir, but anyway, this one's on automatic, and its gone dumb as alpha brass." She twisted her mouth. "Sorry, sir."

Eli let it lie. "Name?"

"Corporal Badri Nazim, third infantry, Baker Camp." Then: "Fucking hells," she growled as a hammering volley pressed them farther into the ground.

They watched as the bot disappeared down the other side of the hill.

"Where's your unit?" he asked.

Nazim glanced at him, taking in his new clothes, his shaved face. Then she turned away, sighting through her rifle eyepiece again. "I'm it. Baker Camp. I'm all that's fucking left."

The words took their good time soaking in. All that's left. One out of sixty-three. After Charlie Camp he was prepared for grim news, but he kept on, determined to find the ones too mean to die. Now he'd found one. And, apparently, another, up in the bunker. The thought that there might just be the three of them cooled his heart. And if the bot had gone after the shooter, there might soon be one less than that.

"I'll hear your story, soldier," Eli said. "Right now, we're going to follow that bot."

"That dog kept me alive, I'm not going to take it too well if the asshole up there kills it."

Eli saw how Nazim would take it, and figured he'd better be on hand to mediate. "Go," he said, directing her over the top, then following.

They ran, hunched down, but no fire followed them. There was no sign of the bot. Nazim ran alongside the saddle, picking a place to scramble up that wasn't too steep. Eli took a more direct path, coming up on the opposite side. He topped the rise, ready to fire, but the bot had already arrived and taken a long-nozzled aim at the shooter's forehead. The shooter was tucked back into a makeshift trench, pointing two guns at the bot, afraid to move his eyes from the multilegged machine.

"Make him stand down," the soldier whispered, voice hoarse.

"Drop your weapons, Private."

The soldier—dressed in transport blue—spared Eli a quick glance, then focused back on the bot. "They must've took the bots, reprogrammed them. Or why is it trying to kill me?"

"Because you've been shooting at your commanding officer, that's why."

"No, the valley's full of pocks and ghouls. They've been killing us off, one by one." He looked up at Eli, licking his lips, eyes staring hard. "Pocks and ghouls. Lemon's a ghoul now, same as Perez." He panned his gun in Eli's direction, squinting. "Maybe you are, too." He recoiled, visibly. "Yeah, you been dead for weeks!"

"Drop the gun, or the bot will figure out which one of us has rank. And it isn't you, soldier."

The private licked his lips. Then he was flying forward, sprawling at Eli's feet.

Nazim jumped into the trench. "You mucking bastard son of a whore." She advanced on him, still aiming her gun.

The soldier scrambled to grab on to Eli's ankles. "She's one of them, gonna kill me, Captain, then she'll eat us both.

She's Baker Camp, they're all dead, everybody knows Baker Camp never made it through the Sticks!"

"Tie him up, Corporal."

"Oh, sir, don't tie me up, the hummers, sir, we need all our guns." As Nazim bent down, yanking his arms behind his back, he jabbered, "You haven't seen them, sir, but I've seen them, they got us up on the ridge. And the rippers, they're fast, real fast. Don't tie me up." He started to cry.

Nazim muttered in his ear, "Shut the fuck up, or I'll give you a chance for a regen prick."

Eli bent over him. "Name?"

"Private William Vecchi. They call me Chi Chi, you remember, sir? We come down on the *Lucia* together, sir, you remember?"

"I remember." Eli knew this Vecchi, but he was so covered with grime, so bristled with beard, he hadn't been sure it was the weasel-faced whiner of second platoon. Too mean to die. Eli had the feeling that was going to prove horribly true.

Vecchi's eyes glittered. "You've seen the pocks?" He looked from Eli to Nazim and back again. "You've seen them?" A small frown appeared between his eyes. "I'm not voided out, am I, seeing pocks?" He waited, mouth open, panting from the heat.

Nazim nodded at Eli. "There's pocks, sir. I saw one. It was alone, as far as I could tell."

Turning his back on them, Eli looked down into the valley. "Yes," he said. "There are ahtra here." He turned partway around, eyeing them both. "It doesn't mean we're at war. And it doesn't mean we fire on them."

Vecchi gaped. "But they're armed!"

"So are we. Doesn't mean we're breaking treaty."

Nazim said, "What are they doing here, sir?"

Eli gazed out over the valley. "Trying to survive, same as us."

The view was remarkably like Nefer's virtual lookout. Not so high, and the terrain below was more open. In the distance he could see a herd of animals bunched between two rivers, hardly moving in the blistering heat.

A shadow passed over the bunker. The bot whined, as one of its firing arms followed the drifting shape.

"Chopper," Vecchi said. "They drop in for meals." He giggled. "Drop in!"

Nazim curled her lip at the huddled private. "He means they can dive-bomb, sir. Floating rats, is what they are. There's no birds here, you notice?"

A dark swarm of the creatures sailed over the crest of the hills, swooping in toward the pinnacle. The bot erupted with pulses of fire.

"Kill 'em, doggie, kill 'em," Vecchi shrieked as a pack of choppers glided down on them, riding a thermal. Rats began dropping onto them, and the bot was firing into the bunker and the air at the same time, as Eli shouted, "Nobody move!"

The bot was a crack shot, picking off the rats in mid-leap as they sprang for the nearest victim, which was Vecchi. From his screams, Eli thought the bot had hit him, or more likely, that Vecchi had moved into the bot's line of fire.

The swarm passed, leaving dead and dying choppers behind. Nazim and Eli methodically finished them off. Vecchi was rolling on the ground, jabbering, "Here doggie, doggie!"

Nazim pressed a boot into his middle. "Nobody chomped you, so shut up."

From under his arms, where Vecchi was still shielding his face, came the muffled rant, "We should of had us the magic lamp. We're all rat food. No way we're gettin' to the *Lucia,* not without the lamp!" He peered out under his arm. "But its gone. Blew to hell and gone, along with the general's brat . . ."

Eli slowly turned to regard him. "What was that?"

"The lamp; oh, they don't like those bright city lights. . . ."

"That's true, sir," Nazim began, but Eli waved her silent.

He knelt by Vecchi. "Tell me what you know about Sascha Olander."

"The brat?" Vecchi asked in surprise. "Dead. They're all dead, like I said."

Eli grabbed him by the collar. "When I ask you a question, you'll give me a clear answer, soldier."

Vecchi sneered into his face. "Clear, you want clear? Dead, that's all."

Eli slapped him. "That's not all. Answer me."

Vecchi paused. "Untie me?"

Eli turned to Nazim. "Next order of mine that Private Vecchi doesn't obey, shoot him."

Nazim grinned. "Yes, sir."

"Fell!" Vecchi blurted. "She fell; the lightning struck her. Right in the middle of the path. I'm not lying. There was a storm, and she exploded right on the path. It knocked her into the valley. Sir!" He looked wildly up at Nazim's steady rifle barrel. "Her and the lamp that keeps the critters away."

"You saw her body?"

"Yes. She was fried right to a crisp." At the look on Eli's face, Vecchi began to babble, "Black and charred, sir, and sorry. I was up on the next ridge, and I looked down, and saw her standing there, and then lightning come and struck right at her. Then up comes a hummer and kills Lemon with an arm as long as a shovel, and another was crashing after Sergeant Juric, and I was pumping it full of shells, but nothing stopped it, and Pig came running up behind me, but all I remember is, I slipped and fell off onto a ledge and when I crawled back up they were all gone."

"Took your time getting back to the ridge, did you?" Eli asked softly.

Vecchi's breath stank as he gaped at the Captain. "No, sir, no such thing . . ."

"Figure he's lying, sir?" Nazim cocked her rifle.

Eli did indeed. And hoped to God. But even if Sascha weren't struck by lightning, what chance did she have, on her own in this place?

"What about Sergeant Juric and Private Platis? Did you see their bodies?"

Vecchi bit his lip, considering. "Not exactly. Saw lots of body parts. Some of 'em could've been them." He looked at Nazim. "Make her point somewheres else, Captain. You can trust me." He blinked, in a parody of innocence.

Eli gave the merest nod to Nazim, who sighed deeply, moving off to scan the flanks of their bunker.

Evening was coming on, draining color from the valley. Then, in the far distance, Eli thought he could hear gunfire . . . gunfire. There *were* more.

Nazim said, "You hear guns now and then. Sometimes, it's pocks, their weapons. I didn't hear our guns until asshole here decided to use us for target practice."

Vecchi protested: "That's not it, not target practice, no, sir! But the hummers morph into humans. You could all be monsters. Even me!"

Wearily, Eli turned from Vecchi, thinking maybe the private *had* gone void, and wishing like hell he'd found somebody other than William Vecchi. Beside Eli, suddenly the bot looked like it had turned on a lightbulb inside itself. Light sprayed out of a hundred cracks in its surface.

"That's what it does at night, sir," Nazim said. "The critters don't like bright light. At night, it keeps them away. Some of the predators make bright light; it attracts insects, and its a pretty good sign of poison. I think some of the animals avoid the bright light, 'cause they think of poison. The dog's got it figured out."

Eli pulled out his satchel of food, throwing it to Nazim. "Eat some of these."

"Sir?"

"I've been eating them, they're OK."

Nazim paused only a moment before stuffing her mouth full. Vecchi watched, knowing better than to ask.

"Sascha carried a lamp, you said?" Eli was looking into the valley.

"Yeah, and it was a good bright one, too, sir," Vecchi said in a calmer voice.

The first shadows of evening flowed over the valley, turning the rivers from gold to gray, the patch of woods into a wall of obsidian. The primary sun had sunk behind the hills, leaving the dwarf star commanding the sky like a minor officer in over his head. It threw a reddish tincture over the land, and over Eli's hands as he held his weapon. Here and there, dots of light bloomed in the valley. They might have been campfires or bunker lights if this were a different planet. But on Null, he knew them for wandering creatures, hoping to attract a meal. He found himself following the lights with his eyes, thinking he might see a young girl, against all odds, the last survivor. . . .

His chest felt heavy enough to crush him. The thought of passively keeping watch through the long night oppressed him. He had spent too many passive hours, longing to fight, his arms sore from the tension of holding back, thinking of his people under ambush while he ate his meals and paced and conducted verbal duels with the queen of DownWorld . . . and learned to be friends with her servant.

Somewhere in the jungle was Maret, a friend—but if the story of the war fleet was true, his enemy once again.

The second sun set, sprouting more roving lights in the valley.

"Tell me about Baker Camp, Corporal." Eli crouched into the makeshift bunker, facing out with his gun.

From the darkness came the pummeling buzz and chatter of the night's insects. Amid them, Eli listened for snapped twigs, the tread of predators. Nazim's voice was so soft, it formed merely a thin net over the jungle's noise.

"It started slow, sir," she said. "And got worse." Her voice sounded very young. She couldn't have been much more than nineteen—and already a seasoned soldier. When had CW started recruiting children? Sometime, no doubt, in the last decade of the war, when losses took young lives faster than the eight worlds could replenish them.

"Worse . . ." Vecchi mumbled, low, chomping on some of the polyps from Eli's satchel.

"We had three years of boredom," Nazim said, "boredom so bad we thought we'd go void. Now, what I wouldn't give for some boredom. That's what they say, isn't it? A soldier's life is pocking boredom in between moments of sheer terror?"

"Tell your story, Corporal." He said it kindly, knowing she didn't want to tell it, maybe not in front of Vecchi, maybe not to anybody.

"Yes, sir." Beside Nazim, the bot had opened its seams, spewing more light and creating the look of a fragment bomb frozen at the moment of detonation. All Eli could see of Nazim was her crew-cut hair, its white stubble bright in the bot's glare.

"We lost twelve in the woods. Lieutenant Roche ordered us into Charlie Camp, we were going to debark on the *Lucia,* once Captain Marzano brought it in. She was going to land it next to Charlie. I guess she never did."

Vecchi snorted. "She took the *Lucia* and bopped. Sure! Why wouldn't she? Think she cared about a bunch of patches like us?"

Nazim's voice sounded forty years old. "I sure hope I

don't sneeze and pull the trigger accidental, in your direction."

"You heard her, Captain. If she kills me, it's premeditated."

"Can't court-martial someone for a sneeze," Eli said. "Go on, Corporal."

"So we took the southern route, hoping to find a place to ford the rivers, and steer clear of the woods, where we couldn't see more than a couple yards in any direction. Charlie Camp said they'd wait for us. We were worried they wouldn't. We talked about it all the time, how they'd give up on us. We kept watching the western sky. If we'd seen the *Lucia* take off, we would've lost it, right then.

"Took us three days to get across two rivers. The bridges had to be wide enough because of the bastards in the water. Sometimes they just threw barbs up. People fell into the water, paralyzed. The worst thing was, we couldn't drag them out. We couldn't get near the water, so we watched them float until something grabbed them. That was the worst thing I ever saw, worse than the Great War, and I saw some fights there. We had to hold some of our own back, from running to help. I saw older guys cry that never did in battle."

She stopped for a long while. Eli held the silence, and for once so did Vecchi. He couldn't prevent the thought that the men that still knew how to cry died first. That could mean, in the long run, that a long war left only the cruel and the numb at the end. And the inept. It was possible that Vecchi was all three.

"We all died the next day," came Nazim's whisper.

"See, I told you she was a ghoul . . ." Vecchi muttered.

"All but three of us. It was raining so hard we could hardly see. Everybody was trekking across a funny round crater, with steep sides, like a meteor impact site. We three were the last to go over the gully ridge. All of a sudden the mud was boiling, kind of with what looked like walruses, different sizes of them, twisting out of the ground, grabbing people. We were shooting like crazy, but it was like shooting into a can of worms; we couldn't hit the things without hitting our own. The dog threw down a sonic, and that stunned everything. Then we tried to pull out our guys— but they were chewed up bad. . . ." She stopped, turning to Eli, as though he were passing judgment. "Sergeant Addi told us to go on. He lost both his legs below the knee. We didn't want to. But the crater began to stir again."

Vecchi sneered. "So you left them, didn't you, you black runt?"

Nazim's answer came quietly. "We didn't want to. The sergeant, he ordered us to, before he died."

"Son of a bitch," Vecchi whispered.

"But we could hear their screams, all the while the bot was building us a bridge over the next river. It was a good bridge, but from then on, I was alone."

After that they were all quiet for a time.

Finally Vecchi piped up: "So now I guess you wanna hear Charlie Camp's story."

"No, Private," Eli said. "I don't." He'd listened to Lieutenant Roche's log, and he didn't want Vecchi's whining voice soiling the hard, honest story. It had been bad enough to hear a brave man's version. "I'll take the first watch. Sleep if you can."

The other two settled down as best they could, as the stars snapped into view like exploded kernels of corn. Oddly, there were sources of light everywhere: the stars, occasional photophoric animals in the valley, the powerful lantern of the bot—but the light didn't illumine anything. It was dark as space.

Eli was sure Nazim would not sleep quickly. After a few minutes, he said into the dark, "You did well, Corporal. I'd have been proud to be at your side." And he wished he had been.

*   *   *

When Eli awoke the next morning, the muzzle of Nazim's rifle was pointed at his shins. It was a casual pose, maybe the gun was aimed at him, maybe Nazim was just careless where it pointed.

Vecchi was staring at him, as though Eli had been the subject of a long conversation.

"So, Captain," Nazim said, her face blank, "where *have* you been all this time?"

33

Vod looked nervously at the fine rug hung over the portal, closing off Zehops' den from the way. A rug hung in that manner meant a recent death; in gomin sector it might mean an *upcoming* death: his own.

Zehops noted his gaze. "We need secrecy. The rug may help for a while."

The airy cloth of the gomin robes felt strange against Vod's ribs. If Nefer's troops discovered him now, he doubted he would pass for one of Zehops' dwellers.

She picked up his cast-off digger clothes, bundling them together. These she handed to another gomin, saying, "Get rid of these, Aarn-as."

Vod said, "Leave my clothes. I may need them."

Zehops was very outward with her sarcasm. "Afraid you'll become a gomin without your digger clothes?"

Before he could respond, a gomin ducked in from the way. Breathlessly he said, "They're coming."

Vod looked up in alarm. "They know I'm here?"

Zehops conferred in low tones with the messenger, who left as he had arrived, on the run. Turning back to

Vod, she said, "Not everything revolves around Vod Ceb
Rilvinn these intervals. They're coming to assault gomin."
She gave him a challenging look. "It might be dangerous
to be in those robes. What tends to be worse, Vod fleeing
Nefer, or an unnatural in Red Season?"

Shouts came from down the way. The den emptied as
each gomin dashed out. When they pulled the rug aside to
depart, angry voices surged louder in the way.

"Follow me," Zehops hissed.

She moved to the back of the den, and into a narrow
corridor, Vod following. Crawling into a cramped storage
gallery, past stacks of supplies, she stopped suddenly. In
the shadows, her face was lost in the dark patterns of the
season.

"I'm about to commit an act of trust, Vod Ceb Rilvinn.
Would it be foolish to trust you?" She looked past him, listening. Muffled cries came from nearby.

Vod wasn't sure what he was being asked to do, but he
had enough trouble of his own without compounding it
with gomin troubles. "Why are you helping me?"

"We want something, certainly."

"Something I can give?"

She stopped, listening again. Then she whispered, "This
is my gamble. That you can help us."

Loud voices echoed through Zehops' quarters. Thinking fast, he responded: "I won't betray you. More, I don't
promise."

She leaned forward in the dim recess. A section of the
wall slid away. They moved through, crawling into an odd
tunnel. The walls were smooth and blank. This was not
the hab.

"Zehops-as, what is this place?" They were able to
stand, but barely.

"The SecondWay. We hide here when they come to kill
us."

"Who? Who comes to kill you?"

She turned to fix him with a calm gaze. "You. You all do. But especially statics. The worst statics whip dwellers up against us. Sometimes a mob comes down to our quarter to beat the unnaturalness out of us. And always during Red Season, as now."

Sometimes the diggers grumbled against the gomin, and at times dwellers talked about correcting gomin ways, but he'd never thought it came to violence. "I thought that no one was hurt by such . . . events."

"Merely gomin," Zehops said.

It wasn't only digger ills that were never discussed DownWorld, Vod realized.

"Come," Zehops said, leading him onward.

Their shoes clicked against the floor, creating a clatter. Vod reached out to touch the walls, finding that his fingers slipped from the surface. "Where is the hab?"

Moving quickly ahead of him, and turning into a side tunnel, Zehops said, "You think our ships in the Far-Reaches carry the hab? Not all ways are of the hab. These walls avoid detection, keep us separate from Ankhorat."

They came to a large gallery where gomin lay on pallets, bandaged and tended by medipractor devices.

Zehops knelt by one pallet where a gomin lay, his face bruised and swollen.

"How do you tend now, Uril-as?"

Vod saw a pulse of bright chemicals thread through the medipractor tube into Uril's arm.

The injured gomin whispered, but his throat was nearly swollen shut.

"They beat him on just the right side, so they thought themselves kind," Zehops said, rising.

Vod counted twenty wounded, but all of them suffered silently. It shamed him.

"Several intervals ago, they came without warning."

"Do you fight back?"

"It's worse if we do. We sustain their beatings, then

they leave. If we're lucky, nobody dies." She watched him closely. "You wonder why we don't report it?"

After a pause he said, "No. Not to Nefer." And not to Hemms Pre Illtek, lost in his preoccupations of ritual and dynasty. "I never knew."

"You never wanted to know," Zehops said simply.

All his life he had lived DownWorld—a world, he was beginning to realize he apprehended less than perfectly.

Leading him out of the sick gallery, Zehops continued into the maze of the SecondWay. The corridors were narrower than the dwelling he knew, but extensive, running in long stretches. Zehops explained that it was possible to slip into the SecondWay at many points DownWorld. They passed a DreamGallery, where dormant gomin rested in safety. In other dens and galleries, the scent of sex was strong. Vod averted his eyes, but chanced to catch Zehops' gaze. She stopped in the corridor, and faced him with irritation. "You are surprised to note sexual contact? Perhaps you thought that we clung to each other only out of season?"

"No," Vod answered, automatically. But then, the truth: "Yes, that's what I thought." They were gomin, after all; even they did not deny it.

"Digger," she said with some heat, "I will tell you what makes us unnatural to you: that we want each other in all seasons." She looked at him with a scouring stare. "And that includes Red Season."

Chastened, Vod followed her as she led him down the way. Now the clatter of feet grew louder, and down the far end of the corridor came a press of gomin, helping the injured walk, or carrying them. To let them pass, Zehops pulled Vod into a side lobe.

"We can't all disappear during the raids," Zehops said. "Some must stay visible, lest they come searching for our hiding place. These are such volunteers."

She gestured for him to sit on the low platform hugging the wall of the lobe. Drawing up one leg and circling her arms around it, as though such mayhem happened every day, she said, "It is a great service we perform, is it not, for the gomin to allow violence such a harmless release?"

Her bitterness showed its bulky form beneath the softness of her words.

"Do we need a release for violence?"

"Yes, during peacetime, as now. Though some purge the inclination with ronid. Others prefer better odds."

Zehops seemed to be implying that dwellers needed war or they turned on each other. She was cynical and suspicious, perhaps with reason. But Vod could not subscribe to such pessimism. That was not the kind of world he was fighting for.

As though Vod had spoken his doubts, Zehops said, "The Well carries our history, where you can see how gomin were tolerated during the Human War. It was a better time, in some ways, for gomin. It's all in the Well. Usually Data Guides aren't paid to explore such topics."

Vod wished Maret were here. She had left him with a world crumbling around his shoulders, and all for a lineage that might be prime, but that could not matter for many years. *Here and now, Maret, this interval. This is what matters. . . .*

That much he knew. Yet he felt he had little grip on the rest. "What do you want, then, Zehops Cer Aton?"

She traced a finger along the hard shell of the tunnel, as though probing for the softness of the hab in the lifeless white lining.

"Honor," she said.

"Few of us have that."

"No, you *all* have that. Honor is different than position. Gomin—static and fluxor alike—find their level of ability, and we ask for no preference."

The last of the wounded limped by, leaving the way quiet. Zehops' voice was very low. "You have heard that the human, Eli Dammond, was sent UpWorld?"

Vod blinked in surprise. He hadn't heard, but cared little for the human's fate.

"He honored me in the PrimeWay. He called me by name. Every gomin heard, and dared to hope for the first time." She looked at him, dark and steady. "Even some diggers rallied to us." At his look of confusion, she said, "You heard of Eli Dammond's wager with Nefer Ton Enkar? He won a gamble with her. For his prize he chose the fate of a mere gomin. Tirinn Vir Horat engaged both you and me to help Eli leave DownWorld. I was caught and banished from the flow. Now I am gated back in, because of Eli Dammond."

She stood, looking down on him. "That is what we want. A public acknowledgment. Not your secret tolerance. We want honor."

"If it were mine to give, so I would, Zehops-as."

She looked at him with indulgence. "Vod-as, there are statics among the dwellers of the SecondWay who say the static cycle has ended. The fluxors among us have long thought so."

Her silent blue stare kept on and on.

"But Maret . . ."

"Forget Maret. We want to know if we should support *you*."

He could not have been more dumbfounded.

Forget Maret. Maret of the fine lineage, Maret of deep learning, Maret of high judgment. He was only a digger, had ever been the least of the fluxors. But now, with Nefer's dark fleet ready to burst from hiding . . . there was no time to wait for Maret. Perhaps Vod would have to do.

In backmind, he saw the vision of the hundred diggers arrayed in front of him in the AncientWay, carrying their axes, shovels, and prods. He saw, in clear backmind replay, that they looked eager for a fight. Eager to fight by his side. He had never spoken to any of them about his vision of how the digs should be, of how their lives would be better. No, they knew nothing of that; they wanted to fight for *him*. Even Harn would have died to defend Vod, to defend the thing that Vod stood for.

In that case, he must certainly decide what he did stand for. Could he in any way seek redress for diggers and exclude the gomin?

Zehops gripped his hand.

"We will fight," she said, "alongside the diggers and any others who incline to see the last of Hemms Pre Illtek and Nefer Most Prime."

"It's revolution, Zehops-as." The thought shook him powerfully.

"It would tend toward disorder." Zehops, no coward, smiled.

He looked down at his gomin robes. Colors flashed from the creases of the fabric in a most undiggerlike way. He would have to get used to this. So would they all.

34

Maret ran for the OverWoods. It was farther than it looked. It seemed that she had been running this race ever since she could remember. But it had only been since the *Recompense,* that ship whose name she now knew— since the *Recompense* avenged its kin by taking all of hers . . .

The woods beckoned. She had seen the worst that Up-World could present, and it was bearable: the sky, the fruiting land, the cold, black gullies of moving water, the vone with their terrible appetites. So far she had survived by luck and mercy alone, and though she longed to test her courage, she was buoyed by the discovery that there *was* luck and mercy in the world.

As she ran, she passed a carrier, and wondered how its occupants fared. Since the carrier was still here, it might bode ill for them. Musing on their fate, Maret lost her concentration for a moment. When she snapped back to watchfulness, her skin chilled.

The shapes up ahead were not bushes, as she had

assumed. They were large, furred creatures on stalklike legs. Dozens of heads snapped up all at once, swinging on long necks to rivet her with their eyes.

She stopped instantly, mav lights blinking *ready*.

The creatures had seen her, and there were many of them, all frozen still. Very slowly she turned her head and saw that she was three-quarters surrounded by the furred creatures, possessed of such claws as could leave no doubt as to their diets. She noted, too, the four-toed feet, with three slashing claws pointed forward, and a far larger one pointing backward. At any moment the claws would flash.

She was retreating in slow motion. It wasn't a move she had planned. In fact, she couldn't think at all. Both her minds were as blank as the sky. But she was backing up. She had lifted one foot far enough that it just cleared the ground, and moved it behind her, setting it down. That action took several increments. Then her other foot, slowly, moving backward.

One of the claws jerked its head to the left. It was eyeing her foot.

She held her foot poised above the ground. If she moved, they would attack. She might take out ten or fifteen before the main group was upon her. After a moment, she succeeded in lowering her foot to the ground, almost without moving it at all.

Incredibly, some of the claws seemed to lose interest, and bent to munch on grass. Perhaps they had recently feasted. Or perhaps they didn't recognize prey that was stationary . . .

She moved at the pace of lorel growing, of bones thickening, of memories fading. After many increments she realized that her feet were leading her to the carrier, though her mind had not the wit to think of the carrier, or the faith.

The day was dripping hot, and her skin burned with

the suns' blackening gazes. Her body felt like a stone pressed in the earth. She feared if the claws charged, her arm would be too paralyzed to raise the mav.

Backward, slowly, slowly. More of the claws returned to feeding, but the foremost one was not fooled. This leader watched her for a signal. Any jerky movement would do. This one played with her.

Where was the carrier? She dared not even look down to follow her own trail. Blind and slow as a tree root, she moved.

The lead claw took a step toward her. She blinked. That seemed to inspire another step toward her. Still, she held her fire, held her pace.

Her mind remained clear, but empty. It was as though nothing else existed in the whole world but this backing up, this calm certainty of moving slowly. It took more strength than anything she had ever physically done. But she felt she could continue forever, until the water ran out of the gullies, until the life of UpWorld sank back into the sand.

At last a moment came when, with her peripheral vision, she glimpsed the carrier. It was closer on her left than she had dared hope. Her mind, sluggish until now, began to calculate the odds, the distance, and the moves.

The claws were now advancing with her, very slowly closing the distance. She knew which one she must kill first. It was the one that had never taken its eyes from her. This one now turned to look at the carrier. Its movements were jagged and sudden, causing Maret to pale. But she had no need of camouflage now, only time, a few more increments. She crept toward the door of the carrier.

That was when the leader made its decision. It sprinted from a standstill, furred arms tucked into its body, screeching, in human Standard: *"Run! Vucking hell!"* Her mav was firing, missing. Her hand was on the latch.

Throwing open the door, she fell backward into it, firing,

kicking the *close* mechanism, but not before the creature's head poked in. The hatch slammed shut on the claw's long neck, squeezing the head from the body, leaving it inside with her. She scrambled to the back of the cell, away from the gory appendage.

She began to shake. Her elbow was thrumming against the bulkhead. Then her tremors were answered by drumming noises outside. The claws were hammering against the carrier with what sounded like their beaks. She heard them screeching, "*Here! No!*" She heard her own cries, but she didn't know what she was saying, if anything.

After a time, her throat was raw, and the outside noises diminished to the occasional hammer tap. She seemed to be floating, though she lay on the hard metal floor. Her muscles slumped, and her minds flowed downward like water.

Her backmind was shutting down. She sensed it disengage, releasing her, leading her into a deep unconscious state.

With persistent beaks still hacking at the carrier, Maret fell dormant.

Sascha awoke early, before dawn, just as Madame Singer was leaving the nest. Madame was the largest of them, except for perhaps Demon Singer, whose true size was hard to judge, as he was always on the outside, looking in.

Madame Singer strode out most mornings before dawn and didn't return until late—unlike the other adults, who tended the young. She bore home carcasses of meat for Triplet and Watchful, who daintily ate their allotments, sharing with Brat and the three cubs. Brat and two of the cubs were the lone males in the grouping. Brat's maleness reared up at times, most often around Sascha, and on these occasions he quickly lost enthusiasm as Watchful sang out her anger, driving him away.

Sascha stared at the slab of bloody flesh that Watchful had offered her. She couldn't bring herself to eat flesh, although her benefactor hummed impatiently. Watchful even demonstrated to her slow learner how to eat meat. Enterprising, Watchful also brought Sascha various kinds of fruit. Sascha looked at the scarred and patient Singer with some affection, uncertain why she had been adopted. Or did every mother recognize an orphan when she saw one?

Remembering her manners, Sascha thanked Watchful for the food, singing a melody that Watchful was trying to learn, a lullaby from Dalarri, her mother's home world. The old Singer could now hum parts of that song, in an odd key.

Watchful bent low to smell the pieces of fruit that Sascha had tied to her leg with coils of vines. In places, her leg was splotched from food reactions. After making herself sick on fruit, Sascha was determined to be more careful. Meanwhile, she drank the milk that flowed freely at times from Watchful's shoulder.

Demon, she felt sure, saw past her ruse of cub-in-the-nest. When she tired of Demon's great blue eyes spying at her through the stockade, she flashed her lamp at him, which, if done up-close, would cause him to veer away, humming a high-pitched protest.

As the light saturated the dawn gloom she could see the bot perched atop the stockade, looking into the Gray Spiny Forest, its periscope extended to command a better view. Sascha worried about the bot. It had reconciled itself to the Singers, but it was clearly not happy. Day after day it kept a vigil high on the wall, watching for an enemy to fight, or perhaps a human who might more value its services.

Sascha would be sad to see it go. It was her last connection to a world that seemed to retreat from her by the hour. Beyond this, the bot did provide some protection:

from boisterous cubs, from Demon, from amphibs that sometimes conducted suicide raids into the den. Even Watchful grew comfortable with the bot. Now she occasionally left the nest; first for short intervals, and last night for a good part of the evening. Sascha had recorded with the bot how the Singers didn't sleep, which Sascha theorized was due to the brevity of the wet season, when every hour must be spent consuming or mating. . . .

Sascha was working on a theory that the ahtra had two stages of their lives, one as humanoid ahtra, and one as the great Singers. The Singer stage might have to be accomplished on Null, but while in ahtran form, they might roam the stars in ships. She hadn't yet told the bot her theory.

"We publish when we're ready with our facts, Sascha," her father would say when she urged him to rush to print.

"But what if somebody beats you to it?"

"It's not a race, Sascha," he would say. And then with a grin, "Or not entirely."

But a more promising theory had to do with the tree boles. There were two boles within this nest circle, both hanging limp against the sides of the trees, as though they had softened, split, and sagged after disgorging their contents. The sacks looked large enough to hold the likes of Watchful or Triplet, if curled up. Perhaps these creatures had lain folded up within the Sticks all the while the army had camped next to it. Now, in wet season, animals had come from all the hiding places that the world could devise: from boles in trees, from the mud of dried-up rivers, from the rocklike carapaces thrown up by animals that made their own calcified dens, from the millennial mats of vines on the floor of the Gray Spiny Forest. Null afforded myriad retreats from the hammering drought, and as many ways to revive, to drink the sudden waters.

Watchful was leaving again. Eyeing the back door where Demon lurked, and humming angrily in his direction,

Watchful pulled up several long strands of vines and, bundling them together, pushed them over Sascha, with a gesture that conveyed, *Stay in bed until I get back.*

As Watchful left, Triplet—for the first time—roused herself from tending the cubs to follow.

Now, with no adult Singer in the nest, Sascha considered escape. Brat was entertaining himself by pulling down vines bearing his favorite polyps, and she wasn't sure he would try to stop her in any case. She felt almost strong enough to confront the forest. But it was many miles to the *Lucia,* and the remnant of the crew might well have left by now. Besides, there was the guard at the door—the hungry one: Demon.

A commotion came from Triplet's nest.

Rising up, she saw the three cubs worrying at the new infant.

She threw off the blanket of vines and rushed to Triplet's nest. The cubs had drawn blood from their sibling, which kicked reflexively, rather like a human babe.

"Stop!" she shrieked at them, waving her arms and stomping.

The cubs hesitated before her as she gesticulated and shouted at them. They were intent on killing their younger sibling, perhaps for food, or perhaps just to remove competition. When they dove for the baby again, Sascha surged forward and turned her lamp full into the face of the nearest one. The forward cub hummed in a low-throated rumble, a junior approximation of the sound she'd heard from Demon. It faced off with her, cocking its head. Pushing past it, she flashed her lamp in the eyes of the other two, but as she did so, the first cub made a lunge for the baby, and broke its neck with a sickening crunch.

Now the three cubs turned from their kill to face Sascha's lamp. Looking at their cold blue eyes, they didn't seem harmless cubs anymore. With Watchful out, they might look for larger sport. She backed away.

At that moment, and woefully late, Triplet returned through the front door. She stopped, staring. Sascha hoped she wouldn't be blamed for the killing. As the cubs bounded away, Triplet slowly approached, gazing intently at the dead babe, her forehead crest crinkling in a Singer's approximation of worry. She nudged it several times, trying to get it to move.

Though Triplet had been careless, Sascha couldn't doubt that she was upset by the death. The Singer began a soft humming, such as Sascha had heard her use with her cubs to soothe them. Saddened, Sascha crept back to Watchful's nest.

She closed her eyes in weariness, as her belly cramped over and over, as it had for days now. She listened to Triplet humming a melody that seemed part dirge, part lullaby. Sascha found herself crying, though with so much else to grieve for, it seemed silly and useless.

Late that night she awoke to see the sky stained with a red and gold light. As she watched, it quickly faded to nothing. But then again, incandescence splashed the sky. It was a flare, a military flare. Sergeant Juric, she knew, had no flares. It was someone else.

Watchful sometimes tolerated Sascha's climbing of the stockade, and made no move to prevent her this time. She used the close weave of the vines to crawl to the top. She joined the bot at the top of the stockadelike circle of sticks. Although at times one of the cubs climbed up to join her, she had no wish for their company today, and to her relief, none was offered.

From below came a rustle and huffing noise that told her Demon was close by. Ignoring him, Sascha gazed outward, seeing another plume of light shoot upward from its source in the valley. *Someone still lives out there*, she thought. It was a heartening notion, and she gazed at the flare as though it contained a message for her alone. If she could just discern the code, she could decipher the message:

I said I'd come back, didn't I?

What will he find, Father?—Abandoned war bunkers, perhaps.

Your hat, Sascha, your hat.

See you in a little while, then. . . .

Next to her, the bot had extended its periscope the highest it had yet mustered, swiveling the eyepiece, searching, searching.

"Go," Sascha whispered to it. "Bring my field notes home."

Small screams issued from deep within the bot, perhaps some complicated strategic thought, or an expression of frustration.

"Go," she repeated. "Save someone else."

She had the distinct impression that it was considering doing so. If it did, she thought, her research would come to an end. Left alone, she would become a denizen of the forest. Already she drank the milk of monsters, buried their dead, defended her status, slept in an animal nest.

As she stood watching the last of the flare fade into the night, she was aware of the night breeze lifting her long hair and spreading it out behind her like a mane.

35

During Eli's telling of his DownWorld tale, Nazim's rifle commanded his attention. She held it casually, pointed at his foot. They both knew she did, and that she had a right to.

He told of the underground fastness; how they had kept him, despite all he could do, until his final escape. He thought Nazim smiled a little at his outwitting of Nefer—the cunning of it. But Vecchi never left off staring as though he expected Eli to discard his human disguise at any moment.

As he came to the end of his tale, the rifle gave way a couple inches, perhaps showing Nazim's provisional judgment.

She said, "We wondered, was all."

It wasn't all. Not a simple matter of *Where have you been?* It wasn't his being missing that troubled them, of course. It was that he'd come back unscathed, save for a bruise or two. Wearing a nice uniform, looking like it had been laundered—as it had.

"*Still* wonder," Vecchi threw in.

"But it squares with seeing pocks," Nazim said. "And why they don't fire on us."

"Still," Vecchi muttered.

Eli had had enough of this ad hoc court-martial. He owed them an explanation. And they owed him an officer's due. He stood up and Nazim turned aside then, as though the matter was settled.

If it had been anyone else, maybe the matter would have been. But for the likes of Eli Dammond, the standard of proof was higher, always higher. They would obey, but they'd watch him, weigh his every move. Like before the hexadron and the tunnels. Only worse.

Now, in mid-morning, rain washed over the bunker in successive curtains as a storm scoured its way down-valley. While Vecchi huddled in the far end of the bunker, still bound, Nazim went collecting edibles on the lower flanks, where fog created dangerous camouflage for predators. But she was hungry, and it gave her an urgent courage, though she hardly needed any more than she was born with.

During a lull in the deluge, Eli realized it was not just rain he'd been hearing, but the staccato burst of an L-31. He squinted down the hillside, seeing only lumps of fog floating in lethal silence.

Then came a shout. "Hold fire, Captain." Nazim's voice. "Some of ours!"

He peered into the gray murk. Here and there, lights flickered, like glowing vacuoles in the cells of fog. From one of these cells three people emerged. In the front, Nazim, followed by two men, one tall and lean, the other tall and beefy.

Sergeant Ben Juric, no surprise. The other, from Vecchi's description, must be Private Platis, of Marzano's infantry.

The newcomers scrambled to the lip of the bunker, and the two groups faced each other.

Ben Juric's left arm rested in a bloody sling. His clothes

were torn and filthy, his boots and ankles caked with layers of mud melting in the rain. One side of Juric's face registered a notch of surprise. Pig Platis stared at Eli with round eyes in a round face. He wiped the rain from his eyes, leaving a new swath of mud there.

Whimpering behind Eli, Vecchi could contain himself no longer. "Sarge! Alpha Captain's got a pock gun, and a bag full of food. Don't trust what you see, could be a big surprise!"

"Captain," Sergeant Juric said.

No salute. Everybody stood in a watery tableau.

Never one for amenities of conversation, Juric said, "Saw your flares."

Vecchi was thrashing, trying to stand up with his hands tied behind his back. He managed to get into a crouch. "He won't let us kill pocks! We saw one this morning, sneaking down the valley, Nazim had it in her sights, but he says, no, we're not at war!" He giggled. "Guess we're dyin' on vacation, then!"

A flash of lightning froze the image, of Pig and Juric standing like gargoyles on the lip of the bunker. The moment stretched on; Juric opened his mouth, but the sky rumbled, garbling whatever answer he gave. Nazim adjusted her L-31 in the crook of her arm, her eyes lit up by lightning. Then Juric clambered into the bunker.

Eli spoke his first words to Juric. "Sergeant, this private here is confused about the chain of command. Give him the benefit of your correction."

One-armed, the sergeant advanced on Vecchi with a look that could have frozen boiling water. If there was a moment when Juric would have taken control of the unit, it had just passed.

"Where's your gear, Chi Chi?" he said, his voice barely audible.

"Gear?" Vecchi glanced at a mud-sodden pack at the edge of the bunker.

Juric stood his L-31 against the mud wall. Glancing at Eli, he said. "Out of ammo." Then he knelt by Vecchi's pack and started yanking out the few items stuffed inside it, muttering, "I find a lamp, Chi Chi, you're a dead man."

Pig watched as if he expected an execution at any moment.

Presently Juric said, "Well, now, you don't have the lamp. Only thing is, you and her went missing at the same time. Gives me a funny feeling."

"I never did anything to her, honest, Sarge."

Juric said with elaborate sweetness, "I ain't your mother, and I ain't your *sarge*." He glanced up at Eli. "He needs correcting, you say?"

"Shutting him up is good enough for now."

"Pig," Juric said, "You know how to count?"

"Yes, sir."

The sergeant nodded. "Figured you maybe did. Infantry's got its standards." He stood up, cradling his bad arm, a grimace jabbing at one corner of his mouth. "You count Chi Chi's words. Every time we stop, he does that many push-ups."

Pig knotted his forehead. "What if I lose count?"

"Estimate."

Then Eli repeated for Juric and Pig as much as they needed to know of DownWorld, the presence of ahtra, both down and up. Juric listened, clearly not liking parts of what he heard. Eli wasn't sure *which* parts. Pig blinked again and again, like an overload light flashing.

Rain clattered down in another volley, hitting the foliage like buckshot. It was time to put his command to the test. The bot was pivoting relentlessly, pointing at one invisible target after the next. This spot was relatively safe, but there was no future in it. Eventually a rescue ship would come— they'd make that effort for Cristin and Sascha, at least—but *eventually* they'd all be dead, and at the present rate it would be sooner rather than later.

Eli looked at Juric. "You got a reason to think anybody else survived out there?"

"No, sir."

Eli had to admit to himself that these five were possibly the last of them. Two days of flares, and they had snared two people. It was time to leave. If what Tirinn had said about Nefer's plans was true, CW Command needed to hear as soon as possible.

"We're heading out to the *Lucia,*" Eli told them. "Looks from here like we've got some rivers to cross. The bot will build us bridges, I'm hoping. Like I said, this planet is a major underground habitat of the ahtra. Whether that breaks treaty or not isn't for us to decide. They won't shoot at us, I'm betting. And we won't be shooting at them." He let that sink in, like oil into the ground, leaving a stain. "We'll be collecting food as we go. Nazim will show you how." He nodded at her. "Untie Private Vecchi."

Nazim looked reproachfully at Eli, hesitating.

"He'll walk unarmed. Pig, you carry his loaded weapon. Under attack, he fights."

Vecchi looked hopeful, but clamped his lips together.

Turning to Vecchi, Eli said, "You're starting fresh, soldier. I don't remember anything that's happened up to now. But we won't hear any more about ghouls." He took everybody in with his glance. "You see something that looks half-human, kill it. That's an order."

Juric spoke low: "We should split into two units, split the ammo. They're attracted to big groups. Sir."

"That's a good instinct, Sergeant, but we'll stay together. The more local food we eat, the less we smell like dinner. There's three of us who don't smell"—he was going to say *human,* and thought better of it—"who don't smell like a meal anymore. We'll do better together." He held Juric's gaze. The sergeant's eyes were so radically different from each other, that the tendency was to look from one to the other. Eli held his gaze steady. "Nazim, hand out the ammo."

"I'm with you, Sarge," Vecchi whispered.

"Five," Pig said.

"That was four!" Vecchi spat.

"Nine," Pig intoned.

Juric growled at Vecchi, "Drop, soldier, and give Pig his due." Vecchi obeyed, scowling.

To Juric, Eli said, "I figure we'll follow the foot of the hills south, Sergeant, where the rivers don't flow as broad. Any suggestions?"

The answer came out more like a growl than words. "No, sir."

As the others were packing up and handing around the last of the food, Eli spoke to Juric in a lower voice. "You have any questions, Sergeant?" He didn't say *questions about me*. But left it open.

Juric spit to the side, looking down-valley at their planned course. "No, sir. No questions."

Eli held back on saying more. Held back on saying, *I would have gladly died up here with everyone else*. It was too easy. He and Juric both knew there was no anchor for such words, no tether to the flesh.

Then they scrambled, each in turn, out of the bunker, heading down the steep slope into the folded gullies of the plain. It was a slipshod remnant of the crews of the *Lucia* and the *Fury:* a nineteen-year-old with the foul mouth of a master sergeant; an ox of a guy, none too bright; the meanest sergeant in Sixth Transport Division; and a mewling coward with a penchant for mutiny. Leading them, a captain who had sojourned with the enemy, and was now hopelessly compromised—in his soldiers' eyes, and maybe his own.

*   *   *

Maret emerged from dormancy. In the dark, all she could tell was she lay curled into a tight ball. Around her hung a stench thick enough to shovel. She moved her aching limbs, trying to shake the lethargy that had settled over her like warm mud.

Her first thought was, *A carrier. I'm in a carrier.* The second was: *I've dreamed my way through Red Season.*

Backmind dredged up for the length of her dream period, and mercifully, it had been only a few spans. She rose into a crouch, staying well away from the rotting carcass near the door. Each lung full of superheated air felt like she was eating something foul.

A ping of sound needled into her awareness. Something outside had scraped the hull. Maret listened for the claws. It might have been the hot sun expanding the hull, or a seed pod exploding and hitting the carrier.

Despite the minimal rest, she felt strength flowing into her limbs. It would be enough to propel her to ronid. It had to be. She reached for the hatch-door mechanism, pausing. Perhaps the claws waited outside. She pushed the hatch mechanism, and swung the door wide.

Cool, bright air flowed over her, yanked on her vision. She sprang out of the hatchway, mav at the ready.

Pivoting, she scanned her surroundings. The live claws were gone. Dead ones lay nearby, hosting small creatures that made the most of the free meal. They looked up in alarm at her sudden appearance, springing away to the bushes. Blinking, Maret tried to orient herself. The primary sun pressed down on the land, suppressing all shadows, draining colors, leaving only a lashing heat. Her sweat-drenched clothes dried instantly. As the scavengers began to creep back out from their refuges, Maret headed out toward the wall of gray-green in the distance.

She ran between two streambeds—a clear, relatively dry way to the heart of her journey. Now, so close to her purpose, all else was forgotten: the vone on the bank of the river, Firan, the attack of the claws. She ran until shooting pains coursed up her legs. And ran some more.

The OverWoods was farther than it looked. She had no reference for the distances of UpWorld. But eventually the gallery of trees loomed closer. She stopped to eat from her pouch, gathering her strength.

At last, and after a final push, she came up to the wall of the forest. It parted before her and she entered, seeking its cool shadows and her heart's desire.

A matrix of sun and shade surrounded her. Amid the green-stained shadows, shafts of light created cisterns of dust and pollen. Her eyes lapped up every stray photon, so adapted was her sight to the dark ways of the hab, and its counterpart forest. From overhead, where the vines braided into a filigree canopy, a festoon of light fell upon her arm. It was in the exact shape of her arm markings, an oval defined by the coiling braid of creeping tendrils.

The bushes and hanging mosses trembled with hidden life, while insect life-forms swooped and buzzed in packs through the air. Many creatures strove here for food and mastery, including the one that she sought. And including her. She fired on creatures that charged, fell from trees, sprang from the ground. She plunged on, but no vone appeared.

As she grew weary, she hatched a new strategy, one of watch and wait.

Sizing up the trees as she passed, she inspected the drooping husks of vone sacks, split and hanging limp. Then, finding one less torn than the others, Maret climbed inside. A small pool of water had collected at the bottom, but mercifully, it wasn't inhabited. Through the rent in the sack, she could peer out into the woods, from a pod that hid her mostly from view and surrounded her with the scent of vone, a musk avoided by all but such as she.

From this small gallery, Maret gazed out at the OverWoods and its denizens: all the living beings, animal

and plant, than ran, lurched, dropped, crept, and flew to
their consummation. Throughout the long afternoon, she
watched as a tree root grew imperceptibly up a small
stalk, entwining it in a fatal hug. She saw gray-skinned
runners no larger than her hand take down a cousin five
times their size. She saw mating of every sort: animals
coupled while running; languorous snakes plaited their
length; insects flying in mated chains of individuals;
plants from which a long central spadex emerged, arching over into a female plant; all the varieties of joining
and exchanging genetic potential. No one noticed her
watching or paused under her gaze. It was, an active,
single-minded time, that brief span between dry seasons,
when the bloodlines flowed forth, or dried up forever. Patiently, she waited.

At times, she thought that, through the chaotic patterns of green, she could make out a tall pale creature with
fur on its head, one who went abroad in the blue uniform
of a captain of Congress Worlds, who sought a good death
that could have no lasting purpose. She saw this vision,
as the humans said, in her *mind's eye*. She willed it to be
so, that Eli had won his freedom, his ascension. *Because
he is remembered in the flow, he is one of us.* How Nefer
would despise such an idea! How Maret would have despised it, so short a time ago.

In the late afternoon, as the primary sun threw vertical
stripes of light through the forest, she saw a tall shadow, a
bulk walking in stately cadence toward her. A vone.

One moment the clearing before her had been full of
pink-winged insects, flapping in a rosy broth of air. The
next instant, a vone was standing there. Luck was with
her; it was a male. Slowly twisting his great head back and
forth, he crinkled his forehead crest in successive waves.
He was close enough to display for Maret his silvery oval
markings, and the concentric, fainter ones within.

He was humming.

The deep song filled the forest depths like a swirling tincture in water. It was a long melody, with one series of familiar repeating notes, just out of reach of her memory. The melody, the slant of sun on the vone's skin, was all she could hear and see. It filled her. Even the bright slash of blood on the vone's thigh was no blemish. This was Up-World: both death and life.

He turned toward her. If he was hungry, and she paled before him, he would kill her.

But there were no two minds about this encounter. She stepped from her hiding place, her skin dark and lush. She stood waiting, hungrily, helplessly. . . .

The vone saw her and approached, his great feet crushing vines and sticks underneath his weight. He towered over her, close to twice her height. Then one long arm descended in a gesture she had seen before. But this time the arm swept down slowly, no death slash. He crouched slightly, laying his arm along the forest floor. Instinctively, she knew what to do. Stepping forward, she straddled the forearm, facing the muscular shoulder.

Then, tucking his arm behind him, the vone began to stride away from the clearing. Maret clung to him, gripping her thighs tightly against the vone's arm as he struck out into the heart of the woods, his easy gait dipping her up and down in an undulating wave. *Yes. Yes,* came her intoxicated thoughts.

The forest knelt before them as they passed. Before the vone, all others gave way, retreating into hiding, as though he threw a long shadow ahead, clearing the way. Thoughts dropped away from her like dead skin. There existed only the riding, riding. She was safe for the first time UpWorld, under the protection of the prince of the woods, his smell soaking into backmind, dissolving every barrier. He stayed well clear of the streams, not engaging the dark waters, not risking his passenger. She hugged herself even tighter to his arm, watching the world unfold in drunken beauty, the chance convergence of light and substance.

They passed many rounds of trees, circular stands of reed and tree, each similar to the next. Except for one: a bizarre tableau came into focus. There in the heights of a tree round she saw a human, a young girl placidly gazing out. The girl stood on a limb as long as a vone's arm, the black hair of her scalp shooting into the breeze like mycelium. Sitting by her feet was an immature vone. Even more bizarre, a mechanical construct clung to a nearby branch, a tall pole extruded, with an ocular on the end, swiveling in Maret's direction. Maret's vone paid no attention, but strode on, its humming so deep she felt her skin vibrate.

When they arrived at the nest, the vone lowered his arm, creating only the slightest indentation among the bed of leaves. Slowly she dismounted. Everything was slow: his movements, and hers. Shadows thickened here, the primary sun a weak memory. Overhead the dwarf star rose over the jagged wall of the den, beginning its traverse of this tree-bound circle of sky.

The vone sang to her. She didn't know the melody, but she sang a counterpoint, as the vone's bass humming reverberated on the drum of her chest wall. The vone lay on his back, a posture both passive and sensual. Dropping her clothes like fallen leaves, Maret climbed on top, finding the pedestal that was, as it must be, just her size. The red sun rolled overhead, squeezing the breath from her. In the vone's embrace, she learned to breathe the green shadows, and she learned to sing his song.

36

Vod stepped into the PrimeWay. It seemed a new place to him. The vibrant, blushing hab enfolded the great Way as it always had; data pedestals nubbed out from the walls, stewards called out the odds on wagers, statics and fluxors mingled without touching, the glint of a gomin robe appeared in the throng like a charged crest in the data flow. But it would never be the same, not after his sojourn in the AncientWay, not after his awful tour of the gomin's SecondWay.

He couldn't venture into the digs. Nefer's forces would watch for him there. Whatever he did toward revolution it would be here in the PrimeWay. A small, rolled package under his arm reminded him that he had yet to give away one gomin robe. He stepped forward to speak to a fluxor watching the latest display of kin wagers.

Beside him, Zehops, holding two more packages in her arms, urged him on with a thrust of her chin.

The fluxor ignored his greeting. Of course, Vod wore the garb of an unnatural.

He tried again. "One wagers on that traitor, Vod Ceb Rilvinn?" Vod asked her.

"He is no traitor," the fluxor responded, flicking her data tendril to signal her interest to the data steward.

For a moment Vod's mood improved, but then, the fluxor spoiled it, adding: "He forces concessions from Nefer Ton Enkar, who has released disbursements by lottery."

"So he is a hero for making you marginally richer?" Vod could barely contain his sneer.

The fluxor turned to Vod. "Follow your own way, gomin."

"I am no gomin."

The fluxor eyed Vod, then Zehops.

"But I hide as one." As the fluxor stared at him, Vod thrust his package forward. "This is a gomin robe. The more wear it, the more we register our discontent."

But already the fluxor was backing away. "You have gone down an up way," she said. Her expression said the rest. The fluxor kept watch on him as he turned to others in the PrimeWay. He didn't think she would betray him. But if she did, if any of them did, Zehops and her cohorts were threaded through the crowd, preparing to cover his escape.

Zehops whispered, "Backmind her. She is a fool." She gripped his elbow in encouragement.

Around them, other gomin—clutching packages of their own—circulated through the PrimeWay. It looked as though no one was accepting a robe. And in turn, Vod was still failing to divest himself of his package. Dwellers were starting to stare at him; he had revealed himself as he approached each one, and now a rumor flew through the Way: *Vod Ceb Rilvinn is among us; Vod has become a gomin.*

Harn approached him, looking decidedly awkward in

the pastel caftan. "I'd rather chew my way through granite. It would be more pleasant. And more successful."

Vod was aware of the nearest portals, keeping his escape in view. "Give it time, Harn-as. We do not tend toward change." He felt it was the thing to say, but it didn't impress Harn.

"I could change more minds with a shovel in the side of a few heads than with gomin costumes." He narrowed his eyes at Zehops as though she were to blame for his embarrassment.

Vod stood with his package under his arm, feeling less and less like a leader. Nefer was bringing war and ruin upon them, while he dithered with robes. . . .

It was then that they felt the tremor. It began with a tingling of their feet. The clamor of the Way subsided, and dwellers came to a standstill. Perhaps the vibration would crest and fade. Harn turned to stare at Vod, no doubt with identical thoughts to Vod's own. The tremor grew to a distant, barking rumble. Zehops plugged into the nearest gate, searching for information, but Vod needed no data. He knew what that sound was.

Now the PrimeWay exploded with motion. Dwellers flooded out of the minor ways, shouting. In the boiling crowd, Vod was pinned into immobility. Nearby someone yelled that it was the digs, a major collapse. The rumbling of DownWorld subsided, but PrimeWay was chaos. Vod saw Nefer appear on a screen, urging calm. It was a minor tube, she said. Lives lost, yes, but minimal. All threat had passed. All that tended toward needful action tended to be done. Next to Vod a dweller was shouting, gesturing. When Vod focused on what this dweller was doing, his skin grew cold with fury. The craven static was betting on the number of rugs that would be filled today. Turning, Vod saw the flurry of arms and gestures, the fast wagering, with data stewards happily sweeping up the commissions.

Without consulting Zehops and Harn, Vod shoved his way to a stall where he could stand on a platform, above the crowd. Scrambling to the top of it, he raised his arms, shouting, "Listen! Listen! The digs have killed some of us!" He shouted it again, and a few dwellers turned to stare at him. "Killed!" he roared. "And you wager! Is that all digger deaths signify?"

Hands were pulling at him; Harn and Zehops were urging him to come down. But he was done with indirection. Vod plugged into a data gate, and entered his fury. His words appeared in the flow: *Diggers will leave these tunnels wrapped in their kin rugs. Diggers who renew the ways for you. Where is the honor diggers have earned, to accept all risk to keep you safe?*

Across the PrimeWay, a familiar static turned from a data pedestal and gazed at him. Her sculpted face and fine oval lines were unmistakable: Nefer Ton Enkar. She was gated into the flow, but she was physically present, a stone's throw away from him.

"Run!" urged Zehops, while Harn tried to grab at him. Furiously, Vod shook off Harn's entreating hands.

Gated in, he read Nefer's message: *Bold words, gomin. But what can a digger's path mean to such as you, dressed in an unnatural's cloak?*

He answered: *We all share the Way. The Common Way.*

Truly? One has been confused, then, for all these spans. One thought a gomin tended to defilement, and a digger to—know his place.

You have indeed been confused, Nefer Ton Enkar.

She was watching him with a tunneling gaze. Beside her, a rustle of movement, and Vod saw her henchmen making for him. He fell backward into Harn's waiting arms, and they ran, with Harn plowing a path through the crowd.

"The SecondWay," hissed Zehops.

"No. The digs."

The three of them sprinted to an upway. Vod listened for the pounding of feet behind him, but, choosing a circuitous route, they lost their pursuers.

When they arrived at the digs, it was a scene of riot and confusion. The air was thick with dust and shouts. Dwellers ran in all directions, some bearing digging instruments, others helping the wounded. Blood and moans colored the scene.

Then Vod noticed flashes of white spotting the dark haze of the tunnel. Vod passed a gomin, covered with blood, helping a digger who could still walk. Gomin were in fact everywhere, shoveling, scrambling amid the rock and soil, some scooping the dirt out with their bare hands. By their sides, diggers in blackened and torn work clothes struggled mightily to clear the cave-in.

Harn grabbed a spade and began shoveling like one gone berserk.

Vod paused for a moment to savor the picture of these white robes of mercy amid the dirt and blood. Then he dove into the fray, digging for signs of life.

37

The rivers were swelling. Even as Sascha stood on her lookout watching the endless rain, she thought she could see the rivers eating into the forest floor. The ground could not absorb any more water. Soon the broad rivers would join hands and turn the Gray Spiny Forest into a vast swamp.

The nearest river was just within view. Over the last few days she had watched as animals hitched rides on broad leaves, tree branches, and other flotation devices, captives of the river's slow journey. Amphibs, she noted, were all but gone, their eggs by now fertilized and tucked into their wet beds with silty covers. The waters bristled with other swimmers, whose backs and tails emerged like probes from another world, then sank away from sight.

The world was changing, but as yet Sascha could not quite say how, except for the distended rivers. She herself was no longer what she had been. Her hair hung in grimy ropes around her face. Her skin was browned from the sun, and her belly cramped. It was a gravid swelling, an ache that bloomed and receded, and bloomed again. Her body had signaled her for days that it was changing, but she was too bruised from her fall on the ridge to realize that her first blood was coming. Not that she would have recognized what it was. . .

Now the final change came: the bot had left her.

Perhaps it was the sight of the rising rivers that convinced the bot to leave. If it was to fulfill its programming, it could travel faster on land than in a swamp. And, if it listened at all to her, she had given it her blessing to go.

Still, watching it trundling into the forest made her throat catch, a little.

Demon and the bot engaged in a mutual ignoring when the bot passed him. The lurking Singer was neither one thing nor the other to the bot: Demon might be ominous, but he was also a Singer like the nurturing Watchful. It had apparently resolved its dilemma by deciding Demon did not exist. The bot picked its way past him with an air of studied indifference, like a snub imparted to an old enemy.

When the bot left, it took her field notes, her record of all that happened, and her only human connection. The one to her father.

Last night she had told the bot, "Remember this: Lots of the rocks and pebbles we saw in the dry season were really pods and eggs. The Singer nest is littered with their cracked shells, so the disguise doesn't fool them, at least. When we came here, we didn't pay attention. We went by what infantry said, that in three years it never rained. We never thought there might be different length cycles—years-long cycles. We saw what we expected to. There's probably lots of times like that, when we don't see things as they really are. I wonder what we could discover about all the worlds if we could look past what we expect. Or would that ever be possible?"

That was her last entry. The rest of her notes contained her every observation about the Singers, surely the most interesting animal she had yet seen. Perhaps their bearing of ahtran young was an important scientific discovery. All this went forth with the bot.

But did the bot remember anything, regard anything, she said?

Just before the machine disappeared into the forest, Sascha called out to it, through the silver wash of rain, "Bot of Congress Worlds!" Her voice sounded like the screech of a bird, high-pitched and nonsensical. From below, Demon raised his face to stare at her, rainwater cascading off his huge face.

She thought she saw the bot stop by a stand of trees. In the distance its dark matte housing looked like water in shadow, like a tunnel in vines. She imagined it turned around to regard her, but logically she knew it had no need to turn around to see her.

"Remember me!" she called out. *Remember me.*

The flash of undergrowth, the parting of vines. The bot was gone.

Later that day, when Sascha tried to nuzzle against Watchful's shoulder to drink, the Singer gently but firmly pushed her away. The push was a light one, but Sascha found herself sprawled on the floor of the sodden nest. When she tried again a few minutes later, Watchful pushed again, eyeing her with annoyance, humming a new tune.

But then, when Sascha looked more closely, she saw that there was no milk in the grooves of the Singer's skin anyway.

Eli and his squad stood on the bank, gazing at the river. It was more of a slow-moving flood than a river. But they would have to cross it.

Each hour the water rose, as the barrage of rain added

tons of water to its volume. Carried along on its surface was a dense cargo of leaves and vines and shards of fruit, and an occasional animal passenger.

Bad enough, the crossing of such a wide expanse of water, and now there was Pig's injury to compound their dilemma. Pig had made the mistake of sitting on a rock to rest. When the rock unrolled its carapaced surface, the animal whose shell it was had time to latch on to Pig's hip before he bolted. Despite the fibrin patch with its clotting agents, their hard march kept the wound ripped fresh. The smell of his blood drew attention, though Pig dutifully stuffed himself with yellow polyps. Vecchi now went armed, with Pig struggling mightily to keep up, with a makeshift crutch. Nazim kept the domino gun, though it was nearly as big as she was.

But the bot took no interest in bridge-building, despite the pointed suggestions of the enlisteds. Nazim coached it with her repertoire of mind-curdling epitaphs, but nothing could force the construct to depart from its own AI logic. The gist of it seemed to be: *River. Dangerous.*

Eli peered through the lashing rain to look up at the steep hills, considering a trek closer to them, where the river might be narrower. Juric said the hills did have narrower streams, but they were also deeper, cradled in the folded gullies.

It was at that moment that they saw the ahtra. Appearing out of the foliage on the other side of the river, the figure stopped and gazed at them through a tight scrim of rain.

Vecchi's gun snapped into position, but he stood behind the others and delayed his shot.

"Easy now," Eli said. He nodded at Vecchi, and the man lowered his weapon with insolent slowness.

The ahtra looked small at this distance—all muscle and dark hide, like an animal, but in torn clothing, carrying a mav. Eli squinted hard to see its facial markings, scanning for the cheek swirls of Maret Din Kharon, but such detail was lost at this distance. No reason it should be Maret.

The ahtra stood still, watching them. Then the individual raised a hand in a sideways salute and set off again. In another moment the figure was gone. Though he couldn't be sure, Eli thought the raised hand was a gesture of greeting aimed at him.

When he turned to face his four companions, there was no doubt *they* thought it had been for him.

Juric's face streamed water as he gazed at the place where the ahtra had disappeared. "Now, that was a right friendly gesture." His voice was casual, unlike his stare.

"Pocks for friends," Vecchi mumbled.

"Twenty-three," Pig's voice came, causing Vecchi to twitch.

Nazim was still pointing the domino across the river, as though she expected a swarm of ahtra to appear. By her expression she had the same doubts as the rest of them about why the ahtra were here. Eli's explanation of the ahtran tradition of mating UpWorld left out the role of the vone, but it was all they needed to know right now of information that was for Command's ears, first. They all knew there was more than he was telling. Their worst suspicion might be that he'd made friends with pocks. It left an uneasy feeling among them, but the river was their problem now, not personal regard for their commander. They didn't have to love him, just follow him.

He peered at the moving green hide of the river. Eli guessed that the river was shallow enough to wade. But even if forced to swim, they must cross it, and soon. So far the only initiative the bot had taken was to incinerate any creatures floating by within jumping distance. A bot on automatic was no strategist. Lacking any clear enemy it took a strictly defensive posture. If the AI programming couldn't formulate a sensible goal besides *preserve, protect,* they might well sit at the river's edge until starvation—or something worse—took them.

He made up his mind. He'd force the issue with their metal bodyguard.

Juric, also staring at the river, muttered low, "Too bad that pock didn't throw us a rope."

Eli let Juric's comment pass. "We'll cross, Sergeant."

Nazim overheard, giving him a nervous look.

"It'd take the bot all day to build a bridge, if it ever does. So we'll have to wade."

He challenged Juric to say something. If the man was going to break ranks, he'd rather know sooner than later. But the sergeant's bifurcated gaze was steady, both sides.

"I'll go in first," Eli said. "Maybe the bot will figure out how to defend me." He turned to the quiescent AI. "Let's see what it's got in its toolbox."

Nazim stepped forward. "Begging the officer's pardon, but why not send Vecchi? He's useless, anyway." As if in proof of her statement, Vecchi lay face-first in the mud, exhausted from his push-ups.

Eli answered, "Because I'm the only one that doesn't smell like liver pâté to the sharks, Corporal. I might walk out alive, but he won't."

Vecchi turned a muddy face to Eli, looking startled at his good fortune.

Juric muttered, "You go down, that dog can't help you."

"That happens, Sergeant, you will carry out my orders in all detail. That includes not firing on the ahtra." He figured Juric might need reminding.

"Sir." The sergeant nodded, scowling in what might have been pain from his lacerated arm, or simple contempt.

Trying to defuse the tension among the five of them, Eli repeated the old army maxim, "A good plan now is better than a great plan later." By the expressions on their faces, he could see they rated his plan something lower than *good*.

The bot was still watching where the ahtra had last been seen. Eli gave a whistle, and the bot turned its head, surprisingly like a dog.

"Sir." Nazim's voice, behind him.

He turned.

After a pause she mumbled, "Good luck, sir."

He nodded at her, grateful for the goodwill. Then he waded into the pulpy water.

The bot trundled closer to the shore, watching. It whirred—Eli could hear it whirring as he pushed through the mat of vines at the surface. The river pushed at his legs, embracing him, sending a chill through him. Surprisingly cold, that water. Things brushed against his submerged shins as he pushed farther in, going deeper than he hoped he'd have to.

To kick-start the AI's thinking, Eli shouted and waved his arms.

In the next instant the bot laid down a salvo of pellets that hit the water in a pattern around Eli. He just had time to plug his ears with his fingers when the brindled hide of the river clutched into a convulsive seizure from the sonic blast.

Eli staggered, and fell to his knees. His ears reamed out and aching, he tried to turn around as he heard thrashing noises behind him. Then he felt himself lifted up, Juric on one side, Nazim on the other. They dragged him along, his legs useless beneath him. Before them, Pig was clearing a swath, like an icebreaking vessel through an arctic shelf.

Alongside, the bot had extended an extra dozen legs, daintily tiptoeing atop the river's green lid.

38

🌿

Vod rushed up to PrimeWay to see if the rumor was true.
With Zehops by his side, he saw that it was: a procession
of the dead wound its way down the center of PrimeWay,
against all tradition.

It was a long procession, for the jaws of DownWorld
had swallowed fifty lives. Rolled rugs on the shoulders of
diggers told, in clear and ancient patterns, the lineage of
those gone to live in the great Well. The PrimeWay fell to
silence. The tread of those bearing rugs thudded in unison,
like a drumbeat. *Rugs we will never see again . . . never see
again.* Dwellers turned from the data nubs, and even the
data stewards stood at full respectful attention. Some by-
standers averted their eyes, unaccustomed to displays of
death. But no one could escape the heavy tread of the long
parade.

Then, as Vod and Zehops watched, the gomin began to
proliferate.

White robes flickered throughout the Way. A few more
than usual, more than might normally be seen in the Way

at any one time. Here a cluster of white, there another pocket, and there.

Zehops noticed it first. "Cousins I never knew I had," she whispered.

From many portals flowed streams of white. Colors winked in the folds of fabric, charging the Way with a nontraditional glitter.

Seeing some of the gomin at closer range, Vod said, "No cousins of yours, Zehops-as. These are diggers."

"But cousins indeed," she chided him. All the packages of robes given out, that Vod had thought were cast away, were now in full use. He saw diggers he knew well: Ooan, Belah, Hute, Irran . . . and joined by gomin now, all surging into the crowd, saying, better than any speech, *As dwellers, we are one.*

Zehops gripped Vod's arm. "Now we begin."

Vod couldn't have been more astonished if the dead had rolled out of their rugs and walked in the way. It had always been said, *Dwellers do not change their patterns.* Now it might be said, *Tradition must give way to necessity.*

In his excitement, Vod found he had embraced Zehops, and she clung to him in turn. For his own part, it was with some heat. He inhaled her response, backmind saying, *Gomin, gomin,* foremind saying, *And so?*

Zehops pushed him away with good humor. "Later," she said. She pulled him into the crowd to join their white robes with the others.

Harn hailed them from a distance away, working the crowd—Vod's good lieutenant, now that Vod was the general. Or, as Zehops insisted, the Prime To Come.

The Way filled with voices. No one could be silent. Some gambled frantically in the wager fields, but most turned from the data plugs and spoke to their neighbors, their kin, every passing robe of white. Here and there insults pierced the clamor, and angry responses hurled back. These were no timid dwellers of the SecondWay to be censored and silenced.

Then every data screen within Vod's view went blank.

Hemms Pre Illtek appeared. A hundred faces of Hemms Pre Illtek, repeated down the Way in decreasing size.

Dwellers turned to stare. It had been long and long since the Extreme Prime had been seen in such a display. His face was puffy with distress. Though his markings were surely of the highest degree, it must be admitted that they were unfortunately pale for the season. His data tendril drifted to one side, sucking on a plug by which he dominated the flow, as was his extreme privilege.

He was pleading for calm. Vod saw how the Way deepened into quiet, dwellers mesmerized by the spectacle of Hemms condescending to speak so publicly.

Vod grumbled, "This will tend against us. Oh, to shut the fool up!"

Zehops set her mouth, watching the nearest screen.

". . . through normal streams in the flow," Hemms was saying. "So we have our immemorial converse in dignity and inwardness. No need, attend me, to drift toward such things as white robes and unnatural inclinations. Now, then. You will all tend to resume your normal clothing, as you are predisposed to be my faithful adherents, despite what one's servants may whisper in one's ear."

He closed his eyes, murmuring, "Rumors and lies . . ." Opening them again, his color improved. "But one knows that you love us, and would not flaunt my will. So then, one will be waiting to see such things relent, and you all return to your places and your habitual garments. Though where such robes can have come from deeply disturbs one."

His tendril jerked, as though in a spasm. "Yes, white robes . . . While one thought you had been content with your natural work and the exigencies of the Season, now one finds looms have been busy with white robes. Gomin robes!" The Extreme Prime's color faded to chalk. "This, one will not tolerate. No looms will produce white cloth. That is what one meant to say from the first. No looms will produce unnatural cloth. Perhaps if one had made this clear earlier, one could be spared such an aggravation." His voice swerved upward. "One will know what colors your looms bear. My servants will inspect all looms, and we must find no white cloth, attend me!"

Now the PrimeWay filled with low rumbles of talk, angry muttering and halfhearted cheers.

Hemms' attendants could be seen trying to pluck at him from the side, but he irritably shook them off and continued with greater vigor.

"Who studies their kin nets among you? Who can recite the degrees, and so forth, and who among you can recite your high prime's net to the twelfth? All, all, attend me, should do so! Should be able to do so, and would be more fitting a demonstration than white robes and carping on a few rugs rolled in the tunnels!"

Shouts of derision greeted this shocking statement, and Vod whispered to Zehops, "He is digging his own doom." He looked about him at the astonishing spectacle of dwellers grumbling about their Extreme Prime.

Meanwhile, the screens showed frantic grabbing at Hemms' sleeves. Hemms looked at the side, as though his own servants were his enemies. "Yes, even you, you short-tendriled progeny of vanishing bloodlines. Stand back and recite!" He was bellowing and waving one moment and the next his voice trailed off as he looked to one side. Dismay crept over his drained face. In a weaker, more uncertain voice, he continued: "All . . . kin nets . . . to the twelfth degree . . . in proper respect . . .

The screen went to black.

When it came back on, it was Nefer Ton Enkar's face on every screen.

"One is very deeply sorry to note Hemms in poor health, as you observed." A slight dusting of snuff still dotted her upper lip, such had been her haste to seize the moment.

"Hemms must surely regret his regrettable comments about our sacred dead. One is distressed by such—illness— which must excuse him from censure. And from his duties. It is one's happenstance to become your Extreme Prime during this—temporary, one is sure—lapse."

Behind him, Vod heard Zehops moan. Now, in the Way, a melee broke out, and hands were raised against the demonstrators. In a single stroke, Nefer had stolen the moment, turned the crowd from rebellion back to tradition. A blow landed on Vod's shoulder. His companions shielded him, moving him toward the nearest portal, as Vod saw his advantage squandered.

As ever, DownWorld loved its stability—even if it meant choking to death on it.

Rushing toward the refuge of the SecondWay, the three of them could hear Nefer's voice trailing behind them: "One has never looked to lead, but only to serve. . . ."

They fled the purring of her voice. But it was everywhere.

39

Three ahtra lay dead at Juric's feet. He knelt next to one of the bodies, examining the wounds.

"Bot-fire, sir."

Eli turned to look at the bot at his side: an innocent bot—if such a concept could be applied. This bot hadn't been out of their sight for days.

Nonplussed by the sudden attention, the AI peeled off a slug of fire at a scavenger creeping back to resume its meal on the ahtra.

Vecchi and Pig stood guard, eyeing the bodies and the hexadron, perhaps thinking how close these three ahtra had been to safety, only to be cut down. Or maybe just seeing dead enemies.

Looking at the mangled bodies, Eli thought how vulnerable the ahtra were, to put themselves in harm's way every four years, their cyclical war of procreation. Maret had said even the ahtra world ships sent shuttles home bearing the latest candidates for ronid, receiving the shuttles at a well-hidden portal to DownWorld. So this home

world was the ahtra Achilles' heal. They needed UpWorld
and its season. Once Congress Worlds knew this, the tide
of war might well change.

*Which will force Nefer to launch her ships sooner rather
than later . . .*

Nazim appeared from behind a small copse of trees.
"Found it, sir."

The second bot trudged forward, at her side. Its housing was punctuated on all sides by a full array of armament. Vines and moss hung around it, dragging behind it
like the tattered wraps of a mummy. To Eli it looked weary
beyond caring. And guilty as hell.

"No one else around, sir," she reported, crushing any
hopes they might have had for human survivors accompa-
nying the bot. But from the expression on her face, it was
clear that Nazim considered the bot a wild stroke of good
fortune.

The second bot trundled toward their own bot as though
happy to see it. The AIs rustled with movement. Eli saw
the new bot extend a narrow cylinder, inserting it into a
port in the other bot. They were exchanging information.

No.

Eli strode forward, aiming a hard kick at the bridge between them, hoping to break the contact. It held with im-
pervious strength.

A fresh nozzle emerged from the new bot, pointing at
Eli.

Swiftly, Nazim aimed the domino at the machine. "Order, Captain? I can melt this bucket of bolts."

But already the bot's threatening tube had retracted,
then the bridge between the two machines.

"Never mind," Eli muttered. "Too late."

Juric and the others looked at him in confusion.

"This bot has got it figured out," Eli said. "About the
enemy. Who it is."

Pig stepped back from the bots as though he thought it might be *him* they decided on.

"Only problem is," Eli said, "the bot's got it wrong." He looked with a kind of sadness at the new bot. "And now he's told *our* bot."

The soldiers shuffled uncomfortably, waiting for their superior to make sense of things. All but Juric. He was watching Eli all this time. "No act of war," he said, "if our machines go nuts."

Juric got it, of course. Nailed it.

Eli spoke low and steady. "These bots are under my command. I'm responsible for what they do. And what they *will* do." On automatic, the AIs were. To be sure. There was that little detail, but it wouldn't absolve humans from the blame for a clear act of war. Eli turned away from the group and walked a short distance to clear his head.

If ahtra saw that CW bots had attacked their people—had attacked them during ronid—oh, the fury Miss Nefer could whip up. A clear act of aggression. How many had the bot already killed?

Nazim, Pig, and Vecchi eyed him nervously. Something was up. And they suspected that they weren't going to like it.

A narrow shadow fell across him. Juric stood there.

The sergeant sat down, bracing his gun on his knee, light winking *armed,* muzzle pointing down-valley. He spat out a wad of fiber, residue of the yellow polyps. As a comment, it was eloquent enough. "Dead pocks never were a problem, far as I ever knew."

"They're a problem *now,* Sergeant."

Juric's regen side was toward Eli, making him about as easy to read as a bot. "The peace," Juric said, making it sound like a wad of polyp fiber.

A jagged wall of dust arose from down-valley. It looked

like a curtain of orange rain, a spasm of dust, in an atmosphere scoured of dust every few hours. But Eli had seen the like before. It was an enormous cloud of insects, all hatched at once to improve their mating success.

"How many enlisteds have you seen die, Sergeant?"

The scent of rain rode the air, making each breath heavy. "Enough," Juric answered.

Eli thought of the battles the man had known. It was a full list, holding a lot of blood.

"Is it? Enough?" Eli still gazed out at the plume of insects.

"Not a matter of what I think."

Oh, but it was. Now it was. The master sergeant must concur. Two officers or two noncoms, or one of each, was what it took to decommission a bot in the field, if put on automatic. If AIs were put on automatic, it meant desperate straits. So it would take more-than-ordinary measures to stand them down. So it was very much a matter of what Sergeant Juric thought. What he thought of *Eli*, most of all.

Eli went on, "How many you figure will die if the ahtra avenge their dead here?"

It was a clear and ugly choice: pull the plug on the AIs, and maybe not make it back to the ship. Or leave the two killing machines free to sweep the area of pocks.

Juric hadn't blinked for a very long time. That side didn't blink very much. Eventually the master sergeant said, "Guess us five don't matter, live or dead."

Eli wouldn't have put it like that. They mattered. But soldiers got paid to die, every one of them knew that. Now maybe they'd earn their pay.

Clouds scudded overhead, as though fleeing from something up-valley. Their shadows swept over Eli and his troops, bringing a few seconds of relief from the dual blaze of the suns. Rains would form up again, within a couple hours.

Eli set out the choice, saying it simply. "Figure a short trek will kill us without the AIs?"

"Done a good job so far."

"Yes. Cut us down to five. Three Transport, two Infantry." He would have had it otherwise, but it was as Maret had said. "The worst of us in the whole unit. That's who's left. The meanest, most self-serving, paranoid bastards of both divisions."

Juric turned a quick look on Eli, what might have been a smile of relish at the edge of his mouth. "Maybe so. Maybe we are." He looked in the direction of Nazim, Pig, and Vecchi. "Good enough to get two miles, or die trying."

As they gazed down-valley, a band of rippers could be seen galloping after something, all in silence at this distance.

Juric stood up, the act taking a little longer than it had in the other direction.

Eli knew Juric had no reason to love him; much the opposite. But the man was looking at him long and steady, maybe trying to take the measure of this captain as Eli was of the sergeant.

Then Juric nodded, his voice low and calm. "You ready to put those dogs down?"

Eli hoped he didn't show his relief. He covered by getting to his feet and brushing the dust from his uniform. "I'm ready, Sergeant."

They passed the enlisteds, who watched them, brows wrinkled.

As they approached the two AIs, one of the bots backed up a step. It wouldn't do to ascribe human motives to them, of course.

Juric stepped close to the bot, placing his hand on the command panel. "Too stupid to know an enemy when it sees one." He grinned at the unit. "Me."

The panel was reading the sergeant's DNA.

The thought came to Eli as he reached out to the bot's panel: *Were you with Sascha? Did you see her die? Was she dead?* The thought still nagged at him, that she might be out there somewhere. . . .

From deep inside the bot issued a high, stinging tone of the processors deactivating. Having read Eli's genetic signature, it stood down.

The other bot—the one they thought of as "theirs"— also went meekly into sleep mode, emitting its own long whine, and then what sounded like a shudder, it seemed to Eli, of relief.

Then they left the bots behind, resuming their journey, with Eli on point, four good soldiers coming behind.

Along the perimeter of the woody den, Sascha dug another hole and buried the soft, bloody moss. In the torrential rains, the moss would soon have been clean again to use against her body, but moss was plentiful, and she feared the smell of blood would draw predators—those witless enough to enter the den of the king predators. There had been a few, to the delight of the Singers.

Madame Singer had left at first light, as was her habit. The others sat in the pitiless rain, watching the tumble play of the three youngsters, whose main targets of mock battle were each other and Brat. Watchful sat her place, chewing on a haunch of meat while observing Sascha digging her hole, blinking now and again to wash the rain from her eyes. Watchful hadn't left the nest for days, acting irritable, staring at Sascha as though brooding over some awful lapse.

Sascha patted mud over the hole and pulled the vines back into place. The odor of rich mud mixed with the smell of Singer dung and the overripe fruit that had become her diet staple. She inhaled the soupy air, almost nourishment in itself, it was so heavy. She stood, wiping her muddy hands on her shirt. She imagined her mother's disapproving look. A lady did not wipe her hands on her clothes. And she was now, in truth, a lady, a woman grown. Not a feral child.

She longed to be clean again. The clothes she had worn for weeks were rotting from her frame. The buttons of her shirt were long gone. It was a simple matter to have done with the tattered things. As she freed herself from her shirt and long pants, they tore like seaweed. She stood naked in the forest shower, wearing only her boots and lantern, letting the rain pelt her skin while Watchful put down the bone she was gnawing on and stared as though she had never seen a naked human before.

Around Sascha the rain clattered, needling the leaves and puddles of the bower and the deeper woods. The sound was almost the crackle of fire, a conflagration feasting on the Gray Spiny Forest.

With her eyes closed, the sound became the roar of a two-man log in the great fireplace of the family hall. In another life she would have known her body's change in a different way. With silk, and white velvet, and the creamy pearls of her maternal grandmother's necklace. With tables of savory dishes, with meaty main courses, buttery side dishes, with food as decoration: carved, julienned, fanned, layered, and molded. Iced smallcakes heavy with candied fruits. Mutton and fragrant cheeses and shellfish stews with great loaves of herb bread. The young men, stiff in Officer Candidate uniforms too heavy to sit in, would be nudged on by their fathers to make nice to Sascha Jaizelle Olander. Her hair would glitter with spikes of light from a jeweled hair net, and at her bosom the symbolic long pin, resting in her gown's fabric, capped with a diamond. In the old days, one drew out the pin at one's breast and drove it into the eye of a conqueror taking

spoils. So her grandmother had told her with relish, knowing that Sascha thought the young bucks in their uniforms
both silly and threatening.

The nest occupants were on edge, humming shrilly.
Everyone had been upset since the death of Triplet's baby.
They let Sascha bury it, but regarded her with something
that felt like blame.

Now, one of the youngsters was at Sascha's elbow.
In the clatter of rain, Sascha hadn't heard it approach. He
snatched a fruit that she had by her side, scampering off,
shredding the pod in a trail of yellow pulp. Casting the seed
stone aside, he collected his two siblings, and the three of
them bounded viciously toward her.

She rose, clutching her lamp. Flipping it on, she sprayed
them with light, causing one of them to veer away. The
other two slowed, but advanced.

They had grown during her stay here. Now they
needn't stretch their necks far to look her in the eye. She
shouldn't have stared at the lead youngster, it inspired him
to move. He leapt forward, but collided with his sibling
who had the same aggressive thought. As they extricated
themselves from their tangle, Sascha backed up toward
the nest wall to protect her back.

Now Brat was among them, droning in excitement,
shoving them with his long arms, but playfully. One of
the young ones bit him. This wasn't play anymore. Brat
screamed, and Triplet's head rose from the nest. Her hum
filled the enclosure, a short burst of melody. The three siblings now advanced on Sascha, heedless of Triplet's song.
Brat worried the hind legs of one of them, and a small skirmish broke out, sending hums through the nest and causing the vines to tremble with the noise.

Sascha's ever-present light was losing its power over
the youngsters. Now it was only a direct pulse of light
that made any difference. She swerved her lamp from one

to the other of the two foremost creatures. They moved apart to make it harder for her, circling to each side.

Behind the woody wall in back of her, she could hear the droning bass thrums of Demon, always a counterpoint to the events in the nest.

The cubs charged. Simultaneously, Watchful erupted from her placid seat. Sascha had never seen her move so fast. She vaulted, her hum pitched so high it sliced painfully into Sascha's ears. The floor of the nest trembled with her landing, and she crashed forward, ripping up vines and hurtling them at the youngsters, smashing a paw into Triplet's face as the mother advanced to protect her young.

The three young ones fled to the farther side of the enclosure as Watchful stomped and screamed. Triplet relinquished the center of the nest to Watchful, who raised her head and sent a long, soaring note into the sky. Every Singer now stood frozen, staring at the old denizen. A stream of drool fell from the side of her mouth as she stood there, panting at her exertions.

The uproar was over. Now Watchful turned her great blue eyes to stare down on Sascha. Sascha waited, stick-still. Something in the eyes of her protector had fled.

Watchful advanced toward her. It was a slow, jerky advance, punctuated by hard stomps of her great feet. Sascha knew to back up. And then Watchful moved to one side, forcing Sascha to retreat along the perimeter of the nest. The creature was still panting, her warm breath hitting Sascha in the face, smelling of baking bread. They were headed in the direction of the back door.

Watchful stomped closer, sending Sascha into the opening in the viney wall. The Singer stomped again, leaving no doubt that Sascha's welcome had run out.

Sascha stood on the border between den and forest. Her mouth parted, to say something to Watchful. But what could she say? *I'm sorry for the blood. I never meant for it to come.*

Now it had. And just as she had always feared: disastrously.

Sascha turned from the Singer and walked through the hole in the nest wall.

Demon was waiting.

40

Vod stood up from the watch he had been keeping over Ooan, fellow digger, erstwhile rebel for such a brief span. The physiopath disconnected the tube in Ooan's windpipe. There was need of it elsewhere, as dozens of fluxors lay here in the SecondWay, driven from the usual ways and bloodied from skirmishes.

At his side, Harn muttered, "Another rug we will never see again."

Vod heard the message below the words, *We are dying, fluxors are dying, while you wait.*

The sick lobe was crowded, overflowing into the narrow tunnels of the gomins' secret world. Vod went from pallet to pallet, encouraging the wounded, paying respects, while Harn kept to his side like a bad conscience.

Nefer had used restraint against those flaunting gomin robes—she was no fool to provoke a reaction among the fluxors—but when she made a show of her troops in the PrimeWay, the fluxors, in an excess of zeal, provoked her guards, who retaliated. There followed a surge of agitated statics who moved against gomin sector, and deaths occurred.

Zehops then opened the SecondWay to the wounded, perhaps jeopardizing the ancient gomin retreat, but proving her mettle. Now fluxor guards stood at every hidden portal into the SecondWay. Well, Vod reasoned, if they had not gained much, they were at least holding on.

Vod and Harn walked the crowded tunnels, barely able to pass among the pallets and those ministering. Voices echoed strangely in these ways devoid of the hab, where smooth, unfeeling walls seemed more like tubes than home.

This is the ThirdWay, Vod thought. No longer a hideout for gomin, it was now the gallery of his revolution.

But Harn interrupted his reverie, boring home his point. "How long will you wait, Vod-as? If they but knew, they'd turn on her faster than you can say *Nefer Ton Enkar*."

He'd heard it before. He'd said no before. But Harn would not leave his side, and there was no lobe of privacy, no escaping Harn's voice.

Vod answered, "What ships she has, she'll launch. And then what will we have loosed?"

Nefer wasn't ready. If she were, her ships would have burst through their confinement DownWorld and be cruising the Neymium Belt by now. Harn made a sour look, not wanting to hear the rest. "Then we'll have a new enemy: Congress Worlds. Where will our struggle be then? Backminded, Harn-as, backminded."

Vod accepted a morsel of food from a digger in a tattered white robe. They served him as though he were their prime leader, they looked to him for answers, for direction. He thought they would not long follow him if they comprehended how little he knew, how little he had of the certainty they needed. He nodded in courtesy at the digger, as though the plate of food was his due, acting the part even in front of Harn.

"You talk of containing her, Vod-as," Harn responded, "but she is containing us! She is controlling us, controlling you. The longer we wait, the more flock to her. We need to be outward, as she is!"

"That is a wager we'd lose. How many turned on Nefer's guards to protect us? How many urged against Nefer in the flow? Plug in, Harn-as, wager for our cause, see how many join you." He locked gazes with his co-worker. Then, challenging him, he cocked his head to a data trunk clinging to the wall. Harn looked at the trunk, then at the floor, acquiescing.

They had been in the flow, reading its crests and surges. Every span, Vod was plugged in, contending with the self-styled Extreme Prime. He fought Nefer for the fore and backminds of the dwellers, a battleground where he could test himself without ultimate risk. He and Nefer traded speech for speech, argument for argument. This struggle dominated the flow, with Vod reminding the dwellers of the many dead from the reign of Hemms-Nefer, the many injustices endured by the gomin.

But it wasn't enough. He must give the dwellers more than digger and gomin grievances. There had always been digger deaths. They sacrificed so that others could dwell in security. It would be tradition.

For revolution he must have something more powerful than complaint. He must have a vision. A vision tied to the prosperity of the kin nets and the strength of the blood-lines.

There grew within him a vision of a new time of out-wardness; of a new alliance with humans. Ahtra security would be based not on arms, but on trade and renewal. It would extend beyond DownWorld, encompassing the FarReaches, their galactic home. It was not, he admitted, the absolute security Nefer promised. It was relational, a process of ahtra becoming secure in relation to human security. As the Data Guides said, all matter, all life was a process. No thing was fundamental in itself. There is no foolproof security. It made Zehops and Harn nervous for him to say these things publicly. But it was his vision.

He might be no philosopher, but it would have to do.

Down the way, he saw Zehops hurrying toward him. For all her personal courage, he saw her pale for the first time. *Well, if Zehops falters, she brings a dark strand of news, indeed,* he thought.

"Come," she said, breathlessly.

"With arms?" Harn asked, clearly sharing Vod's alarm.

"Just hurry!" she urged. Dwellers, those who could walk, followed the three of them in a jumble of voices. Weapons were drawn, rumors flowed, and the odor of fear stained the air. "An army . . ." someone said. Vod and Harn were running now, close on the heels of Zehops Cer Aton.

They came to a hidden entrance, tucked in the back of a lobe. The guards stood aside, and Vod and his companions crawled through.

They were in Zehops' den.

Now, with the clamor of the Second Way muted, they stood in the quiet apartment, looking to Zehops for the cause of such a rush.

She took Vod by the arm, murmuring, "We ran out of robes."

As he turned into the way, a ribbon of light caught his eye. Down the path were two bright ranks of dwellers, lined against the hab walls, in military order. Stretching to the next bend in the way stood dwellers wearing armbands of white, holding such weapons as mavs and knives, and lengths of hose. Slowly turning in the other direction, Vod saw the same banners extending to the limit of sight.

He caught Harn's slow blink. They were witnessing the gathering of his army. The White.

Zehops whispered in his ear: "Say something to them."

He *was* trying. But his voice had fled.

Turning to Harn, he murmured, "Now we will move against her." Harn nodded.

"But first, I'll talk to them, one-on-one. You, Harn-as, walk down the way, speak to them, know their names."

Harn smiled, and turned to the fluxor beside him, first in line.

Vod and Zehops walked the other way, taking the long walk down the length of the armed ranks, learning their names.

41

They crept through the night, not stopping to rest, the five of them, the last of the contingent of the *Lucia* and the *Fury*. With Juric and Pig wounded, the defense fell to Eli, Nazim, and Vecchi. Vecchi fought like a madman, an ahtra mav in one hand, an L-31 in the other, firing alternately, or two-fisted, at anything that moved.

By dawn they were staggering, and pressing on through a light rain that evaporated under the crushing light of the two suns. Juric looked like the walking dead, his face rigid and blanched. His arm smelled like it had been dead a long time.

Then they heard Vecchi shouting up ahead. Nazim strode forward, the domino raised for action. In another moment she was back.

"Sir. It's there." Her grin looked positively feral. "The *Lucia*."

They walked out of the tall grass to see Pig standing at the edge of the clearing, gazing on the *Lucia* with something close to religious rapture. Vecchi was prancing around the ship, slapping its sides and hooting. Even to

Eli the squat, gray transport ship was a vision of beauty. The industrial housings of the external modules were sculptured and symmetrical. A profusion of rivets dotted the craft like stitchery, interrupted by tanks, ports, casings, feed lines, forward and aft fuel tanks, and landing/take-off assemblies. A work of Congress Worlds art.

And swarming with vines.

Vecchi jumped up and swung on one of them that draped from the radio array. He warbled like Tarzan, then jumped down, managing to convey his thoughts without accumulating push-ups.

"That will do, Private," Eli said, grinning despite himself.

"Goddamn fool," Juric muttered. He eyed the perimeter of the clearing, as though expecting one last assault from Null.

"We have made it," Pig pronounced solemnly. He looked like he might cry.

A quarter mile off, the remains of the *Fury* protruded from the rampant green. It might have been in a previous life when Eli had stood here last, gazing at that ruined ship, thinking that his unpleasant duty was to know whether it had failed with honor or without.

The world had changed since then. As had his duty.

Nazim called to Eli from a short distance away, where she knelt in the grass.

When Eli joined her, he saw the remains of a soldier. Nazim examined the ID chip. "Corporal Nuninga, Infantry."

Vecchi raised his hand, jumping with excitement.

Eli nodded at him.

"That's Bill Nuninga, Captain, he went with Captain Marzano, he was one of her unit that went to bring in the ship." He stared down at the gnawed bones. "He got chomped ten feet from the fucking ship!"

Pig frowned at the volley of words. Looking at him

with fiendish delight, Vecchi continued, "Ten feet from the fucking ship!" To shut him up, Juric set him to cutting away the vines probing the ship's vents and nozzles as he and Nazim searched the grass, finding three more bodies.

Then, with Pig standing watch toward the sea of grass around them, Eli, Juric, and Nazim clanked up the access ramp of the ship. Nazim touched the commands into the hatchway panel. The ship crooned a smooth, panel-release sound, and the hatchway slid open.

The fetid odor of putrefaction met them. As Nazim turned right toward crew quarters, Eli and Juric headed left down the grated corridor to the flight deck. They passed the blackened scar of plasma fire on the bulkhead, and Eli steeled himself for a view of the flight controls. But as they came onto the bridge, another sight commanded their attention.

There on the floor, propped up against the back of the navigator chair, sat Luce Marzano, dead a week or more. Her body bore savage wounds. An L-31 lay in her lap, one of her hands still fixed on the trigger.

Eli's heart felt inert in his chest. He'd had no reason to believe that Marzano had survived, but it hadn't stopped him from hoping.

The flight deck instrumentation looked in good order. Chances were, the ship was serviceable. They would go home. Some of them.

Juric knelt next to the body, where he picked up a folded wad of paper.

"Sir." He stood, handing it over to Eli.

One side was a ship readout. On the other was a scrawling note, written in pencil.

He read through it once. Then he turned and gazed out the nearest flight-deck port, encompassing a tidy circle of gray-green, brilliant in the tropical sun.

Then he read the note again.

Sitting in my own blood, guarding the hatch access. If my people come through that hatch, I'll kill them. In their favor, it was a bad seven miles, about the worst any of these young patches ever saw, and no sleep for three days, so they went a little nuts. No excuse.

We lost half our number in the first day. Hard slogging. Bad rivers. Came upon a great humming beast who killed Veracruz. The patches were crazy with fear. It made a likeness of Hammond Farley, who they all knew. Seeing Farley, they couldn't fire, and they died, Privates Reese and Corulian. We fled while it ate them. The beast didn't follow us, but one by one we went down. By the time we crossed the last river we were six in number, and so tired we were careless. Private Loeb walked right into the arms of a tall, wingless bird. The rains didn't stop. When we found the Lucia, they all thought we couldn't fly into the jagged valley of Charlie Camp and land. The men demanded to go home. All a little crazy, but I killed Private Nuninga when he turned his gun on me. I cleared the ship, but took a gut wound, then a slug in my hip, so I can't move. Nothing works from the waist down. Keep them from coming in the hatchway. Cold.

Sounds outside. I sent them out to die, God help me. Don't trust them anymore. Hope to outlast them.

Dying. Now, on my honor, tell you and swear my ship failed and limped into orbit. Decayed. Brought us down, is God's truth. No deserters. We were all ready to die for our Worlds. So we have.

God bring you to the ship, though it be

without Captain Eli Dammond, a brave man. The first to die. God bring you home.
  For Congress Worlds, Capt. L. Marzano.

Eli handed the paper to Sergeant Juric, who read it in silence, then passed it to the others when they came in from their duties.

As Eli stared out the port, Juric supervised the removal of Captain Marzano's remains to the body freezer.

Pig volunteered for meal prep. He coaxed the meal processors into cranking out beef stew, creamed corn, and apple pie. The standard gripe about army onboard beef stew was no bread. Processors never could make leavened bread. This time they ate in silence, no comments about the bread, grateful just for the stew, and their lives.

That accomplished, Eli called for systems checks, and Juric took over the control panels, one-handed, not trusting the job to anyone else. They lit up, real pretty.

From deep in the grasses, Maret watched the ship as the launch systems whined to life. Now that the humans had come, she faced a dilemma, whether to help them or not. She did not forget her promise to Eli Dammond. But then she had seen the bodies of the dwellers, massacred by Congress Worlds soldiers or their robotics.

Maret watched as, inside the ship, people passed in front of the ports in the forward cabin. One of them was Eli. Was this the same captain of ships that she had known Below? It was possible humans changed their patterns with ease, one guise among captors, another among their own.

She had waited here in the grass, knowing the survivors would come. When she saw them, she watched them intently as they searched the field, and cut vines away from the ship. They looked ugly and desperate, all but Eli. But no matter how hard she stared, their patterns became no clearer, her foremind became no more resolved.

Maret had come to tell Eli she had seen the young human, the girl that he hoped to save. And that the vone kept her.

She didn't think the vone capable of mercy. But perhaps more unfailingly than either human or ahtra, they recognized one of their own.

From the high ground where she had been walking, Sascha looked down on the swamp waters. Shafts of light plunged through the mosses and trees, spattering the water's surface with freckles of light. Standing in a deep well of sunshine, she let the heat dry her back. Butterflies alighted on her skin and hair, also drying themselves, as she had seen them do on the Singers. Perhaps by now she smelled like a Singer, or looked like one. She hoped so. In this world it was better to be one of its denizens than a foreigner.

For all that had happened, she couldn't blame the world itself, only that they had come here ignorant and unprepared. It was, like every living thing, wondrous and perfect in its own right. She hoped it wasn't a betrayal to think so.

She covered the body of the soldier with layers of moss. It was an imperfect burial that wouldn't last long, but it was the only respect she knew how to give the body after she had taken the clothes and the equipment. Nearby, the soldier's shirt now hung drying on tough, upright canes. Laid out before her on the ridge were a canteen, water-sanitization kit, utility knife, and handgun.

The flares four nights ago came from the west. She judged she was heading northwest along the ridgeline, not the right direction. But surrounded by teeming swamp waters, she had little choice but to follow the dry land. She hoped it would lead out of the forest. And before nightfall.

It seemed that Demon preferred the dry route as well. He had been following her all morning.

She looked along the spine of the ridge where, forty yards away, the creature stood, always keeping the same distance between them. He toyed with her. Maybe he wanted her to run, for the sport of it. She'd lose that race. Her defense was to ignore him, as she usually had in the nest. She might have used the L-31 against Demon. But the big weapon lay buried under the moss with its owner. It hadn't saved that soldier, and it would be heavy to carry. Besides, she saw how the forest creatures deferred to Demon, quieting and slinking away, or rushing head-long for the uncertain refuge of the waters just to avoid him. With this great beast a few paces away, her path was oddly safer.

It hurt that Watchful had turned on her. But Sascha knew she hadn't been entirely innocent. It wasn't long before she'd figured out that the old Singer needed a babe to nurture—still living with the bones of the real one as Watchful was—and Sascha had played along. She still remembered the rage in Watchful's face at having to confront the truth. That Sascha was no child. And no Singer.

The air colored with the green wings of butterflies as they arose from her back. Pulling on the army-issue shirt, she belted it with the soldier's web belt. Then she took a swig of water from the purified contents of the canteen and hooked it to the belt, stuffing the first-aide pouch in her breast pocket. Her boots were still better than what this private had worn, and with the shirt long enough to hang to her thighs, she had no need of the trousers. She had gone past the time she needed moss to catch her blood. She considered cutting her hair, now that she was a woman grown, but instead tied it behind her neck with a length of vine.

Around her for as far as she could see, lay the water-colored world of greens and browns, woven with silvered water. Amid the chittering of the forest animals she could hear Demon's humming, a more assured melody than when he had been an outsider, at the nest where Madame and Watchful held sway. Sascha thought she caught strands of song that she had taught Watchful, but oddly revised, decaying into other, deeper songs.

It occurred to her that at any time she could turn and walk toward Demon. She could choose her own moment. That choice calmed her nerves, and her dread of Demon evaporated in the streaming sun. All the worst had happened. Everything that she had hated to lose was already lost. Even Watchful's protection and the uneasy truce of the Singer nest had fallen away. Lost, too, was her bot, departed with all her research, perhaps to sink into a permanent slurry of mud. A calm sense of freedom coated her thoughts. It wasn't that she no longer cared. Indeed, she cared more than ever before. Each moment held all her care, her memories of her father, her observations of the watery world—held it all. If she stayed in this moment, and then this one, everything remained.

Her equipment thumped gently against her as she resumed her trek along the ridge. Her flashlight sprayed its light around her and she moved in an easy stride, hearing Demon's footfalls behind her.

By late afternoon she came to the end of the ridge, where it sloped gently toward swirling water.

The slope pulsed with movement. There in the shade afforded by the ridge, hundreds of amphibs slumbered. Heads bobbed up at her approach. The nearest ones jumped onto two legs, watching her, swaying. Long tongues darted out, tasting the air. Now the entire hillside stood up.

Sascha pointed her light, her heart thudding. Stopping transfixed, the nearest amphibs blinked into the light. Then advanced.

The ridge rumbled behind her. Whether it was the ground shaking or a rumbling sound in the air, she had no time to discern before she felt herself shoved to the ground. Demon passed by, stomping into the midst of the swarm.

In the next instant he was flicking the amphibs away with savage swipes of clawed hands. Sascha heard the whoosh of his jointed arms as he sliced the air and the amphibs' bodies. The water boiled as the farthest of them plopped into that refuge. Others were stomped beneath great, flat feet. Within moments the ground was littered with small bodies. Demon casually ate several as he watched the remnant leap into the river.

He turned then, eyes scanning for further assaults to his command of the ridge. But there was only Sascha. She shut off the lamp hanging by its strap on her chest. Demon hated her lamp, and she judged him in none too fine a mood as it was. The crenelated folds on his forehead quivered as he sampled the smells around him.

You don't smell too good yourself, she thought. Then, reliving the scene of the living hillside, she slumped to her knees, shivering. She looked up at the monster of the Sticks as it approached. But she couldn't move, and besides, it was far too late.

When his arm draped along the ground in front of her, she stared at its rough hide, its circular pockmarks. She knew the difference between Watchful and Demon, and considered her options. Then, making her choice, she climbed on Demon's arm.

Raising her up into the air, and tucking her against his body, he strode down the slope into the dark water.

*   *   *

Engines thundered, vibrating the flight deck. The whine of the hydraulics sang of systems at the ready. Sergeant Juric, still able—but barely—to sit copilot, toggled the switches for departure.

Eli had delayed as long as he could.

"Advisory check," he said over headset to Juric.

"Satisfactory," Juric responded. "Cabin pressure nominal."

"Nitrogen supply switch—on. Cabin vent complete."

"Crew secure? Corporal Nazim?"

From aft, at crew stations, "Yes, sir."

From Juric: "Main engine pressure at 93 percent."

"Looks good, Sergeant . . ." Eli stopped in mid report, his gaze caught by a movement in the field, in front of the ship.

"Stand by."

Then: "Throttle down, Sergeant."

"Sir?" from Juric.

It was an ahtra. Standing in view of the near port, a spot where the blast thrust would blacken the ground. Standing gazing at the ship, clothes fluttering in a brisk wind. In a clear human gesture, the ahtra beckoned.

Looking closer, he recognized her. It was Maret.

"Abort launch, Sergeant." He nodded at the port, as Juric leaned over him to stare, seeing what Eli saw, or seeing an ahtra, anyway.

Eli nodded to him. The sergeant powered down the engines, a twitch in his good cheek the only comment.

In another instant, the crew pounded up to the flight deck, stopping in the corridor, worried faces poking through the hatchway.

He turned to face them. "Corporal Nazim," he said. "Here is an ahtra that we will have reason to speak with. Escort her to captain's quarters. With all courtesy."

"Sir," the astonished Nazim managed to say. Vecchi's

face had gone closed and narrow, while Pig looked like he
had just lost the last thought he ever owned.

She stood facing him, small and dark, eyes so large they
must take in a wider world than he could ever know. Her
skin markings, affording such excellent camouflage outside, set her into sharp relief against the bulkheads.

He reached out his hand. "Maret." It surprised him,
how much it pleased him to see her.

Looking at his hand, she answered, "Eli."

The low register of her voice made her hard to hear
when she spoke softly, as now: "You have done everything
we told you was impossible," she said. "It gives me two
happinesses to see you yet alive."

"And me, I'm more than glad. I never thought to see
you again." He couldn't know what she had endured, but
saw her scars, here and there. "Are you well? Would you
like water, anything?"

"No, but one thanks you."

Not wanting to embarrass her about ronid, he carefully said, "Do you have everything you hoped for?"

"Yes," was all she answered. She was looking around
his cabin, observing his personal space.

Seeing it from her perspective, he thought the place
should be more than it was. It had no decoration, no art,
nothing personal. A photo of his parents and brothers was
all. It was this she looked at for a long while. Then she
waved her hand at him. "Please sit down, Eli. You tend to
be too tall."

He sat and they faced each other in silence.

"Your people are not happy to see me, Eli."

He smiled. "They don't want to be here longer than
they have to."

"Neither do mine."

At her level stare, he knew her suspicions. The bots.

"We stopped them," he said. "We shut them down and left them disabled."

Her face acquired a softer expression, if he could remember from what now seemed a very long time ago, and very deep underground.

"But now we have a harder job," he said.

"War . . ." she said. "Your people dead. You must tell your generals we raised no hand against them."

He shook his head. "That doesn't matter now. Nefer has changed the game. Raised the stakes."

Maret closed her eyes for a moment, as though just the sound of her old nemesis' name brought dismay. She sat on the extra chair, hands resting on her knees. "Tell me."

He said what he knew, which was only as much as Tirinn had told him. They sat a long while in silence. Her skin had paled, and Eli realized how much better she looked in her clear, dark markings. Finally she said, "Vod has challenged her. Perhaps he will prevail." Her voice betrayed how likely she thought that was. "He demands fluxor rule. But such a thing has never been seen in ten-thousand cycles."

This was news. "How does Vod fare against her?"

She shrugged. "It has been three intervals since I had any news from those ascending."

"Go and lend him your support, Maret." He didn't know much about Vod, but he thought of Nefer and wondered who could prevail against her.

"Yes, one will, soon. But first, there is my promise to you. That I would help your people . . ." She blinked, one of those slow ahtran blinks.

"What is it, Maret?"

Another blink. Then: "The young one lives, Eli."

As his eyes locked on hers she continued, "The one you call Sascha Olander. I saw her."

He sat very still. He whispered, "Where?"

"In the OverWoods, in the nest of the vone."

His voice came out scrappy. "Nest?"

"Yes, in their kin grouping. They keep her."

He took a deep breath to replenish the air he'd been holding in his chest for the last while, maybe the last weeks.

"Tell me. Tell me what you saw."

He listened to her story—the gray-green swamp, the young human in the trees, with black ropes of hair—but in his heart, he was already on his way back to the forest.

The crew would not be happy about this.

The crew be damned.

It was news best told quickly. "We're going back," he said.

Nazim, Vecchi, and Pig stared at him, each with their own thoughts, but not hard to parse out. Juric slept on a bunk some paces away, finally collapsed. Maret waited outside, on the access ramp, Eli's concession to the crew's long history of killing ahtra and being killed by them.

He told them about the granddaughter of the general, alive out there in the woods. They didn't seem as relieved as he was.

Vecchi raised his hand. At Eli's nod, he said, "That pock could be lying. Sir."

"I judge otherwise, Private."

"It's a bloody pock!" Vecchi's mouth quivered with more words itching to get out.

"Shut up," Nazim snarled at him.

Vecchi turned on her as though she had struck him. "Shut up? Shut up? That's all I done is shut up for the last bloody ten miles!" He turned vacant, urgent eyes on each of them. "We'll never get home, you know? We'll never get out now. Pitch your tents, boys and girls, and slit your throats!"

Pig shook his head sadly. "Now you went and made me lose count."

"Enough, Private," Eli said.

"Enough? You think it's enough?" Vecchi looked startled, like a vessel had blown somewhere in his head. He turned, lunging for the gun belt slung on the post of the nearest cot.

Pig fumbled for a gun, but before he could fire, Vecchi stopped short, gulping.

He took a step backward. Swiveling around to face the others, he looked surprised. A knife protruded from the front of his neck. He ripped it out, clutching his bleeding throat, then sat abruptly on the bunk. Then he slid to the floor, slowly, as though careful not to hurt himself.

Juric was propped up by one elbow, staring at Vecchi as he twitched on the floor. "Should have killed him days ago," he mumbled.

Eli nodded at Nazim to attend to Vecchi. She went for a med kit, and by the time she got to work, Vecchi was unconscious. Nazim applied pressure to the wound, but it streamed blood between her fingers.

Juric managed to sit up on the edge of his bunk, cradling his arm and staring at his knife on the floor as though it were a damn shame he'd have to clean it again.

Pig was fumbling to get his pistol back in the holster.

Noticing, Juric caught Pig's eye. "Boy," he said almost gently. "No call to fire a gun shipboard, now, is there?"

"No, sir," Pig answered, eyes wide.

Juric nodded. "Just so you remember. We got a long flight home."

Nazim stood up from her position by Vecchi's body. "Dead, sir," she said to Eli.

"Chi Chi was scared shitless of going back out again. Guess he died anyway."

"Then he died for nothing," Eli said.

Pig looked at him, a furrow between his eyes.

"I'm going alone. I never thought to take any of you. That ahtra and I are going back for the girl by ourselves."

A coughing sound came from Juric's cot. He lay back down, very slowly, favoring his arm. After a few more rumbles from that quarter they realized that Juric was laughing.

42

It had become a violent struggle between the White and the Red. Nefer had appropriated the sacred red for her own banner, leaving ignominious white, with all its gomin implications, for Vod's ragtag rebellion.

With his white robes swirling around him as he walked, Vod went abroad freely, striding through the ways. Under-Prime was his. OverPrime was Nefer's.

The PrimeWay was the zone of struggle. It lay empty now, the latest skirmish having left fleshy wounds in the hab, the data pedestals and screens flashing their chaotic messages. And on those screens, the wagers still flowed, even now, after many deaths. Odds had it for Red.

Harn raced into the SecondWay, huffing with the effort.

"She's out," he said simply.

Vod was on his feet and down the corridor; Zehops was at his side, thrusting her gun into her belt.

"You're ready?" he asked Harn.

Harn nodded, glancing at Zehops. Their joint command of troops was an uneasy compromise; she for the gomin, he for the diggers.

"More than ready. What say you, Zehops-as?"

She grinned. "Gomin have been ready for a thousand cycles."

They rushed through UnderPrime, collecting their forces. It was no secret he stalked Nefer Ton Enkar. Now he had found her. His spies were among the Red, as he had no doubt their spies were among the White. Nefer sometimes left her dead-end galleries, the collapsed tunnels surrounding her lair. This time they would snare her.

At the portal to PrimeWay, Vod turned to his lieutenants. "For the White Reign," he said, "or may we never sit our rugs again."

"The White Reign," Harn growled.

"And for Vod-as, White Prime," Zehops said, looking even more fierce than Harn.

With a hundred count of armed Whites, they poured into the deserted PrimeWay. In the dim promenade, the screens flickered, lending a jerky quality to their movements as they hurried across to the one portal they thought they might penetrate. It had been blocked, but a snaking tunnel remained in the debris, work of their allies in OverPrime, in preparation for this moment. One by one, Vod's force entered the portal and began crawling.

A skirmish at the head of the upway. By the time Vod emerged, three Red had fallen.

Vod changed into his old clothes. "My own troops will think me a Red," he muttered.

"They know you, Vod-as. No one will mistake you."

"If I am killed, Zehops-as, it falls to you."

"But Harn-as . . ."

"He will follow you. Harn follows, it is how he tends. Promise me."

She jutted her chin to the side. "We're not ready for a gomin Extreme Prime."

"But we are for a digger?" Vod grinned at her. "Zehops-as, you may have no choice."

He saluted her, then turned and ran, with his fighters—disguised, as he was—following at a distance to avoid drawing attention.

At a branching in the way he slowed to a walk. Here, avoiding knots of Red, he followed the ways, taking the least crowded, circuitous routes to his destination: the Over-Prime forward edge of Ankhorat.

To a DreamGallery.

Here, his supporters caught up with him. There were no guards at the portal. That meant they either were inside with her, or Nefer was no longer in the gallery.

Vod and his fighters entered the gallery. Not many slots were full. Of those that were, just the rounded skulls could be seen, as the dwellers lay in dormancy. And standing at the far wall, Nefer Extreme Prime.

She stood there, still and calm, watching him. He managed to retrieve his voice: "Do you lie down to dream, Nefer Ton Enkar?" His voice came to his ears muffled, eaten up by the gaping honeycombs.

"Certainly not, one assures you." Still not moving, she said, "Perhaps you, however, grow weary of the fight, Vod Ceb Rilvinn."

He advanced, gun drawn. "White holds this portal. Times tend toward change, Nefer-as."

"Sweetly put. A poet revolutionary."

Her body was so completely still. He had to admire her inwardness, here, where his own hand was shaking as he held his gun.

"Nefer-as, I believe you are my prisoner." He gestured toward the portal. "This way, and move slowly."

"Do you know where we are, Vod-as?"

"Will you come now, Nefer-as?" She saw his fighters. She was no fool.

She continued, disregarding his question. "On the other side of this wall would be the birthplace of ships."

"I know about your war plans." A chill floated around him. The empty slots of the gallery reminded him of a reliquary, where dark holes waited for the bodies that would fill them in war.

Nefer smiled, her white teeth very delicate in her dark face. "Yes, certainly. You chanced upon my foundry. You left your name tag—so clumsily, one must point out. But all you were apt to see was a glimpse. One is willing to show you all."

Behind her, a bank of slots disappeared. They were projections. Now a narrow passageway was revealed.

"All my ships might be yours, my young White Prime." She looked at him with jewel eyes, beautiful, cutting. "Perhaps you will deign to look upon this new kingdom." She glanced at his followers. "Of course, you tend to worry for yourself. Bring your soldiers, then. How many shall you need to be safe from one small ex-Prime?"

He kept his face neutral. "I do not pretend that you are harmless, Nefer-as. But it is a charming pose." Her eyes glittered at him as he backed away from her to the portal, calling a few soldiers to join him. Nefer was not giving up; he was not so foolish to think so. He had not surprised her in this gallery. She had been waiting for him.

Now, standing with a group of five soldiers, Vod faced her again. "What do you have to show me, then?"

"A time tending toward change," she murmured. "Heralded now by a fleet of twenty-four fast ships. Twenty-three are finished. One regrets that the last one is unready. No matter. You may watch them leave the birthing den."

Vod's hands felt cold, sculpted from ice. He knew now that he had misjudged dreadfully, misjudged everything. She was indeed ready. "No ships will leave, Nefer-as," he said, bravely enough.

As his gun leveled toward her, she said, "We will see

what the dwellers choose. Your guards will bear witness to what they will see." She gestured into the narrow corridor, and when none of her captors moved, she calmly turned and walked into it.

Vod followed her, gun drawn, his escort close behind.

They emerged onto a high balcony overlooking a great bay: the foundry. Its vastness was deserted, empty of the machinery and skeleton ships. A breeze wafted through the cavern, rippling their clothes. Vod's skin cooled in dismay.

Directly across, in a tunnel so long it disappeared into blackness, the warships were lined up, one behind the other. The foremost ship sat like a ghost, its metal sides reflecting no light, its body hiding the secrets of distance and stars and domination. They could have the galaxy. Humans were no obstacle once ahtra were truly and finally geared for war. If there were twenty-three such ships as this one, human surrender would soon supplant armistice.

In the next moment a sustained cracking sound filled the cavern. Clouds of dust scuttled along the floor far below them. Then the floor of the foundry collapsed. Howling vents kicked in to suck up the maelstrom of dirt. Through a scrim of dust, Vod saw a gaping hole in the floor.

Then he understood why they must dig out the floor, for ships to leave DownWorld. He slowly raised his head to the overarching ceiling. Above them was the riddled soil of tunnels dug too close together, tunnels meant to collapse.

Nefer noted his gaze. "Yes. A digger by trade, aren't you?"

"You can stop this, Nefer-as. You will die when the first ship leaves."

She turned to the dwellers jammed into the balcony, saying: "There is a human warship approaching HomeWorld. The humans will avenge their dead comrades, certainly.

Even now, they could fire weapons—world-destroying weapons, erasing our germlines."

Behind him, Vod could hear his soldiers reacting in horror to this news. One muttered, "You said nothing of a human fighting ship, Vod-as."

Vod fought back. "A convenient lie, this ship. Like the *safe* tunnels."

"No, so regrettably true, Skilled Digger." Nefer gestured toward a data screen on the balcony. An image assembled of a ship, a human warship, or at least a non-ahtran ship.

"Our long-range sensors tend to report all that approaches." The view narrowed in on the armament ports. "It is of a class of weaponry sufficient to wreak satisfactory havoc."

"Such a Skilled Liar," Vod exhorted to his guards. But their eyes were all on the ship.

She went on. "We go to meet this threat. For your Extreme Prime, you dwellers may choose a tested war leader from the HumanWar, or a tested digger from the tunnels. I am susceptible to your wishes."

In another instant a ringing crack pierced the air. A puff of dust shot along a network of lines in the ceiling. The cavern rang with an ear-wrenching blast, and another. The ceiling began to fall. And all the world above it. Great chunks of rock and clay cascaded into the waiting declivity in the floor. Then the whole chamber ignited for a moment, as dust fired to life, and receded. An avalanche of dirt and rock fell amid thunder, billowing up onto the overlook where they stood.

Someone was pulling Vod backward. He had clamped onto Nefer's cape, yanking her back with him.

As they fell back through the passageway, dust poured after them, as well as the clattering sounds of the last of the rock debris.

There in the narrow rock passage, Vod stood with Nefer's empty cape in his hands.

He hesitated only a moment before summoning his wits, his counterstrike. "To the foundry, lads—stop them from launching. Stop them...." He led the way, shouting his orders, hoping that they followed.

Back through the passageway, and then onto the balcony. Nefer was gone.

Calling for rope, he and the nearest Whites secured their lines and dropped over the sides, rushing into the dust-filled cavern.

In the smoke of the ruined foundry, Vod groped his way over the avalanche of rocks and soil toward the great tunnel of ships. His battle cries sounded thin and small compared to the amplified, bodiless voice of Nefer, repeating: *"The humans come to destroy us. Even now, they approach ... to destroy us...."*

He didn't believe her. Why, after all the lies, would anyone believe Nefer Ton Enkar?

He clambered over the mighty fallen rocks, his hands bloodied, side by side with a few White stalwarts, rushing to block the ships' maiden flight. Dust choked his vision. He pushed on, shouting for others to follow, hoping that they did.

The warship loomed over him. In the haze he saw a cluster of Red, armed and braced for the attack. Cries of fighting erupted from points in the cavern behind him, but now he faced off in silence with a cadre of Nefer's supporters.

He was alone. In the white-out of dust, he stood on a chunk of the fallen ceiling, staring at some twenty dwellers who thought him a traitor.

"Nefer is wrong," he called to them. It was not the profound thing he might have hoped to utter.

They stared at him.

"That ship isn't coming to attack us," he went on.

A dweller stepped forward. "Nefer says they will kill us."

"*I* say she is wrong." He wasn't sure what provenance

his own word had, but he would have to test it now. "*I* say she is a liar. The same liar who told us to dig those tunnels, who sent us to die there." He looked overhead, and felt the shock of daylight on his face. "The same liar who planned a war and played at peace."

"Then why is the ship coming?" someone shouted, and many added their supporting shouts.

Vod drew himself up. He made his best guess, gambling that he was right. "It comes for its missing crew," he said, and suddenly *believed* it. "For their lost kin. Let them have their dead. And go home."

He was aware of several White standing nearby, and others of his band moving up to join him from the rubble of the cavern. But this couldn't be a contest of force. In the long haul, it would never be enough.

Vod threw down his weapon, and made his way forward over the debris, to the waiting Red. Their ranks opened and he walked into their midst. He moved among them, saying their names—those he knew—exchanging a comment here or there.

"Let them have their dead," someone said. And then others. The air cleared, revealing the ruins of the foundry and the quiescent warships in their long bay. Behind him, Vod heard his own followers cast aside their weapons. Then Red and White were milling together.

"And you, Vod-as," one of the Red asked, "what will you have?"

Vod looked him square in the face and said, "Bring me Nefer."

43

Just after dawn it began to rain. The tall grasses lay over, yielding to the rain, affording Eli and Maret what might have been a good range of view had it not been for the hugging white fog. They walked with weapons drawn, straining to hear any threat as the staccato drone of rain ate all other sounds.

Hours later, they were still pushing through rain and ankle-deep mud, putting feet down softly, careful not to wake the burrowing habsen.

They came upon another hexadron, the second since their departure from the ship. Once again, as he had with the first hexadron, Eli said, "Go back, Maret." *Go down, down to safety.* It would have done his heart good to see her safely tucked in and descending.

Maret kept walking. "There will be more carriers, one is certain."

"One is a fool," Eli muttered. She was determined to accompany him. They had argued it in his cabin, and the resolution was no different now. She would keep her promise to help his people, despite his insistence she had already fulfilled it.

"You risked your life to come to the ship and tell me."

"It was little."

"It was enough. I release you from your promise."

"You cannot go up a downway, Eli. The promise remains. Besides, here you are a babe in the river. We must help each other."

"A babe in the *woods*."

"That, too."

He bit his tongue. The truth was, he didn't want Maret's help. This task was his to do. Without troops, without more deaths . . . Sometimes he thought a rescue ship might come and a full search-party would go out for Sascha; but he didn't hope for it; hoped the opposite, if the truth were told. He would do this on his own.

"I am sorry that my company displeases you, Eli."

He turned to her, wiping the rain from his eyes. "Damn it to everlasting hell, Maret!"

Her lids covered all but the top fraction of her eyes, as though she narrowed them in anger. But she watched him impassively.

"Your company doesn't displease me. Your place is below, that's all, and mine is up here, getting my people home."

She looked away, as much as to say, *It's a little late for that. . . .* She nodded, scanning the mist behind him. "You have a desire to die the good death."

He grabbed her arm, making her look at him. "And you have a desire for progeny, to replace the line we killed in the goddamn war that will start all over again unless you get down there and stop those ships!"

He slowly released her. She hadn't even jumped. Either she was that much in control, or she had learned not to fear him. He felt himself flush hot despite the dousing rain. "I'm sorry."

"I will go, Eli. After we find your Sascha. First things will tend toward first."

They pressed on. Lights flickered now and again in the curdled air, signal fires of photophoric animals, some with poison, some pretending poison.

By mid-morning they passed another hexadron. Eli refrained from comment.

At first they thought it was thunder. Distant booms sounded, muffled, erupting from behind the jagged hills. No lightning followed. And again, concussive blasts, deep-bellied, despite distance, rain, and fog.

Eli and Maret stood on the hilltop bunkers, where three days ago—God, had it only been three?—he and Nazim had released flares, hoping for troops to rally to him, hoping for something simple, like survivors. Now that seemed such an innocent hope. Small, by current standards.

"That was not thunder." Maret looked at Eli for confirmation.

"No, I think not. She had to dig the ships out of their tunnels. To blast away the lid." He sat on the floor of the bunker, unutterably weary. Raindrops indented the soft mud, forming a regular and meaningless pattern of divots. He listened for the roar of warships, but then they heard thunder in earnest and were left none the wiser.

Maret crouched down beside him, holding a flare casing in her hand, examining it. At last she said, "Sascha is not here, Eli."

He looked into Maret's eyes. She was clear-eyed, still focused on the mission, though now it was only for the sake of one small girl.

He hadn't really thought to find Sascha here. It was only a remote possibility that Sascha would have seen the flares, much less come this far on her own. But they were in the business of remote possibilities.

Maret stood, hiking her mav up on her shoulder.

He joined her on the lip of the bunker and, with another glance toward the serrated hills, they began threading their way down the steep slope, in the direction of
Charlie Camp, in case Sascha went to the only place she
knew.

They walked into the old settlement, the place that had
been Charlie Camp, now a green and soggy ruin. Each
time Eli returned to this place it lost a little more of its human component. Last time it had been deserted, stinking
and torn, sagging into the rain. Now, washed daily with
the colors of Null, it was half a swamp. Here and there,
broken tents elbowed up from the shallow water like great
webbed feet. Some tents remained intact, on slightly higher
ground. Light poles still rimmed the outpost, the only
thing left with a proper military bearing. As for the dead,
the bones had washed away, been dragged away, sunk
into the mud. The smells were now of clean mud and rotting foliage, and fruit gone past its prime.

Thunder broke out nearby. Eli knew the Sticks were
close, obscured by quavering mist. Lightning inflamed the
swamp waters for an instant. Then the water went gray
again, hammered flat by raindrops.

Maret looked at him. "We are lucky to have come so
far, Eli. Nothing challenged us the whole way. The season
is ending."

She meant to cheer him. He put his hand on her shoulder, wordlessly.

"One will check the remaining tents," she said. He
nodded, and they struck out separately to search the place.

So quiet. In the background, the silken rustle of moving water, the crackle of rain.

Photophores played among the dead branches of the

swamp, winking on and off. One remained a steady glow. Eli approached it.

There, behind an abandoned generator, the source of the light lay on the ground. An oddly fashioned lamp. Affixed to two long straps.

And it was turned on. Shining into the fog.

Eli knelt down, resting his rifle on the ground. He picked up the lamp. It shook in his hands, as though trembling with the effort to stay lit. Vecchi had said Sascha wore a lamp strapped onto her chest. Its light flooded out in a strong beam, probing the white void. Drawing a ragged breath, he stood, spraying the light in a new direction.

There, a tall, upright beast stood watching him. One moment, it had been only thick, sticky fog. The next, there materialized a muscular giant of a creature. Thirty feet away. Now moving slowly toward him, humming.

The thing advanced. One step, another, great feet so gentle against the ground, arms too long, claws winking in the melted light. No time to reach for the rifle, lying on the ground. Eli drew his knife.

Still the monster lumbered toward him, in no hurry, or time itself drifted to a standstill. Now, stopping before Eli, one arm upraised, the beast paused, forehead rippling as though an index of its rampaging thoughts. The gray skin was a version of Maret's, pocked with circles within circles, the blue eyes were ahtran, the arms, a prodigious length, past which no other arm could hope to thrust.

"Release her, you son of hell," Eli growled, knowing the beast as a vone, knowing it kept her, knowing, suddenly and with perfect clarity, everything.

As though in answer, the vone's head crumpled in on itself, changing form and color. In the mist, Eli thought he saw the very likeness of Sascha. Without her hair, she looked oddly ahtran. . . . But it was the same Sascha he knew from before, gone wild, half starved and bruised. The moment before her death. She had been brave, to stare so defiantly.

So it was over. But then he felt a howl moving up his throat. Not over. Not yet.

He charged. His mouth was open, and he was bellowing, charging the monster. His feet took two strides, bringing him forward into the long arms, close to the broad belly. He would kill this monster that had killed her. By God, he would kill the beast. He rammed forward his knife. As he did, a long arm with gleaming claws came between his eyes, ripping his skin and skull.

Maret heard him scream. Bursting out of the tent, she came running.

There was an enormous vone. It turned now, to face her.

Eli lay crumpled there. Whether there was blood or not, Maret couldn't see. But of course there was blood. Humans bled, like real dwellers.

She strode forward. Having killed Eli, it would be content. It would eat him, and leave her in peace. But she walked closer. All she had worked for, longed for, now given away. She walked within the vone's striking distance. Now if it all ended, it would still be for kin. It would be for Eli.

She was so close, she had to strain her neck to look up at the great vone. It displayed the human girl for her, and, shocked as she was, her color held.

It dipped its head closer, breathing her in. It paused. The pause stretched past the breaking point.

Maret felt a smile pull at her face. The vone could smell her quickening with new life. She hadn't thought of that protection. She wasn't even sure it *was* a protection. But the vone hesitated.

"Go back," she whispered. "Enough. The season is over."

One clawed hand lay on the mud next to Eli. The vone tucked its arms in close to its body, looking with steady, fearless eyes over Maret's head to something beyond her. Then it turned, slowly, magisterially, and walked away. It faded by degrees, passing one curtain of mist after another. It was a ghost, then a shape, then a tremor in the fog. Then gone.

Maret was holding Eli in her arms. He was alive, but his face was flowing blood. She wiped at his wound, a terrible gash that appeared to have sliced his temple in half and crushed part of his face. She dug in her hip pack for dressings, pressing them into his ragged face. They filled with blood over and over.

His garbled words were at first unintelligible.

"Dead," he seemed to be saying.

"No, Eli, a wound. You will live."

"Sascha. Sascha. Dead."

Maret was fumbling for more bandages.

"The vone keeps her," he whispered.

Maret found herself smiling again. "Eli, one is confused. Understandably." She took the compress off his face long enough to hold his attention with her gaze. "Sascha is alive, Eli."

Humans could be so outward with their expressions. She read him, as she had learned to do, below. Then she repeated the words.

After struggling with him whether he could move yet or not, Maret managed to affix a bandage to his face, and helped him to stand. He leaned heavily on her, swaying. Moving slowly through the ankle-deep water, she steered him to the place where she had found Sascha Olander.

* * *

As Eli stood inside the tent, at first he couldn't see in the dimness. Maret braced him up as he swayed, unsteady from shock. Slowly, he began to pick out details in the enclosure. Cots, computers, a litter of clothes on the floor.

She lay on the farthest cot. Or something lay there. Black hair hung down from cot to floor, a heavy drift of tangled strands. As he walked closer, he saw her huddled there, mud-caked, curled up like a creature in a burrow. Legs bare, she wore a belted army shirt with a private's insignia, and heavy army boots encrusted with mud. Her deeply tanned face and hands were covered with scratches—small blows, as though the forest had branded her.

Her chest rose and fell. In the circle of her arms she held an assortment of things: her father's hat, a gold-rimmed mirror, and a geologist's hammer.

"Sleeping," Eli said. The word came out silently. His throat was raw, words got stuck rather far down.

"Ronid," Maret replied, "will do that." At his stare, she continued, "The vone held her essence, after mating." A pause. "And she is—pregnant, you would say."

The words didn't want to sink in, but they did. He whispered, "Mother of God. Maret, no . . ."

She eyed him coldly. "It is all that kept her alive. That vone's protection. I saw this great one patrolling the nest. Then he took her and kept her."

"She's only a girl. . . ."

Maret looked at the sleeping huddle of hair and mud. "Not anymore."

He thought of the vone's shaping of her features. Her clear blue eyes, fearless, wise . . . the flat plane of her cheek, no child's . . . but he was beyond thinking. Whatever had happened to her, he would take her home now. He shook off Maret's arm and moved to the cot.

As he sat on the edge of the bed, Sascha stirred, still not waking, clutching her pile of objects.

"Sascha," he whispered. "Sascha, wake up."

She burrowed her face into the blankets. He put a hand on her head, onto hair so matted it felt like a nest of twigs.

At his touch she opened her eyes. She looked at him for several long seconds. Then her eyes looked beyond him, scanning the tent, as though, if he were here, others might be as well. Noting Maret, Sascha stared hard, but said nothing. Perhaps she had seen other ahtra, or perhaps she had seen far stranger things.

As she sat up, her pile of treasures clattered to the tent floor, where eddies of mud and silt had thrown down a wet carpet. She reached over to retrieve the hat, brushing at the mud on the brim, smearing it.

"We must clean everything," she said. "You've all tracked in mud." She looked again at Maret as though trying to decide if bringing in mud was her worst offense.

"Yes," Eli said softly. Looking at the hat, he said, "We'll clean it." He took Sascha lightly by the shoulders. She turned to face him. When he was sure he had her attention, he said, "I'll take you home now, Sascha. It's time."

He thought she understood him. But her face was smooth and closed as marble.

She reached up to touch the bloody bandage on his face. "What happened to you?"

There were several questions there. He answered, "A battle."

"Did you win?"

For a moment he couldn't speak. Then he said, "Sascha, I don't know. But I'm back."

Around the rim of her eyes glittered a store of tears. "I've been waiting for you." Her voice finally wavered.

He wasn't sure if it was a reproach or proof of faith, but he held out his arms, and she moved toward him, burying her face in his chest, the hat crushed between them. Her ragged breaths emerged from the mass of muddy black hair as he held her.

"I know," he whispered. "I know."

Eli awoke to find the hatchway fully open, sun streaming inside. They had cocooned in the refuge provided by a hexadron. They had been lucky to find a remaining one. Red Season was ending, Maret said, and now there were fewer working craft. In a last gambit, Eli led them to the copse of trees where he had found the slaughtered ahtra, where he had left the bots. Here, the hexadron remained, opening to them. Maret kept watch while her human companions rested.

Next to him lay Sascha, sleeping fitfully as she had for the better part of two days. He left her to her dreams and climbed outside, finding Maret gazing at the early-morning sky.

"One admits it is impressive," she said. "An awful beauty? Would that be sensible?"

"Yes." He accepted some food from her, mercifully not a yellow polyp, but a half-decent dried mushroom. "I think I could say the same thing about this place."

She smiled. "And not about DownWorld?"

"Not the part I saw." As he chewed, his face felt like it had been cloven in half and glued back together.

Maret said, deadpan, "We did not put our best hand forward, in your case."

"No" was all he could say.

"You slept a very long interval, Eli." She smiled. "And therefore you have missed all the news."

By her expression it was good news. They had need of some.

She continued, "Vod has won. Gomin and Nefer's troops all rallied to him. The ships rest in their slots."

A breath filled his chest, deep and cleansing. It was good news indeed.

"There are still stragglers coming UpWorld. But these were the last. Now, if we would access the flow, we must go Down."

He wouldn't argue, for the moment, who she meant by *we*.

"You were right, Eli." At his questioning looks she said, "About the gomin. She brought all her people over to Vod. Because of you."

He thought of Zehops Cer Aton, blessing her. "Now we can talk peace," he said. "Now Congress Worlds may listen."

"No, I think not." Maret turned away, looking up to the patch of sky.

"It's a start," he insisted.

She was still looking at the sky. "All our world is now at the mercy of your Congress Worlds forces. Our hidden, sacred world—is no longer hidden."

So she hadn't given up her argument, the argument they'd been having from the moment they'd found Sascha.

Steam rose around him, dissipating in the morning heat. He knew what Maret was going to say: how Sascha's place was DownWorld, as evidence of peaceful human intention. She would be safe; after all, the vone accepted her. Could DownWorld do less?

He circled around the subject, looking for handholds. Sascha had sacrificed enough. It was out of the question. He shook his head.

"You protect her, Eli Dammond, as though she were your own kin." Maret shrugged, to show how odd this was.

"That's not the point."

"How does the point tend to be?"

"It tends to be . . ." He sighed. "The girl's grandfather

will take it highly amiss if I don't bring her home. He may
be inclined to retaliate. He has the further excuse of all our
deaths. You will have broken the armistice, after all."

"Which we have not."

"Which is impossible to prove." Now they were at the
same point as they had come to so often over two days of
arguing.

"One piece of this you have wrong, Eli."

He figured he was going to learn which piece.

"You think you will be a peacemaker. Your sole mind
is full of what you will do and say to keep a peace between
us. But you are not the peacemaker. Sascha is."

From behind them they heard a stirring. Turning, Eli
saw Sascha standing in front of the hexadron, disheveled,
but awake.

In a soft voice, she asked, "What will my child be?"
She locked her gaze on Maret.

So Sascha knew. Eli had hoped to spare her until she
was stronger. And more, he hoped Maret was wrong, that
a life had not quickened from the mating. How could it?

Maret looked steadily at her, unblinking. "One does
not know. The vone, as you have seen, play with forms."

Eli concealed his dismay. He was sure she *meant* to be
reassuring. . . .

Sascha walked toward them, accepting a drink of water from Eli's canteen. "If the baby is Singer or ahtran—or
other," she said, "how will Congress Worlds accept us?"
As Eli struggled to answer, Sascha pressed on: "If my child
is one of these, how will we fare, do you think?"

Sascha had changed into her mother's camp clothes.
With her hair pulled back into a clasp, she looked not so
much like her mother but her father. She spoke logically
and clearly, as though, after what she had been through,
this part was easy.

He answered her. "Better than below, Sascha. What
choice do we both have other than to go back home and

face what comes? . . ." But from her expression, he thought his words fell flat.

"That's not home anymore."

He didn't like this heading. Home was home. Null was Null. This was no time to blur the two.

"Sascha," he began again, "you won't be in the forest. The forest will go away, and you'll be in the world of tunnels, among strangers." It had gone far enough. "I can't allow it."

"Captain Dammond." She stood taller. "I know the forest will go away. I'm not a child." He had trouble meeting her steady gaze. *Not a child.* But should be, still . . .

"Maybe I am . . . what Maret said."

"This is war, Sascha, not chess," he said with some heat.

A small smile greeted his comment. "You think Grandpa will blow up Null if I'm down below?"

He gave her the courtesy of a moment's silence. The moment stretched on. Was he thinking to relent? Had the vone knocked all sense out of him? No . . . but yet, could he bear to force her?

Maret watched them, immobile, unblinking, not arguing, but watching him with those damn placid eyes.

When he didn't answer, Sascha strolled over to the bots, which stood deactivated near the hexadron.

Eli and Maret followed her out of the copse and across the muddy flat to the gentle slope where, days ago, he and his unit had left the bots to rust.

Sascha stood by the bots, looking closely at them. Then she nodded and said, "This one," indicating the nearer one. "This one is mine." Her fingers traced a dent along the upper housing, as though she well knew where it came from.

Maret put a hand on Eli's arm. "Let her descend, Eli. After the youngster is born, I will send her back to you."

"And the baby?" Eli asked.

"We will see what happenstances bring." The deal, all unspoken, was: *If human, the progeny is yours. If not . . .*

He watched Sascha crouched near her bot, probing it, perhaps looking for a way to turn it on.

Eli thought again how like her father she was. He didn't know what Geoff Olander would have decided in his place; sometimes the price of command was to decide between two bad outcomes. Eli knew it was a terrible risk to let her go. He would not permit it, except for the child she bore, and the reception it would have among humans for whom ahtra were *pocks* and Singers would be . . . worse. And as for any *combination*—well, that possibility was beyond him right now. All he knew was that Sascha was too young to make this decision. But she was too young for everything that had happened.

The rules had changed. It was a different season.

Eli walked a few paces off with Maret. "I want messages from her, Maret. Regularly. I don't care how they get to me. Every month, I want her to speak to me. Promise me." She nodded, and he believed her.

Maret said, "Eli, take the robotics back to the ship. Few ahtra remain here. And you must survive. To tell your story."

"When the general hears the part about his granddaughter, he'll have my head."

Maret's eyes grew large. "That is a punishment among you?"

Eli smiled.

She nodded. "Figure of speech, one hopes."

Eli shared that hope.

44

Vod stood with Zehops and Harn in the middle of the PrimeWay. The smell of burnt hab flesh threaded into his awareness, a scent that reminded him, more than the deserted Way, that their world was turned upside down. They had fought and killed each other, kin against kin. It was over now, but the eerie silence of the Way held the strong memory. Dwellers were slowly clearing out the barricaded portals, but most still avoided the late battleground.

Now Maret had come home, come home from ronid to this altered place, bringing with her the young human female, touched by UpWorld, passing its strict tests. . . .

They would meet here, in this most sacred of places where the great shaft to UpWorld bounced the captured tracked light of the red sun from mirror to mirror, and fell upon the hab: the sunline. It had grown smaller, now barely the length of Vod's arm. The season was passing, so the ocular confirmed.

Two figures approached. Harn touched his sleeve. "This human is even uglier than the first one."

It was true that the human sprouted long shanks of hair from her head, down over her shoulders, giving her a pronounced aspect of disorder and unpredictability. If he was not mistaken, there might even be bits of twigs and dirt in it. The female was not so disconcertingly tall as Eli Dammond had been. Vod tried to see her in a favorable light, but Harn was right. She *was* ugly. Still, it must be remembered that the vone took her as their own. And that she was bearing young. This had been confirmed, and when Vod released it into the flow, the response nearly shut down the Well.

A few dwellers could be seen hovering near portals, come to gape at the spectacle of a human, returned from ronid.

Dwellers began to gather along the walls of the Way, trickling in to watch what would befall. Vod suspected every other dweller DownWorld observed as well, plugged into the flow.

Now Maret was close enough that he could see her face. She was still the old Maret, Data Illuminator, and friend. But by her markings, she had changed: she was bearing young. Leading her strange companion, she stopped a few paces from Vod.

"Extreme Prime," she said, so perfectly calm, so Maret-like.

A hitch caught in Vod's throat. "Not yet, Maret Din Kharon. But I thank you. One has—I've missed you with two sadnesses."

With a graceful turn, Maret brought the human slightly forward. She pronounced her name.

Vod heard the dwellers murmur, "Sazza Ol Ander, Sazza Ol Ander. . . ." There were many more than the last time he looked. They began to spill into the PrimeWay from the restored portals. Some still wore the uniforms of Red, but no one was armed, he was relieved to note.

This Sazza stepped forward. Zehops stirred beside

Vod, and he knew what caused her to lose her composure. It was the eyes. This human had eyes of the deepest ahtran blue. Small, certainly. Eyes like small stones. But so blue . . .

The human was handing him something, presenting him something with both hands outstretched. Maret indicated he should take it from the human. He did so.

It was a large implement, made of fiber and glass and metal. Though he didn't know what it was, it felt strangely familiar in his hands. Harn whispered in his ear, telling him the thing he would have soon figured out for himself, were he not so nervous.

It was a lamp. Not so very different from a digger lamp. Larger, not meant to wear on the head. He switched it on. As the light bled across the Way, it struck the sunline on the hab. A collective sigh came from many throats at once. The lamplight was of the primary sun; the sunline was of the red. Combined, it was the light of UpWorld, as every veteran of ronid would attest.

A wave of emotion rolled through the spectators, cresting at the same time in the data flow. From all sides, the PrimeWay filled as dwellers left their viewing screens to come in person.

To her credit, the human remained calm. Perhaps Maret had coached her in ahtran ways. Or perhaps this was how such a one as a vone accepted would act. Vod passed the lamp to Harn for safekeeping.

"One is grateful for such a fine gift," he said to Maret, who murmured a translation to the girl.

Footsteps behind him caused him to turn. One of his lieutenants whispered to Harn, and in the next instant the crowd began to move down the Way. Dwellers surged for the upways. It seemed everyone had heard a message of great import, everyone but their leader.

Harn nodded at him. "Nefer," he said.

Vod bid Zehops take the human into the SecondWay

for safekeeping, and she led the girl away. Around them, the PrimeWay was rapidly emptying. Vod put dignity aside and ran to catch up.

The huge Paramount Borer came roaring down an industrial way. Behind the massive cutterhead, Vod could see Olton, the semiskilled digger, driving with glee. Others clung on to the machine, riding it in an extreme display of disorder. Vod stood in front of it, causing it to lurch to a halt.

"Stand aside, Vod-as," Olton yelled, "we're going to smash through!"

Vod thought he would never live to see the day the Paramount Borer came from the digs to Nefer Ton Enkar's apartments. But it was an interval of strangeness, all in all.

"I thank you, Olton-as. But it will not be required."

Olton drooped noticeably. Boring through to Nefer's gallery would have made Olton an instant celebrity in the flow. "Not required?"

Vod gestured for him and his fellow diggers to look ahead, where from their vantage point high in the borer, they could see over the heads of the throng gathered in front.

For word had just reached him that Nefer's own static guards had brought her out from her impregnable lobe, where she had fled, for what little good it could do.

As Vod pushed forward, the crowd parted for him.

A small clearing lay between him and Nefer. She stood among her former guards. They had not dealt gently with her, or she had fought hard. Her clothes were torn, and she bore the sign of a bruise on her famous patterned cheeks.

She shook off the restraining hands of her captors, but stayed rooted in place, head held high. "One concedes you have won the grand wager, Vod Ceb Rilvinn," she said, her voice husky, perhaps from an excess of shouting.

"It was never a wager. It was a revolution."

Her teeth flashed very white for a moment as she savored her next words. "If you didn't wager on yourself, you bypassed a very great fortune, one regrets to observe."

"And if you *did* wager on yourself, you have lost more than power."

She looked like she would have paid much for a wand of snuff at that moment. Or perhaps a mav.

"Now you will deliver us to our enemies, one is given to understand." Nefer still acted her part, though she would be lucky to keep her life.

"Your sources were ever behind in the flow, Nefer-as. But the warships will not fly. We will find a better use for your great foundry. I envision a different time. We have tried isolation and war. Now we will begin something new."

"New," she sneered. "You would tend toward *new*."

Vod spread his hands. "I am a fluxor."

At this, a cheer went up from the crowd, loudest from Harn, at his side.

"One has noticed." She could dismiss with her tone of voice, and the merest hint of her face. "Pronounce your sentence, then, digger-fluxor," she said. "One is in haste to be done with this."

He was happy to do so. "You will leave, Nefer Ton Enkar, on a world hexadron, the next to come within shuttle flight of HomeWorld. It will be dispatched to the DeepReaches, for distant exploration. You are stripped of your resources, and you must earn your way into the flow of that ship by honest labor. With you goes Hemms Pre Illtek. You may work out between you any disagreements your actions have provoked. You will not return here ever again."

If she was relieved at his leniency, she gave no sign. Rather, she looked to his side, at someone else.

"You," Nefer said.

Maret had come up from the crowd to stand beside Vod.

"You." A look of bafflement came over Nefer's face. For the first time she seemed like a small static in custody instead of a high prime with her retinue. Vod heard her say in a whisper, "I thought you were a danger to my rule. Your genotype showed . . . it showed . . . but you are nothing."

Maret spoke softly, but in the hush of the crowd, her words carried as far as Nefer's: "I am all that I ever wished to be, mistress."

Vod thought it was well said of Maret. Nefer had ever been blind as the hab to Maret's true worth. He gestured for the guards to take Nefer away.

As the guards led Nefer off, he heard her say: "All the while, it wasn't Maret, it was Vod. Vod. A *digger* . . ."

Vod allowed himself to throw after her: "Diggers and gomin, Nefer-as. Don't forget that part."

Maret looked across the makeshift rug at Vod Ceb Rilvinn, seated opposite her. It would take many intervals for his kin net to be woven into a proper rug for an Extreme Prime. For now, a humble rug would have to do. Knowing Vod, he might prefer it. She hoped he would warm to his new role. Seeing Harn and Zehops sitting in firm support nearby, Maret felt he would not feel far out of category.

Vod was considering her suggestion. He had already retired with his lieutenants twice to discuss it in private. Always, he returned with more questions. Maret answered and waited. DownWorld, the idea seemed more audacious than when she and Eli considered it UpWorld.

She thought Harn would burst from indignation when he first heard the proposition. Zehops—the gomin that had done so much to help Vod—seemed more amenable.

The Congress World ship had landed. She trusted that Eli had done his best to explain happenstances. But neither she nor Eli—nor Vod—felt the armistice would hold. Who had first broken it could be argued, but who struck first in an act of war would be the only thing worth wagering on.

Vod cleared his throat. "Here is what we—I—have decided." He looked at Maret with more calm than he might have felt. She herself was losing the markings on her hands, turning cold with apprehension.

"I will present a gift to the general of Congress Worlds."

Maret closed her eyes. So. She smiled across at him. The technology of ahtran ships, their star speeds so desired by humans. It was the one thing humans desired—and never thought to receive from the ahtra.

"But," he noted, "there is one condition."

Condition? There was not much room for conditions, given their happenstances. . . .

"That is, that we bestow an understanding of these star speeds—in increments." He looked at Harn for a moment, and Maret discerned that Harn was the cautious one, and perhaps not inappropriately so. "An eight percent improvement in human speeds every eight-year increment, as they would measure it."

"That is a cautious gift, Vod-as." Maret said it respectfully, looking at the floor. He was, after all, the Extreme Prime.

"Yes," came his voice. "But it will keep us in relation with humans over a longer span than they might otherwise tend." He still wore his white rags, but already he sounded like a Prime to reckon with.

It was a conducive gift. The key to the FarReaches. On an equal basis, eventually, with the ahtra themselves. It would require that they come to know each other. And each would suffer change, as a result.

"They are the children of this world, as we are," Vod said. "This is the ancient truth that Tirinn Vir Horat revealed. Kin, we might say, though distant." Noting Harn's scowl, he added, "Very distant."

"Still . . ." Maret murmured. Kin was kin.

45

It was an odd feeling, staring across thirty feet of grassy field at Congress Worlds soldiers, and seeing them as the enemy.

Eli stood with the two bots at his side, facing a squad of soldiers in front of a shuttle with a CW major general's crest. Didn't take a mastermind to figure which major general that would be. Didn't take a genius, either, to figure they'd come looking for the Olanders. No way they would have come this far, at this much cost, for just anyone. Eli wondered how Ridenhour felt now that he knew exactly whom he *had* rescued.

In the late afternoon sun, the squad's twenty guns winked red, announcing themselves armed to fire. It was the bots that made them nervous. Each bot held the equivalent firepower of a full platoon and was far more lethal.

"Stand them down, soldier," an officer barked at him across the landing field.

"I can't. They're on automatic." Eli hadn't even been sure he could activate them all by himself, back where they'd been abandoned. But army designers made sure that the "fight" command was easier to activate than "don't fight."

In short order, an AI specialist and a newly-minted second lieutenant moved in on the bots. As they worked to bring the AIs under command, Eli struggled with his reaction to having a CW vessel here. He'd planned on having more time to prepare for a debriefing. Now they'd have the whole story, all at once, and the part they'd hear the loudest was the foundry and its war fleet.

He didn't know what class of warship the general had come in on. Likely it was a cruiser of limited armament. Maybe he should be hoping it was a battle-class destroyer. It was an odd feeling not to know which side he was on.

Eventually he walked across that field, following the bots and the specialist, with the second lieutenant behind him; three men and two bots moving through the corridor formed by the squad. As he walked the ramp to Ridenhour's lair, they watched him with faces as frankly ambivalent as his own must be.

Gordon T. Ridenhour was a fighting man's general. He stood almost eye-to-eye with Eli, not as tall as his reputation, with silver hair cropped close. Brilliant and ambitious, the bantamweight general had a penchant for going for the jugular, and expected his officers to do the same. Eli didn't have to wonder how the general would be disposed toward him, and he was not disappointed.

It was a long debriefing. At times it seemed that the presence of Ridenhour's aide, Lieutenant Colonel Foss, was the only reason the general kept his temper. Or perhaps Ridenhour was still reeling from the news of his daughter's death. At least Eli didn't have to tell him that part; the general knew about Cristin from debriefing Sergeant Juric. He also knew that Sascha had been alive three days ago. It didn't give Eli much opportunity to provide the context for what had happened. Unfortunately, it sounded rather bad as a bald fact.

"She went below. With a reliable ahtra, sir."

Lieutenant Colonel Foss kept a stony neutrality throughout the first minutes of the debriefing. But when Eli explained he'd had Sascha in his care and given her up again, the colonel could only stare in disbelief.

"Below?" the general asked, altogether too quietly. Eli would rather have had some fireworks than this quiet, neutral gaze. Eli had seen that look before, in the eyes of men with desperate plans—and the means and mettle to carry them out.

It took a while for Eli to explain what happened, with the general interjecting all too frequently, "Below? You sent her below?"

There was nothing for it, but to tell it straight out. He asked for permission to tell about the ahtra, and their mating practices. How was it relevant to Sascha?

Sir, if I could just tell this in the order it needs to be told.

You won't be wasting my time, Captain.

No, sir. I'm sorry to report that it is relevant.

The look on the general's face was morphing from contempt to worry.

Eli told it in order. Pieced it together, this fact, and the next one. If you start at the beginning, then you can just pull on the thread and it keeps coming, until the end. He made himself look at the general. Sometimes he glanced at Foss, whose face had that locked-up look of someone who needs to hold a perimeter against emotion. Like horror. Or like pity. Mostly he did Ridenhour the courtesy of looking him in the face. He didn't use the words he might have used. He wasn't obliged to describe what he hadn't seen. Didn't need to. She was pregnant.

So Maret had said.

Eli saw the misbegotten hope in Ridenhour's face. The kind of flimsy thing you held on to if you were desperate enough. That Maret lied. That Maret guessed. He let the general suggest that. He listened until the general finished.

No, sir, I don't think she was wrong. They can smell these things. Scent is a major sense. And the vone had her DNA. It morphed into her shape, sir. He could have gone along with Ridenhour, held out some hope. But he gave him the respect to say the truth.

They brought Eli a flask of water. It tasted like champagne compared to the chemically altered swamp water he'd been drinking. After weeks of mayhem, the ordered surroundings of the general's quarters looked odd—the upholstered chairs, the spanking-clean bulkheads, the rosewood desk, the plush carpet, the straight row of medals on the general's pressed shirt pocket. Strangest of all were the chemical smells of wood polish and disinfectant, recalling, more than the ordered cabin, his life from Before. Eli noted these things like a newcomer. As though he'd spent his life in the killing wilds and not a place much like this.

Colonel Barada, ship's surgeon, was brought in. Eli repeated his story. He answered some questions. Most questions the surgeon put to him, he couldn't answer. *You need to talk to Maret,* he held off saying. That part would come later. Barada, small and dark, took refuge in science, giving the general some technical explanations and theories. Not a courageous man, Barada was giving the general hope.

In the end, Eli thought the general believed *him,* not Barada. It came of leading troops in battle, believing the worst, preparing for it.

Ridenhour walked to the portal, gazing out. As the dusk deepened outside, his face reflected in the glazing, showing a worried grandfather trying not to look like one. He stood thus a long time. And everyone in that cabin waited.

When at last the general had composed himself and turned back to the group, Eli said softly, "She'll be coming home, General." He believed it. Against all odds, he had, hadn't he?

"She damn well better," Ridenhour said, the words almost out of hearing range.

They both left unsaid the matter of *when*. Congress Worlds and the ahtra were in a standoff, with young Vod Ceb Rilvinn sitting a new post. And this was a *fluxor*, no less, for the first time in millennia. As the ahtra measured dynasty, he was young and untried. Add to that, he had warships, and possibly static factions who might lean toward Nefer's old policies.

Sascha, however, would show them a human face. To the religious, she might come trailing the glamour of ronid, but to the secular she could show what humans were— what the best of them could be. To the cynical, she would be a comforting deterrence to a CW strike against the home world. So in truth, though he didn't say it to the general, the longer she stayed, the better.

He was sure that Ridenhour wouldn't attack Null while Sascha was below; but the general might not sway others at Command. For that, other inducements were needed. Such as the matter of certain technologies—technologies of war, and also trade—that the ahtra were willing to put on the negotiating table. Depending on Maret. And even more, on Vod. It was a possibility, and he did bring it forward—knowing it was no answer to a daughter's death, a granddaughter's ruin. But more was at stake than anything either of them had to lose. He had no illusions that Ridenhour completely believed him. But surety would come only from more formal exchange with the ahtra— and for that, Ridenhour was willing to wait.

But now the general sat behind his desk with hands steepled in front of his face. "Let's get one thing clear, Captain," Ridenhour said. "I don't like you. I didn't like you before I met you, and I sure as hell don't like you now."

Eli held his gaze. There was something about keeping eye contact with this man. If he let Ridenhour cow him, it would go worse for him. It was a fighter's instinct.

Ridenhour muttered to himself. "Down *below,* is it?" The man hated to be thwarted in his military instincts; it stuck in his craw. "We can drop a few pulsar bombs down those shafts and flush the lot of them to the surface." He looked up at Eli. "How'd they like that?"

"There are no shafts, sir."

"Goddamn it, I know there aren't. Do you take me for a damn fool?"

"No, sir." You couldn't blame the man for grasping at straws.

Irritably, Ridenhour dismissed the surgeon. When more coffee arrived, Colonel Foss poured for the three of them, and the general let an unhappy silence reign for a few moments.

Eli's hand was shaking when he brought the cup to his lips.

"Maybe some food?" Foss suggested.

The general responded, "I've lost my appetite, Colonel." At the colonel's quick glance at Eli, Ridenhour said, "Soon. We're almost finished."

A rainsquall was beading up on the portal. He continued, "The fact is, Captain, it doesn't matter whether I like you or not. It doesn't matter one damn bit." He tapped a finger on the rosewood desk surface. "What matters is what we decide happened here."

"What happened, sir?" Eli asked.

Ridenhour's face stretched into a facsimile of a smile. "Yes, the story of what happened. This slaughter of 153 soldiers. People will need to know what happened here."

Here comes the politics, Eli judged.

"Do you think you're the only one branded by this little

debacle, Captain? It happened on my watch, you know. My watch. Now, we can either say that 153 ill-trained CW troops failed a test of camping out"—here he noted Eli's expression—"of however demanding a nature, or that 153 brave men and women engaged the enemy and plugged the dam, holding back a galactic war." He turned to Foss. "Which story do you like?"

Foss mumbled, "Plugged the dam, sir."

"I agree. Plugged the dam." He pointed at Foss. "Take notes, Colonel: 'plugged the damn,' or some such . . . The odd thing is, it's the truth." He stopped Eli from speaking. "Do you think there's just one truth? Can you be so damn stupid?"

"I know about *versions,* General. The army's take on things doesn't always match the individual's." *Like the* Recompense, *you son of a bitch. Which* version *did you hear, General?*

As though reading his mind, Ridenhour said, "I followed that investigation, Dammond." Across the gulf of the polished desk, he did Eli the courtesy of eye contact. "I would have blown those ahtra to kingdom come, that's a fact. No decision to leave to a Captain, though. You learn in this service, Dammond, not to see two sides of everything. That was your mistake, seeing it from the enemy's point of view. I've made a career out of not second-guessing myself. I recommend it to you." In a different tone of voice, softer, he said, "You showed great courage boarding that world ship. There would have been a medal in it for you if Suzan Tenering had managed the story better."

It was unexpected. Eli took it at face value, this token of begrudging respect from a man who didn't like him. He knew better than to read too much into it.

Ridenhour rose, signaling the interview over. He pulled his jacket down to firm its line, and nodded at the doorway. "Know who's out there, Captain Dammond? Two of your survivors. Waiting in the corridor to see how much of you is left after our chat. It doesn't impress me, you know. Those youngsters are grateful to be alive, God knows. They credit *you* with their survival. I don't. Sergeant Ben Juric is in quarters, smoking stogies. And I'll put more stock in *his* appraisal, I assure you."

"As to that, sir," Eli said, "I recommend Sergeant Juric, Corporal Nazim, and Private Platis for the Medal of Valor."

Ridenhour waved at Foss. "Good, good, see to that. Make it with nova, the medal with nova." He muttered, "Add Captain Dammond to that list, just to make it a foursome."

Eli winced. "I don't want the medal, General."

"I'm sure you don't." The general glanced at Foss. "Get this soldier his supper, Colonel." Then, as Eli was moving to the door, the general said, "We can't give the medal to your people if we don't give it you."

When Eli didn't answer, he went on. "You're lucky you'll never have another promotion, Dammond. The politics are ugly at the top."

Eli was dismissed, but then he remembered. There was one thing more. It had slipped his mind, the thing he'd kept in his fatigue pocket. He didn't look forward to explaining how he'd gotten it. Eli groped to find the locket and chain. Found it.

When he reached out toward Ridenhour, the general put out his hand. And recognized the locket: Cristin's.

The old man made a barely perceptible nod. Nothing need be said. And already the general had turned away, holding on to the chain, standing very still.

At the door, Colonel Foss said in a low and not unkind voice, "Have the surgeon take a look at that wound, Captain."

"Thank you, sir. I will."

As Foss opened the door, Eli stopped for a moment, gazing into the corridor.

There, Corporal Nazim stood, coming to attention at

the sight of Eli. Next to her, Pig saluted, letting one of his crutches lean against the wall. On the other side of the corridor, Sergeant Juric stood ramrod straight, his sleeve pinned up where his arm used to be. With his good arm, he snapped a smart salute.

Eli returned the salutes, hearing the door close softly behind him. He nodded at the three of them, deciding not to trust his voice.

The way they looked at his bandaged head, they must have wondered how rough the proceedings were.

Rough, Eli thought. *But we've seen worse.*

They followed him back to quarters.

The surgeon peered closely at Eli. He had removed the temporary dressing and was prepping him for microknits. Turning his head toward Sergeant Juric's bunk in the med lab, he grumbled, "Next time you leave that bed without my permission, I'll have your stripes, Sergeant."

"Okay, Doc," Juric mumbled from his cot, where he was again connected to tubes and monitors. His tone conveyed massive impudence or drug-fogged incoherence. Eli figured he knew which.

Nearby, Pig, confined to bed rest, was kept company by Nazim, a chessboard between them on the bunk.

She snorted. "You can't jump pieces. You occupy the square where it was, that's all."

"Not like checkers?" Pig responded.

Nazim's muttered response, inaudible at Eli's surgery table, was harsh enough to turn Pig's ears bright pink.

Colonel Barada had finished cleaning the wound and was bending in now to begin subcutaneous regen. He smiled reassuringly at Eli. "By the time I'm through with you, Captain, you'll be good as new." He reached for the plasma wand offered by his assistant. "The remarkable thing is, the wound traveled from your hairline down the

bridge of your nose and into mid-cheek, and missed both
eyes. I'm surprised it didn't take your face off. But not to
worry, Captain. Good as new."

From Juric's bunk came the suddenly lucid growl,
"Leave it like it is."

The surgeon bent in to his task. But Eli gripped his arm.
"You heard him, Doc. Just sew it up. Nothing fancy."

Barada coughed daintily. "Captain. That would leave
quite a bad scar." He exchanged glances with his assistant.

"I know," Eli said. With the grisly wound denting the
center of his face, his smile took on a decidedly menacing
cast.

While Badri Nazim stared at this interchange, Pig took
the opportunity to jump two of her pawns with his rook.

The mirror wasn't a reflective surface, but rather an imaging screen that functioned like a mirror. Zehops paused at
Sascha's side, holding a very sharp knife.

"It would not be required, Sascha-as," she said again.

Sascha smiled, trying to reassure her. "It's OK, really.
Go ahead and slice."

"And it would not tend to hurt, you are quite certain?"

"No. Cutting hair doesn't hurt. Go for it."

The sight of Sascha's hair, especially as much of it as
she had, was distressing to the dwellers here. Though
Zehops was reluctant to insult her, Sascha had managed to
learn that with her long and rather tangled hair, she looked
repulsive to the ahtra. If she was going to be DownWorld
for a while, Sascha had decided that hair was not an asset.
And from what she was viewing of herself on the screen, a
good haircut would be an improvement.

Zehops cut a strand of hair, her expression conveying
her reluctance to touch it. The lock fell to the floor, and

Zehops sucked it up into a vacuum hose. She plucked at another strand. At this rate, it would take hours.

"Zehops-as, you speak Standard CW very well. It's hard to believe you just learned it."

The ahtra looked with hesitation at Sascha's tresses, as though overwhelmed where to cut next. "One absorbs information easily. But meaning is harder."

"My mother always insisted I learn languages of places we stayed. I have French, Latin, Dalarri, and Parth, besides Standard. I hope I can learn your tongue."

Zehops sliced another hank of hair, backing out of the way as it fell. "Though I am an imperfect teacher, I will help you, Sascha-as. Your sole mind is strong. You will learn fast."

"Will the hab eat my hair?"

"Certainly. It consumes all our organic wastes."

"Does it excrete?"

"There are small tillings left in the trailing edge of Ankhorat. These would be wastes, but of small proportion. Living as we do, all must be used efficiently."

"I have many questions, Zehops-as."

Her beautician had become more bold with her knife, now cutting steadily away at great falls of hair. "Relative to the hab?"

"Relative to everything. Of fluxor and static. I must learn everything about fluxor and static. And about the hab and the mycelium . . ." She wanted to add the Singers, but she knew Zehops would avoid discussing them. She put her hand on her belly. As a scientist, being here was a great opportunity to learn about cross-species breeding. As a young woman, she was not quite so eager to find out. Once she was rested she might have time to be afraid, to wonder what she would bear.

Zehops had cut a short bob around Sascha's head and now stood staring at her.

"How do I look?" Sascha asked.

Zehops blinked. "It . . . would be hard to say."

Sascha smiled. "Not so hot, huh?" At Zehops confirming expression, she said, "Cut it all off, then."

Zehops looked pleased at the assignment. She bent to her task, saying, "I would not be suitable to answer all your questions, Sascha-as. But you will have a conducive Data Guide, Nemon Es Marn, who studied with Tirinn Vir Horat. Vod Extreme Prime will spare no expense for you."

Looking at the screen, Sascha saw a young woman. A woman rather like her mother, but with darker hair, and blue eyes instead of brown. The short hair was the very emblem of womanhood. But as Zehops continued her shearing, the image began to change. Now, with her head bare, she looked more like Zehops than Sascha Olander, which was to say she didn't any longer know exactly who she was—or who she would become.

When Zehops had finished, she vacuumed all wisps of hair from Sascha's clothes and from the floor.

"Now, one is very deeply conducive," Zehops said, looking at Sascha's smooth skull on-screen.

"You realize that we have to do this every few days?" Sascha said mischievously.

Zehops' face fell. "It grows thus, so rapidly?"

"No. Not so fast. But there will be tiny hairs all over in a few days."

Zehops flashed her knife. "I will tend to be ready." She smiled at Sascha. "One has a question for you, in exchange for your many questions." She sat down opposite Sascha. "Eli. Tell me how happenstances are disposed toward Eli, UpWorld."

"He will be well. He saved my life. That will count in his favor."

"He saved my life as well, Sascha-as."

Sascha turned to face her. "While he was a prisoner among you?"

"Yes."

"Well. I told them he was a hero." She had only been a child then. But she had known the truth of it.

Sascha looked at her image. It wavered in front of her. She saw dun-colored sand, gray spiny trees with minor green ridges bulging between cracked bark . . . the world before it changed, before everything changed.

She turned back to Zehops, conscious of the missing hair, but not regretting it. "I'm ready," she said.

And Zehops led her from the den into the ways.

46

≈

S eems peaceful enough," General Ridenhour said.

Standing on the shuttle ramp, taking some air, the general looked across the grassy field and beyond, to the distant hills, where clouds were massing for an afternoon squall.

"Looks that way," Eli responded. But he noted the platoon had set up small artillery at the base of the shuttle and were keen on the watch.

Colonel Barada had joined them, bored waiting, no doubt.

The general nodded in the direction of Marzano's *Fury*. "That ship was loaded with firepower. Still is. Even a laser cannon, they tell me."

"It was seven miles away," Eli said evenly.

The general shook his head at the irony of the *Fury*'s armament lying fallow while good soldiers died. Eli didn't venture to disabuse him of the notion that firepower would have saved them.

He thought of Maret's prediction that only the merciless would survive. She'd been right about a lot of things, but maybe not that one. What did the survivors have in common? They were by turns smart and simple, young and older, dark and light, man and woman, officer, non-com, and enlisted. Each brought a different brand of endurance to the killing valley that he gazed out on. But from what he knew of mercy, he thought he saw it in Sascha, Nazim, Pig, and even Juric, if mercy was what you forgave as well as who you spared. Sometimes what you forgave was yourself.

He touched the swath of bandage, stretching down from brow to cheek, feeling the pull of tissue binding one thing to the next, re-creating his face as best it could remember. An approximation would do. Beyond that, all he wanted for himself was the army. Maybe even a decent command. But, in any case, if they made him a hero, they'd have a damn hard time drumming him out.

"Do you believe the claims, Captain?" Ridenhour gazed out over the clearing, gone to extreme green from the monsoons.

"Claims, sir?"

"The ahtra. Original DNA, all that."

He'd been thinking about it, talking about it with the ship's surgeon. But the general had asked *him*. So he answered. "Why else has all other life we've found been based on the same DNA?"

Ridenhour stepped back into the last piece of remaining shade on the ship's ramp. "Damn hot," he commented.

Barada threw out, "We still had to climb up the ladder of evolution. They didn't help us with *that*." He looked at Eli as though he was still resentful that Eli had ruined a nice surgery.

Continuing his line of thought, the general said, "Some would say that God made it all from one mold."

Eli knew he was treading on thin ice, but said, "Miracles aside, General, it's one hell of a coincidence."

The doctor spat into the grass. "It's an impossible

coincidence. It's either a divine miracle—and I have to say I'm not a believer—or it's panspermia, rather like the ahtra claim. Someone broadcast the precursor molecules."

"I'd sooner thank God than the ahtra," the general muttered.

Eli heard the message. *I'd rather not be beholden. And don't care to be related, thank you.*

It was no surprise. Thirty years of war, and the CW worlds were content with their enemy as he was. Some—perhaps like Ridenhour—would never accept a new viewpoint. For others, a billions-of-years-old debt of creation was too remote to matter. Even the ahtra had forgotten their act, their original impulse to share the universe with other sentient beings. Then, when they met their progeny at long last, they took up arms. And when humanity met its parents, it raised a collective hand to strike them down. It had been a mutually agreed on war. Sadly, it was far easier than a mutually desired peace.

He looked at Ridenhour calmly surveying the territory around the shuttle, and saw a man comfortable with his enemy. It would take more than a creation story to mold the peace. Whatever it took would begin with Sascha and Maret. Sascha with the ahtra, Maret with Congress Worlds.

She had said that she would come. So they waited.

Eli hoped she would bring the ahtra starship technology, as a peace offering. But even more, he hoped she would come herself, to live among them. So they might know their ancient kin, their recent foe, in a new way.

He would be glad to see her, whatever she brought.

Just at dusk, a soldier came to fetch Eli, bringing him to the ship's ramp. The last fragments of soil were still cascading from the hexadron as its engines shuddered to a standstill forty yards away.

Eli noted the guns trained on the hexadron.

"Sir," he said to Ridenhour, "Maret Din Kharon is an ambassador, not a soldier."

"Stand down," the general told his commander.

"I'll escort her, sir. It might be best if she saw me first."

Ridenhour nodded, and Eli set out across the field. It hadn't rained in forty-eight hours, and the mud beneath his feet had cracked into tiles. The primary sun, setting now, was half-buried in the horizon, like an ancient hexadron. The red sun lingered above, small and fierce, following the yellow star down the sky.

He waited as the hatchway swung open. Maret emerged gracefully, climbing down to stand next to the carrier. She was dressed as he had seen her the first time, in cropped shirt and simple trousers of a red and brown pattern of squares within squares. Everything had changed since that first time. She was pregnant, for one thing. Amid all their obstacles, he thought a child might be an advantage for their mission. Depending on what *kind* of child it was . . .

There was no way to figure all the possible happenstances.

She looked around her warily. Not at the ship and the soldiers, but at UpWorld: its grasses, soil, and suns.

"One goes against tradition, Eli," she said in a brave voice.

"I suppose we will," he replied. There would be a season of going against the tide, for everyone. In rough waters, he'd want an ally, a friend. Like Maret. As they walked toward the shuttle and its waiting officers, Maret looked with concern at the wound his face bore.

"You would be well, Eli?"

"Yes," he said, and for all he knew, it would be true.

About the Author

Kay Kenyon began her writing career as a copy-writer at WDSM-TV in Duluth, Minnesota. She kept up her interest in writing through careers in marketing and transportation planning, and published her first novel in 1997. *Tropic of Creation* is her fourth book, following the release of *Rift*, *Leap Point*, and *The Seeds of Time*. She lives near Seattle with her husband.

She can be found on the web at:
www.kaykenyon.com

and on e-mail at:
tko@kaykenyon.com

Printed in the United States
70255LV00004B/67

9 780553 763171